Of Relationship & Storms

A Novel

By

Mark MacMillin

Narration Publishers

Newport Beach

Narration Publishers

1400 Quail Street, Suite 210
Newport Beach, CA 92660
narrationpublishers.com

Narration Publishers Edition, January 2014

ISBN-13: 978-0615963976

For my brother Brad,

Who fought great and terrible storms

Forward

That was a long time ago, the past is the past. It doesn't affect me.

Most weeks I hear these words. I used to hide my cringe. These days, my whole body seems to revolt: I close my eyes, turn my head, double over, grimace, grit my teeth, and sometimes put my hands over my face. Like Lincoln.

It's funny because those words can seem so obviously true. A quick glance at the calendar proves it. The only problem, they are not true. Not even close. In fact, these words will steal your life.

The truth is our early story teaches us "the rules" of life. What we can expect from others and from ourselves. Is it safe to love? Will I be loved? Can I trust other? Depend on them? Will I be betrayed, abandoned, unnoticed, lonely...and on.

The past is not only present, but it is impacting, distorting, coloring, even determining the next moment.

Our choice is merely, do we accept this or deny it. Most of us, to our own peril, deny it. And because of this, we suffer. As do our loved ones. Any field that I am not actively cultivating from my earlier life will harden. Nothing of value or beauty will grow there. Think of someone you know who can both belly laugh and weep with sorrow. They have a twinkle in their eye when you talk to them. You can feel they are open and present, fluid and not afraid. You bask in their warmth and in their presence you are a free, alive version of yourself. This person works their story.

Contrast this with someone you know who is only half present when you speak. They listen…sort of, but you can easily stop mid-sentence and they won't notice. In fact, maybe they are relieved. This person cannot be wholly and fully present. Parts of their soul are hardened and not accessible. You feel bored and boring, dropped and alone. This person is trying to forget their uncultivated fields.

MacMillin is a story teller. He observes truths of the human condition, of what leads to the flourishing life and, what leads to hard packed soil, dead save for the weeds. And then he tells story. Find yourself in these characters and let it guide you to your plow.

Dr. David Pickens
Psychologist

Acknowledgments

I have had the opportunity to join many souls in their battles with storms of various forms. Some have fought with internal storms of great emotion, some with relationship storms, and most with the rough seas of both. I have gleaned much learning from these experiences, for which I am thankful to these many courageous people. I respect all who brave to tell their heart-felt story.

I want to thank Kathleen O'Dell, who offered valuable help with grammar, word usage and spelling. I value her great skill with word-smithing. I appreciate Dan Meisel, who provided essential feedback on the initial form of this novel, which needed improving. Dan's patient, kind and honest thoughts provided me with an important new direction. David Pickens read several drafts, and gave me priceless input on both character and story development. He generously gave many hours to this novel, and offered many insights into how the story and characters may better tell their tale. And to Catherine Loquet, who refined my words, making them read more easily and smoothly. She's given my novel a sophistication that it would have lacked without her help.

Lastly I'm thankful to Brad, my brother, who showed me a great example of enduring in the face of overwhelming storms.

Of Relationships & Storms

A Novel

The River: Day 9

Kathy and Stacy no longer paid much attention to where they drifted. It no longer mattered, since they didn't have the strength to do anything about their direction anyway. They clung to each other, afraid of getting separated. Having been in the water a long time, they were cold and constantly shivering. Whatever energy they had left went into keeping their heads out of the water. The small waves often filled their mouths with water, leaving them spitting and sputtering.

They drifted in silence, neither talking. At first Stacy monitored her surroundings, trying to find a familiar landmark. The desert river landscape all looked about the same to the unpracticed eye, and Stacy soon gave up trying to figure out where they were and surrendered herself to wherever the current took them.

A wave washed over Stacy and she awoke. She glanced around and saw they were still roughly in the middle of the river. Stacy noticed Kathy's eyes closed. "Hey Kathy, you still awake?" asked Stacy. No response. Stacy asked more loudly, "Kathy, you still with me?" Kathy's eyes fluttered but remained closed. "My God Kathy, don't leave me! Come back to me!" Kathy moaned softly, but remained unconscious. Dread arose in Stacy. "Oh my God, I have to get you to shore, you're freezing!"

With one hand holding onto Kathy's life jacket, Stacy swam for shore with the other. After a few minutes of making little progress, Stacy felt light headed and stopped. "It's no use

Kathy, I don't have it in me to get us to shore. Oh my God, help us! Mike, where are you?" Stacy cried. She shivered, and held onto Kathy tighter. Stacy felt herself drifting towards unconsciousness, but fought to remain awake.

The ranger piloted the boat just above idle speed, carefully scanning the water as she stood. "Go faster!" urged Mike.

"No! Two bobbing heads are tough to see in the water. I might hit 'em," said Ranger Barb.

Mike stood in the stern of the boat, bracing himself against the gunwale, scanning the water's surface. "Come on, you won't hit 'em at this speed. They might be drowning. Let's go!" said Mike.

"Take it easy! We'll find 'em," said Ranger Pete. Mike hit the gunwale in frustration. He sat down and took his water-spotted sunglasses off and cleaned them on his shirt. He put them back on and resumed his scanning. Then he spotted something.

"There they are! I can see something in the water up ahead," shouted Mike. The rangers followed his pointing finger, and Barb gave the boat more throttle. As they neared Mike could clearly make out two heads bobbing above two orange life jackets. "That's definitely them! Stacy! Kathy!" Mike's heart sank when they didn't respond.

Once the boat finally reached them, Mike dove into the river before the boat even stopped. He reached them in a few strokes. "Stacy, I'm here!" Mike grabbed Stacy and swung her around. Her brown eyes opened briefly, and then closed without seeming to recognize him. Mike reached for Kathy, who didn't respond at all to him.

Mike held onto the women's life jackets and swam them to the boat. Pete grabbed the back of the lifejacket and dragged Kathy around to the swim platform, and then pulled her into the boat. When he came back for Stacy, Mike already had her at the swim platform. When Mike climbed into the boat, both women lay in the bottom of the boat with thick blankets over their unconscious bodies. "Have a seat! Let's go," said Barb.

The boat roared to life and sped the short distance back to the marina. On the way Pete shouted something into the marine radio, and was answered by a voice that competed with static. They reached the dock and Pete jumped out to tie off. "Hand me the first one," he shouted. Mike and Barb lifted Kathy to Pete on the dock, who carried Kathy off in his arms. Mike and Barb lifted Stacy onto the dock. Then Mike picked her up and followed Pete up the dock.

By the time they reached the ranger station the sound of the approaching helicopter could be heard. Two helmeted paramedics leapt from the helicopter just as it hit the ground. They loaded Kathy and Stacy onto stretchers and then into the helicopter. Mike began to climb into the helicopter, but was stopped by a hand on his chest. "We can't take you with us. No room." Mike hesitated, and then reluctantly stepped out. A minute later the helicopter lifted off for the hospital.

Mike drummed his fingers on his knee as he sat in the passenger's seat of the ranger truck. "How long did you say till we get to the hospital?" asked Mike. Barb smiled, "I've told you three times now. We'll be there in another thirty minutes. And no, I won't drive any faster, in case you were about to ask me again." Mike grinned and looked out the window and sighed.

"No word from Pete yet?" asked Mike. Pete had stayed behind to organize a search party for Jack.

"Have you heard anything on my radio yet?" she asked rhetorically. After Mike shook his head Barb added, "I'm sure Pete will radio as soon as he knows anything. Be patient. These search and rescues take time."

"Yeah, I know. I just can't stop worrying about Jack, or the women. You know?"

"I'm sure the doctors will be able to tell you something soon enough."

They crested a hill and then surveyed the small town of Marble. It lay in the valley below, framed by red rock and a low mountain range behind it. The hospital was easy enough to pick out, being the only large, multi-storied building in view. Only a handful of other buildings made up Marble. The helicopter still sat on the roof of the hospital. Mike shifted in his seat again and again, barely able to wait the last five minutes. Before the ranger had the engine off Mike bolted out of the truck and into the hospital.

The waiting room was decorated with stiff, plastic chairs providing little low back support. Two particle board tables each contained a few magazines. Fluorescent lights gave the room a sterile glow. A kindly older nurse sat at the nurses' station, giving Mike a warm smile each time he anxiously glanced her way. By now he felt assured she'd let him know the moment she had any news of Stacy or Kathy. They were still being attended to in the ER.

Mike stood and paced the room back and forth. From pacing earlier he knew there were fourteen steps from the door to the window at the end of the hall. He crossed his arms over his chest and watched his feet as he paced. The only information the nurse had provided was that Stacy and Kathy were badly dehydrated. Badly dehydrated, badly dehydrated, Mike kept repeating in his mind. So what does that mean will happen to them? he wondered. It seemed strange that they were dehydrated after being found floating in water. However, Mike knew enough to know it meant they hadn't drunk enough water. It's a tall order to ask yourself to continue drinking when all you want is something to eat.

Tired of pacing, Mike sat down and picked up a magazine to thumb through. He glanced at the front page and his eyes zeroed in on an article entitled, "How to Survive in the Wilderness." Mike tossed the magazine back onto the table and looked for another one. The second magazine's cover article read "The Top Ten Ways People Die in the Desert," which he quickly threw back. He picked up a third magazine which was plastered by pictures of a half dozen celebrities on the cover. Mike leafed through it. He found an article that caught his interest, but when he tried to read he couldn't make his mind concentrate on the words. A moment after his eyes ran across the page he'd already forgotten what he'd seen. After several attempts to re-read the first paragraph he gave up and discarded the magazine onto the table.

Mike sat with his head in his hands and his elbows on his knees. He looked up when he heard the door open. A young, tired doctor walked through the door and conferred briefly with the nurse, and then approached Mike. Mike stood to meet the doctor and held his breath and braced for the news. "The good news is they're stable. Unfortunately, they've yet to regain consciousness. We're rehydrating them with IV drips. They don't appear to have sustained any injuries. I think we're dealing with a case of simple dehydration and heat-stroke, but we might be dealing with hyponeutremia as well," announced the doctor.

"Hypo what?"

"Hyponeutremia means low salt. Out in the heat the greatest dangers are dehydration and heat exhaustion, but a close third is salt depletion."

"So what does that mean? Are they going to be okay?"

The doctor hesitated before responding, "I can't be sure yet. We're replenishing their salt and water, but we'll have to wait and see when they regain consciousness."

"Wait and see what?" asked Mike.

The doctor hesitated before responding, "We really can't know anything more until they're conscious."

"Oh God, are you serious? We can't know what?"

"Let's just take this one step at a time. You'll have to be patient until they wake up."

Mike collapsed into the chair. He struggled to get his mind around the information he'd just received. What is the doctor not telling me, Mike wondered. Maybe there's bad news that he's holding back? The doctor sat down next to Mike.

"Look Mike, I know you're worried. There's a good chance they'll make a full recovery. Let's just hope for the best." The doctor watched Mike struggling with the news. "Is there somewhere you can go and get some sleep? You look exhausted. I can give you something to help you sleep."

"No. I want to stay here until they wake up. I can't sleep until I know they're okay," said Mike.

"You're not doing your friends any good exhausting yourself with worry."

Mike turned his head to the window, "Anyway, I have nowhere to go. The park ranger dropped me off here."

"There's a motel across the street. Go check in and get some sleep. I promise I'll call you as soon as they regain consciousness." Mike studied the doctor while he pondered the suggestion. The doctor added, "Go, there's really nothing you can do for your friends until they regain consciousness."

Across the street lay a single line of one-story motel rooms. The dull orange paint appeared to be at least twenty years old, peeling back at the edges. The color seemed to match the orange and brown dirt of the desert. Mike brushed his mated hair back and slowly plodded across the almost deserted street. He didn't bother looking before stepping into the street. Fortunately there were no cars within a mile in either direction.

The motel room featured an orange bed spread, faded yellow wallpaper, and a small cardboard table and plastic chair. The room contained no television, only a metal wall-mounted brace where a television once sat. The bathroom was small, with only enough room to open the door without hitting the commode or the shower.

Mike dropped the room key on the table and fell onto the bed, without bothering to pull back the covers. He stared at the cottage cheese ceiling. Images of Stacy lying in her hospital bed with tubes coming out her arms and nose filled his mind. He hadn't actually seen her, but pictured her in her hospital bed just the same. When he shooed those thoughts away, they were soon replaced by pictures of Jack collapsed on the hot sand, an empty beer can in his hand. Mike tried in vain to push both fears from his mind.

He sat up and reached into his pocket, pulling out the pill the doctor had given him. He unwrapped a plastic cup and turned on the faucet. Water fell from the faucet a murky brown, and then slowly cleared. Mike filled the cup and swallowed the pill.

Staring into the mirror, he was surprised at the haggard man looking back at him. His face was sunburned, his lips badly chapped, his eyes dull and the skin around his eyes hung loosely. He turned the water back on and washed his face. Collapsing on the bed, he soon knew no more.

The River: Day 10

Mike awoke to what sounded like an alarm clock ringing. He opened his eyes and looked around the room, wondering where he was. The alarm clock stared at him with bold numbers 9:57. Mike hit the "off" button. Nothing happened. He unplugged the alarm. The ringing continued. A red light flashed on the phone next to the alarm clock, and Mike lifted the receiver. "Hello?" Mike said into the phone.

"Hello Mike, this is Dr. Painter from ER. We spoke outside the nurses' station in the ER wing?"

"Oh yeah, I remember. Have they woken up?"

"Yes, Stacy's regained consciousness."

"And?"

"And there's no sign of brain damage. I think she'll be okay."

"Oh thank God. And Kathy, is she okay?"

After a pause Dr. Painter said, "She's still unconscious. We don't know about her yet."

"So when will she wake up?"

"Of course I can't know for sure, but I would think within 24 hours."

Mike thought for a moment and then asked, "Can I see Stacy?"

"Sure, but only for a brief visit. She's still weak and needs to rest."

The door opened with a creak, as Mike slowly pushed it back. His palms were damp and his heart beat rapidly. He looked through the opening at Stacy, whose eyes were closed. Mike soundlessly approached her and stood at her side. Her chest gently rose and fell as she slept peacefully. An IV protruded from the inside of her left elbow. Stacy's brown hair lay flat against the sides of her face, but her coloring seemed almost normal. Mike sat down in the vinyl chair in the corner and waited. Red and brown dirt, scraggly low brush and gnarled cactus filled the view out the window. A few scattered clouds created a collage of blue and grey skies. Mike glanced back from the window to Stacy, who continued to sleep. He put his head back against the wall and waited. A few minutes later he slept.

Mike drove his boat down the river, frantically searching the water while he stood in the cockpit. He repeatedly called out to her, but she didn't answer. He opened the throttle wide open. The engine made more noise, but the boat failed to move any faster. Off in the distance Mike spotted something in the water that appeared to be a person, yet as he neared the spot it was only drift wood gently rocking in the waves. Then up ahead he found something else in the water. As he neared he could discern the arms of someone waving at him. When he got closer he could see that it was Stacy in the water, struggling to keep her head up. Mike positioned the boat alongside Stacy and reached over the gunwale for her arms. His hand slipped off her fingers. Mike grabbed for her again and again, yet was unable to get a firm hold of her, as she continued to slip away. Stacy sank under water. Mike dove into the water after her. The faster he swam down for her, the quicker she sank into the depths. He heard her cry out for him, and he helplessly called back to her. "Stacy! Stacy!"

"Mike. Wake up Mike, I'm here." Mike opened his eyes to see Stacy smiling at him from the bed. His eyes darted around the room and then they returned to Stacy. He focused and refocused on her face.

"Mike, you were talking in your sleep and you woke me up," said Stacy. Her voice was weak and her face fatigued. Stacy reached out her hand to Mike. He took her hand and sat on the edge of her bed, caressing her hand and arm.

"Thank God it was only a nightmare! I had this terrible dream that you were drowning and there was nothing I could do to save you. My God, it was the worst feeling…"

"I'm okay…at least I think I'm okay…but how did I get here?" asked Stacy.

"Oh my, we found you and Kathy drifting in the water with life jackets on, and unconscious."

"We?"

"The park rangers took me out in their rescue boat."

"Where's Kathy? Is she okay?"

"She's still unconscious."

"Is she going to be alright?" asked Stacy with a look of alarm.

Mike made a face and then said, "The doctors don't know yet. I mean she'll live, but we don't know if she'll have brain damage."

"Oh my God," Stacy whispered. "So how long were we floating in the river?"

"I don't know. We found you sometime after two o'clock yesterday drifting near the marina."

"Really, near the marina?"

"Yeah, you were just upriver from the point by the marina."

"I can't remember how long we'd been in the water. All I remember is being cold," said Stacy.

Mike smiled and squeezed her hand. He bent down and embraced her. "I'm so glad you're okay. I kept worrying that you'd be left with some kind of terrible…well let's not think about that now," said Mike as his eyes teared up.

"And you! Thank God you made it back. I was afraid you didn't make it. Did you have to hike all night?" asked Stacy.

"I must have gotten to the marina sometime after midnight. I don't know what time. I knocked on the ranger station door, and then…and then I must have passed out. I woke up the next morning on a cot in the ranger station." They were interrupted by the nurse coming into the room. "Excuse me, are you Mike?" the nurse asked.

"Yes?"

"There's a phone call for you at the nurses' station."

Mike ran out of the room and was panting when he reached the nurse's station. He knew the call was from the rangers; after all, no one else knew he was here. Mike threw up a desperate prayer and picked up the receiver. "This is Mike."

"Mike, this is Pete calling from the ranger station at the marina."

"Yes, is there any word on Jack?"

"Yes, well yes and no."

"What the hell does 'yes and no' mean?"

There was a pause on the other end of the line. "We found an ice chest. It had a few empty beer cans in it. It's red and white, with 'Strand' written across it."

"Oh God, that's my ice chest! And what else? Is that all you found? What about Jack?"

"I'm sorry, Mike. That's all we found. No sign of Jack. There weren't even any footprints. We found the ice chest on rocky terrain. We combed the area for any signs of fresh prints, but...look Mike, with the weather we've had recently we can't tell how fresh any of the tracks in the area are..."

"So what are you trying to tell me? That he just vanished into thin air? Where the hell is he then?"

"Mike, I'm sorry. That's all I can tell you."

"You mean you found his ice chest and you can't track him from there? How incompetent are you people?"

"Now look here son, before you go off and say something stupid, there are a few facts you ought to know. After it rains anything more than a sprinkle we can't effectively track. Whatever tracks may still be there are useless. And not only that, do you have any idea how many people in a given season hike in the area surrounding that marina? Of course there were tracks, but there were dozens of them, and all washed out to the point of being virtually worthless. We can't tell what's fifteen minutes old and what's fifteen days old after a good rain. And lastly we've had a helicopter search the area twenty miles in all directions that side of the river, and we got nothin' but an ice chest. I'm sorry, I wish I had better news, but we ran a search and rescue by the book. So before you go off and take cracks at me and my team…"

"Okay, okay. I was out of line…I'm sorry. But isn't there anything else that can be done about Jack?"

"Look, the ground S and R is still under way. That's all we can do. The helicopter's done what it can. If he's out there, he can't be seen from the air. I'll call you if there's anything else." And then Mike heard the line go dead.

Mike replaced the phone. His head spun. He felt faint and set himself down on a chair while he still could. Mike tried to focus his thoughts, but couldn't. He held his head in his hands, begging the dizziness to stop. It was as though his computer just kept spinning and wouldn't boot up.

Mike felt a dull pressure on his shoulder, yet he didn't move. Then his shoulder shook back and forth. He next became aware that he stared without seeing out the window in the lobby. "Young man, can you hear me?"

Mike looked up to see a kindly older woman wearing all white with her hand still on his shoulder. "Uh yeah," he said.

"Do you know where you are?" asked the nurse.

Mikes thoughts came rushing back to him. "In the Marble Hospital…I just got some news…"

"There's a young lady in room 238 that's awfully worried about you."

Mike stood, holding onto the chair while his head settled. "I can't…I'm not ready to…Tell her I'll see her later."

He slowly walked down the hall. Mike wasn't aware of walking or opening doors. He crossed the street and found his way into his motel room. Once the door was shut he slumped onto the carpet. Mike sat with his back to the bed and his head in his hands, slowly shaking his head from side to side. "He can't be gone. They must've overlooked something. Maybe they'll find him in…or maybe he'll be hurt, but…or maybe he's asleep somewhere…It'll be alright. It has to be alright."

The River: Day 11

A knock on the door jarred Mike from sleep. He looked around the room, wondering where he was. Someone knocked again. Mike stared at the door before comprehending the noise, and then opened the door. Dr. Painter stared into Mike's eyes, and then a smile formed on his face. "How are you doing?" asked Dr. Painter. Mike searched his mind, finding no answer. He waved Dr. Painter into the room and sat down on the bed. Dr. Painter remained standing and watching Mike. "When I came in to see Stacy this morning she told me you never came back after taking a phone call. She got worried and asked me to check on you. Did you get bad news?"

Mike nodded, "They found some of Jack's gear, but no Jack."

"Oh…I'm sorry."

Mike nodded as he stared at the floor. He pulled his knees up into his chest and leaned back against the wall.

"Is there anything I can do?" asked Dr. Painter. Mike shook his head.

"Why don't I walk you back to Stacy's room? I think you should be with someone."

Mike nodded and followed Dr. Painter out the door.

As soon as Mike walked through the open hospital room door Stacy's eyes blazed as she said, "Where in God's creation did you go?"

"I was so shocked that I…I didn't know what to do, so I went"…

"When you never came back I feared you'd left," said Stacy.

"Left? Where would I go without you?"

"I don't know, but I can't believe you just left the hospital without telling me."

Mike looked out the window while he took in Stacy's words. "I get that...I'm sorry. I was just so...so shaken up when I got the news."

"What news?" asked Stacy.

Tears flowed down Stacy's face as she absorbed the news about Jack. She pulled Mike close and held him. The vacant look on Mike's face worried her. She'd never seen him like that. "I know he's your best friend...I feel so...I'm sorry," said Stacy. Stacy waited, but received no response.

"Mike, say something. You're scaring me."

"I don't know what to say...I just can't believe they can't find him." Stacy held him tighter, and rubbed his back.

"But isn't there still a chance they'll find him?" asked Stacy.

"I don't know. I don't know how long he can last without..."

"Oh my God...does Kathy know?" asked Stacy.

"I don't think so. I didn't tell her. Has Kathy woken up yet?"

"Dr. Painter didn't say, and I forgot to ask I was so worried about you."

"I can't tell her. I don't know if she's strong enough to hear something like this," said Mike.

"But I think she'd want to know," said Stacy.

"Yeah, I know you're right. I just hate to be the bearer of this kind of news. I don't even like saying it out loud." Mike sat up, pulling away from Stacy's embrace.

"I know. I don't envy you."

"Do you think I should tell her right when she wakes up?"

Stacy thought for a moment, and then said, "Yes, I do."

"You're probably right...but I don't want to scare her too much. I mean you ladies almost died. And we don't even know much yet."

"I know Mike, but I still think she'd want to know whatever there is to know."

Stacy and Mike sat with their private thoughts. Mike rubbed the sides of his head, while Stacy watched her man with concern. "You know Mike, I thought I'd lost you the other day. I was so worried when you didn't come back that morning with help. I argued with Kathy to stay and wait for you longer. I was afraid you didn't make it back. I couldn't bear the thought that...I mean you're the best thing that's happened to me in a long time...well, probably ever. I think that's why I was so upset when you didn't come back to my room yesterday."

Mike smiled and squeezed Stacy's hand. "It'll take more than a storm, a shipwreck and no food to get rid of me." Stacy grinned and pulled Mike into an embrace. They sat quietly talking for the next couple of hours until Dr. Painter came into the room. He stood leaning against the door frame.

"I have good news. Kathy's regained consciousness, and does not seem to have suffered any brain damage."

"Oh that's terrific, thank you, doctor!" responded Stacy. Dr. Painter smiled and nodded, and then left the room. Mike maintained a grim look on his face.

"What is it, Mike? Aren't you glad that Kathy's okay?"

"Sure, but that means I have to go tell her."

"Oh, right."

"I suppose I ought to go tell her now. She has a right to know. Damn, I wish I could put it off longer."

Stacy squeezed Mike's hand. "Come tell me how she takes it."

Mike nodded, sighed and left to deliver the news. As he walked down the corridor to Kathy's room he felt like one of the armed forces guys who knock on doors and tell people their loved one has been killed in combat. But then he thought that he might be overreacting, since he didn't really know where Jack was yet. Jack might be okay.

He reached Kathy's door and paused. Mike searched his mind for the right words to say. Then he shrugged, took a deep breath and entered her room. Kathy lit up when she saw Mike, and reached her hand out for him. He gave her his hand and sat on the edge of her bed.

"You made it back to the marina!" said Kathy in a tired voice. Mike nodded solemnly, "Yeah, barely I suppose."

"What do you mean, barely?" asked Kathy.

"I woke up on a cot in the ranger station...I guess I fainted at their door," said Mike as his face grew grim.

Kathy noted his expression. "Why the sad face? Are you still recovering?"

"No, I'm okay."

"Is Stacy alright?"

"Yeah, Stacy's okay. She's resting down the hall."

"So then what is...? Oh my God, it's Jack? What happened to Jack?" said Kathy with an air of alarm.

Mike shook his head from side to side. "I'm sorry Kathy, but Jack hasn't been found."

"What do you mean 'hasn't been found'? Where else can he be? But they're still looking for him, right?" Mike nodded.

"But where is he then. He couldn't have gone too far."

"I don't know, Kathy."

"They'll find him, won't they?"

Tears formed in Mike's eyes. Kathy turned her face away from Mike and put her hand up to her mouth. She cried softly. Mike waited and continued to hold her hand. Finally she turned back to face him with wet eyes.

"What exactly did they tell you?"

Mike exhaled and told her, "They found my ice chest. You know, the one that he was carrying the beer in. They found it with a couple of beer cans...empty."

"My God, I hope this didn't kill him," Kathy whispered.

"What?

"I worried that this would kill him."

"Kill him? What are you talking about? You make it sound like you had something to do with it. Don't do that to yourself Kathy," urged Mike. Kathy appeared to not have been listening. She continued looking out the window.

"Kathy, did you hear what I said? Kathy?" However, Kathy was unresponsive and her grip of his hand had gone slack. Mike reached over and gently turned her face towards him. Her eyes focused on him briefly, and then turned back to the window. Mike gave up and left the room.

Mike paced the corridor several times. He'd been shaken by Kathy's reaction to the news. He returned to Stacy's room, where she waited watching the news. Stacy turned off the television when Mike entered. Mike sat down in the chair with his head down. "Well, how'd she take it?" Stacy asked.

"Not well at all. I'm not sure, but it seemed like she blamed herself for Jack being missing."

"No! We can't allow her to do that to herself."

"I know. I tried to talk her out of it, but it was like she was in some kind of trance and I couldn't get her out of it."

"Oh poor Kathy," said Stacy.

"What else can I do for her? I don't know if I should go back and try again, or if it'd be better to just give her some time, or what?"

"She might need some time to absorb the shock...but I wouldn't wait too long. That's such awful news to take in alone...Lie down next to me. I want to feel you next to me." Mike smiled and sat down on the bed next to her. Stacy turned the television back on and leaned on Mike's shoulder.

Mike glanced at his watch. Two hours had passed since his visit with Kathy. He stood, crossed his arms and then looked at Stacy. "Well, I figure it's been long enough. I'll go check on Kathy...and see if she'll talk to me now."

Stacy nodded and said, "She probably needs somebody with her...And Mike, go easy on her." Mike set his jaw, nodded and left the room.

Mike pushed the door open a crack and peeked inside. Kathy's head faced the window, turned away from the door. He wasn't sure if she was awake, and approached the bed cautiously. She didn't stir. Mike walked around to the far side of the bed, and Kathy looked him in the eye and said, "Oh, I didn't hear you come in. Is there any more news of Jack?" Mike shook his head. "I've always had a dark fear that Jack wouldn't make it through...I know I'm being too hard on myself, but I feel like I've done this to him. That I've so deeply wounded him that he couldn't rebound. When you told me about him not being found and the ice chest it hit me like a strike of lightning. I kept thinking 'I knew it'. There's the evidence that my worst fears are true." Mike sat on the edge of Kathy's bed.

"Jack always seemed fragile to me…like a boy who's stuck in childhood, never having really made it to adulthood. And I made it worse by how I treated him…I think it's actually what I liked about Jack in the first place, at least in part. Maybe I thought I could make a man of him. Maybe I imagined he was asking me to help him grow up…Maybe he was just…I don't know. Whatever it was, I see now that I don't like how I was with him."

"Kathy, aren't you taking on too much responsibility here for Jack?" asked Mike.

"Am I? I don't know. I suppose I might be, I mean, I know Jack's made his own choices and all. I just can't stand the thought of being one of those people who blame their spouse for their problems and all their unhappiness."

"Of course you don't want to blame anybody."

"Oh my God no. I so want to figure out where we went wrong. Something's not working between us. There has to be more than I can figure…I guess I also am struggling with my guilt over our marital problems, especially with what's happened now. I don't know how I'm going to take it if he turns up dead."

"Now Kathy, nobody made him do what he did."

Kathy smiled and squeezed Mike's hand. "It's sweet of you to say so. I know what you're saying is probably true, but I'll need time to…time to deal with…I guess with my guilt over whatever happens to him out there."

Dr. Painter entered the room. "So how's my patient feeling?"

"My head doesn't hurt as much, but I'm really hungry. Can I get some real food?" asked Kathy.

"Maybe something light; we don't want to shock your system with too much at first."

"Well, I'm heading back to Stacy's room," said Mike as he walked towards the door.

A nurse brushed past Mike on his way out of the room. She took Kathy's hand and said, "So, how's my favorite patient doing?"

"Oh, hi Alex. I don't really know."

"You've been through quite an ordeal, even the little that I know of it," said Alex. Kathy averted her eyes before saying, "I don't think I want to talk about it anymore."

"Okay dear, I won't pressure you, but I do think you need to talk to someone about this when you're ready," suggested Alex.

"I suppose I'll talk to my sister when I get home."

"That's not what I mean. I know it's none of my business, but you have something serious on your mind," said Alex.

After a pause Kathy said, "Well, I suppose I do, but..."

"Kathy it's plain to see that you are distressed...and I mean more than just the medical situation you're in."

"How do you know I'm distressed?" asked Kathy.

"Look I know this must sound strange, but I've faced enough of my own suffering to recognize somebody in pain. And you seem to be suffering alone."

The woman's words opened the flood gates and Kathy cried involuntarily. The woman put her hand on Kathy's arm while she cried. Kathy surprised herself with her flood of emotion. My God, can this woman see right through me? I don't know if I want her to. I don't feel ready to talk about this to anyone, and especially to a stranger.

As Kathy's tears slowed she glanced up at the woman, expecting to see impatience. The woman smiled with eyes of compassion. "I know you're right, but I don't know what to say," Kathy began, "Some things happened out on the river...and I think maybe even before the river trip...but I don't know if I'm ready to get into it. I can't even say what it is."

"When the time is right, you will need a friend. You need a confidant to whom you can say anything. Everybody ought to have one," said Alex.

Kathy turned away towards the window. She was tempted to open up more to this kind woman. Yet something held her back. Kathy wasn't used to talking to anyone in such a personal manner, with the exception of her sister. "I'll give it some thought. I appreciate your…kindness," said Kathy.

The next day when Kathy woke up she found herself looking for Alex. However, Alex didn't work the morning shift. By the time Alex came on duty in the afternoon, Kathy was ready to talk. Kathy said, "I've been thinking more about what you said. It's partly that my husband's missing…I'm really worried about him. But there's more to it. I feel like there's something wrong between us and…I don't know what else to say."

"Your marriage isn't okay," said Alex.

"Yes, it seems like we have a lot of conflict, but I don't know, maybe that's normal. I mean, I know marriage isn't supposed to be a walk in the park. But somehow, I thought we'd be able to work it out in some way. I don't know why…"

"Yes, there's something deeply troubling about your relationship with your husband, and I think you need to get to the bottom of it," said Alex.

Kathy stared off out the window as she pondered Alex's comment. Nothing clear came to her. "I don't know what's going on. It still seems like I just need something to be different between us…I don't think I know what else to say."

Alex paused before saying, "Well, think about it more, and let me give you my number in case you want to talk again." Alex pulled a pen out and wrote on the back of a business card and handed it to Kathy. This is my cell number, call me whenever you like."

"Do you often give out your number to patients crying in the hospital?"

Alex laughed. "No I don't, but I enjoy helping out when I can. Please call if you want, it would be a pleasure for me to help you again." And with that Alex got up, smiled, and walked out of the room.

Kathy watched her go. She wondered about her question, "What might the deal be with me and Jack? And what in God's name happened out there on the river?" Again nothing clear came to her. She shrugged her shoulders and turned over and fell back to sleep.

Kathy awoke to thoughts about her conversation with Alex. At first she brushed these thoughts away as a distraction, yet they kept coming back. When Kathy eventually allowed herself to pause long enough to think about it, she realized she wanted to talk with Alex again, but felt embarrassed to bother her. Alex had gone off duty while Kathy slept. She dialed Alex's number several times, only to hit cancel. This time she allowed the call to ring through. She was relieved to get her voice mail and left a brief message.

Alex surprised Kathy by calling her back within the hour. "Hi Kathy, I'm so glad you called. I was hoping you would. What can I do for you?"

"I don't really know. I just wanted to talk again. I keep thinking about what you said. I mean I think I have been through something big. I don't know though, in some ways it just seems like another one of our vacations."

"Do you normally almost die on your vacations?" asked Alex.

Kathy laughed nervously. "Well no, I guess I don't. But except for that part, it seems like a regular trip for us."

"That's sad," said Alex.

"It is?"

"It is to me. From the little you told me, you and Jack weren't having that good of a time, even before the problems of the river trip began."

"No, I guess we didn't," agreed Kathy. "So what do I do now?"

"It might help you to talk it through with someone. You might need help," suggested Alex.

"What kind of help? I tried asking Jack, and it didn't seem to help to talk to him."

"I wasn't thinking of Jack. You might try seeing a therapist."

"A therapist? You don't think I'm a nut case do you?"

"No, nothing like that," said Alex with a laugh. "Maybe I should tell you some of my story. My husband left me eight years ago. I was floored. I had no idea why he'd left. I kept myself in shape and I was available to him sexually, so I couldn't imagine why he'd want to leave. If he was having an affair I didn't know about it, and so I wasn't asking him to give anything up. Looking back on it later, I saw that he spent most of his time at the office or out with the guys. Anyway, when he moved out I was so devastated that I didn't leave the house for a week, and I only went out then because I needed groceries. I didn't return phone calls from my friends either. Finally, after a few weeks of this, a friend knocked on my door. I wasn't planning to answer, but when I looked out the window and saw her I melted. After listening to me for hours, she handed me a business card and told me to call this person. I looked at the card and was surprised to see the name of a therapist.

Anyway, to make a long story short, after seeing this therapist for awhile everything began to make sense. I began remembering things that Larry said, like 'Alex, I don't even know who you are.' My therapist helped me see that I didn't even know me. If I didn't know me, how could Larry. Larry was married to a body with nobody home. I would have left too. It's taken me a long time to find out who I am. As painful as it was at the time, Larry leaving me was the best thing that ever happened to me. Now I'm hardly suggesting that you leave Jack, but I strongly encourage you to get into therapy and figure out what is going on."

"Well, you don't seem like a nut case."

"I'd like to think not, but I sure had a lot to work on," said Alex.

"So what can a therapist do?"

"If you find the right fit, a therapist can help you understand the dance between you and Jack, and begin to look at your part in the dance. I came to understand that I didn't have a chance to make a relationship work until I looked at my role in my marriage. If I hadn't, I'd probably have ended up in the same kind of relationship again. Anyway, you won't be able to do much about it until you can see the dance steps."

"What you're saying sounds kind of good, even though I don't really understand what you mean. But I don't even know anyone that's been to see a therapist. I thought that was just for crazy people."

"Well if that's the case then I must be crazy," laughed Alex.

"You don't seem crazy, although I keep wondering if you're going to get weird on me. But I have to admit that something about what you're saying intrigues me. I tried talking to my sister, and she told me to leave him. And I don't want to leave him."

"Give this therapist a call and let me know how it works out," said Alex.

"I'll think about it, but I'm not sure I'm ready for that. I don't know if it will help."

"Only one way to find out," said Alex.

7 Weeks after the River Trip

It had been almost two months since the fateful river trip. Kathy's life still seemed strange to her, although she'd be hard pressed to say why. Something about the river trip had changed her. On the outside, life seemed to be getting back to normal, which may be good, or perhaps not so good.

Kathy came into the condominium from the garage. She set her purse and day timer down and found Lily watching a video in the family room. Lily's face lit up and she ran into Kathy's arms saying, "Mommy, you're home!"

"And how's my little teddy bear tonight?"

"I'm good."

"And how was school?"

"Fun. I played dodge ball with Melinda and Lacy and Bridget."

"That does sound like fun. Did anyone bean you with the ball?"

"Yeees, they always do, silly."

Kathy carried Lily into the master bedroom and set her down on the bed next to Jack. He looked up from his Sports Illustrated magazine and said, "Oh, hi babe." Kathy smiled and got into the shower. Lily climbed into her daddy's lap and snuggled against him. Jack hugged her tight, gave her a kiss on her forehead, and stroked her hair while he read his magazine.

When Kathy got out of the shower Jack was reclining on the bed, but Lily had gone to watch the rest of her video. He glanced up, "Hey Kath, what are you doing home so early?"

"Oh tonight I have my first therapy group, and I wanted to shower first."

"Is this that guy that the nurse turned you onto?" asked Jack.

"Yeah, that's right. Alex gave me his number."

"You sure you want to do something extreme like that?" asked Jack.

"I don't know that I'd say it's extreme, but I do have my doubts about it."

"I still don't get what you need help with," said Jack.

"Jack we've been over this. I need help dealing with…us. Something just isn't right."

"Come on Kath, are you still dwelling on the other night? I thought we'd gotten past that. You've got to let it go."

"Maybe something is wrong with me. I don't get how you can seem to let it all roll off your back like water."

"I just don't think about it anymore and it goes away. It's gone and I've moved on. Come on Kath, things are pretty good between us. I think you'd see that if you would just lighten up. You hold onto things."

"Maybe you're right, Jack, but I don't know. I try to let things go, but they keep coming back to me. I have to find out if somebody can help me with this, because I don't like how we fight."

"Well, suit yourself," Jack said with a shrug of his shoulders. "I don't know what time I'll be home, but I'm going over to Mike's with Lily to watch the ball game."

"Okay."

On the way over to Dr. Aragorn's office Kathy wondered what the group would be like. She tried to picture what the people might be like. She'd met with Dr. Tim Aragorn earlier in the week for an interview, so at least she had some idea what he was like. Dr. Aragorn was in his mid-forties with kind and unblinking eyes. Kathy felt uncomfortable with how he seemed to look right into her. She wondered how much he saw, and if he was thinking she was crazy. However, he'd been kind and welcoming of Kathy into his group. Kathy pulled into the parking lot and took one last look in the mirror. Satisfied with what she saw, she grabbed her purse and left the car.

The waiting room was good sized with seven small chairs

arranged around the perimeter. Four of the chairs were occupied, and each of the occupants looked up at Kathy when she walked in. Three of the people simply glanced her way briefly, but one woman sized Kathy up for what felt like an hour. Kathy sat down self consciously. Her eyes darted around the room, trying to avoid eye contact with the others. She was curious about each of them, assuming they were the other members of the group, but she didn't risk a close examination as she didn't want to attract attention, or appear to be staring at anyone. Instead she inspected the room, which had chocolate carpeting and wood chairs with two matching end tables. Both tables had a lamp and several magazines scattered on top. The walls were painted with a cream color and were hung with a picture or two. Kathy thought, My God, how long has it been since somebody redecorated this room. It looks like it belongs in a 70s sit-com. I hope this group isn't going to be lame. Maybe I should just get up and leave. I didn't commit to anything…well, I suppose I'll just see how it goes.

Soft classical music played in the background. Kathy excused herself as she reached over a woman sitting next to her to pick up a magazine. She had no interest in the contents of the magazine, but was thankful for something to pretend to focus on. Through her peripheral vision she monitored the other people in the waiting room. Two of them were men, the other two women. Then another woman quietly entered the room from the outside door.

After ten awkward minutes in the waiting room, Dr. Aragorn opened the door and with a smile and a nod invited everyone in. Kathy waited for everyone else to go into the consulting room first, not sure if there were assigned seats. Since only an end spot on the couch remained vacant, Kathy knew her place and sat down. Her palms felt moist, her ears and throat felt hot, and her stomach flip flopped. Kathy glanced around the room to see the same chocolate carpet and similar décor and thought, who decorated this cheesy office? Does this guy have no taste or what? What kind of strange guy is he? Who does this weird kind of work anyways?

After an anxious moment Dr. Aragorn finally spoke, "Tonight we have a new member, so we'll start by introducing ourselves. I think everyone knows me," and looking to his left, "Tom, will you start?"

"Uh yeah, I'm Tom, but I guess Dr. Aragorn already said that, and I been coming for over a year now. I started because I was down a lot. I've figured out that I'm depressed. Dr. Aragorn and the group are helping me learn that my depression is just the tip of the iceberg." Everyone laughed but Kathy.

"I'm Susan and I've been in group for two and a half years. I came because I was getting a divorce," said the next person with a smile.

"My name's Karen, and I'm here because I get too caught up in details, and it was driving me nuts, not to mention my boss. I almost got fired, and I was on probation for six months at my job. I'm realizing that I'm pretty nervous. I've been in group for almost two years," she said without emotion.

"I'm Jake, and I've been here for almost a year. I started coming when my wife threatened to leave me," he said with a sad grin.

"Evelyn is my name, and I'm in group to deal with my overeating and my weight problem," she said as Kathy quizzically eyed her average looking figure. "Well I started in group because of my weight, and now am dealing with all the things that were going on behind the scenes, and I've been here over three years," Evelyn said with a warm smile.

"Evelyn is our old timer," said Dr. Aragorn. "Okay Kathy, why don't you introduce yourself, and don't feel pressure to say much yet."

Kathy shifted in her seat and uncrossed her legs and then crossed them the other way. She cleared her throat twice and licked her lips before saying, "I'm Kathy, as Dr. Aragorn said, and I'm here because I need help…uh…I guess we're all here for help," she added with a nervous laugh. "I need help with my marriage. I'm not sure what else to say because I don't even know what's wrong." Kathy looked around the room to see if it was okay to continue. All eyes were patiently on her.

"You can tell us some about your marriage, if you like," said Dr. Aragorn.

"I don't know what to do about my husband. He can't seem to get a career going for over five years, and then the moment that he does he wants to quit. I guess he expects me to keep supporting him indefinitely. He also doesn't do what he says he'll do. Jack will tell me he'll handle an issue with the bank or a bill, and then I find out later that he didn't and I feel like I'm about to go crazy. And he's irresponsible. He'll hurt himself or get sick and not go see the doctor to take care of himself, until I tell him again and again to go in for it." Kathy stopped and glanced around the room nervously.

Susan said, "How long have you been married?"

"About seven years now."

"Oh yes, the play time is over and now you're in the thick of the hard part of trying to make a marriage work," said Susan.

"We did have a great time the first year or so, but it's gotten worse since then," said Kathy.

"Have you had anyone to talk with about your marriage before now?" asked Dr. Aragorn.

Tears welled up in Kathy's eyes, "No, not until a woman approached me in the hospital a few weeks ago."

"You were in the hospital?" asked Jake.

"Oh that…we were on vacation and something…well, something bad happened and…well, I think I'll save that for another time."

"Getting back to not having anyone to talk to, that's quite a burden you've been carrying on your own, Kathy," added Dr. Aragorn. Kathy nodded and cried silently. She pulled a tissue out of her purse and blotted her eyes. "Hopefully we can help you sort out what's happening in your marriage, but the most important help the group might offer you is a place to bring yourself and not be alone in your struggles."

Kathy nodded, "That would be nice," she whispered, not yet having her voice back.

"Before I started group, I didn't know if I was crazy or my husband was crazy, or both. The group helped me feel sane…well, at least a little sane," said Susan.

"I didn't have the first clue how to change when I first started," began Evelyn, "and group helped me to realize there were all kinds of issues going on inside me that I was completely unaware of. I feel like a different person now that I've begun getting to know myself."

"What does getting to know yourself have to do with getting help? I don't care if I know myself, I just want to fix my marriage," said Kathy.

Several group members laughed or smiled. "That's what we all think when we start, and then after a while we find out it has everything to do with getting help," said Jake. The others nodded their heads in agreement. Kathy looked at Dr. Aragorn blankly.

"Don't expect much to make sense yet, it's enough for now just to be here. Just keep coming and you'll do fine," said Dr. Aragorn.

"Don't worry about it, I didn't get that until I'd been coming at least six months," said Susan.

"So how does it feel to be here so far?" asked Dr. Aragorn.

Kathy stared at Dr. Aragorn and then said, "I don't know."

"Is group about what you expected, or were you thinking it'd be different in some way?"

"I didn't know what to expect, or what to even talk about. I guess I wondered if you'd all seem crazy to me," said Kathy with a smile. Everyone laughed.

"I thought I was crazy when I first started coming," said Karen.

"You are crazy," said Jake with a grin. Karen made a face at him. Dr. Aragorn turned his gaze back to Kathy.

"I think I'm mostly confused about my marriage," said Kathy as she began to cry again.

"Be patient with yourself, you'll get there. We all started out about where you are," offered Evelyn. And then the group moved on to Jake. Kathy tried to follow what everyone had to say to Jake, yet her mind went in and out of focus. Her head was spinning slightly, and she felt strange.

Kathy felt strangely calm as she drove home from group. She certainly didn't have any new insights, but she somehow felt better just being there. What they said rang a faint bell deep within her, yet she couldn't say what that was. Kathy took a leisurely shower, and then settled into bed with her book. She liked to read novels.

When Jack got home he carried Lily into her room. She'd fallen asleep on the way home from watching the game. Jack came into the bedroom and asked, "So how was it?"

"Pretty good, I think."

"You liked it?"

"Yes, I think so. I'm definitely going back."

"Oh that's great," said Jack flatly as he turned his attention to the TV, which he'd just turned on. Kathy set the book down on the bed. She studied Jack's face. He turned to her and said, "What?" Kathy paused and considered saying more, then changed her mind and said, "Nothing. I'm going to turn off the light and go to bed. Would you mind watching TV in the other room?"

"Well don't feel the need to wear anything to bed on account of me," said Jack. Kathy chuckled and slipped into bed wearing only a thin t-shirt. Jack immediately recognized her invitation and turned off the TV and set the remote on the night stand, and slipped his fingers under the covers. Kathy moaned in delight, which increased Jack's excitement.

Afterwards Jack held Kathy as they lay in bed, gently stroking her arm. Kathy lay content in his arms. "Wow Kath, maybe those people have already fixed you."

"Oh yeah, definitely. It was so easy. All they had to do was throw a switch inside me, and viola, I'm healed," she said with a smile.

"It sure seems like it. You haven't made love to me like that since I don't know when," said Jack.

"Besides, I'm going to group to fix you, Jack."

"What, me? I don't need no fixing. I good just the way I am," said Jack.

"Well, we'll see about that," said Kathy with a chuckle.

"So what made that great sex happen? I want to figure it out and bottle it." Kathy laughed and rolled over and turned out the light.

"Oh by the way, my mom called and wants to have Lily's birthday party over at her house," said Jack.

"Oh that's sweet of Gran-gran to offer, but I want to have it here. I don't want her to do all that work."

"Kath, don't kid yourself, you'd be doing her a favor by letting her host the party."

"You sure it wouldn't be too much for her? It's a lot of work to host a party with a dozen kids."

"Trust me, I'm SURE it wouldn't be a bother for her. It'll give her something to live for next month," said Jack.

"I'll call her back and talk to her about it."

The next week Kathy felt more comfortable driving to group. She wasn't quite as nervous. However, Kathy didn't know if she'd want to say anything tonight. She exchanged smiles with the others when she sat down in the waiting room. Five minutes later she took her same place on the end of the couch in Dr. Aragorn's office. Evelyn started group by bringing up something that happened between her and a friend, and the group was off and running. It wasn't until the last fifteen minutes that there was a pause and Dr. Aragorn turned to Kathy, "So Kathy, what's on your mind tonight?"

"Um, I don't know…"

"How did you feel after your first group last week?" Dr. Aragorn asked.

"At first I liked it, but then later I wasn't so sure. I don't know if this is the right place for me. I mean I guess I liked coming okay, but it didn't really help me."

"What kind of help did you expect?" asked Evelyn.

"I don't know…I suppose I thought you'd tell me what to do about my marriage," said Kathy.

"You mean you thought I'd give you some kind of advice?" asked Dr. Aragorn.

"Yeah, I guess so. I thought you'd tell me what to go say to Jack."

"It doesn't work that way. There's nothing to go home and do yet," said Susan.

"But then what good is coming here?" asked Kathy.

"You're probably confused about how this works," said Evelyn.

"Yes, so explain it to me."

"You have to start by getting to know yourself. There's nothing else to do before that," said Evelyn.

"Just like I told you last week, I'm not interested in getting to know myself! I just want my marriage to be better," said Kathy.

Jake laughed, and then said, "I think that might be exactly what I said the first month, maybe word for word."

"It took me three months before I liked coming," said Susan. "I hated it at first."

"What changed it for you?" asked Kathy.

"At first I felt worse when I'd come here. It took a few months until I could let myself take in anything from the group. I was pushing everybody away at first."

"I didn't like it for awhile either," began Tom. "I thought everybody here, including me, just needed to suck it up and deal with life. I almost quit every week the first month." Several people laughed.

"I still don't like it. I keep wondering why I keep coming," said Karen with a smirk.

"I don't want to keep coming if I don't like it. I don't see how you keep coming if you don't like it," said Kathy. Karen frowned and looked away.

"How are you doing with your marriage?" asked Dr. Aragorn.

"We didn't fight as much this week…but I don't think that anything's changed."

"Maybe it helped just starting with us," suggested Dr. Aragorn.

Kathy wondered if Dr. Aragorn might be an idiot, or perhaps self deluded. She stared at Dr. Aragorn a moment before saying,

"I don't see how that's possible." Several people laughed and nodded.

Dr. Aragorn smiled and said, "Just give it time."

Kathy thought a moment and added, "In fact, I don't see how merely coming here will do anything for me. It seems like a waste of time and money."

"Well, we'll just have to see," said Dr. Aragorn.

"Although I don't know what else to do; I have to do something about my marriage," said Kathy.

"Why is that?" asked Susan.

"Well, it's kind of like what happened the other night…I got home from hanging out with my sister all day. Jack had been home with Lily, our daughter, all day. I walked into the kitchen and almost gagged when I took a breath. I've asked him a hundred times to clean up after himself in the kitchen. The dishes from breakfast sat on the sink, and at least they made it that far. But the lunch was still all over the kitchen table. When I said something to Jack, he told me to give him a break, and that he would have gotten to it if I'd given him a chance. At that point I told him to get in there and clean up right now! I tried to say something to Jack after Lily was in bed. He just said to not worry about it, and that it was no big deal. When I tried to get him to sit down with me and talk with me, he just said to let it go. At that point I threw my hands up in the air and left the room."

"And did he have any other response?" asked Susan.

"He tells me to just let it go and get over it," said Kathy.

Several people groaned. "That doesn't work for me," said Evelyn. "I tried that."

"I've tried to just let it go, and I can't. I don't know how he does it. It seems like Jack is usually over our fights the next day, sometimes even the same day, or even the moment after the fight. It's almost like it never happened to him. It seems so stress free, I wish I knew how to do that."

"It looks good, and it might work for Jack, but there's a cost to operating that way," said Dr. Aragorn.

"What cost?" asked Kathy.

"He has to get rid of his feelings somehow to be able to pull that off."

"How does he do that?" asked Kathy.

"I don't know. I don't know Jack, but there are many ways to cut yourself off, which is fine if you don't want to feel," explained Dr. Aragorn.

"It sounds pretty good to me right now. I don't want to feel either…in fact I hate feeling!"

"Yeah, but Kathy, you would just stay the same if you did what Jack's asking you to do. Would you be happy with that?" said Evelyn.

"You're in pain," said Dr. Aragorn.

"I don't want to be in pain. I don't want to deal with my feelings. I don't particularly care about them. I just want my marriage to be better. Why do I have to do anything with my feelings?"

"Because they don't just go away," said Evelyn.

"What do you do with your feelings about your marriage?" asked Dr. Aragorn.

"I don't even know. It's not like I keep track of my feelings or anything. No offense, but to me honest, that seems like a stupid question to me," said Kathy.

"You're probably getting the same feelings again and again because you can't do anything with them. You've probably never learned how to process feelings with somebody. And you're not sure that I can help you," said Dr. Aragorn.

"I don't even know what you're talking about. And I'm not sure I want to process any feelings. And you're right, I don't know if you can help me. You haven't done me any good so far," said Kathy.

"If you stay in group you'll find out," said Susan.

"Getting back to the fight you had with Jack, you sound a bit controlling with him," suggested Karen. A couple of others nodded their heads, including Dr. Aragorn.

"You think so? What am I supposed to do, give him a high-five for leaving the kitchen a war zone?"

"Are those the only two choices? You either ignore it, or make Jack fix it?" asked Dr. Aragorn.

"Of course it is! If I don't get on Jack, then we live in a pig-sty."

"There are other ways to confront an issue. I mean no offense, but if I were Jack, I wouldn't like your approach either," suggested Karen.

"Well then enlighten me. What else should I do?" asked Kathy.

"I don't know, but I don't see how your approach will work," said Karen.

"Well, we're out of time for tonight, but we'll have to take a closer look at this," said Dr. Aragorn.

Two weeks later Kathy arrived early for group. She was the first one in the waiting room. This would be her fourth group, and she'd been contemplating telling the rest of the story of her marriage since the first week. Now she felt ready, and was planning to jump right in and begin. At first she'd been afraid of what the others would think about her marriage, but at this point she felt like the others misunderstood her anyway. While she sat in the waiting room she thought again about where she might start. She was still pondering various options when Dr. Aragorn opened the door to let them in.

Kathy waited until the last person sat down and started, "I want to go first tonight." She surveyed the group and saw expectant welcome. Reassured, she continued, "I haven't said much about my marriage yet, and I don't think you all got what I was trying to say a couple of weeks ago, so here goes."

Kathy took a deep breath and exhaled slowly, "Jack and I were introduced by mutual friends eight years ago. We were both twenty-four. We had a lot of fun the year and a half we dated before marrying. Jack was really entertaining to be with. I loved how he was game to be adventurous. We went skiing and hiking, and other stuff like that. I'd never been with a guy that fun, so when he asked me to marry him I said 'yes' right away. When we were first married everything was great. We kept having a good time together and still went out regularly." Then Kathy frowned and continued, "I don't remember us fighting at all while we dated, so I was surprised when we started, but at first I dismissed our fights as just having a bad day or something. Then we had Lily, and for a little while that seemed to help. But then we went back to the fighting...I kept getting more and more upset about his career."

"What about his career? You mentioned it briefly, but we don't know much." said Susan.

"He worked about twenty hours a week testing prototype new video games when we were married."

"Didn't that concern you at the time?" asked Evelyn.

"Not really. He told me that he would work up to a full-time position after we were married, but that he wanted time to help me plan the wedding for now...I suppose I liked that answer at the time. But when he still worked about twenty hours after we'd been married for a year, I started getting upset. Here I was working full-time since before the wedding, and he's still working half-time."

"So did you say something to him?" asked Evelyn.

"Yes. That's when the fights started. When I'd ask him about getting a real job he told me I was nagging, and to back off. I thought that maybe he was right, so I tried to back off for awhile, but I couldn't help myself. I started bringing it up again and the fights got worse. Jack started calling me 'Nagila', and I got even by calling him 'Playboy Peter'. I told him that it was time to leave Neverland."

Several members of the group laughed. Dr. Aragorn smirked. "I'll bet that set him straight," said Jake sarcastically.

"Not really," said Kathy. "As a matter of fact, that's when the fighting reached an all time low. I remember calling Jane, my sister, and crying on the phone for two hours that I wanted to get divorced. I didn't think I could take it much longer. I hated him calling me Nagila...I don't know how I've lasted as long as I have. I probably wouldn't have made it if it weren't for Jane."

"You're angry with Jack," suggested Dr. Aragorn.

"No, not really; I'm just frustrated with our marriage," said Kathy.

"You don't think of yourself as angry with him?" asked Susan.

"Not at all, I mean, I get a little frustrated at times, but not angry. I'm not an angry person."

"Just talking hypothetically, would it be so bad if you were angry with him?" asked Dr. Aragorn.

"Of course, I don't want to be a bitter person," said Kathy. Everyone was quiet for a moment before Susan broke the silence.

"Do you talk to Jane regularly?" asked Susan.

"I talk to her several times a week, mostly about Jack. And she can relate since she fights with her husband too."

"And does it help much talking to Jane?" asked Dr. Aragorn.

"Yes."

"How so?"

"I'm not sure what you're asking."

"I mean, what is it about your talks with Jane that helps?"

"I guess just that she knows what it was like to fight with her husband and be called names, and would tell me that Jack has a problem."

"Was she able to offer you any feedback?" asked Susan.

"Feedback? Yes, like I said, she told me that Jack had a problem."

"No, that's not what I mean. Could she help you make sense out of your conflict with Jack?" asked Susan.

"She would tell me that I was right and that Jack should get a real job, and that it was time for him to be a man now, that it was unfair of him to expect me to support him. That's pretty much it I guess."

"And did that help?" asked Dr. Aragorn.

"I don't know. I don't understand what you're asking me? I mean I liked hearing it."

"I'm glad you've had Jane's support and listening ear through all these years, and yet I don't hear that you and Jane were able to make much sense of the conflict with you and

Jack," said Dr. Aragorn.

"Well we sure didn't fix it," said Kathy with a laugh.

"Seven tough years of marriage is a long time to endure something that's not working. You did well to tolerate it," said Dr. Aragorn.

"I'm not sure how well I tolerated it."

Dr. Aragorn smiled and nodded. Evelyn added, "But you have somehow coped until now."

"I suppose."

"And I suppose it's now time to see if we can help you do better than cope," said Dr. Aragorn.

"Oh my God that would sure be nice!"

Jack sat in his favorite leather chair watching football and sipping on a beer. Kathy walked into the room and hugged Jack over the back of the chair. Lily sat next to Jack in his chair, watching the game with him. Kathy patted Lily on the head. "What was that for?" asked Jack.

"I just wanted to hug you, no special reason."

"Hi mommy, you're home!" said Lily.

"So what did the head shrinker have to say tonight?" asked Jack.

"Don't call him that! He's a nice man."

"So you're going to keep going to the crazies group?"

"Jack! You're calling me a crazy."

"Come on Kath, you don't need something like that, it's for people with problems, and for those that ain't playing with a full deck."

"What if this group helps our marriage? Wouldn't that be worth it?"

"I don't know Kath, I think we're doing just fine. The truth is, a head shrinker like that might make things worse."

"What makes you say that?"

"Come on Kath, you hear things."

Kathy thought about Jack's comment, and then decided to let it go. "Have you given Lily a bath yet?"

"I gave myself a bath, mommy."

"Yeah, it was maybe an hour ago," said Jack.

"Well, I'm going you bed, you coming soon?"

"Yeah."

"Oh yeah, I'm going over to your parents' a couple hours early to help set up. I'll bath Lily and do her hair, but don't put her party dress on till right before you come," said Kathy.

"Yeah yeah Kath, I got it handled."

"Jack, I want Lily to look nice for her birthday party; it's important to me, okay?"

"No worries Kath, I said I'll handle it."

On her way to the bedroom Kathy stopped at the kitchen counter and flipped through the mail. She opened the credit card statement and immediately saw red. "Jack, I thought you said you were going to get the credit card bill paid on time this month?"

"I know, I did."

"Then why did we get a twenty-five dollar late fee for the third month in a row?" Kathy asked with increasing volume.

"Come on Kath, it's no big deal. I'll bet they made a mistake on it, but even if they didn't, twenty bucks won't make or break us."

"Twenty-five."

"Whatever Kath, let it go." Kathy opened her mouth to say more, but then thought better of it. She shook her head, exhaled deeply, and walked into the bedroom.

Kathy looked up as Jack and Lily entered the party. Lily wore her party dress, including a grape juice stain down the front. Kathy darted her eyes at Jack, who shrugged his shoulders. Kathy rolled her eyes and took Lily by the hand into the bathroom. They emerged with Lily wearing a wet, but clean dress. Lily ran over to Jack and sat on his lap. He wrapped his arms around her and kissed her hair. Lily snuggled her head into her dad's shoulder. Kathy smiled and went to put candles on the cake.

Lily's eyes lit up as Kathy set the cake in front of her at the table. "Now honey, make a wish before you blow them out. And don't tell us what you wished for." After Lily blew out the candles Kathy pulled them off the cake and cut pieces for everyone. Once all the guests were eating cake she pulled a plastic trash bag out of the pantry. Kathy systematically scoured the living room for discarded wrapping paper and quickly filled two trash bags. She dragged them out to the trash cans, and then went into the kitchen and started working on the mountain of dishes.

Twenty minutes later Jack's mother came into the kitchen looking for her. "Kathy, what on God's green earth are you doing washing dishes! Come on out and enjoy the fun. For heaven's sake, I can wash the dishes at my own house."

"I've got it Gran-gran, I'm not going to leave these for you. There must be a hundred dishes, not to mention all the utensils and other random items to clean," said Kathy.

"Nonsense, come out and join us and we can do them after all the kids leave."

Kathy reluctantly dried her hands and followed Joanne, Gran-gran's given name, back to the dining room. After the two women sat down, Joanne turned to Jack and said, "My God Jack, don't ever let this one get away. She's the best catch you'll ever lay eyes on!"

"Oh believe me, Mom, I know."

"She must be the best wife in all of California!" gushed Joanne.

"I've thought of entering her in one of those contests for mom of the year, but the problem is I can't write a good essay," said Jack.

"Well, contest or no, you keep her at home."

"If she ever tries to leave me I'll hunt her down and fix her good," said Jack as he looked over at Kathy and winked.

Kathy gave Jack a quizzical glance. He responded with a sly smile.

The next day Kathy sat at her desk, responding to the last few emails. Thoughts of the mall came to her mind. In fact, she'd been thinking of the mall throughout the day. She called Jane to see if she wanted to meet her there on her way home from the office. Jane enthusiastically agreed to come, which worked out well since Kathy had to pick up Lily from Jane anyway. Jane usually picked Lily up from school at least one day a week. Kathy loved to hunt through the sales racks, searching for the hidden great deal, while Lily liked to hide in the racks and see if mommy could find her.

Within the hour Kathy and Jane each had a number of outfits on hangers that they took to the dressing rooms. They shook their heads at some, complimented the fit on others, and ended up buying a couple outfits each. While standing in line at the checkout Jane checked her cell phone for messages and noticed the time, "Oh my, guess what time it is?"

"I'd say about 6:30," answered Kathy.

"Try 7:10. We've been here for two hours!"

"Oh my God, Jack will wonder what happened to me."

"Oh he'll get over it," said Jane.

"Probably, but he's going to be mad…but that's okay I suppose," Kathy said with a smile.

Kathy walked Jane out to her car, and chatted for a few minutes at her door. Then she sighed and said, "Well, I really should be going now. Jack will be hungry."

"Okay honey, I'll see you soon," said Jane and she hugged her sister and got into her car. Kathy slowly walked to the car with Lily hand in hand and drove home.

When Kathy first got home she didn't see Jack, but she knew he was there because she'd seen his car in the driveway. Jack sat in his favorite chair when she emerged from the bedroom. He glanced up with eyes ablaze, "Where the hell have you been?"

"I met Jane at the mall."

"You were at the mall until 7:30? I've been starving here waiting for you to get home. I called your phone twice and it went to voicemail."

Kathy looked at the end table next to his chair, which was draped in the sports page, and served as a coaster to three empty beer bottles. "It looks like you started dinner without me," Kathy retorted.

"What are you talking about? I haven't had a damn thing to eat since lunch."

"But you've had plenty of liquid dinner just the same."

"Now don't start with the beer thing, Kath. I don't want to hear about that tonight. So what's for dinner?"

"I was thinking I'd just heat up some soup."

"Soup? That's it? You mean I've waited two hours for a can of soup?"

"It's late and I'm tired, and that's all I have the energy to make."

"Yeah you're tired because you were out late at the mall. If you'd gotten home on time you wouldn't be tired, and I'd be getting a decent meal."

Kathy glared at Jack, who didn't notice as his eyes were on the T.V. She banged the can of opened soup on the edge of the pan, and dropped the pan on the stove. Jack turned at the loud noise, but didn't say anything. A few minutes later Kathy set a bowl of soup on the sports page next to Jack, and retreated to the bedroom to change.

Kathy waited for a break in group, and jumped in first chance she found. She recounted the events of the previous evening, including her impulse to drop the soup in Jack's lap while he sat in his chair.

"Do you always cook for Jack?" asked Jake.

Kathy thought for a moment. "I always make him breakfast and dinner."

"And what does he do for lunch?" asked Jake.

"On the weekends I make it, but he goes out for lunch during the week."

"So he never makes his own meals," said Susan.

"I guess not," agreed Kathy.

"You complain about Jack not being responsible, but you do a lot for him," suggested Susan.

"Don't most wives make their husband's meals?" asked Kathy.

"Kathy, you work too! Maybe most wives who don't work outside the home might, but you work as many hours as Jack does, and probably more." said Susan.

Kathy looked at the floor and swung her crossed leg back and forth. Finally she looked up and said, "Are you saying that it's my fault that Jack is like that?"

"Heaven's no, but we are suggesting that you might be playing a part in feeling like a nag with Jack," said Evelyn.

"So what am I supposed to do?"

Dr. Aragorn set his drink down and said, "I think there may be another piece to this puzzle. I wonder if you might have been sending Jack a message by staying out late last night."

"Like what message? I just wanted to meet Jane and have some fun at the mall."

"Maybe that too, but I wonder if you were trying to tell him something as well," suggested Dr. Aragorn.

"Like what?"

"Like how angry you are with him," suggested Dr. Aragorn.

Kathy laughed nervously. She looked around the room and several people were nodding their heads. "I guess everybody thinks so. I mean guess I get mad at him on rare occasions, but it's not like I carry around a grudge." Kathy looked around the group, as nobody spoke. "What is it? Why aren't you saying anything?"

"I think you're more angry than you know," said Evelyn.

"Really? I don't know about…" began Kathy.

"You've been telling us how disappointing your marriage is, and you're not angry about it?" said Dr. Aragorn. Kathy glanced out the window. Her stomach churned.

"I don't want to be angry at Jack," Kathy said softly.

"And yet nothing is more likely," began Dr. Aragorn.

"It's ugly to be angry," said Kathy. "And how come it doesn't seem like I'm angry with Jack?"

"You're probably not allowing yourself to know. But it might show up in unexpected places. Where else has it gone?" asked Dr. Aragorn.

The first thought that came to Kathy was her credit card bill.

"I do like to shop, probably even more after I got married. I guess I do charge a lot at the mall."

"There you go," said Susan.

"There might be several reasons you enjoy going to the mall," said Dr. Aragorn.

Kathy laughed aloud, "My God, I go to the mall several times every week, and I always buy something."

"And how does Jack react to the bills?" asked Dr. Aragorn.

"He gets mad and tells me I am overspending."

"You've found a way to let Jack know how angry you are, and he's getting the message," said Evelyn.

"Oh my God," said Kathy with an uncertain smile. After pausing to consider she asked, "I don't know, I think you guys are getting too Freudian on me. I think this whole anger thing is a bunch of crap. I mean, I do get a little frustrated, but it's not as bad as you all make it sound."

Dr. Aragorn merely held her gaze.

"You're learning to look in the mirror, and some of what you see won't be pretty," added Susan.

"But I don't want to see ugly stuff! What's the benefit of that?" said Kathy.

"There's more benefit than you can possibly know," countered Susan.

"I'm here for help with my marriage. So what do I do about that?" asked Kathy.

"You keep showing up for group," suggested Evelyn.

"But that's not doing anything!" said Kathy.

"Just showing up is plenty for now," said Dr. Aragorn.

"But I have to do something, what good is just thinking about it?"

"More than you know yet," said Evelyn.

"But if I don't do anything, then thinking about it is wasted. Tell me what to do," said Kathy.

"Be patient with yourself. It takes time for genuine growth. You might be able to slap a band aid on it real quick and do something, but I don't know how helpful it would be. You're starting an important work that includes looking at your part in the dance with Jack. It's enough for now to just be looking inside," said Dr. Aragorn.

Kathy put her finger nails in her mouth, and began to gently nibble. Her eyes darted around the room, but no one said anything. The others gently gazed at her, in no hurry to move on. She shrugged her shoulders and sighed. "I'm done for tonight. This has been a waste of time."

Kathy set down her pen, straightened her papers, and packed up her satchel. The deposition had gone reasonably well, but it had taken all morning till 12:30. She stood, shook hands with the opposing attorney, made a reassuring comment to her client and left. A sandwich shop caught her eyes a few blocks down the road, and she pulled in for a bite. While she waited for her order she checked her cell phone for messages. There was one, "Hi Kathy, it's Alex. Just thought I'd call and see how group's going for you. I know you've just started, but I hope you're finding it helpful. Anyway, I'm off to my reading group. Give me a call when you feel like it."

Tears formed in the corners of her eyes, which she dabbed with a napkin. It warmed her heart to hear Alex's voice. She was the reason Kathy had even considered getting help. Kathy went up to the counter and retrieved her sandwich and iced tea, and sat down in the corner where she'd have some privacy. The sandwich looked so good after the long morning, and she took a bite and then hit the call back key. Alex picked up on the second ring, "This is Alex."

"Oh hi Alex, it's Kathy. I'm so glad you called. I'd been thinking about you, and was planning to call myself."

"So, how's group going?"

Kathy paused as she didn't know how to answer. "I'm not sure."

"Yes, you're probably still trying to figure out what you're supposed to do there."

Kathy laughed and said, "I not sure what to talk about, and I don't even understand most of what they tell me."

"Welcome to therapy, dear," said Alex with a chuckle. "Has anything been helpful yet?"

"Well, I don't know, but I keep thinking about what they said last time. They told me that I'm angry, and that I might be controlling with Jack. What do you think of that?"

"I don't know you well enough to know for sure, but you do feel angry to me. Does it ring any bells for you?"

"Well maybe, I sure wish Jack would take care of his own clothes. Last night when I was getting out of the shower I saw his clothes thrown into a ball on the floor. I wish he wouldn't do that...I guess it did frustrate me. But I think most women would hate that."

"Well, that might be something for the group to help you take a closer look at," said Alex.

"I felt stupid in group. It seems like they're so confident in their feedback, but I don't think it's helping me," said Kathy.

"Well, I can see that the adventure has begun for you. I think your life will start changing, if you stay with the work."

"Really? I don't think I can keep living like this much longer."

"I know how that feels. I thank God for getting help myself, and that I'm still getting it."

"You're still getting help? How long have you been in therapy?" asked Kathy.

"It's been six years, so far."

"Six years? My God, that's so long."

Alex laughed. "Six years doesn't seem that long to me anymore. I feel like I still have years of work that I could do on myself."

"I don't want to go that long. I just want to fix my marriage."

"We'll see how long it takes. Maybe it will be quicker for you. How do you like Dr. Aragorn so far?"

"I think I like him, but...but I don't know what he can really do."

"Why not?"

"He doesn't say much, and he's not telling me what to do."

"You might talk to him about that, but he'll probably almost never tell you what to do. That's not how therapy works. His job is to help you get to know yourself and to understand your marriage, and develop your skills, and then you'll be in a better position to decide for yourself what to do."

"But why can't he just tell me what to do to fix my marriage? It would be so much faster. Getting to know myself might be fine for later, but what I really want is to fix things with Jack."

"It doesn't work that way. You can't fix things with Jack until you understand yourself better."

"That's the same damn advice I got in group, and it makes no sense to me. Why doesn't it work?"

Alex paused to think before saying, "I'm not sure I can tell you, I just know it works that way for me. I went into therapy because I was anxious and a mess after my husband left me, and it interfered with my work. I'm a nurse, and some weeks were so bad that I was missing days of work. When I first went in for therapy all I wanted was a pill to take away the pain. My therapist told me that we might pursue medication, but that she wanted to help me understand why I'm anxious and depressed. I didn't care why I was anxious and depressed. I just wanted it to go away. But as the work went on I started to see connections to my pain that made sense. The better I got to know myself the less paralyzing my feelings became. And I can't overemphasize how safe I felt with her."

"Do you still have anxiety and depression?"

"Oh sure, but not like I used to. I have my moments, but I've learned to listen to myself and work with what I hear."

"Listen to yourself? What possible good can that be? I just want the pain to go away."

"You'd be surprised. But be patient with yourself, you're on the road. I'm sure things with Jack will change if you stay with the process. I know it doesn't make sense to you, but trust me on this," said Alex.

"Well I suppose I'll give group a few more times and see what happens."

"That isn't long enough, try giving group six months and

then reevaluate. If you stop before then you might be stopping before you really know if it's working."

"That just sounds so long to wait. Oh I just wish the marriage problems would go away."

"I know," said Alex.

"Well, I better get back to the office. I'll call you later," said Kathy.

Kathy sat in the waiting room flipping through a gossip magazine. She hated waiting for group to start. She tried to arrive just before Dr Aragorn came out. Sitting in the waiting room felt like waiting for a final exam to begin. And yet she sometimes looked forward to coming, but didn't like admitting that.

Dr Aragorn finally came out and they all filed in. Kathy had made up her mind to start group, and did so just as everyone took their seat. "I want to go first tonight."

Dr Aragorn nodded at her. Kathy said, "I'm thinking about quitting group. I don't think it's helping…It actually makes me more frustrated. I wonder if I'm wasting my time, and need to try something else."

"What else would you try?" asked Susan.

"Maybe I just need to get better at staying on top of Jack, but without being too much of a bitch," said Kathy.

Dr Aragorn said, "So tell us about how group isn't helping."

"My marriage isn't any better. And that's the whole point of me coming to this. I'm here to make my marriage better, and so far nothing has changed. If that isn't a waste of time, I don't know what is."

"So what had you expected would actually be different by now?" asked Dr Aragorn.

"I expected that you'd tell me what to say to Jack. I expected you'd help me to make us get along better, and stop the fighting that I can't stand. And none of that's changed at all."

"It doesn't work that way," said Evelyn simply. "You can't change your marriage until you change yourself."

"What the hell does that mean? That's the kind of confusing crap you all have been feeding me all along. I've been coming to this group for several months now, and all this wise counsel you all give just doesn't make sense. I'm not here for any Buddhist parables. I'm here to fix my marriage!"

"Well, let me be plain. I don't see how your marriage can be much different while you're being controlling with Jack," said Dr Aragorn.

"The one thing you keep telling me that I do understand is that I'm being a controlling bitch to Jack. And the only thing I understand, I don't agree with. How else can I be with an irresponsible husband like Jack? Can anyone tell me? So I suppose I should just let the bills go unpaid. I suppose I should just allow us to get late fees month after month? And I suppose I should just sit back and patiently allow him to quit job after start-up job like a college student? What kind of worthless advice is that? I suppose you just sit back and watch your wife ruin your credit, Dr Aragorn."

"You think your problem is that you married an irresponsible man," suggested Susan.

"Of course I do! Isn't it obvious? How many of you don't worry about paying your bills? How many of you don't worry about your kids being picked up in a timely manner? Do you all just meditate and hum?"

"You see the whole problem being your husband, and that you have no responsibility in your marriage," said Susan.

"I know, I know, I'm a controlling bitch. Isn't that the correct answer?"

"Yes you're controlling, but you have a bigger problem than that. You're blaming your husband. Just as you're blaming me right now," said Dr Aragorn.

"Yes, I blame you for not offering me any kind of help. And of course I blame my husband. I lay blame where blame is due. I'm not the one forgetting to pick up our daughter. I'm not the one who doesn't pay the bills on time. I'm not the one who can't get an adult career off the ground. The way I see it, you have to call a spade a spade, and lay blame where blame is due."

"You're trying to wipe all your fingerprints off the glass, as though you play no part in how your marriage is constructed. As if only Jack leaves fingerprints on the glass," said Dr Aragorn patiently.

"That's the kind of confusing mumbo-jumbo you've been giving me all along. So enlighten me doc, where exactly are my prints?"

Susan interjected before Dr Aragorn could respond, "Let me make it simple Kathy, cause it pisses me off the way you're trashing Dr Aragorn. You and Jack together made the marriage you have. Jack hasn't done it by himself. Marriage is always a dance of two. He can't screw it all up on his own. You've helped him. And until you start taking some responsibility for your part, nothing is going to get better. Is that clear enough?"

Kathy rolled her eyes and looked out the window. Then she stood up and said, "I'm out of here." And with that she left the room.

The next morning Kathy woke up thinking about group. She tossed and turned all night in bed, and woke up tired and anxious. A shower and cup of coffee helped some, but she kept thinking about it. I can't believe I lost my cool enough to actually leave. I've never walked out of anything before, Kathy thought. She thought about calling Dr Aragorn and apologizing, but decided against it. Kathy called Alex.

"Alex, I'm struggling with group. I know you told me to give it six months, but I don't know if I can stick it out. I hate it, and it isn't helping me. And I feel like a jerk about last night," Kathy explained.

"So what happened last night?" asked Alex. And so Kathy recounted last night's experience.

"Oh I see…so let me see if I have this straight. So everyone in the group is telling you you're angry and blaming Jack, and not taking responsibility for being controlling?" asked Alex.

"Uh, well yes, I suppose that's about the size of it," acknowledged Kathy.

"So the feedback from group is pretty consistent," said Alex.

"Yes, so what are you getting at?" said Kathy warily.

"If everyone's telling you the same thing, then you're probably in denial," explained Alex.

"That's the same shit one of the group people said."

"You're fighting looking in the mirror they're holding up for you," said Alex.

"But what if it's a false mirror?" asked Kathy.

Alex chuckled before responding, "Kathy, think about what you just said. Mirrors don't lie. They merely reflect what there is to see."

"Damn it, Alex! I was hoping you'd take my side on this. I thought you were the kind of friend I could count on. And this isn't Sleeping Beauty and the Wicked Witch!"

"That's exactly why I'm saying what I'm saying. Because I am your friend and I care about you, I'm telling you the truth. Look Kathy, I know this isn't fun to hear. And I know it isn't what you wanted to hear from me. But will you consider that it might be what you need to hear? Dear God I know, sometimes the truth is a bitter pill to swallow. And it might just be the medicine that you need to swallow."

Kathy paused and pondered Alex's feedback. Then she said slowly, "Well, I do trust you, Alex. It's tempting to reject what you're saying, and I probably would if you hadn't been really helpful to me in the past. But I also just can't fully accept what you're saying either."

"Then maybe you need to think on it," suggested Alex.

Kathy sat in her car in the parking lot and waited until she saw all the other members walk into the waiting room. She looked at her watch and saw that it was one minute before 7:00. Thankfully Dr Aragorn was almost always right on time. Kathy stepped into the waiting room just as Dr Aragorn opened the door. Kathy walked in behind the others with her eyes on her shoes. As everyone sat down Jake said he wanted to talk about something, and group was off and running. Kathy breathed a sigh of relief to have the focus off of her.

Looking at her watch, Kathy realized there wasn't much time

left. The next opportunity she spoke up. "Okay, I'm dreading this, but I have to say something." Kathy looked up and all eyes were on her. She searched their faces for signs of judgment, but wasn't sure if she saw any. Then she continued, "I want to apologize for walking out last time…I was mad, really mad. I still don't agree with what you are telling me…but I made a commitment to a friend to give this group six months, and it's only been four…so I guess I'll give it another eight weeks and then probably stop…unless I change my mind, but I doubt that I will."

There was a brief anxious pause before Dr Aragorn spoke, "I'm glad you came back. I respect you sticking to your commitment. We'll see where you are in two months."

Jake said, "I was really defensive the first several months I was in group. I almost quit about five times."

"At least five times," said Karen.

"Okay, it might be closer to ten," said Jake sheepishly. "I hope you hang in long enough to get your mind around what we're telling you. I know it's a rough go at first. But it's totally worth it if you can make it past the first part."

"I know you have to make your own decision, Kathy, but I'd hate to see you quit now or in eight weeks. I'd like to see you be patient with us and yourself. It's a painful surgery, but the healing is hard to put a price on," said Jake.

"I thought about you more after last week, and I wonder if you feel like we're saying the marriage problems are all your fault?" suggested Dr Aragorn.

"Yes, that's exactly what it sounded like to me. That's what made me so mad. As though you think I'm making Jack act the way he does."

"Oh goodness no! We believe you and Jack are causing the problems together," said Susan.

Kathy stared out the window, looking for inspiration. And then Dr Aragorn added, "Kathy, I don't believe ANY one person is at fault for their marriage problems. It truly takes two to tango."

"Then why does it feel like you're saying that I make him

behave that way?" asked Kathy.

"Maybe you think it has to be either your fault or Jack's," suggested Evelyn.

"Of course I do. What other option is there?"

"Both. The other option is that you both are at fault, if you want to call it that," said Dr Aragorn.

"But how can it be both of our faults?" asked Kathy.

"Maybe thinking of it in terms of fault isn't too helpful. It's not really about fault. It's about everyone taking responsibility for themselves," said Dr Aragorn.

"That doesn't make sense to me," said Kathy.

"Any kind of relationship is co-created," added Dr Aragorn.

"What does 'co-created' mean?"

"It means you dance as two partners. A couples' dance is always a dance of two. Even if one person leads, the other partner influences the dance steps," explained Dr. Aragorn.

"So help me understand how I dance with Jack so that he pays the bills late?" asked Kathy.

"Jack's responsible for when he pays the bills, just as you are responsible for how you respond when he's late," suggested Dr. Aragorn.

"I don't see how I can DANCE any different when he can't get the damn bills paid on time."

"You're never going to be happy about Jack paying the bills late, yet we can help you look at the rest of the steps that make up the whole of the dance. There's more to it than Jack being late and you being angry," said Dr. Aragorn.

Kathy paused and peered out the window. She looked Dr. Aragorn in the eye and then made a decision. She said, "Okay, since I'm only going to be here for eight more weeks, maybe this is a good time to tell you all about how I ended up in the hospital…It started with Jack and me going to the river with friends…"

The River: Day 1

Mike's view of the road blurred. The next thing he knew a honking horn jolted him awake. A fraction of a second later he jerked the wheel back to the right, narrowly evading a catastrophic head-on collision. "Damn, I've got to get me a shot of caffeine! Shit, that was too damn close."

"Hey, what the hell was that?" cried Jack from the back seat. Mike looked in the rear-view mirror to see Jack and Kathy staring at him wide-eyed, having been ripped back to consciousness by one yank on the steering wheel.

"Sorry guys, I guess I fell asleep for a sec," said Mike. He eyed the dash clock which read 3:29 am.

"Look, if you weren't okay you should have woke me up. Give me a cup of coffee and I can drive," offered Jack.

"Look, I'm really sorry. I'll pull over and get a coke. There's a mini mart right there," said Mike.

"Whatever you do, don't kill us before we get there," said Kathy.

Stacy reached over and touched Mike's arm. "Hey babe, you sure you're all right to drive?" whispered Stacy.

"No, but I will be once I get another coke in me. That scared the shit out of me. I should have realized the caffeine from the last one already wore off," Mike responded.

"Hey it's okay, just get that caffeine in you," said Stacy.

Back on the road equipped with a 32 ounce coke and a bag of pretzels, Mike felt confident he could drive the last 75 miles to the launch ramp. His heart still hadn't returned to resting rate, but was slowing with each pretzel and each coke injection. The three passengers were back asleep, and Mike had the dawn patrol to himself.

An hour later Mike eased off the gas as he piloted his pick-up into sleepy Backlight City, population 1248. He knew these small towns were often speed traps to provide income to local public treasuries. Mike checked his mirror to make sure his boat still looked okay, and then turned right down towards the river.

Mike turned on his brights, as there was not a light anywhere to be seen on the two lane road. He piloted the truck through the winding curves as the road wove between mounds of small hills and ravines. Minutes later his headlights lit up the sign, "Marble Canyon Marina". The words of the metal sign were mostly covered by a second sign made out of plywood that stood directly in front of it. The sign read, "Marina closed until May 25."

"Hey babe, what's that sign all about?" asked Stacy. The winding road had awakened her.

Mike turned to his girlfriend with a mischievous smirk on his face. "That sign is exactly the reason we're risking our lives driving in the middle of the night to launch before daylight. Remember me telling you that this section of the river is closed for another two weeks, and the Rangers don't patrol the marina until after dawn. So we should have the launch ramp to ourselves."

"But won't they see your truck?" asked Stacy.

"They might if I left it at the marina," said Mike.

"So, where will you leave it?"

"You just wait and see. Old Mike didn't fall off the turnip truck this week, and he's got a couple of cards up his sleeve." Stacy shook her head. She knew how he could be.

Once they'd loaded all the supplies into the boat, they launched and tied it up at the courtesy dock. Mike looked up at the Eastern sky, which evidenced the beginnings of a graying sky as he unfolded a map of the river and turned on his flashlight. "We have to get out of here, quick. Okay Jack, come here and take a look at this. I want you to pick me up in this cove right here. See where the dirt road dead-ends at the river?"

asked Mike.

"Yeah, I see it. It's just a few coves upriver from where we are, isn't it?" asked Jack.

"You got it. I'll see you there in about twenty minutes," said Mike over his shoulder as he jumped into the cab of his truck.

Mike drove slowly, not wanting to miss the turn off to the obscure one-lane dirt road. "There you are, you son of a bitch," said Mike aloud. Mike turned right onto the dirt road and slowed down even more. He knew parts of the road could be sand, and he couldn't risk getting stuck with no way for the others to get to him.

As he came around the last curve he almost drove right into the water. Fortunately, enough of the coke remained in his veins that he was still alert enough to brake in time. Not to mention the added stimulation he felt about the possibility of getting caught doing something illegal. The truck came to a stop with the front wheels in three inches of water. Mike shined his brights onto the river, but couldn't see much since his lights angled downward. He backed the truck up fifty yards so that it was hidden from view of the river, and set the parking brake. He grabbed the flashlight from his glove compartment and swept the beam out across the cove. No boat. "Damn, I hope Jack didn't go down river."

A moment later his boat was illuminated by his flashlight, idling towards the narrow swatch of sand. The familiar crunching sound of boat hull sliding onto sand beach greeted Mike as he stood in knee deep water. "Glad to see you landlubbers didn't get lost driving a whole mile upriver," needled Mike.

"No, we aren't quite the idiots you take us for," quipped Jack good-naturedly.

Mike jumped onto the bow as he pushed the boat off the beach. He dipped his sandals into the river, and then stepped into the cockpit. Jack stepped away from the helm, and both men looked back towards where the truck was parked. "Well, you think this is gonna work?" asked Jack.

"Yep, don't see any Rangers yet. Let's hope it stays that way," replied Mike. Mike steered his 22 foot cuddy cabin out into the middle and headed upriver. He accelerated enough to get the boat onto plane, but no faster. Dawn was just making her appearance, and Mike couldn't see far. Mike knew there could be rocks barely submerged, and close enough to the surface to do serious damage to a boat's hull.

"You think we're okay now?" asked Stacy. Mike turned to look to the east to see the rising sun's first rays flickering over the horizon. "I'll feel a lot better once we get a few more miles upriver. I don't think the Rangers will go more than a mile or so from the marina. Even they're supposed to stay out of here," said Mike.

Kathy slid down in her seat so that her head rested against the top of the bench. She sat against the starboard side of the boat with Jack sitting on the same bench leaning against the port side. Mike drove a bit faster now, and the thirty five mile an hour winds on Kathy's face felt surprisingly refreshing. Kathy had been quite leery of agreeing to this trip, not being the camping type. Not to mention that she and Jack have had some rough vacations in recent years. She had told Jack that she would come and try to enjoy herself, but for him to not expect her to be excited about the camping thing. Several times she'd reminded Jack that she made no promises. Kathy closed her eyes to stop them from watering in the wind, and thought, this might end up being alright. And Stacy seems pretty nice. I hope Lily will be alright at Jack's parents' for the week. This would be the first time she had left her for a whole week.

Kathy opened her purse and fished out her sunglasses. Even though the sun was not yet bright enough for glasses, she wanted to enjoy the beautiful scenery and not have to keep her eyes shut. Rocks, bushes, small trees and sandy beaches took turns dotting the passing shoreline. No two spots seemed the same. And the hills and cliffs framing the shoreline were equally varied. The changing colors of the rock, dirt and sand surprised Kathy. She hadn't remembered how bright the desert colors could be. Kathy had been to the river a couple of times in college when her friends invited her over summer break, but that was many years ago. And even then she'd only been downriver of the marina, and they'd stayed in hotels.

Marble Canyon is the marina furthest upriver. Only Mother Nature stations anything permanent further upriver. Most boaters head downriver where most of the human activity gathers. It's mostly fishermen, and the occasional serious boater that ever ventures upriver, which is exactly why Mike piloted the boat upriver.

Jack stirred as if just awakening. Kathy glanced over at Jack and smiled weakly, and then turned away. Kathy folded her arms across her chest and went back to taking in nature. Jack started to reach out to Kathy, and then changed his mind, putting his hand back in his lap.

Surprised birds flew off away from the boat, being interrupted from their morning routines by the noisy boat rounding another bend in the river. Mike glanced over his shoulder, and not seeing anyone, breathed a sigh of relief. "I think we're in the clear now. We have to be at least forty miles upriver by now. We can pick out a nice beach to make camp," said Mike.

"Hey look at that beach in the middle of the river. Let's set up camp there," suggested Kathy. She pointed to a large sand bar on the right side of the river.

"No, that wouldn't work," said Mike.

"Why not?" asked Kathy.

"Because the water might rise and overrun our camp. And it's too exposed to the elements," answered Mike. They continued upriver with Jack, Kathy and Stacy taking turns pointing to possible camp sites. Mike eyed each prospective beach with a critical eye, being the veteran of numerous boat camping trips. At each suggestion he shook his head, until Kathy pointed to one on the east side of the river that met Mike's approval.

Mike grew up going to the river regularly each season, starting when he was about ten. His family owned a lake boat similar to Mike's current cuddy. They boat camped at least once yearly, and often went house boating as well, which was Mike's favorite kind of lake camping. There's nothing like waking up to the sunrise on the river. The only thing better than that is waking up on the river with a floating condominium underneath. Lake boating had been Mike's favorite vacation for as long as he could remember. He had bought his own first boat shortly after college, as soon as he'd had the income he needed to pull it off.

Mike beached the boat onto the sandy cove. Barren sand covered the first thirty feet of ground coming down to the water, with small trees and brush behind as sand merged into dirt. The ground rose quickly with hills flanking the river on both sides of the cove. All four campers worked at getting their site set up. The men set up the tents side by side. Mike pounded stakes into the ground to secure them well. Then they set up the awning right in front of the tents, creating something of a sun protected porch complete with chairs. Meanwhile, the women created a make-shift kitchen with ice chests of food, dry storage containers of cooking implements and a stove.

Mike and Jack hurried over as the smell of frying bacon filled the air. All four campers fell to their breakfast of bacon and eggs as though they hadn't eaten in days. In truth, it had only been about twelve hours since they stopped for dinner last night.

After breakfast they all sat down in contentment. "Oh man, isn't this the life?" suggested Jack.

"This is great. I could stay here a month," said Mike.

"It is beautiful," added Stacy.

Jack looked at Kathy, who remained silently sipping her second cup of coffee. "What about you, Kath?"

"Huh?" Kathy answered. Jack tilted his head as he looked sideways at her. "Do you like it here okay?" asked Jack.

"Yeah, it's nice," she replied.

"Just nice?"

"Hey, nice is good. I like it," Kathy said. Jack looked over at Mike, and shrugged his shoulders. Mike nodded. The four sat in silence, taking in their surroundings.

Kathy thought, does he think he brings me out into a beautiful place and everything's okay between us? I'm still upset about the fight we had a couple of nights ago…maybe I'm being too hard on him. I do want to try to have a nice time with Jack this week.

Mike awoke to a dull pain in the left side of his face. He'd fallen asleep with his head leaning against the hard aluminum bar of his beach chair. He rubbed his sore jaw. Mike heard snoring, and saw Jack asleep on a towel a few feet away. He scanned the campsite and found the women quietly chatting on the bow of the boat, sunning on their towels. They had changed into their bathing suits. Mike glanced at his watch. "My God, I've been asleep almost two hours." Stacy looked over at Mike and waved. Jack stopped snoring for moment, turned over and went back to sleep.

Mike stood up, stretched and walked down the beach. He rounded a point and saw a trail leading up a low hill. Mike made his way back to the ladies. "Hey, you wanna go for a hike?" Mike asked.

"Yeah sounds good. I could use some exercise after being cooped up in that truck all night," said Stacy.

"Did somebody say something about a hike?" Jack called out.

"Even in his sleep he hears about hikes," said Mike.

"That's right. I never miss out on a chance to go exploring. How about it, Kath?" asked Jack.

"No, I'm going to catch up on my People Magazine, you go and have fun," answered Kathy with a smile. Kathy turned around and searched through her bag.

"Are you sure, Kath? It might be fun to go exploring," offered Jack.

"No, you go ahead, I want to rest. I don't have much energy after that all-nighter," said Kathy.

Jack shrugged his shoulders and went to his own bag. He pulled out river shoes, a hat and a water bottle. "Alrighty, let's go," said Jack. Stacy and Mike headed out towards the trail, while Jack turned back towards Kathy. She was already settled into one of the boat seats with her magazine, and didn't look up. "Do you need anything before I go?" asked Jack.

"No, I'm fine," Kathy said while keeping her eyes on the magazine. Jack turned away and caught up with the others.

The three hikers reached the top of the first low hill only to see a larger hill behind it. They faced the river. "Oh my God, look at that view!" said Stacy.

"That sure is nice. I wish Kathy were here to see it with us," said Jack.

Mike put a hand on Jack's shoulder along with a grim smile. "Hey, let's climb that higher hill up there," said Mike pointing up.

Thirty minutes later they stood at the top of the second hill breathing hard, but they were rewarded for their efforts with an even more magnificent view. They could see at least ten miles upriver and downriver, and there wasn't a soul or a boat in sight. "Man, we really do have the river to ourselves. I can't see anything but Mother Nature," said Mike.

"This is so fun," said Stacy as she sat on a rock and put her hand in Mike's hand. Mike rewarded her by squeezing her hand. One of the traits that had drawn Mike to Stacy right off had been her child-like enjoyment of life. He sat down next to her and put his arm around her waist and pulled her tight. She responded to him with a kiss on the lips.

Stacy released Mike and ran off back down the trail, sliding as she went. When Mike and Jack got back to the campsite the ladies were making sandwiches. "Great, I'm starved. Let me at one of those," said Jack as he hoisted a sandwich to his mouth. Mike cracked open a couple of beers from the ice chest and handed one to Jack. After putting away two turkey and cheese filled French rolls, Jack stood and faced the others.

"Okay, time for some skin diving. Who's with me?" asked Jack.

"I'm in," said Mike. Kathy shook her head.

"I think I'll stay back with Kathy this time," said Stacy.

"Maybe we can find some lost treasures. This beach probably gets a lot of traffic," suggested Jack.

"Yeah, probably so; we might find something as exciting as a dirty towel," said Mike.

"Come on, we've found cooler stuff than that before," countered Jack.

"Like what, empty beer bottles," said Mike.

"Get out of here, I found some nice sunglasses last summer, and a Swiss army knife the year before," said Jack.

"Alright, so you've gotten lucky twice," agreed Mike.

"With that attitude you probably won't find anything," said Jack.

They dove off the back of the boat and the cold water sent a shock throughout their bodies. They hadn't expected the water to be that cold. They recovered and started exploring the sand and mud bottom. As Mike predicted, at first they only came across discarded bottles and cans of varied type. Mike had seen enough and climbed back on the boat to warm himself in the hot sun. Thankfully, the sun warmed the air to a comfortable 90 degrees. Not easily discouraged, Jack kicked his fins further out into deeper water. Mike wrapped himself in a towel and lay down on the sun pad.

Mike was just drifting off to sleep when he was interrupted by shouts from Mike. "Look at these! I told you I'd find something, I always do." Mike looked up to see Jack holding up a pair of black sunglasses, in surprisingly good condition for probably being under water since last summer.

"You lucky son of a bitch," said Mike shaking his head.

"Hey man, we make our own luck," Jack responded. Jack pulled himself into the boat and cleaned his new glasses before trying them on. "So Kath, what do you think," asked Jack?

Kathy grinned and shook her head, then said, "That's great, Jack. Well, I've had enough sun for now. I'll sit under the sun shade for awhile."

Jack sat down next to Mike on the sun pad. "I tell you buddy, Kathy is such a kill-joy. She can never give me credit for anything I do. Maybe this whole trip was a bad idea," Jack complained.

Mike glanced over his shoulder at the women before responding, "Be patient, man. We just got here. Give her a chance to settle in and enjoy herself."

"Yeah yeah," mumbled Jack.

Both men sat in silence. Jack pulled the fins off his feet and tossed them into the boat.   "So how long you and Kathy been married now?" asked Mike.

"Uh let's see, I think it's been seven years. Yeah, about seven," answered Jack.

"Do you have a good marriage?"

"Yeah, we have a really good marriage. Of course we have our tough moments, but all in all, I think we have a great marriage," said Jack.

Mike nodded and pondered Jack's response for a moment, before saying, "It seems like things are a bit tense between the two of you."

"Oh really…well, maybe a little. We had a few words the other night, but no big deal…maybe Kathy's holding a grudge or something."

"Give her a chance. She's got to be tired after last night," suggested Mike.

"But with that attitude we don't have a chance to have a nice week. She's blowing me off no matter what I do."

"Again man, we been here what, six hours already? Chill out and be patient. Maybe she feels like you're pressuring her," said Mike.

"Pressuring her? I'm just trying to have a nice time with her. How is that pressuring her?"

"Look man, she knows you want her to like this trip. Didn't you have to talk her into going?"

"But that doesn't mean she has to be a bitch and blow me off no matter what I say," said Jack.

"Hey guys, what's a girl to do when she's got to go, know what I mean?" called out Stacy.

"Let me get you the shovel," said Mike. He opened up one of the seats and pulled a folding shovel out, holding it up in the air.

"Tell me you're kidding," pleaded Stacy.

"Get out of here, there's no way I'm using that thing. That's fine for you boy scouts, but you better have a better plan for us ladies," chimed in Kathy.

"Of course there's more," said Mike. He rummaged under the seat some more and produced a roll of toilet paper. "There you go, nothing but first class on my trips." Both of the women rolled their eyes. "Sorry ladies, this is it. There's nothing else; what'd you expect out here in the wild?" answered Mike.

"I expected at least an outhouse," said Kathy.

"Well hand me the damn shovel then," acquiesced Stacy.

"Come on girl, have some self respect. You got to expect better that that. You mean you can't even drive us to an outhouse out here?" asked Kathy.

"Sure, but the nearest one's probably fifty miles downriver at the marina," Mike said.

Stacy grabbed the shovel out of Mike's hand, ignored his grinning face and marched off to find a private place to do her business. Kathy shook her head and turned her attention back to her magazine. Jack put his hands up in the air by way of apology to Kathy. Kathy shook her head and waved him over.

"It would have been nice if you'd warned me about this. Did you know there'd be no facilities out here?" Kathy asked.

"Come on Kath, what did you expect on a boat camping trip, miles from nowhere?" pleaded Jack.

"Exactly my point, what are we doing out here, miles from nothing, out in the damn sticks?" said Kathy.

"Come on Kath, let's make the best of it. This might even be fun if you let it," said Jack.

"Jack, you know I'm not a camping person. For me camping is staying in a motel."

Jack shrugged his shoulders and walked away to get another beer. He popped it open and sat down in a huff, crossing arms and legs. Ten minutes later his beer contained only air. He got up and went over to get another out of the ice chest.

"Hey man, slow down on those. I don't want you to miss the party," warned Mike.

"I'm under control, don't worry about me, man," returned Jack.

Mike scrutinized his friend for a moment. "Hey man, you want to go off somewhere and talk?" asked Mike.

"Talk? No, I'm good," said Jack.

Mike reluctantly left his friend to be with his own thoughts, and found Stacy putting the shovel away. "Stacy, I'm worried about Jack," Mike began. "I don't think the trip's going too well for them so far."

"No doubt, I got the same vibe. The tension's pretty obvious."

"I hope they can rally and enjoy the trip. I mean we've got another six days out here together," said Mike.

"I know, if things don't get better we may want to consider going back early," suggested Stacy.

"Damn, I'd hate for it to come to that. Jack is so counting on this trip to be great for him and Kathy," said Mike.

"That seems like a lot of pressure to put on this trip," said Stacy.

Both Mike and Stacy turned and saw Jack in the same position, his arms folded with a beer in one hand, and eyes drilling into the sand. They looked the other way and found Kathy sitting under the canopy, People Magazine across her lap. "Do you think we should try to talk to them?" asks Stacy.

"Naw, I already tried with Jack. I say we just let them be for now and see how it goes. It's got to be tough for both of them. I think they've been having a rough go," said Mike.

"Okay, he's your friend. I barely know Kathy. She probably wouldn't talk to me anyway," said Stacy.

A gust of wind blew across the campsite. Mike looked up and scanned the river. Moments later a second gust ruffled their canopy and tents. Mike turned his head upriver from which it came. "Hey Stacy, we might be in for a good blow tonight, let's get going with dinner while we can still cook. I'll get the stove started," said Mike. Stacy nodded and walked over to the ice chest for the steaks.

"Here's the steaks," said Stacy as she set the steaks on the table. "Wow, that marinade sure smells good."

"Okay great, I'll put 'em on right now. The grill should be hot enough," said Mike.

The steaks sizzled as Mike place each of the four on the hot grill. Stacy opened a can of beans and set it next to the grill. She then pulled four russet potatoes out, pre-wrapped in tin foil and placed them on the grill.

"How do Margaritas sound tonight?" asked Stacy.

"Sounds perfect. I'll help you mix those," answered Mike.

Stacy handed a Margarita to Kathy and Jack, and Mike went back to check on the steaks, Margarita in hand. He was surprised to not hear much, and pulled off the lid to find they'd barely begun cooking. Looking underneath, he couldn't find a flame.

Damn, the flame's out. I'll bet the wind blew it out, he thought. Mike relit the stove and replaced the lid. He waited a minute and then looked under the stove to see if it was still lit. He took a swig of his Margarita and sat down next to the stove to keep an eye on it.

Ten minutes later he opened the grill and turned the steaks over. "Hey don't forget to turn those potatoes also," yelled Stacy from the tent opening. Mike waved, and did as requested. Just as he'd set the lid back on, a stronger gust of wind come up and blew the stove out again. "Damn!" Mike fumbled with the wooden matches and relit the grill, quickly setting the lid down to keep the wind from getting to the flame again.

Mike wandered over to Jack, finding him keeping guard in the same position. Mike pulled up a chair and sat down. "Hey man, we might get some wind tonight."

Without moving Jack replied, "That right?"

"Yeah, we're going to have to tie everything down so we don't lose it," suggested Mike. "Uh huh," said Jack.

"Look man, I get that things are rough for you with Kathy. Is there anything I can do?" offered Mike.

"No, it just pretty much sucks. There's nothing can be done about her. She's just the way she is, you know," said Jack.

"Come on man, don't give up so easy. There's got to be something you can do to make this trip work for you," said Mike.

"No man, it is what it is," laments Jack.

Mike looked out at the river, searching for something else to say. He felt helpless, not coming up with anything. "Alright, well at least come and help with the steaks," said Mike. Jack got up and followed Mike back to the stove.

Everything tasted great, and the good food mixed with Margarita's blessings seemed to bring the mood of the campers up. S'mores capped off a perfect dinner, just as dusk gave way to dark. Dusk brought increased winds with it, and Mike scampered around tying down everything in sight. He checked the anchor lines first, making sure the boat was well secured for the night. Mike had two anchors sunk a foot or more into the sand, with a third line tied around a pile of heavy rocks. Satisfied that the boat was okay, he turned his attentions to the tent and canopy.

The winds prevented the use of the lanterns, and the campers broke out their flashlights. Jack remembered he'd left his hat on the boat. And this isn't any old throw away hat. This hat had belonged to Jack's dad. Jack's dad passed away five years ago. The passing was sudden. He died of a massive heart attack in the middle of the night. The one mercy was that he didn't suffer. Richard had been asleep, and never woke up. He had played several years as a pitcher in the minor leagues, and had made it to the major leagues for three seasons. The Cincinnati Reds had brought him up as a relief pitcher. Jack still remembered sitting in the seats behind the dugout, brimming with pride as his dad stuck out the side to win the game. When Richard died, his mother asked Jack if he wanted any of his dad's things. The only thing Jack took was the red Cincinnati Reds hat. Jack's dad wore this actual hat during that game.

Jack's interest in baseball started before Richard made the big leagues. Jimmy, Jack's younger brother, had never been right. Richard and Joanne had known something was wrong with their second son soon after birth. Jimmy didn't walk until well into his second year, and never really learned to speak King's English. Jimmy had his own made up language that the whole family understood.

Richard started his boys out on baseball at age two. Both his sons received a baseball and glove on their second birthdays, and began playing catch with him from then on. Jimmy wasn't coordinated enough to catch the ball on his second birthday, as Jack had been, but Jimmy was content to fetch the ball whenever Jack or Richard dropped it. Richard often pretended to drop the ball accidentally, and Jimmy eagerly ran to fetch it. Jack looked forward to catch with his dad and brother. Sadly, Jimmy never became skilled in throwing and catching a baseball. He could catch a ball thrown underhand from a short distance, but never overcame his fear of a ball thrown overhand.

Once Jimmy was old enough to be in school, Richard and Joanne enrolled him in a school for developmentally delayed children. Whenever Richard was in town, he and Jack would go down to the school and play baseball with Jimmy and the other kids. Richard became quite a celebrity amongst the kids, especially after he wore his professional baseball uniform to school for the first time. There wasn't a dry eye amongst the adults the day Richard showed up with his uniform on and a souvenir hat for each kid. All of the kids lit up immediately, as though it were Christmas.

Jack always looked forward to these visits to Jimmy's school. Not only did he love to be with his dad, but he came to genuinely care for the kids. Once Jack was in high school he played on the high school baseball team. Throughout high school he went to Jimmy's school even when Richard was out of town with the team. Every time Jack showed up, Jimmy would run to him and call out, "Jackie's here! Jackie's here!" Sometimes he almost knocked Jack over. Although Jack was strong and six foot tall in high school, Jimmy had grown to weigh well over two hundred pounds.

Jack continued to visit Jimmy's school on most Saturdays. He still taught the kids to play baseball. Jack amazed the staff with his patience with the kids. Jack even organized baseball teams amongst the kids, and umpired the games. He loved the pure joy on the kids' faces when they actually hit or caught the ball.

Jack always wore his dad's hat to Jimmy's school. He never let the hat be far away. It was either on his head, or within reach at almost all times. Even when Jack went to work he brought the hat, and set it on a peg in his cubicle. At home and at the office Jack had installed a special wooden peg to hold the hat. One time Lily played with her dolls, and decided to put Jack's red hat backwards on one of her bears. The bear had been a rapper, of course. When Jack discovered his precious hat wasn't on its special peg, he nearly tore the house apart looking for it. Kathy thought Jack might be having a nervous breakdown when she found him tearing through their bedroom.

Jack waded out to the stern of the boat in search of the hat. He tripped over the upriver anchor line, almost spilling his drink. Jack stepped over the anchor line, while he held his third Margarita up out of the water. Then his shirt caught on the cleat of the boat, just as he tried to climb aboard. Jack pulled to free himself, but for his effort only received a slight tear of cotton. He took a step back and fumbled to pull his shirt tail off the cleat in the dark. Getting more frustrated at his failed efforts, he untied the rope from the cleat and managed to free his shirt in the process.

"Hey man, you need some help out there?" asked a laughing Mike. Jack waved him off with an indiscernible grunt. He climbed into the boat and found his hat after searching around for ten frustrating minutes.

The winds became even stronger, with the gusts peppering their faces and eyes with sand. Even with a flashlight it was difficult to see much. The almost constant flying sand prevented them from opening their eyes for more than fractions of a second. Tiring of this sport quickly, all four campers changed into sleeping apparel and turned into their respective tents.

Mike tossed and turned in his sleeping bag. He kept thinking about the wind. He wondered if everything was battened down well. Mike rolled over and started to get up, then stopped himself. Oh man, I'm still a bit tightly wound. I just need to chill and let it be. I know I tied everything down good. Mike laid back down and finally relaxed enough to sleep.

Mike awoke with a start to a strong gust of wind. The winds had increased in intensity. He sat up and reached for his flashlight. He flipped it on and shown the light on Stacy, who blinked in the sudden light and shielded her eyes with her hand. "Hey Stacy, did you hear that?"

"Hear what?" she asked.

"I could have sworn I heard something."

"Of course you heard something, the damn wind is blowing hissy fits," returned Stacy.

"No, something doesn't feel right. I'm gonna get up and take a look around," said Mike.

"Knock yourself out," said Stacy as she turned over and closed her eyes.

Mike unzipped their tent flap and rezipped it after stepping out. A sudden gust punished his eyes, bringing his arm up to shield him. He tried to close and reopen his eyes several times, but each time he was instantly blinded. He went back into the tent and retrieved his sunglasses for some protection. Not having to blink every half-second, Mike could now see their campsite dimly. At first everything seemed in order, even if half buried in sand. Then he realized what was wrong.

"Shit! Where in the hell is my boat!" He ran down to where it should be anchored to the beach. Mike shone the flashlight out into the river, searching for any signs of his boat. After several minutes of sweeping the flashlight beam up and downriver he gave up, not being able to catch even a glimpse of his boat. Then he inspected the downwind anchor. It had been dragged into the water. Then Mike checked the center line. It was gone! The rope had been ripped right out from under the heavy rocks that had held it in place. Then he searched for the up wind anchor, the most important anchor, and found it strangely in place.

"What the..?" Mike pulled on the line and discovered that it came right to him, loop and all. He examined the entire length of rope, and found it sound. "What the hell happened to this rope?"

Mike swept the flashlight out into the water again, hoping to find it just offshore. He found nothing. Then he trained his light further out into the river, but still found nothing. He started hiking down river, praying he'd come across it any second. However, instead of finding his boat he tripped over some low brush and fell into the river. The only good thing was that his flashlight was waterproof and undamaged. Mike slapped at the water, retrieved his light and made his way out of the water.

"Stacy! Stacy, wake up!"

"Huh, Mike? What is it?"

"It's my boat! It's gone!"

"Gone? What do you mean gone?" asked Stacy.

"Beats the hell out of me."

"How can it be gone? Where is it?"

"I don't know!" growled Mike. "That's what I'm trying to say. It's just gone. Maybe it was blown away."

"Oh my God! How do we find it then?"

"Don't know…I guess we'll just have to wait for first light," said Mike.

"Should we wake up Jack and Kathy?"

"No, I don't think so. There's nothing they can do. Let 'em sleep."

Mike lay down next to Stacy, with his hands over his eyes, rubbing them. Stacy reached out and put her hand on his chest. "I'm sorry, babe," offered Stacy. Mike nodded, and reached out and pulled her close.

24 Weeks after the River Trip

"I want to go to the river. That sounds like fun! At least so far," said Jake.

"Yeah, take me with you next time," said Susan.

"Well, before you all sign up, you should probably hear the rest. Things got worse," said Kathy.

"We'll have to stop there for tonight. We're out of time," said Dr. Aragorn.

The next night Jack had plans to go to the ball game with a couple buddies. When Kathy heard the news she made plans for her and Lily to meet Jane for dinner. Kathy and Lily arrived at the restaurant first and sat down at the table and ordered an appetizer and glass of wine for herself, and a Shirley Temple and crackers for Lily. She stared into the wine as she swished and twirled the red liquid in the glass, with her other hand holding up her head with her elbow on the table. Jane took Kathy by surprise, sneaking up behind her and engulfing her in a bear hug. Kathy started, spilling the last two swallows of the wine. "Oh my God, you scared me," said Kathy.

"Well I guess so. Have you considered switching to decaf?" said Jane. Kathy smiled and hugged her sister.

"Hi Auntie Jane!"

"Give me a big hug, my favorite little niece." Jane spent a few minutes and listened while Lily explained the drawing she'd made on the children's menu.

Midway through dinner Kathy stared off at nothing. Lily kept herself entertained by drawing on a second paper menu.

Jane followed Kathy's gaze over her shoulder. "Hey Kathy, what's on your mind? You don't seem yourself."

Kathy shook her head and focused her eyes on Jane, "Do you think I could be less controlling with you know who?" Kathy asked as she nodded towards Lily.

"What? You mean Jack? Where's that coming from? What's with the intense question?"

Kathy nodded again in Lily's direction with an emphatic eye nod and a shake of her head and said, "I'd rather we talk in impersonal pronouns."

"Oh sorry. Got it," said Jane.

"My group told me they think I'm part of the problem, and that I control him as though he's irresponsible," Kathy said as she rubbed Lily's back. Lily smiled at her mom and went back to her drawing.

"He does act irresponsible, and of course you have to be the one in charge, or in control, if you want to call it that."

Kathy put her elbows on the table and her chin on her folded hands. "I don't know about that, I mean, he is irresponsible, but maybe I'm making it worse somehow."

"Then what else are you supposed to do when he acts like that, and doesn't pay the bills on time or clean up after himself?"

Kathy paused and reflected on Jane's question. "I don't know."

"Of course you don't know, because there's nothing else you can do. You can't just let him get away with stuff like that. Every time Frank forgets one of his chores I have to remind him. If I didn't remind him, it would never get done," said Jane with her hands above her shoulders.

Kathy pursed her lips. Everything Jane said seemed familiar, and a month ago Kathy would have pounded the table with the same pronouncement, but tonight she wasn't so sure anymore. There was something to what Alex and the group were saying. It felt so good to say it's all Jack's fault, but it just didn't have the ring of the whole truth anymore. "But I wonder what would happen if I could somehow be different with him."

"I can tell you what'll happen. Stuff won't get done, and you'll be letting him get away with it."

"Maybe, but what if my getting on his back makes it easier for him to not get stuff done. Isn't that possible?"

Jane stared at Kathy through narrowed eyes. "You aren't making sense, Kathy. I'm worried about you. Are you sure that group is helping you? Maybe those people are putting some dangerous ideas into your head."

"I don't know, Jane. I used to think I saw everything between me and him so clearly. If he'd just grow up and stick to his responsibilities we'd have a good life. But now I don't know what to think. Part of me still believes that's right, but part of me thinks there's got to be more to the story. It's just so easy to say it's all him."

"Kathy, why do you have to make it so complicated? Now come on, wouldn't your life be a whole lot better if he did what he said he'd do, found a real career and stuck with it?"

"Yes, that would help, but I'm not sure that would really fix everything."

"What else would you need? If Frank followed through on what he said he'd do, I'd be happy. And Frank would be happier too. That sounds pretty good to me."

Kathy grabbed her head with both hands as she shook her head slowly. "I don't know, Jane. I just don't know anymore. Maybe you're right, Jane, maybe if he did that I'd be happy. I'm just not as sure anymore."

"You have to take what that group tells you with a grain of salt. They don't know our family, and they don't understand what works for us. Don't forget that you're a Russell, and we Russells need a strong man who does what he says and lives up to his word. That's what worked for mom and dad. Mom always kept a firm hand on Dad's shoulder."

Lily interrupted with, "Mommy, are you mad at Daddy?" Kathy glanced at her sister and mouthed, "I don't know what to tell her." Jane shrugged her shoulders.

"No my little teddy bear, I'm not mad at Daddy, but sometimes we have to talk about things."

"Like what things?" asked Lily.

"Like mommy and daddy kind of things that you're too little to understand."

"Is Daddy mad at you?"

"No Lily, don't you worry about such things."

Lily looked deeply into her mother's eyes as though exploring for signs of truth, and then said, "Look what I been drawing Mommy, it's a picture of you and me and Daddy."

"That's very nice, Lily. And what are we all doing?"

"We're all playing together and nobody's mad at anybody." Kathy turned to Jane and frowned. Lily continued, "It's cause we all decided to just play nicely and get along. See how you and daddy are sharing nicely?"

It was Tuesday night again, and Dr. Aragorn glanced over at Kathy from time to time. She hadn't spoken yet. Kathy sat with her head in her hands, as if trying to hold it steady. She tried to track what the others were saying, with limited success. Kathy kept trying to figure out if what each of them said made sense, or was crazy. It was as though Kathy sat on a rock above a deep pond. Most of the time the waters below were rough and windblown, only allowing a glimpse of the surface. But every so often the waters stilled and Kathy thought she could see deep into the pool. In those moments the waters appeared so clear. Then a moment later the waters were stirred and she couldn't penetrate the surface. She couldn't be sure the clear glimpse had been real. It was the strangest experience. Then Kathy stared at Dr. Aragorn. She studied his every feature, as if trying to discern a hidden code. Was he the wisest person she'd ever met? Was he a deluded narcissist, imagining he had powers of healing that were illusory? Or was he just trying to fix his own life like the rest of us, using us as guinea pigs? Dr. Aragorn noticed her stare and asked, "What's on your mind, Kathy?"

"Nothing."

"Nothing? Your face suggests otherwise."

"What does my face suggest?"

"That you're troubled."

Kathy looked away. She surveyed the other faces in group. They all waited and listened. "Yes I am troubled. I had dinner with my sister the other night and I don't know what to think. She thinks this group is dangerous. Jane thinks I just need to get Jack in line with a firm but kind hand, and everything will be alright. And I'm still wondering if she might be right. Maybe what you all are saying is crazy."

"And have you tried getting Jack in line?" asked Dr. Aragorn.

"Yes, you know that I have."

"And did it work?"

"Well no, uh yes. I mean sometimes it seems to work and sometimes it doesn't."

"What do you mean sometimes it works?" asked Evelyn.

"Sometimes Jack tries hard and does what I want, for awhile."

"For awhile?" asked Evelyn.

"Maybe he's good for a few days or even a week."

"And then?" asked Dr. Aragorn.

"And then he always goes back to being irresponsible."

"So it doesn't work. Jack might be compliant for awhile, and then he reverts to rebelling against your control," concluded Dr. Aragorn.

Kathy looked out the window and tried to organize her thoughts. It was like her head was in a washing machine, spinning around in circles and never getting anywhere. She felt light-headed and dizzy. She thought of getting up and walking out, and then Dr. Aragorn spoke, "Kathy, I'm sure Jane means well, but she's inviting you to keep doing what you've already been doing for years, and it's not working. That's why you're here, because what you've been trying isn't working for you."

"From what I've gathered you and Jack have arranged your relationship around a parent-child pattern, and if you were happy with that you wouldn't be here. I get that it's confusing to be told that what you've always thought was right doesn't work for you," said Susan.

"I know you're right about one thing. I can't keep doing what I'm doing because it's driving me crazy. But can anyone tell me what to do different?"

Dr. Aragorn answered, "I don't think your marriage will feel much better to you until you give up mothering Jack, but..."

"You think I act like his mother?"

Almost every head in the room nodded, and Susan said, "Yes I do. You treat him like a child, as though you're his mother and have to keep him in line."

"I don't see how your marriage can be much different until you resign from that job," said Dr. Aragorn.

"But how do I do that? What do I do different? Tell me what else to do! I don't know how to be any other way!"

"That's right. You're doing what you know how to do, and you probably can't do anything else until we help you create something else. Kathy, the something else would be an equal partnership with Jack, but I hesitate to say that because I don't think you can just go home and do that. We have to help you create it within yourself. And that involves us understanding why you got yourself into the mothering role in the first place," said Dr. Aragorn.

"I can't do anything else! I've tried!" Dr. Aragorn nodded sympathetically. Kathy dropped her face into her hands and sobbed, the dam breaking in the wake of a flood of emotion. Susan, sitting next to Kathy, leaned over and put her hand on Kathy's shoulder. Eventually the emotion ebbed and Kathy wiped her face and looked up at Dr. Aragorn.

"So how do I learn to do something besides mother Jack? I desperately want to know."

"We start by understanding how it is that trying to control Jack is so natural for you. Got any ideas?" said Dr. Aragorn.

At first Kathy drew a blank. She looked to her fellow group members, hoping for a clue, but they merely held her gaze and waited. Then Jane's words from the other night came back to her. "Jane said something to me about Mom always keeping a firm hand on Dad's shoulder."

"How did she do that?" asked Susan.

Kathy thought for a moment, and then said, "I do remember Mom often asking Dad if he'd done this or that, and reminding him to not forget something. Maybe Mom was in charge of Dad somehow."

"And how would your dad respond?" asked Dr. Aragorn.

"Um, he would either reassure her that he'd done it, or sometimes give reasons why he hadn't. It did kind of seem like Mom was the boss."

"So your parents taught you how to do marriage," suggested Susan.

"Oh my God, I'm just like Mom to Jack," said Kathy. A deep pit formed in Kathy's stomach as she saw some similarities in her parent's marriage and hers for the first time. "So what do I do now that I know that?"

"There may be nothing to do yet, but it's a good start and you keep looking," suggested Dr. Aragorn.

"Keep looking at what?"

"Keep looking at the face in the mirror, and get to know her better and better."

"But I don't know what to look for!"

"You don't have to know yet. We'll help you. And by the way, you've already started looking," said Evelyn.

"What did I look at?"

"You've looked at how you can be parental with Jack, and you've seen how your parents probably modeled that for you," said Evelyn.

"Yes I've seen that, but so what?"

"Be patient. It will come," said Dr. Aragorn.

"I wonder if the trip to the river was typical for you and Jack?" said Jake.

"I don't know…I don't know if it has anything to do with it," said Kathy.

"You started to tell us about the river trip last week…so what happened after the first day?" asked Susan.

The River: Day 2

Jack peeked out of the tent and looked both ways before exiting. The wind had expended itself, leaving the air cool and calm. He spied Mike sitting in a chair and headed over. "Hey man, what're you doing up so early? You really are the full-on river rat," said Jack. Mike turned and showed Jack his face. "Hey man, you don't look like a happy camper," said Jack.

Mike merely pointed to where a single anchor still guarded the beach. "So what'd you do with the boat?" asked Jack.

"Very funny," said Mike.

"No really, where's the boat? Did you put in the next cove or something?"

"It's gone, Jack."

"What'd you mean, gone?"

Mike pointed in the general direction of down river. "What?" asked Jack, getting a bit exasperated.

"You don't see it?" asked Mike. "My boat's about 2 miles downriver, stuck on that sand bar."

"No shit?"

"No shit. Look, all I know is that I woke up about three hours ago and knew something was wrong. I came out and couldn't find my boat. I couldn't go back to sleep, so I waited for the sun to come up. Well, an hour ago I could see good enough to find my boat down on the damn sand bar."

Jack looked hard at the sand bar, and then shook his head. "How the hell will we get it from there? Swim?"

"That's what I've been trying to figure the last hour. The current's pretty strong. I don't know how we'll get it, but we sure have to," said Mike.

"So, when do you want to try?"

"Maybe after I get some food in me. I'm tired as hell. I didn't sleep much."

Jack got up and went over to the stove and started breakfast. Stacy smelled the coffee and bacon and went and helped Jack. Mike didn't move. His eyes remained riveted on the lone anchor. Kathy emerged from the tent just as breakfast was being served, looking like she'd slept like a baby.

"Hey Jack, come here," said Mike. Mike kneeled down next to the remaining anchor, which was still dug into the sand on the beach. Jack kneeled down next to Mike.

"The one thing that bothers me…is that I can't figure out how this rope got untied. The other two lines were ripped out of the ground, but this last one is just untied. Did someone untie it?" asked Mike.

"I don't know, man. I didn't untie it, if that's what you're asking."

"Was anyone out on the boat last night?" asked Mike.

"I don't think so. We all turned in early, due to the winds and all."

"So who was the last person on the boat last night? I'm sure all three lines were secure when I was last on the boat, and that was just after dinner. Jack, these ropes don't just untie themselves. I mean I could understand if the rope had been ripped apart, but this rope is perfectly sound. Somebody untied it, maybe by accident. Who was on the boat last night after me?" asked Mike.

"Look man, are you implying that it was me? I didn't untie nothing."

"Wait a minute, didn't you come out to the boat for your hat right before we turned in?"

"Oh yeah, but I didn't untie any ropes," said Jack.

"Look Jack, I'm not trying to nail you to the wall. I just want to understand what happened. Did anything happen when you came out for your hat?"

"Hey man, I just hopped on the boat, grabbed my hat, and hopped off. That's it!"

"Wait a second Jack, didn't you tell me that you ripped your shirt on the boat cleat?" asked Kathy.

"Well yeah, but I didn't untie nothing," said Jack.

"So did you catch your shirt on the cleat on this side of the boat," asked Mike as he pointed to the upriver side of the boat. The same side of the boat from which the mysterious rope remained anchored in the sand.

"Look man, I don't know. I was a bit light-headed. I didn't pay any attention to what side was what. I just jumped onboard and grabbed my hat. That's it!"

Mike looked over at Kathy, who shrugged her shoulders. Mike glanced at Jack, who averted his eyes towards the water. Then Mike said, "Let's just forget it for now. I'm starving."

Mike finished drying the last of the pots from breakfast and exhaled deeply and said, "Alright Jack, let's go deal with the boat." Jack nodded, and went to change into his bathing suit. Jack put on sunscreen, cleaned his glasses and donned his favorite baseball cap. Then he changed his mind, and put his favorite red hat back into his backpack. Jack took out his expendable black hat, that didn't have the same sentimental meaning, even though it was also bore the Cincinnati Red's famous "C". Jack called out to Kathy, "Hey Kath, I'm leaving my dad's hat in my backpack. Don't let anything happen to it, okay?"

"Yeah ok, I won't touch it," said Kathy.

"No, I mean keep an eye on it. I don't want anything to happen to it."

"Okay, I'll take care of it. I know what it means to you," said Kathy.

"You have no idea what it...well, thanks though."

A two hour hike and numerous leg scratches later, the three campers stood at the end of the point nearest the sand bar. Kathy had offered to remain behind and guard the campsite. Exactly who she guarded the site against was unclear. Perhaps the scorpions or maybe it was the lizards. Although for Jack, she stayed behind to guard his red hat.

Mike wore his backpack, which included several liters of water. It was now near midday and the sun was bearing down on them mercilessly. By Mike's best guess it was already over 90 degrees.

"Don't think we can get any closer than this," assessed Mike.

"Agreed," said Jack. "So, what's the plan? I'll do whatever."

Mike looked from point to sand bar several times. "Well, I guess this is as good a time as any. I figure it's more than a quarter mile out there, probably even a half mile. Stacy, you stay here, and Jack and I will make a swim for it. I sure wish we had life jackets, but of course they're on the boat," said Mike. Mike took off his backpack and handed it to Stacy. He and Jack took off their sandals and shirts. They left their sunglasses and hats on.

"Alright man, I'm ready whenever you are," said Jack.

"Wait a minute, are you sure you guys can make it? That's pretty far to swim," said Stacy.

"We have to try. What else can we do?" said Jack.

"I'm not leaving my boat marooned on a sand bar," said Mike.

"Oh my God, stay together, and do be safe. If you can't make it, come back to shore," pleaded Stacy.

Mike embraced Stacy and kissed her cheek. "We'll be alright, babe."

And with that the two men waded into the river and then began their swim. They swam the breast stroke slowly, trying to conserve energy. They both made good progress the first couple hundred yards, which instilled confidence. Soon their confidence waned.

"Damn, this current is stronger that it looked," said Mike breathing heavily. "Do you think we'll make the sand bar?"

"We're fine. We'll make it," said Jack without emotion.

A hundred yards later they were almost directly in front of the sand bar, but still a good hundred and fifty yards from reaching it.

"Hey Jack, I don't think I'll make it."

"Come on man, we can do this. We have to make it," countered Jack.

"No really, I'm running out of gas. The damn current's stronger than I'd thought."

"Don't give up, Mike. Come on, dig deep and let's do this," encouraged Jack.

"Look man, you're the stronger swimmer; you go ahead and do it. I'll find somewhere to make land," said Mike between labored breaths.

Jack put his head down, losing his hat, and switched to the freestyle. He made better time this way, but it was a risk since it took more energy. Mike settled back into treading water. He scanned downriver for landing options. No point of land looked close enough to reach. A pang of panic shot through Mike's stomach as he thought, damn, what if I don't make it back? I don't have much left…okay don't lose your head. Just pick a target and conserve energy.

Mike scanned the Eastern shoreline again, and a half mile downriver another point jutted out into the river. Mike targeted the point and started swimming towards shore. The current still moved him downriver quickly. He relaxed a little and made better progress. After ten minutes he felt his energy flagging more. Panic began to spread within him, like a fire picking up speed. His fear picked up in intensity that he wouldn't make the point. He realized that he'd be past the point in a few minutes, and put his head down and forced himself to swim harder. He looked up and saw the point just twenty five yards away, and yet the current would push him past it in less than five minutes.

Stacy watched intently as Mike struggled against the current. She urged him on, pumping the air with her fist, as if loaning him her efforts. Then Stacy saw Mike turn back towards shore. She put her hands to her mouth. "My God, what's he doing now?" she said aloud. Is he drowning? Oh my God, should I go in after him? She thought.

As Stacy frantically wondered what to do, she watched Mike begin to swim back towards shore. She followed his eyes and hoped he was aiming for the next point, and picked up his backpack and hurried to meet him. A hundred yards downriver Stacy found her way impeded by a cliff. She wondered if she should turn back or swim around the sheer cliff. Not knowing what was on the other side, she decided to turn around and wait for Mike where he'd left her. Stacy looked for Mike and could no longer see him. He'd drifted around a bend in the river far enough that the Eastern shoreline obscured her view of him. She craned her neck to see around the point, but couldn't find Mike.

Mike lifted his head and saw that the point was almost upon him. It was now or never. He took a deep breath and swam with all he had, which wasn't much. He opened his eyes again to see the point ten yards away, and now he was directly opposite it. He lowered his head for one last push and looked up just in time to grab a tree in the water just as he was being carried past the point. The tree began to give. Mike lunged for a second tree with his other hand, yet his wet hand slipped through the moss on the tree. He grabbed a second time and caught hold of a limb. His hand began to slip again, yet he strengthened his grip with all he had. The limb cut into his hands, creating scratches in both hands, but he held on. He drew his legs up underneath him and tried to find a footing. At the same time he pulled on the branches, ignoring the pain in his hands. His feet merely kicked water. Mike pulled harder on the branch, as his hands began to tire. Finally he grabbed hold of a boulder just under water, safely pulling himself into water shallow enough to get his footing.

Mike collapsed on the dry ground, heaving for air. He fell onto his back as he sucked in air and massaged his arms. He sat up. Finally regaining enough strength, he stood and looked upriver for signs of Jack.

Stacy paced back and forth along the narrow spit of sand. Every few seconds she scanned the shoreline downriver. She couldn't stand still. Although Stacy wasn't a religious person, she found herself praying to God, or whoever might be listening. "Please God, if you're out there, don't let Mike die! Please don't let him die!" Stacy checked her watch, and it had now been forty-five frantic minutes since she'd last seen Mike. She looked up and Mike rounded the point and came into view. Stacy collapsed into his arms, knocking both of them into the water.

"Hey Stacy, you alright?" asked Mike.

"Oh thank God you're okay!"

"Yeah, I'm fine, but I had a hell of a scare."

"You had a hell of a scare? I couldn't see you the last forty-five minutes, and didn't know if you'd made it back to shore!" cried Stacy.

Mike frowned, and said, "I've got to get out there and help Jack."

"You're not going to try again, are you?"

"I have to. Jack can't fix the boat on his own."

"But what if you can't make it again?" asked Stacy. "You almost drowned!"

"I'll be okay. I just have to start further upriver so I don't have to fight the current as much."

Mike took the backpack from Stacy and they hiked upriver. They stopped a half mile further up and assessed Mike's options. "Mike, that's so far to swim!"

"I know, but at least I can ride the current most of the way down river. The worst part was fighting the current."

"Oh Mike, I don't know. Isn't there any other way?"

"No. I have to just give it a go. Jack doesn't know what to do."

"At least eat one of these protein bars so you'll have some energy," pleaded Stacy.

Mike ripped off the wrapper and quickly ate the bar. He washed it down with a few swallows of water. He didn't want to drink too much and get a side ache. "Okay, I'll meet you back here after we check out the boat. But, if it gets close to dark and we're not back, just go back to camp."

"But what are you guys going to do out there after dark?"

"I don't know. I don't know what I'll do until I see how bad the boat is. Just go back to camp before dusk, cause it'll take you an hour to get back. At least that way you and Kathy will be together."

"Okay, I guess. Please just hurry back!" Stacy winced. She wasn't comforted by the thought of being with Kathy. Stacy had just met Kathy recently, and didn't know her well. And Mike was the person she wanted to spend the night with.

Mike turned his hat around and dove into the water. Stacy paced back and forth while keeping an eye on Mike's progress. Mike alternated between free-style for speed and breast stroke for rest. This time he made it to the boat.

Kathy finished reading her People magazine. In fact she'd read one article twice, just to help pass the time. She set down the magazine, put on her visor, and walked down the shoreline. Kathy hiked down to the point just downriver from their campsite and scanned the river. When she squinted she could just make out Mike's boat. Kathy searched and searched, but couldn't see anyone on or near the boat. She walked back to camp. Kathy thought, I wonder how those guys are doing…did they make it out to the boat…it sure looks like a long swim…and where is Stacy…I feel bad for being a bit of a bitch to them…especially to Jack…I guess I don't really feel that way to Mike and Stacy…and now they have to deal with this problem…maybe I can somehow make it up to them…or at least to Jack…of course I don't want to overdo it, and make Jack think I…oh well, I guess I'll figure it out when the time comes…I wish someone would come back to camp, I hate being here all alone…I guess I better make myself lunch, since nobody's coming back for now.

Kathy sat down with her sandwich and coke. She thought of her sister as she ate, I wish Jane was here with me now. It seemed so strange to not be able to see, or even hear anyone else.

Stacy glanced up at the westering sun. She figured dusk was only thirty minutes away and Mike and Jack weren't back. She could see them out on the sand bar, doing something on the boat, exactly what she couldn't tell. Stacy sat in the shade of a small tree, and stood and stretched. Pacing back and forth on the small beach, she desperately wanted Mike to come back before dusk. Although she felt nervous waiting on the strip of sand alone, the thought of spending the entire night without Mike scared her. Dusk came before Mike. Stacy considered waiting longer, but she wasn't sure she could make it back to camp safely after dark. She couldn't see Mike or Jack, although she knew they were still out there. She'd seen their heads pop up twenty minutes earlier. Reluctantly, Stacy headed back to camp.

Stacy found the camp deserted. She searched around until she located Kathy bathing at the far end of the cove. Stacy hadn't noticed had grimy she felt until she saw Kathy with the bar of soap in her hands. She pulled off her shirt and joined Kathy in waist deep water. "Where have you all been so long, and where are the guys?" asked Kathy.

"They're still out at the boat. They've been out there all day working on it without food."

"So what's taking them so long to bring the boat back? Why don't they just drive it back here?" asked Kathy.

Stacy rolled her eyes, not bothering to conceal her face in the dark. "Kathy, I'm sure they would have driven it back if they could. It's probably been damaged in the storm. Who knows, it might even be flooded."

"Of course, you're probably right. I'm just worried about the guys being out there so long. And are they going to sleep out there?"

"I suppose they'll have to at this point. I can't imagine they'd try to swim back in the dark. They'd better not try to swim back in the dark," said Stacy.

Stacy got out of the river and borrowed Kathy's wet towel to dry off. "I'm starving. Let's go get something to eat," suggested Stacy. Kathy nodded and followed her to the ice chests.

Stacy was famished, having only eaten a protein bar and some chips since breakfast twelve hours ago. Kathy helped her make a couple sandwiches each. When the sandwiches were made they looked to each other for answers. "So now what?" asked Kathy.

"I don't know," said Stacy.

"So I guess we're going to have to spend the night alone," said Kathy.

"I'm really worried about them. At least we have the tents and the food. Those guys might have to sleep in the boat, or maybe even on the beach," said Stacy.

Kathy got up, opened the ice chest and cracked open a beer. "You want one?" Stacy shook her head. The two women ate slowly and in silence. Kathy felt bad for not considering the guys' situation, but she'd become increasingly anxious as the day wore on and no one came back till after dark. It was the strangest experience for Kathy to spend twelve hours without seeing another soul.

By the time they finished eating there was still no sign of Jack or Mike. Kathy said, "I guess they aren't coming back tonight. Is there anything we can do for them?"

"I can't think of anything," said Stacy.

"Well, I guess I'll go to sleep then," said Kathy, and then she went back into her tent.

Stacy sat down in Mike's beach chair in the dark. She kept hoping she'd hear their footsteps any moment. They never came. Finally Stacy gave up her watch and went to bed. Her exhaustion was so complete she was asleep just after zipping up her sleeping bag.

26 Weeks after the River Trip

"There's something else bothering me. I had Lily with me at dinner with Jane, and she asked the strangest question. She asked if I was mad at Daddy."

"Why would that be strange?" asked Dr. Aragorn.

"What in the world would make her think that? I mean, Jane and I are always careful to not use Jack's name around her."

"And you think that fools her? Of course she knows you're mad at Jack, she can feel it," said Dr. Aragorn.

"But she's only six, how can she possibly know that?"

"Young children are incredibly intuitive, sometimes more so than adults. I would be surprised if Lily didn't know about the problems with you and Jack. Now I don't mean that she could understand the complexity of the issues, or even put much of it into words, but she knows, and she's known for a long time," explained Dr. Aragorn.

"Oh that's just great! So I'm already damaging my daughter?"

"I wouldn't say you're damaging her, but certainly she's affected," said Dr. Aragorn.

"Oh my God, I'd hoped to keep Lily out of this! I'd hoped Jack and I could work it out without her having to be traumatized! But now you're telling me she knows everything!"

"Now you're adding to what I said," began Dr. Aragorn. "Lily's telling you that she knows you're mad at Daddy, but what makes you think she's traumatized?"

"Because she knows; she knows Jack and I are angry."

"So knowing you're angry is traumatic?" asked Dr. Aragorn. Kathy looked away and rubbed her face with her hands.

"We don't know that she's traumatized by it. It's likely she's not. However, she might need you to help her with her feelings about Mommy and Daddy's conflict," said Dr. Aragorn.

"So how do I do that?"

"What did you tell her?" asked Dr. Aragorn.

"I told her Mommy and Daddy are not mad at each other."

"That's probably confusing to her since she already senses that you are mad," said Evelyn.

"Then what in God's name do I tell her!" said Kathy.

"I would tell her that Mommy and Daddy sometimes do get mad at each other, and that we talk about it to make it better," answered Dr. Aragorn.

"But won't that scare her?" asked Kathy.

"I think it may scare her more to have you pretend what she feels isn't so," said Dr. Aragorn. "What Lily feels is real, and she's bringing it to you to help her with it. She needs you to acknowledge what's going on in a way that she can take in. Don't overwhelm her with any details, but reassure her that you and Daddy are talking it out."

"Okay, I think I can do that. But what if she asks me why I'm angry with Jack?"

"Then you tell her that you don't want her to worry about that, and that one of the good things about being a little girl is that Mommy and Daddy take care of their own feelings so she doesn't have to." Kathy nodded.

"Maybe you're uncomfortable with the whole anger thing," suggested Susan.

"Well, I certainly don't like being angry, if that's what you mean," said Kathy.

"And perhaps you're communicating that to Lily," said Evelyn.

"I suppose I am a bit defensive about it, being angry with Jack that is," said Kathy.

"That would make it harder to talk about with your daughter, wouldn't it?" said Jake.

"An important point, Jake," said Dr. Aragorn.

"I don't want to be defensive with Lily…I suppose I need to think more about that," said Kathy.

The next day Kathy had a full day between case research and the related phone calls, not to mention the ever present emails to return. A hearing deadline approached and she had to dig in to prepare. Normally Kathy hated such dreary days at the office, but today she welcomed the distraction from the confusion that had become a constant the past few weeks. Around noon, one of the other junior partners stepped into her office and invited her to lunch. Kathy hadn't even noticed that it was already that late. Mission accomplished.

On Thursday Jane called. Kathy let it go to voice mail, and later listened to Jane's invitation to meet for lunch. Kathy had mixed feels about meeting Jane. She missed her sister and wanted to see her, yet she dreaded another conversation about her marriage. Kathy was weary of covering the same ground again and again with Jane. After debating with herself for twenty minutes, she called Jane to accept.

Kathy and Jane hugged when they saw each other, as usual. "So, have you found any great clothes since I've seen you?" asked Jane. Kathy was relieved and gladly filled Jane in on her recent acquisitions. They sat down at the table and continued to catch up. Then Jane glanced up from buttering her bread and eyed Kathy for a moment. "So, have you set your group straight yet?"

"I don't know if I want to get into that today," said Kathy.

"Oh come on now, don't shut your best sister out."

Kathy looked out the window and sighed before she said, "I'm still trying to figure all that out, and I'm still not sure I want to get into it with you again."

"Kathy, you're scaring me. You're not going to leave Jack are you? You know no Russell wife has ever left her husband. We Russells always make it work."

"Why in the world would you ask me that?"

"Look Kathy, I'm your older sister. I know you. I know you're unhappy with Jack."

"No, I'm not leaving Jack. I want to find a way to make it work with him. I think the group might help me learn how to do that," said Kathy.

"Don't count on them too much. I'm sure they can offer you some techniques for communication or something, but remember to weigh carefully everything they tell you. What are they telling you anyway?"

"I don't want to get into the details with you."

"Kathy, you aren't pushing me away, are you?"

"No, of course I'm not..." Kathy took a deep breath before conceding, "They're telling me to get to know myself."

"Get to know yourself? You already know yourself, what kind of nonsense is that?"

"I'm not sure that I do know myself in the way they're talking about."

"You're a great sister, a good mom, a patient wife and a terrific attorney. What else is there to know?"

"I'm not sure it's that simple. I mean..."

"Kathy, don't make this more complicated than it has to be. All that psychobabble more often muddies the water than clears the air. Let them help you with communication techniques and leave the understanding the family to family."

"I don't want to talk about it anymore. I'm getting a headache. So, tell me about my precious niece Jessica," said Kathy. Jane gladly filled in her sister on her two-year olds' cute behavior this week.

Kathy hugged her sister and walked to her car. Once safely inside she pounded the dash board, and then collapsed onto the steering wheel in tears. Her head seemed a little clearer after group Tuesday night, but now on Thursday she didn't know which way was up. Kathy looked at the time on her cell phone and groaned. She had a meeting back at the office in fifteen minutes. She briefly considered skipping it, but quickly realized she had to show. Kathy desperately wanted to talk with Alex, but that would have to wait. When she arrived in the company parking structure she brushed her hair, reapplied her make-up and checked to see if it looked like she'd been crying. She put on her game face and stepped into the building.

Three hours later she retreated to the privacy of her car and immediately phoned Alex. "Please pick up, oh please pick up," she said as the phone rang. Then she heard Alex's voice mail and began to cry. "Alex, this is Kathy. Please call me back as soon as you can. I really need to talk to you. I feel like I'm going crazy. Call at any time of day or night and I'll pick up."

Once the garage door closed behind her, Kathy flipped down her visor mirror and dabbed at her eyes. Satisfied, she went into the house. Kathy only made it about three steps into the house before Lily leaped into her arms. "Mommy's home, Mommy's home."

"How's my little teddy-bear? I missed you."

Jack sat ensconced in his usual spot. "Hey Kath, how goes it?"

"Hi. What do you want for dinner?"

"How about spaghetti?"

"Great, I can reheat spaghetti from two nights ago."

"Oh come on Kath, I don't want some warmed over crap. Make it fresh."

"Don't talk like that around Lily," Kathy said as she set Lily down. Jack rolled his eyes. "Give me a break, Jack. I don't have it in me to make anything tonight."

"Why? Did something happen today?"

"I had a tough lunch with Jane, but I don't really want to talk about it."

"Well that explains it. She's crazy enough for the loony bin."

"Jack! That's not fair. Jane's…oh never mind. I don't want to get into it with you."

"Look Kath, I know you love your sister and all, but you have to admit…"

"Don't even go there, Jack! I don't want to hear it."

"Wow! You sure are touchy tonight. Alright, I'm warned."

Kathy threw her head back and sighed loudly, gripping the kitchen tiles tightly as though she held on for dear life.

Kathy glanced over at Lily, who was watching her intently. Once they made eye contact Lily came into the kitchen and said,

"Mommy, I want to help with dinner."

"Okay honey, I'll cut up the carrots and you can pour some Ranch into a bowl for us to dip in.

"Okay Mommy." Kathy opened the fridge, took out the spaghetti and carrots and poured herself a glass of white wine. After a sip of wine she cut up the carrots and turned to Lily, who had already poured the Ranch, half in the bowl and half on the counter. "Okay Lily, do you want to set the table?"

"Uh huh."

"Okay we'll need forks and…"

"Don't tell me! I know, I know what to do," said Lily.

Kathy smiled and looked across the room. Jack had gone back to the sporting news and didn't seem to notice her abruptly terminated conversation with him. She was relieved that he'd let it go that easily. After her lunch with Jane the last thing she wanted was another difficult conversation. "Okay Jack, dinner's ready," said Kathy as she sat down to eat. They ate without talking for a few minutes until the silence was interrupted by Kathy's cell phone ringing. Kathy jumped up and checked the caller ID, and then answered. "Alex, I'm so glad you called back. Yes I can talk, just give me a minute. Kathy turned to Lily, "Honey, I have an important phone call, so I'll be out in the garage for a little while and then I'll be back in to help you get ready for bed, okay?"

"Okay Mommy."

Kathy went out into the garage and turned the light on. "Okay, I can talk now. I'm out in the garage."

"Kathy what's up? You sounded terrible on my voice mail."

"Oh my God, I feel like I'm being pulled apart at the seams. The Tuesday night people tell me one thing, and then Jane tells me the exact opposite. Just when I feel like I'm beginning to get what the group's saying, I talk to Jane and want to pull my hair out. Please tell me that I'm not going crazy."

"Oh you're long past going crazy," said Alex.

"What?" said Kathy with alarm.

"Oh Kathy, I'm teasing you. You're not going crazy. You're disorganized, and your head's swimming with upsetting feedback. You've seen your world one way for a long time, probably the way Jane's telling you, and now group and I are telling you something quite different. You're trying to get your arms around these new ideas about yourself and your marriage, and it's a rough go."

"Oh my God yes. I don't know what to think. I know there's something to what you and the Tuesday people are telling me, but when I meet with Jane I feel like I leave our world and enter another dimension...or maybe entering the world of Alex and group is the other dimension. What do I do?" said Kathy as she sat down, feeling a bit light-headed.

"You need to give yourself time, and it's hard to do that when you're disorganized and anxious. You need time to understand yourself and your marriage. This might be the hardest season when you're so confused."

"Please tell me this season ends soon."

"I can't tell you that. I don't know how long you'll be there, but I can tell you that it did end for me. And I can tell you that it's better on the other side of winter. You're in winter, and spring does come...Kathy, are you still with me?"

"Yes, I'm still here. I don't know what to say. I guess I'm just thinking."

"About anything in particular?"

"Just that I noticed that the room isn't spinning as much."

"Oh yes, I remember what that feels like. Nothing like walking around on a ship tossed on rough seas," said Alex.

Kathy laughed. "It feels good that somebody else knows what that's like. I'm glad you called back. I don't know what's changed, but it just seems a little more okay for now."

"Good, I'm glad it helped to talk. Hang in there Kathy, and don't give up. It will get better."

"Okay. Well, my dinner's getting cold on the table, so I'll let you go."

"Alright girlfriend, talk to you soon."

The spaghetti was cold when she touched it to her mouth. She got up and reheated it, and then sat back down with Jack and ate. Lily was in the family room coloring at her plastic table. "So who was that?" asked Jack.

"Alex, the nurse from the hospital."

"And what did she want?"

"It's more like what did I want. She was calling me back. I'm struggling, and Alex has been real supportive."

"So have you figured anything out yet?"

Kathy eyed Jack carefully and said, "I hesitate to tell you this, but I'm wondering if I'm mothering you."

"You definitely are! I've been trying to tell you that for years. If you would just back off everything would be fine. You treat me like I'm either a child or an idiot who can't go to the restroom by himself."

Tears came to Kathy's eyes. She nodded and looked down at her food. "I wish I wasn't like that. I'm sorry."

"It's okay, Kath…Maybe these groupies can help you stop doing that."

"Yes, maybe they can. I hope so, because I hate how things are between us."

"Well, you admitting that you mother me might help a lot," said Jack.

"I sure hope so. I can't take much more of this."

"Don't make too much of it. It hasn't been that bad. We have our rough moments, but on the whole, it's a good marriage."

"I don't know if I'd agree with that. It hasn't been so good for me. I really hate it when we fight," said Kathy.

"Maybe it'd be better if you'd just back off a bit."

Kathy looked at her glass of wine and took a sip without saying anything. She didn't know what would fix their marriage. She wondered if it was as simple as that. Maybe if she stopped being parental it would radically change their marriage, and maybe it wouldn't. Well, it was certainly worth a try, and Kathy planned to give it a go. Jack interrupted Kathy's thoughts.

"The game's starting in ten minutes, so I'm going to jump in the shower so I can see the tip off." Jack loved to watch the Lakers and rarely missed a game. If he wasn't able to watch it live, then he recorded it and watched it later. Kathy didn't mind since she didn't feel like talking anymore tonight. She washed the dishes and then went to help Lily get ready for bed.

When Kathy went to put Lily to bed, she found her on Jack's lap. Lily often watched the Lakers games with her daddy. While daddy held a beer, Lily held a Sippy cup of juice. "Come on Lily, it's time for bed."

"No, I want to watch the game with daddy," complained Lily.

"No honey, you go with mommy," said Jack.

While she tucked Lily into bed she decided this might be as good a time as any to talk to Lily about what Dr. Aragorn suggested. Kathy thought for a moment and didn't know how to start the conversation, and almost changed her mind. And then Lily said, "Mommy, why are you worried?"

"I'm not...wait, do I look worried to you?"

"Uh huh."

"Well, maybe I am. Do you remember the other night when you asked me if I was mad at Daddy?"

"Uh huh," said Lily.

"Well, Mommy didn't tell you the whole truth and I want to fix that. The truth is that sometimes Mommy and Daddy do get mad at each other, like the other night when we had dinner with Aunt Jane. But I don't want you to worry about it, because me and Daddy talk about it when we get mad at each other. Okay?"

"Are you mad at Daddy tonight?"

"Uh well, yes I am. I am a little bit."

"Okay Mommy. Hey Mommy, read me the Gingerbread Man tonight."

Kathy was eager to talk in group, but Susan beat her to it. Kathy struggled to be patient while Susan processed, and watched for her opportunity to jump in next. Finally, after about twenty minutes, Susan said she felt finished for the night, and Kathy jumped in. "I'd like to bring something up. I talked to Jack about us...He agrees with you all that I've been parental with him. He said he's been trying to tell me that for years...It hurt to hear him say that. I didn't know what to say to him, except that I'm sorry."

"That might be enough for now," suggested Dr. Aragorn.

"But that doesn't fix anything."

"It's a good start. And how did Jack respond?" asked Dr. Aragorn.

"He accepted my apology and said that maybe you all could help me. And then he said that our marriage isn't so bad, that we have our rough spots, but really it's a good marriage. I didn't know what to do with that, because I hate the way things are between us."

"Your marriage may work okay for Jack, but it doesn't work for you the way it is," said Evelyn.

"Definitely not! I have to find a way to make it different."

"Yes, and one way or another we'll help you do that. And I think you've taken an important step towards changing it by acknowledging you're assuming the parent role," said Dr. Aragorn.

"Okay, but now what?"

"Now we look at what made that role work for you, and help you take a look at all the ways that you put yourself above him, so that you can begin to resign from the job of being Jack's parent," explained Dr. Aragorn.

"So how do I figure out what made being a parent work for me?"

"How did you first start being a parent with Jack? Did it come up when you were dating?" asked Susan.

Kathy looked out the window. She couldn't see much since it was dark, but it gave her space to think. "Oh my, this takes me back," Kathy said as she laughed. "I first met Jack when we were seniors at Southwestern State. The night before our first finals together we were studying in the library and Jack said he was tired and decided to go back to his apartment. He said he felt ready for one final, but he hadn't started studying for his communications final, also the next day. Jack said he would make some coffee and then attack the second final before he went to bed. Anyway, I studied for another hour or two in the library and then I decided to swing by his apartment on the way home. I had a key to his apartment, and when he didn't answer the door, I let myself in. I found Jack asleep on the couch with the <u>Sports Illustrated</u> swimsuit edition on his chest. I picked up the magazine and slapped him across the head with it. It worked, I mean he woke up right away, and I insisted that he tell me how much he'd studied for his communications final. Of course, he hadn't even cracked the book yet, and he'd forgotten about the coffee. Well, I made the coffee, and when I got back to the couch he was watching T.V. I turned off the T.V. and told him to get his ass over to the table right the hell now. He sheepishly complied. I stayed for two hours until he'd gone over all thirteen chapters on the final. So does that answer your question, Susan?"

Susan and the entire group laughed uproariously with Kathy. "Alright, so you got an early start on the controlling mother thing," said Susan with a wink. Kathy nodded with a smile.

"So you rescued Jack that night. Why do you think you did that?" asked Dr. Aragorn.

"I don't know...it just made me so mad to find him sleeping, and not only sleeping, but wasting time reading some porno magazine when he should have been studying."

"Okay, but what about that angered you?" pressed Dr. Aragorn.

"Wouldn't it anger you if you found your girlfriend screwing up like that?"

"I don't know that it would. It wouldn't have anything to do with me," answered Dr. Aragorn.

"You mean you could just watch and not care if your girlfriend failed her final?"

"Sure, I'd probably have some feelings about it, and I wouldn't like it, but I probably wouldn't have woken her up. I probably wouldn't have even gone over. Do you see how you were taking responsibility for him?" asked Dr. Aragorn.

"You saved him from responsibility for his own choice," added Evelyn.

"So it's better to let someone you love fail, and even maybe get an F in a class?"

"Yes," said several people in unison.

"But how is that more loving?" pushed Kathy.

"Because it's loving to let someone make their own choices and run their own life," said Dr. Aragorn.

"I don't know...," said Kathy slowly.

"But let's get back to understanding what happened. Why do you think it angered you to see him as you found him? Where did that take you?" asked Dr. Aragorn.

"Well it does remind me how every night my mom would put me to bed. And I remember her always asking me if I'd done all my homework and chores for the day."

"And what if you hadn't?" asked Susan.

"She'd make me get up and do it right then. Oh my God, it's the same isn't it," said Kathy as she put her hands over her face. "I can't believe it! I'm just like her."

"That's an important connection. You did as you were taught," said Dr. Aragorn.

"I hate that! I don't want to be like her that way. Oh my God, I can't believe I've been doing that to Jack. I do that over the bills, I do that over his job, I do that over the house being messy. I do that over everything." Dr. Aragorn nodded with a grin.

"So how do I stop? I can't keep doing this. Please tell me how to stop."

"Give yourself time. Be patient with yourself," said Evelyn.

"Yeah, you're just now seeing something really important, you'll need some time to adjust," said Susan.

"How can I be patient when I see what a mess I'm making of my marriage? How can I give myself time when I'm ruining my life?"

"Kathy it's not like throwing a light switch. You need time to process what you're discovering and be able and ready to be different. The change will come, but being harsh with yourself won't help," said Dr. Aragorn. Kathy rested her forehead against the palm of her hand. Tears silently rolled down her face. She didn't bother to wipe them away. After a few moments Jake asked if Kathy was done. Kathy nodded without looking up.

When Kathy arrived home she was relieved to find Jack asleep on the couch. She cracked Lily's door and smiled at seeing Lily peacefully asleep. Kathy's limbs felt heavy and she half dragged herself into the bedroom. Her whole body felt drained of energy and weighed down as though her weight had doubled. Kathy thought about getting into the shower, but didn't feel the energy for even a relaxing shower. She slowly undressed and went to bed with her make-up on. She was asleep before she knew it.

Mike had been Jack's best friend since college. They pledged the same fraternity together, and hit it off right away. Mike influenced Jack for the better, often suggesting they meet up to study during midterms or finals. Jack tended to wait until the night before the exam to study, and was smart enough to get by with that strategy, but could have earned better grades with better study habits. In contrast, Mike had the self-discipline to keep up with his studies, and his grades reflected this. Desiring to do something in return for his best friend, Jack helped Mike with the ladies, being unusually skilled at meeting women. Many college coeds readily responded to Jack's charms and easy-going nature.

When he entered college, Mike had been determined to become a psychologist, wanting to understand himself. When he found out how much schooling was involved, he changed his mind and studied business, eventually earning his MBA. Being naturally drawn to understanding people and relationships, Mike developed a consulting business for himself. He consulted with management teams, helping them to work out conflict and differences of opinion, setting goals, and finding ways to work together for the benefit of the company and all concerned.

Mike started his training as a boy. His parents fought regularly. As a young boy Mike would huddle under the covers of his bed when his parents screamed at each other, often crying himself to sleep. When he got a little older, he would get out of bed and go downstairs to find his parents. At first they ordered him back to bed, telling him to ignore the conversation that mommy and daddy were having. But Mike was determined to put a stop to the evening shouting matches, and he would patiently help mommy understand why daddy was angry. And then he would explain to daddy why mommy was disappointed. When Mike began consulting with management teams, he found that coaching each member of the team to communicate seemed easy. He'd already been doing it for years.

Jack walked into the sports bar and found Mike on the end, saving the next seat. Jack slapped Mike on the back and ordered something on draft. "You just missed the tip-off, and it's a tie game. You haven't missed much," said Mike.

"Ok cool. Well let's hope the Lakers can rally after that embarrassing loss a couple nights ago," said Jack.

"They will. They pretty much never tank two games in a row," said Mike.

"And it should help when they get Fisher back from the DL next week," said Jack.

"Yeah, no doubt," agreed Mike.

Half-time came and Jack slipped off to the men's room. Both men were in high spirits, as their team enjoyed a nice lead. When Jack came back he pondered his beer and sipped slowly. Jack looked up to see Mike staring at him. Mike said, "You know Jack, you've been quiet tonight."

"Have I?"

"Yeah, so what's up?" asked Mike.

"Nothing really."

"Come on Jack. I know you better than that. The only time you get quiet is when the Lakers lose or you've got something on your mind. And the Lakers are up 10 at half-time, so…"

"Well I guess I'm concerned about this counseling thing that Kathy's gotten herself into," began Jack.

"You mentioned that she'd starting some kind of therapy. So why are you concerned?"

"I don't know…they seem to be putting some crazy thoughts into her head," said Jack.

"What kind of crazy thoughts?"

"I don't know, like we have some marriage problems or something."

"And do you have marriage problems?" asked Mike.

"Of course not! You know we don't."

"So what does Kathy think the problems are?" asked Mike.

"The one thing she does have right is that she can be heavy-handed and act like she's my mother…she admitted that for the first time the other night."

"That sounds pretty good. So then what's the problem?" asked Mike.

"No, that's not the problem, I mean it's great that she finally admits that, but she thinks we have issues or something," said Jack.

"What kind of issues?"

"I don't really know…something about how we have disagreements seems like a big deal to her," said Jack.

"So what kind of disagreements are we talking about?"

"Oh I don't know, no big deal really. You know, like every couple, we have words every once in awhile."

"You make it sound like it's nothing," said Mike.

"That's just it! It is nothing, but Kathy makes it out to be life or death."

"Maybe it is life or death to her," said Mike.

"Then she's making too much out of nothing!"

"Maybe so, but the conflict might be more upsetting to her than it is to you," said Mike.

"Then she needs to get over it."

Mike chuckled, "And how is she supposed to do that?"

"Just shrug it off, like I do. Kathy makes mole hills into mountains. If she'd just stop doing that, we'd be just fine, like every other couple that has normal minor issues."

"I wonder if you're making mountains into mole hills. Have you ever considered that?" asked Mike.

"Hey wait a damn minute! Are you taking her side, or what?"

"Hold on Jack, I'm your friend. And because I'm your friend, it's my job to get you to consider her perspective too."

"What a load of crap that is! I don't need friends to take Kathy's side. I need friends who have my back, and support me when my wife's going a little crazy."

"A little crazy? Jack, isn't that a bit extreme to call Kathy crazy? Yeah, she can be controlling and a bit demanding sometimes, but crazy? I don't think so," said Mike.

"Now wait a damn minute…"

Mike cut Jack off, "Now hang on! You're my friend and I do got your back. And I'm trying to help you deal with your marriage."

"Then how about being more supportive?"

"Is it supportive for me to blow sunshine at you, no matter what you tell me? Is that being a good friend?"

"Well…maybe…"

"Come off it Jack, I'd expect a little more than pure sunshine from you if I was having a rough go in my relationship. That's what friends are for. To help us see our part in something, so we can go back to our lady and make it work," said Mike.

"I don't know man, I sure had your back that night when we were pledges," said Jack.

"Yeah, and thank God for that, blood brother," said Mike.

"So how about getting my back when…" Jack was interrupted by the second half starting, and both men turned their attention back to the big screen above the bar.

Jack and Mike were in the same pledge class as freshmen in college. Each week on Monday nights was hazing night. Of course, hazing is officially illegal, but many fraternities ignore that rule. On Monday nights the brothers lined the pledges up. The pledges were assigned study material each week, and each

Monday night they lined-up and took that week's exam. Brothers would demand the pledges answer questions from the reading material, and require them to recite passages. The penalty for an incorrect answer, or incorrect recitation, was to gulp down a beer.

Most Monday nights found Mike well prepared and Jack not so much. Jack often left the fraternity house well intoxicated each week. On one particular week Mike had forgotten to study, while Jack had studied well. It was probably the only time that had happened. This was the Monday night that left Mike as drunk as he'd ever been. After line-up Mike and Jack walked back to their apartment. There were a couple of dark alleys on the way home, unless you took the long way home and walked through campus. Jack and Mike always took the short way home. As they walked through the dark part of town, suddenly Mike slumped to his knees, with blood wetting his hair. Fortunately, Jack had only had one beer that night, and was sober. He quickly turned around in time to see a bottle coming at his head. Jack automatically blocked the arm swinging the bottle, and countered with his other arm. The fight lasted a short time, and within a minute two men lay groaning on the ground, both holding their own heads. One guy had a broken arm and the other lost a couple of teeth.

Jack had taken years of karate as a kid, and had advanced far enough to achieve his black belt. Although he hadn't been in a fight in years, the training was so ingrained in Jack that he didn't require conscious thought to react.

Although his arm hurt badly from the bottle, Jack carried Mike the two blocks to the campus ER room. The doctors told them that if Mike had arrived much later, he would have bled to death. Ever since that night, Mike and Jack became "blood brothers".

The other positive influence Jack made on Mike was the special school. Once they became good friends, Jack brought Mike to Jimmy's school. It took Mike a few visits to become comfortable with the special kids. Not having any prior exposure to such kids, Mike didn't know what to do with them. At first he merely watched Jack, but eventually he warmed up to them and joined in with the play. Play really best described their visits. Just like any other kid, these children most wanted someone to play with them.

In fact, Jack got their fraternity involved as well. The university required all social fraternities and sororities to volunteer and make a positive impact in the local community. When this requirement came up at their weekly meeting, Jack's was the first hand to go up with a suggested charity. Jack organized a calendar of fraternity brothers' visits to Jimmy's school. Most of the guys put in their time and quietly uninvolved themselves with the special school, yet a few of the guys continued on with Jack and Mike. Mike continued going to Jimmy's school all through college.

The River: Day 3

Just after dawn Stacy awoke to someone climbing into the sleeping bag with her. She started, and then realized who was joining her.

"Mike, you're back! Thank God you're alright!"

"Thank God the morning finally came. I was freezing my ass off and starving to death, all in the same enjoyable evening."

"Oh my God, you guys probably didn't sleep much."

"Sleep? What's that? I might have dozed a few times. The seats on the boat weren't too comfortable," said Mike.

"Hey, you're wet," noticed Stacy.

"I didn't fly back."

"Oh my God, of course you had to swim back," said Stacy.

"Yeah, we couldn't get the boat started. We ran out of daylight, and then the boat flashlight ran out of batteries a couple hours later," explained Mike.

"So what now?"

"Now I sleep. I can't even think about it until I get some shuteye."

"Do you want me to get you a sandwich or something?" But when Stacy turned to Mike for a response, he was already asleep. She closed her eyes and joined him in pleasant slumber.

Crows called to each other overhead. Mike opened his eyes. It took him awhile to orient himself to the sounds that woke him. He rubbed his eyes, and then looked to the right to see that Stacy wasn't there. His clothes stuck to him. Sleeping in wet

clothes isn't the best way to go, and it was now hot. Mike sat up and peeled off his semi-damp clothes. He pulled out a fresh shirt and bathing suit, and put them on. The other three already sat in their chairs eating hot dogs and chips.

"Hey babe, I'll put a dog on for you. You want one or two?" asked Stacy.

"Uh two, at least two. God, it seems like I haven't eaten in days."

"You want a beer?" asked Jack as he opened the ice chest.

"Oh no, that sounds terrible. Toss me a coke."

Jack threw him an ice cold coke.

"Hey man, I didn't mean that literally," said Mike.

Jack flashed a smile, "Glad to see you've kept a sense of humor after yesterday."

"We're on vacation, aren't we," returned Mike.

"Yeah, are we having fun yet?" quipped Jack.

"Absolutely, this is an adventure."

"You guys sound like idiots," said Kathy.

"Come on Kath, don't be like that," Jack responded.

"Don't be like what? I just spent an entire day and night wondering if you guys are coming back dead or alive, if at all, and you're talking about having fun," Kathy fired back. Jack shrugged his shoulders and shook his head.

"Hey Kathy, we're just trying to make the best of a tough situation," said Mike.

Kathy paused while she thought, "Yeah, I know. I guess I was just worried. I'm sorry."

"Forget about it," said Mike.

"What do you want on your hot dogs?" asked Stacy.

"The works," said Mike.

Stacy set a plate in Mike's lap. Mike fell to the food with zeal, often belching his compliments to the chef. Stacy smiled. Kathy rolled her eyes. Jack laughed.

Stacy's face took on a serious form. "Okay, so what are we going to do?"

"We'll have to see what we can do with the boat," answered Mike.

"So for now we have no drivable boat, and we're how many miles from the marina?" asked Stacy.

"I'd have to look at the map, but we're probably fifty miles upriver," answered Mike.

"Fifty miles? Oh my God! It's too bad we came this far from the marina," said Kathy. Stacy and Mike looked at her, searching for signs of seriousness. Jack didn't even bother looking.

"We still got a chance to fix the boat, don't we Mike?" asked Jack.

"A chance, I guess. We ran out of light before we really knew if it could be fixed."

"What's wrong with the boat?" asked Stacy.

"The boat was half flooded when we got to it, with a good sized crack in the hull. It must have hit some kind of rock before it was beached. Anyway, we spent most of the day bailing the water out and patching the crack. Thank God I had some bonding compound in the boat. The thing that took so long was waiting for the crack to dry so we could patch it. We had to do the patch work after dusk. Damn, I sure hope it took," explained Mike.

"I think it took. It was totally dry before we put the compound on," said Jack.

"Well, let's hope so. We're in a heap of trouble if it didn't. That crack is pretty good sized," said Mike.

"So what do we do if the patch didn't take?" said Kathy. Mike looked at Kathy and said, "Let's cross that bridge once we come to it." And then Mike turned to Jack, "Let's get back out there and see how it looks. We've still got a long day's work ahead." Jack nodded and got up to get packed for the day's labor.

"What else is there to do?" asked Kathy. "Look I don't mean to be difficult, I'm just worried about our situation. Do you have to Mickey Mouse some fix-it job?"

"Us Mickey Mouse repairmen have all kinds of work to do. It takes a long time to attach the chewing gum and Popsicle sticks," returned Mike.

Kathy rolled her eyes and crossed her arms across her chest. "Come on Mike, I'm not trying to be disrespectful, I really am concerned about our situation. We're fifty miles from civilization with no serviceable boat." Mike nodded at Kathy.

Stacy stood up, "I hope you brought back an extra life jacket, because I'm coming with you guys today."

"You sure you want to do that? We might be out there all day, and with only protein bars to eat," said Mike.

"No, I've got an idea. I'm going to double bag sandwiches in zip lock bags. We're going to eat well out there today," answered Stacy.

"Alright, whoever's going get packed. I want plenty of light," said Mike.

"Wait a minute, you aren't going to leave me here alone all day again are you?" asked Kathy.

"I need Jack to help me with the boat, and Stacy makes her own decision," answered Mike.

"I'm going," said a resolute Stacy.

Jack shrugged his shoulders, "Hey Kath, I gotta go. And keep an eye on my hat." Kathy stood and nodded slowly.

The three campers headed downriver with hats, sunscreen and two backpacks, one with food and one with waters. Kathy remained behind. An hour later they stood on the point from which Mike had successfully made his swim to the boat. Mike had brought back an extra life jacket, and all three put them on. Jack and Mike put on the two backpacks, and they pushed off from shore.

Stacy proved to be as strong a swimmer as Jack, and all three made it safely to the sand bar, with Mike bringing up the rear. The boat was still pulled well up onto the sand, which Mike and Jack had done to allow the patch to dry. Fortunately the crack was up near the bow, so they were able to get the drying compound completely out of the water. Mike inspected the patch. "It looks good. I think it's going to hold."

"I'll start bailing out the water again; looks like the boat took in some more water over night," said Jack.

"Before you do that, help me pull the boat back into the water. It might take all three of us to pull that off," instructed Mike.

"Why do you want the boat back in the water? Isn't it easier to work on it on the beach?" asked Jack.

"Yeah, but I don't want to risk any water coming in over the stern while I've got the engine opened up. Okay, here's what we're going to do. Pull the boat off the beach, and then walk it around the sand bar to the downriver side of the sand bar," explained Mike.

"Oh I get it, the sand bar will protect the boat from taking in more water," said Jack.

"Exactly. Okay ready, one two three pull," said Mike.

It took several heaves, but they eventually got the boat back into the river, and anchored it to the beach on the far side. One of the anchors had still been attached when the boat was marooned on the sandbar the first night. Stacy and Jack fell to bailing the water out of the boat. Mike began to work on the engine. He pulled out each of the eight spark plugs and peered inside. By the time he was done, the other two had cleared the boat of water.

"Okay, now it's time to see how bad the damage is. Jack, put the key in and turn the engine over, maybe a half dozen times," said Mike.

"Okay boss," answered Jack as he put the key in the ignition.

Jack turned the key and water squirted out of the spark plug holes. Mike instructed Jack to do this several more times, until he was convinced that all the water was out of the engine. Then he sprayed each cylinder with lubricant to retard any oxidation that had begun. Mike replaced the spark plugs and wires.

"Okay, anybody hungry?" asked Mike. "I want to let it sit a bit before trying to start it."

"Yeah I'm starving. Man, we've been out here three hours already," said Jack.

Having polished off the sandwiches and rested, it was time to see if the engine would start. Mike climbed into the driver's seat, pumped the throttle a couple times and looked at Stacy and Jack. "Okay guys, this is the moment of truth. If this doesn't start, we're screwed," said Mike.

"Please God, let it start," said Stacy.

Mike turned the ignition key and the starter motor rotated several times seductively, but the engine failed to catch. He tried again and the engine turned over a few times, and then fell silent. "That sounds hopeful, the water damage must be minimal," Mike assessed.

Mike allowed the batteries to rest a few minutes. He turned the key again and the engine sprang to life for a few seconds, and just as Mike gave it more throttle, it died.

"I don't like how that sounds. There isn't much juice left in the batteries. I'm going to let it sit a few more minutes. We may not have many more chances before we run out of juice," said Mike.

"Oh my God, please!" urged Stacy.

Mike turned the key again and the starter motor labored and groaned, failing to turn the engine over. Mike left it rest a bit longer, and tried again. The starter motor barely turned, and then they heard the fateful clicking sound. Anybody who's had a dead battery knows that awful sound. Click click click, means dead dead dead.

"Ah crap, we're screwed," said Mike.

"The batteries are dead?" asked Jack.

"That's exactly right. And we have no way to charge them or jump them way out here," answered Mike.

"So what do we do then?" asked Stacy.

"Don't know what we can do," said Mike. "Damn!" he said as he hit the dash board.

All three sat in silence, pondering their fate. Mike put his face in his hands. Jack rubbed his face. Stacy stared out at the river. Nobody spoke for what seemed like an hour. Jack broke the silence, "Hey, don't you have two batteries on this thing?"

"Yeah, but I got 'em both turned on," answered Mike. "The one thing that's sure, this boat isn't going anywhere."

"Won't a ranger eventually come across us?" asked Stacy.

"Eventually, but this part of the river isn't even open for another two weeks. The ranger may not find us until then," explained Mike.

Jack gazed out at the river. "Wait a minute, the river flows towards the truck, right?"

"Right."

"So we pack up and float back down to the truck," suggested Jack.

"That might take the rest of the week, or more," said Mike.

"No it won't. The river moves pretty fast," countered Jack.

"Yeah, but you're forgetting that we have to navigate turns in the river."

"How hard can that be?" said Jack.

"I don't know, but we'll just have to deal with it. I mean, what else can we do?" reasoned Stacy. All three sat in silence considering their options.

"Do you have an oar," asked Jack.

"What good's that going to do us?"

"We can paddle the boat to shore, and then walk it back to our campsite," suggested Jack.

"That's our best chance right? I mean, I don't see any other good options," said Stacy.

Mike paused before responding, "You're probably right. One thing's for sure, I don't want to spend another night on this sand bar. I suppose we ought to get paddling while we still have a few hours daylight."

"Let's do it," said Jack.

The boat had one paddle aboard. Mike and Jack took turns paddling, and were both exhausted before they made it to shore. They reluctantly allowed Stacy to take the paddle the last hundred yards. Paddling the boat proved to be more difficult than swimming, and they ended up hitting shore a good two miles downriver.

After a short rest, they walked the boat upriver towards camp. They took turns with one person riding in the boat while the other two pushed and pulled the boat, respectively. After another hour's labor they pulled the boat up onto the sand and rested. Stacy fished out the remaining two protein bars and a bag of chips with only crumbs remaining, and divided up the spoils amongst the three of them. With only water to wash it down it, it wasn't exactly five star quality dining. But it sated their stomachs for the moment.

"Hey Mike, how much farther till we make camp? I'm beat," said Jack.

Mike glanced upriver, "You're not going to like the answer. I'd guess we still got another mile to go."

"Shit. How do we make that before dark," asked Jack.

"We don't," said Mike.

"Oh come off it! We got to find a way to make it back. I don't care if we're doing it in the dark.

"Mike's right. We have to make a plan to spend the night out here," urged Stacy.

"No! I'll make a plan after we do our best until dark, even beyond if we have to," said Jack.

"Jack, you have to face it, we're still a mile off and we're all exhausted. And even if we weren't, I'm not going to risk pushing my boat in the dark when we can't see the rocks just under water. Do you know what happens if we hit a rock on the port side of the bow again?" said Mike.

"Yeah, yeah, I get it. We blow the hole in the hull back open. Don't treat me like I'm an idiot," Jack pushed back.

"Okay, I just want us to be realistic about our situation…tell you what, you go back to camp and bring back the other anchor. I'll need it to make the boat fast to the shore. I won't risk another wind storm blowing the boat off the beach. And you can update Kathy on where we're at," suggested Mike.

Jack pulled his black hat off and scratched his head. "I guess so," consented Jack.

"Okay, so climb up beyond the brush near the river so you can make better time," said Mike.

"Look, I know how to hike, okay? Stop treating me like I'm an idiot. That's all I get from Kath, and I'm not gonna take that shit from you," Jack fired back.

Mike looked at Jack with wide eyes. He wasn't used to his friend jumping on him like that.

"Look Jack, I'm sorry if I'm stepping on your toes. I'm just trying to get us out of a jam," offered Mike.

"So where do I meet you?" said Jack.

"See that beach the next cove upriver, we'll wait for you there. That looks like as good a beach as any to dig in for the night," said Mike.

"And bring us back something to eat," said Stacy.

Jack hiked along the shoreline beyond the second cove and disappeared from sight. "Can you believe how stubborn he is?" said Mike. Stacy merely nodded. Stacy and Mike moved out at a slower pace. The next cove up seemed far with how tired they both felt. Mike walked at the bow where he could keep an eye on submerged rocks. Mike turned back to see Stacy walking with her head down and dragging her right arm in the water.

"Hey babe, you want to stop for a bit?" asked Mike.

"I can't go any farther."

"Hop in and I'll pull for awhile," offered Mike.

It was all Stacy could do to pull herself up the transom ladder into the boat. It was slower going pulling on his own, but Mike needed more time to scan for submerged rocks in the fading light.

At first Jack hiked along the shoreline. He glanced over his shoulder to see if Mike was watching. Once he knew he was out of sight Jack climbed up the hill to the higher ground. It turned out to be easier terrain to travel on, but he hadn't wanted to give Mike the satisfaction.

Jack stumbled and fell as he tried to slow himself from running down the steep sand dune that formed the downriver boundary of their campsite. He picked himself up, brushed himself off and dragged himself into camp. Dusk was just encroaching on the campsite as he approached. Kathy looked up from her magazine.

"Well, look what the cat dragged in," said Kathy by way of greeting.

"Very funny," countered Jack. "Don't start with me. It's been a hell of a day."

The contrast between the two campers couldn't have been much greater. Jack wore a torn shirt, sunburn, scraped knee, bruised elbow, and was covered in sand. Kathy had her hair neatly combed back, was lightly tanned, and wore a pink visor and matching outfit all appearing to be right out of the catalog. Kathy stood, folded her magazine, set it down on the chair and approached Jack with a leering smile.

"Let's see what we can do about improving your day, big boy."

Kathy brushed the sand off Jack's face, kissed his lips wet and tugged on his manhood.

"No Kath, what are you doing…I mean I like it, but…I've got to…"

Kathy put her hand over his mouth, and slipped her hand down his pants and rubbed more vigorously, while ardently kissing his mouth.

"Kath really, they're waiting for me to get back…"

"Don't worry, they'll be fine. They won't even know you were, uh, delayed."

She put his hand on her breast, which was bare underneath her pink t-shirt. She lowered his other hand between her legs. Jack hardened instantly, and obediently followed her back to their tent.

Kathy watched Jack until he vanished from sight, which wasn't long in the early evening low light. She hated to see him go and leave her alone for another night, and yet was relieved he was gone. Kathy threw herself down in a chair. She took a deep breath and slowly exhaled. "My God, what am I doing," she said aloud. I feel like such a tramp for seducing him like that! Why did I do that? Most of the time I'm so sure that I…but when I saw him stumble back into camp I just wanted him. I don't know what it was that got to me…maybe because he looked like he was trying so hard to make the best of a tough situation… but I feel so awful for confusing him. Jack probably doesn't know what to think of me. Oh my God, what am I going to do now? Oh well, maybe it isn't such a big deal, she thought.

By the time Jack started back it was completely dark. He rinsed himself off in the dark, not wanting the others to know what had delayed him. Jack even changed his torn shirt. He walked along the river's edge, as he didn't dare take the dry path up on the cliff after dark. Even though he wore water sandals, Jack stubbed his toes accidentally kicking sharp rocks several times. His guilt quickened his pace to the point of recklessness. He didn't have the use of his arms to balance him, since he carried the anchor with the rope wrapped around it. And his mind was elsewhere, pondering why Kathy came onto him, and also enjoying the memory. In moments he allowed his hope to increase, imagining their marriage getting better. But caution brought his feet back down to earth. After all, the last time he'd gotten his hopes up, things got worse between them. "So what was that all about," he said aloud. Jack brushed caution aside and savored his fantasy of Kathy being available to him almost every night, as she once was. He stumbled over several more rocks as his distracted mind didn't register the danger the rocks presented.

After what seemed like hours of hiking, Jack wondered if he'd passed Mike and Stacy in the dark. It was a crescent moon that didn't give off much light, making visibility about ten feet. After walking another fifty yards Jack called out, "Hey Mike! Mike, Stacy, where the hell are you guys?"

No answer. He walked another fifty yards and stopped to call out again, "Damn it Mike, where the hell are you!"

"Right here, man," returned the nearby answer. Jack turned his head to the left and could dimly make out someone walking towards him in the shallows.

"What took you so long? We were wondering if something happened to you," said Mike.

"No, I made it alright. Try hiking in this kind of terrain with an anchor under your arm. It isn't exactly a walk in the park," said Jack.

"Hey it looks like you got something in that backpack," asked Stacy. She had given Jack one of the backpacks to bring back some food. Mike took the anchor out of Jack's hands and Stacy pulled off the backpack.

"Don't expect much. I just grabbed whatever I could find quick," apologized Jack.

"I don't care what it is, I'm so hungry I was about to eat sand before you showed up," said Stacy.

Stacy fished out a half a loaf of bread, turkey, cheese, mustard and a six-pack of beer. She searched the inside of the backpack, and then turned it upside down. Nothing else fell out. "Hey, where's the knife?"

"I told you not to expect much, I just threw stuff in there and ran," Jack explained.

"There might be a knife under the driver's seat," called out Mike.

"Okay yeah, here's one," said Stacy as she put the seat back on. "I don't know where this thing's been, though."

"Look, I'm sorry about the knife," offered Jack.

Stacy jumped out of the boat and cleaned the knife in the water as best she could. She climbed back in the boat and made everybody a couple sandwiches. They eagerly wolfed them down, and grateful to have something other than water to drink. Jack quickly finished off his second beer. He got out of the boat and made water a few feet away.

"Come on Jack, that's disgusting! That's right next to the boat," Mike admonished.

"That is gross," added Stacy. "I'm not getting off the boat on that side again."

"Give me a break, the current will take it away. Don't be such stiffs," complained Jack.

"If you don't mind so much, then tomorrow morning you can help me pull the boat off the beach from the pee side. We can call it 'port' and 'pee' sides of the boat," suggested Mike.

"Oh, give me a break. You're as bad as Kath," Jack said under his breath.

With their sumptuous dinner over, the three turned in for the night. All they had were damp towels to cuddle up with. Mike and Stacy cleared out the small under-cabin to sleep in. Jack grabbed a towel and settled on the sun pad. With Stacy next to him, Mike slept much better than the previous night. Not only was he warmer, but somehow comforted by Stacy's presence. Mike felt his body relax as he held her tight and drifted off to dreamland. A gentle rocking of the boat helped lull them to sleep.

28 Weeks after the River Trip

Friday evening Jack and Kathy had their suitcases on the bed and Jack was throwing clothes into his. Kathy folded her outfits and set them in the suitcase to avoid wrinkling. Kathy went down on her knees, looking for her overnight make-up bag under the sink. "Hey Kath, how many shirts should I bring for the weekend? I don't see where you laid any out for me."

Kathy stood and walked over to Jack's closet. "I think, wait a minute, pack however many you'd like." And then Kathy thought, thank God I caught myself this time. I almost did it again. She turned around and went back to the sink.

"Come on, Kath, help me out here. You always pack for me. I don't know what to bring."

"Jack, I don't want to be like that to you anymore. Remember we talked about that. I'm sure you'll figure out packing just fine on your own."

"But that isn't parenting me. I want you to help me pack."

"No, I don't want to go there anymore."

"You're taking this too seriously, Kath! Does that mean we can't help each other out anymore?"

"You make it sound like I don't want to do anything for you. It's not about that. It's about changing the way I've been a wife."

"Okay Kath, whatever you say. Screw it! I'll be a big boy and pack myself. Maybe I'll bring my Charlie Brown lunch pail too."

"Come on Jack, that's not fair!"

"Let's just drop it and get on the road." Kathy felt dismissed, but took a couple of deep breaths and decided to let it go for now.

Kathy shrugged and went into Lily's room. Lily sat on her bed cuddling her stuffed bears. "Hey teddy bear, are you all packed for Aunt Jane's?" asked Kathy.

"Mommy, I want to come with you."

"I know honey, but this time it's just a trip for Mommy and Daddy."

"But why can't I come too? I'll be good. I promise I'll mind you real good."

"I'm sorry to disappoint you, Lily. Right now Mommy and Daddy need some time alone. I know that probably doesn't make sense to you. I promise that you can come next time, and we'll do something really fun." Lily merely searched her mother's eyes, and then dropped her chin onto her chest and hugged her bears tighter.

"Do you understand, Lily?"

Lily nodded her head up and down without looking up.

"Okay, well let's get your bag into the car. Do you want to bring your bears with you?" Lily nodded and packed one under each arm as she left the room.

Jack piloted the car to the freeway. A few off ramps later he exited, which took Kathy by surprise. "Hey Jack, where are you taking me?"

"Oh sorry, Kath, I forgot that I had to stop by Jimmy's school for a minute. There was a new kid last Saturday, and I didn't have a hat with me. And I don't want this kid to have to wait until next Saturday."

"What hat?"

"Oh, I didn't tell you about dad's tradition? Dad gave each new kid a souvenir Reds cap on his first Saturday at the school. When Dad passed, I decided to continue the tradition," explained Jack.

"Really? That is so cool, Jack. I didn't know that you were doing that."

Jack pulled into the school's parking lot, and Kathy followed him inside. Now that Jimmy was an adult, he lived on the adult wing. No kid ever got dismissed from the school, no matter their age. They simply got moved to the age-appropriate wing. Jack found Jimmy on the swings. He could swing himself, but not very high. So Jimmy and another resident took turns pushing each other. When Jimmy saw Jack he lit up and shouted, "Jackie's here! Jackie's here!"

Once Jimmy saw the red hat in Jack's hand, he figured out what Jack intended. "So Jackie, who's the new kid this time? Can I be the one who gives him the hat? Please Jackie!"

"Sure Jimmy, you bet." Jimmy and Kathy followed Jack over to the new kid, whose name was Bobby. Jimmy took the hat out of Jack's hand and offered it to Bobby, and said, "Bobby, Bobby, this new hat is from Jackie. This here is Jackie, and, and he's my big brother." Bobby's face erupted into an ear to ear smile and hugged Jimmy, then Jack, and finally a surprised Kathy.

"That's really cool what you do for those kids," said Kathy as they walked back to their car. Jack nodded and wiped away a tear.

A few minutes later they were back on the freeway, heading north to the wine country. The freeway curved towards the West and Jack flipped down the driver's side visor as the sun glared directly into his eyes. He opened up the overhead glasses case and said, "Hey Kath, where's my sunglasses?"

"How would I know?"

"You mean you didn't bring them?" asked Jack.

"Why would I bring your glasses?"

"You mean you let me forget them?"

"What do you mean I 'let you forget them'?" I can't believe he's asking me this, after all the conversations we've had about it, Kathy thought.

"Come on Kath, you know what I mean. You always help me remember stuff like that."

"Not anymore, Jack. That's not part of being a wife. I'll be your wife now, and I'm officially quitting as your mother."

"That's great Kath, but you still could've reminded me to bring my sunglasses. I can't be without them all weekend.

Should I turn around and get them?"

"If you want to turn around that would be fine with me."

"Or should I just buy new ones when we get there?"

"That would also be alright."

"Come on Kath, just tell me what you think." She's taking this groupie thing way too far. In fact, she's becoming even more of a pain in the ass than she used to be, Jack thought.

"I'm okay with you doing whatever you decide is best. I'm not going to tell you what to do. I know you're used to that. I guess I've trained you to not have to think for yourself, as I've been willing to do all the thinking for both of us. Well I'm done with that."

"Oh my God, I don't know if I like you being in that groupie meeting. You were more helpful the old way." Kathy turned her face away from Jack and smiled, saying under her breath, "Thank you Tuesday night people."

They drove in silence for the next thirty minutes. Kathy enjoyed the beautiful country. Jack turned up his rock 'n roll. "So what's the off ramp again, Kath?"

"Coachella Road."

"How far up is that?" asked Jack.

"I think it's about five or ten miles up, so keep your eyes open. Are you still okay to drive?"

"Oh yeah, I'm fine. I'm a little tired, but I can drive the last ten minutes to the hotel." Jack turned on his Jethro Tull disc, which was his favorite when he was starting to fall asleep. Kathy didn't particularly like it, but she tolerated it.

"Oh wait; it's the next off ramp! You have to get over right away," said Kathy.

"Damn!" Jack looked over his shoulder, waited for two cars to pass, and then made his way into the middle lane.

"Hurray Jack, we're about to pass Coachella Road!"

"I know Kath, but there's a lot of traffic." Jack checked his mirrors again, and finally maneuvered into the right lane, just as they passed the Coachella Road off ramp.

"Damn it, Jack! I told you it was coming up."

"I know Kath, and I was trying to get over, but there was heavy traffic. What do you want me to do?"

"You could have planned ahead and been in the right line well ahead!"

"I didn't realize it was coming up this soon. I'm sorry. Hey, aren't you parenting me right now?"

Jack's words hit Kathy between the eyes. "Oh my God, I'm so sorry, Jack. You're right; I'm doing it again… This is going to be harder than I thought."

"Don't worry about it Kath, it's no big deal."

"It's a big deal to me. I can't be like that anymore."

Before they left the hotel the next morning Kathy got out her cell phone and speed dialed Jane. "Hi Jane, how's it going with Lily?"

"Oh she's fine. Lily's been playing with Brian all morning real well. Don't worry about a thing." Kathy felt grateful that Jane had a son the same age as Lily.

"Okay good. Let me talk to her for a minute."

"Hi Mommy, where are you?"

"Hi teddy bear, we're at the hotel," said Kathy.

"Where's the hotel?"

"It's in the wine country, but honey you don't know where that is. So what are you up to?"

"I'm coloring with Brian. We're making some new posters to put up in our rooms. I can't wait to show you! You're gonna be so surprised."

"I bet they look great! Okay, me and Daddy will be home tomorrow night, and I'll see you then, okay?"

"Okay Mommy, bye."

By eleven o'clock they had arrived at the first winery, and by two o'clock they were at the third. The third winery served five generous *tastes* of their wines. Kathy could feel herself being affected by the alcohol, and had taken more time between her sips throughout the day. She pulled out a protein bar to provide her stomach something other than wine to absorb. Kathy set her glass down just as Jack bumped into her, almost knocking her to the ground as he fell.

"Jack, watch it!"

"Sorry Kath, I guess I just lost my balance."

Kathy looked into his eyes and saw his glazed stare. "Okay, I'm the designated driver, and I'm done tasting," she said.

Jack picked himself up, brushed off the dirt he'd picked up while rolling on the ground, and sat back down on his stool. "Hey Kath, did you try this one yet? I think it's the best we've tried all day."

"No, I'm done tasting for today. I've had enough."

"Oh don't be like that, Kath. This is a rare opportunity for us to taste top wines from this area."

"You go ahead. I'll walk around a bit."

"Come on Kath, don't be a killjoy. We're having fun, aren't we?"

Kathy smiled, picked up her purse and walked off. She went over to the parking lot and walked the circumference. I don't like it when Jack gets drunk like that. But I don't want to nag him for it. I'm so trying to stop doing that. I just know if I stayed at the bar I'd be wanting to taste that last one as it drips down his face, after I dumped it on his head. Oh my God I'd love to tell him to grow up and finally learn to drink responsibly, Kathy thought.

Twenty minutes later Jack waved Kathy over to their car. He unlocked the driver's side door and got in before Kathy reached the car. Kathy opened the driver's door and said, "Jack, let me drive back to the hotel."

"No, I'm fine. I can drive."

"I'm sure you are, but I'd feel more comfortable driving."

"How come? Don't you trust me?"

"Jack, we've both had a lot to drink today, but I stopped drinking long before you did."

"No, you didn't. We both drank at all three wineries."

"Yes, but you finished all five tastings here and I stopped after the first one."

"Look Kath, I'm fine. Just get in the car."

"I'm trying really hard to not parent you right now, but it's really tempting. Please just let me drive this time. I'd really feel much more comfortable."

"You've never made this big a deal out of me driving before."

"Jack, normally I'd lambaste you for being an irresponsible idiot for getting drunk and even thinking about driving. I'm trying desperately hard to not do that this time. Please, please just let me drive."

"You don't trust me, and…"

"Never mind Jack, I'm calling a cab. You do what you want." Kathy walked back to the tasting bar and asked for the number of a cab company. The bartender handed Kathy a preprinted card, and when she turned around to walk away she almost ran into Jack.

"My God, Kath, if you're going to make a federal case out of it, then just go ahead and drive," said Jack as he stuffed the keys in her purse. "It seems like you are treating me like an idiot child that doesn't know when he can drive. But if that's how you want to do it, then fine. Did you call the police to come and give me a sobriety test too?" Without waiting for an answer, Jack turned around and went back to the car. Kathy set the cab company's card on the bar and followed.

Kathy's impulse was to yell after him, but she caught herself just as she inhaled deeply. When she sat down in the driver's seat she glanced over at Jack, who sat next to her with his seatbelt on, arms folded across his chest, head against the head rest and his eyes closed. Kathy sighed and started the engine.

Jack kept his eyes and mouth closed all the way back to the hotel. When Kathy parked the car he got out, went into their room and lay down on the bed. Kathy stood next to the bed with her hands on her hips and words on her lips. She started to speak several times, but finally grabbed her purse and went for a walk to think. She wondered if she'd handled things well, and thought over what her options might have been. An hour and a half later she was tired and went up to the room.

She found Jack awake and watching T.V. "Hey Kath, what're we doing for dinner?"

"Jack, maybe we should talk about what happened today."

"Talk about what? It was no big deal. Let's just drop it."

"But you felt like I was parenting you."

"It's over! Don't worry about it. I've already moved on. Let's just go have a nice time at dinner."

"But if I'm being like that I need to know about it."

"Kath really, you take these nothing conversations and blow them up. Everything's fine between us. It's done." Kathy shrugged her shoulders and lay down next to Jack.

"So are we doing that steakhouse we saw today, or should we do the fish place the hotel recommended?" asked Jack.

"I don't know. I'm too tired to think about it. I think I'll lie down for a few minutes and rest my eyes. Why don't you pick the restaurant?"

"Alright, the steakhouse it is. I'm jonesing for a cordon-bleu steak."

"Okay," said Kathy as she turned over and shut her eyes.

Kathy awoke to a sense of sharp pain in her backside. She opened her eyes, but didn't see anything. Then she felt it again, and realized she'd been slapped on her backside, now for the second time by Jack. "Hey Kath, you awake yet? Let's go, I'm starving." Kathy slowly sat up, stretched and yawned. "Okay, let me jump into the shower first."

"Okay, but don't take one of your famous two hour showers." While in the shower Kathy kept thinking about Jack's comment when she came back from her walk. At first she wondered if she was making too much of their interaction at the winery, but now she thought not.

Jack and Kathy sat down in the restaurant and talked casually. She wanted to revisit the winery incident, but decided to wait until after they'd finished their entrées. Kathy wanted to have a nice dinner with Jack. She'd made her decision as she thought, Jack might be okay with today, but I'm not.

Kathy pondered their conversation over dessert, while Jack caught glimpses of Kathy in his peripheral vision, trying to assess her state of mind. Kathy found her opportunity while she and Jack picked at their shared, giant black forest cake. "Hey Jack, I want to bring up the winery thing again."

"Oh Kath, stop with…"

"Wait a minute, hear me out. You may be okay with how that went, but I'm not. I know that I have a problem with being controlling with you. I get that now, and I mean to change that. God knows how hard I'm trying. At the same time, I wonder if you're playing a part in our problems too."

"What are you talking about?"

"Now wait a minute, don't interrupt me. Please hear me out before you dismiss what I'm saying. I'm not saying it's all your fault. I totally get that I'm part of the problem, but I think that sometimes you act like a child. Take today for example, do you feel good about attempting to drive after you'd had that much to drink?"

"Oh come on Kath, I was fine. I told you that and you wouldn't believe me."

"Jack, you fell off the bar stool. Is that fine?"

"I slipped. Just because I slipped doesn't mean I was drunk. Aren't I allowed to make a mistake once in a while? Or do I have to be perfect like you?"

"You think your slipping had nothing to do with how much you'd had to drink today?"

"Of course not; I can handle my alcohol just fine. I always drive after I've had a couple drinks."

"A couple…" Kathy caught herself and took a deep breath as she paused. "Wait a minute, I don't want to go there with you. Look Jack, you decide how much you drink, but getting back to my point, do you think you play a role in the parent-child thing that we do?"

"No Kath, I don't. I think you do that all by yourself."

"I see. So does that mean you see our marriage problems as all about me?"

"First of all, I don't think we have *marriage problems*. I do think you have a control problem. I think you and your sister both have a control problem, and I'm sure Frank would tell you the same thing. In fact, Frank has told me the same thing. I mean, I wish you'd relax a bit more, maybe get off my back some, but on the whole I think we have a pretty darned good marriage. So let's not over blow this whole thing."

Anger surged through her veins. Kathy averted her eyes and took several deep breaths. She didn't want to say something she'd later regret. She thought, you son of a bitch, you think our whole problems are on me, and that you don't have a damn thing to do with it, other than being saddled with a controlling bitch of a warrior wife. Don't say it Kathy, don't say it. You'll just be repeating the whole pattern again. Oh my God, I don't know what to say…I just want to strangle the son of a bitch. Yeah, I'd like to show him control alright. Kathy raised her eyes and said, "Let's go back to the room. Are you done with the cake?"

"Not quite. Give me another minute or two," said Jack.

"You're not mad at me, are you? I hope you're not mad at me for telling the truth. You did want me to be honest, didn't you?"

"Yes, I did want you to be honest. But I don't want to talk about it anymore tonight."

Jack drove back to the hotel and neither spoke. Finally Jack broke the silence, "You're still mad at me, aren't you?"

"Yes, I suppose I am angry with you. But it's not just that, I'm still trying to figure out how to make our marriage work."

"You think too much, Kath. Why can't you just enjoy what we do have, instead of focusing on the minor problems?"

"They may be minor to you, but they're important to me. I can't keep doing this."

"You can't keep doing this? Does that mean you're considering leaving me?"

"No, I don't want that. I want to try to make our relationship work, but do you get it that it's not working for me?"

"Yeah I get it. But don't you think you're a perfectionist? I admit our marriage isn't perfect, but can't you accept it the way it is?"

"No, I can't accept our marriage the way it is. Maybe I'm a perfectionist and maybe I'm not, but I have to find a way to make things better between us. Don't you want things better between us? Or are you content with the way we fight?"

"What fighting? I don't think we fight that much. Yeah, we have our moments, like every couple by the way. I wish you were less controlling, and maybe less angry, but on the whole I guess I am pretty content."

"So you're content with the way you are, but you'd like me to change. Is that it?"

"Come on Kath, you have to admit that you have issues with anger and control."

"Yes, I admit that I do. What troubles me is that you seem to be under the impression that you don't have any issues at all."

"Just because you have issues means that I have to have them too? I'm happy with how I am, Kath. I'm pretty happy with our marriage. You're the one who isn't happy."

Kathy exhaled loudly and turned away from Jack to look out the window. She leaned her head against her hand, her elbow on the armrest. She took deep breaths, trying to contain herself. Kathy was angry, and discouraged. Jack pulled into the parking lot and took the key out of the ignition. "I can tell you're still mad at me Kath. Is this gonna ruin the rest of our weekend?"

"Yes, I'm still angry. Just give me time to be. I think I'll go for a walk again."

"Do you think you'll be safe walking around this time of night?"

"Oh yeah, I guess I'll just stay on the hotel grounds."

The next Saturday Kathy went to Jane's house for lunch. Jane was excited to show her sister her latest acquisitions in her closet. As Jane put away her new clothes Kathy became serious. "Hey Jane, does Frank think you're controlling?"

Jane laughed, "What made you think of that?"

"Oh, Jack thinks I'm controlling and angry, and I know I am, and I'm curious if that's a thing for you too?"

"Frank knows that I have to keep on him or he'll let things slip. So if that's controlling then I guess I am. Sometimes he tells me I'm on him too much, and sometimes he's right and sometimes he's just being lazy."

"Are you happy with how things are between you and Frank?" asked Kathy.

"Yes I am. I wish he had a better memory, but on the whole I'm fairly content."

"What about your marriage makes you content?"

"Kathy, what's with all the intense questions? I don't know, I don't think about it. I just accept Frank the way he is and live my life."

"I used to not think about my marriage much either. I suppose I used to act like everything was fine. At some point that stopped working for me. I have to figure it out. I don't want to wake up at fifty and realize I have the same bad marriage I had at thirty. Maybe I'm just different that way."

"Maybe you think too much. I wonder if it makes it worse for you to pick apart your marriage like that."

"Maybe," said Kathy absentmindedly.

"Honey, is Jack having an affair?"

"Oh I don't think so."

"Well maybe you should ask," suggested Jane.

"Why do you suggest that?"

"Because if you're unhappy, maybe it's because you're sensing that he's having an affair. You know, we women sense those kinds of things. We can feel when something's wrong. You're probably making this more complicated than it has to be with all this worry if you're too this or not enough that. I think you're a terrific wife and Jack's lucky to have you. And if he's not appreciating you then maybe he's fooling around with someone else. You ought to go through his wallet and briefcase and see if you find anything."

"No, I don't want to be like that. Then I'd be snooping around like a nosey parent, and that's exactly what I'm trying to stop doing. I'd rather just ask him straight out, if anything, but I really don't think he's messing around on me."

"Suit yourself, but don't play the fool.

A week and a half later Kathy sat in her Tuesday group. She half listened to the group and half thought about her discussion with Jack the night before. She'd been angry and had said things she later regretted. Kathy came out of her ponderings to the voice of Dr. Aragorn, "Kathy, where are you. I haven't felt you with us tonight."

"Oh yeah, I suppose I'm not really here. I keep thinking about what happened with Jack last night."

"And what was that?" asked Dr. Aragorn.

"I'd just got out of the shower and Jack asked me where his white dress shirt was. I told him that I had no idea. He became angry and said he needed that shirt for an important meeting the next day, and why wasn't I keeping up with the laundry. I wasn't sure, so I went into the laundry room and saw that there were very few dirty clothes in the basket. So I told Jack that I was on top of the laundry. He said that if I was, he would have a clean white shirt. I wanted to blast him, because I felt like he was saying it's my fault, but instead I helped him look around, and we found his white shirt underneath a bunch of his clothes on the chair in our room. Actually I'm the one who found the shirt, and when I did he demanded to know why I hadn't washed it. I told him he ought to know that I only wash clothes that are in the dirty cloths basket in the laundry room. He got angrier and told me that I was being a perfectionist, and that I should wash any dirty clothes that were in our room, like I used to. That's when I started to get angry. I asked him if he thought he was acting like a child, expecting his mommy to wash and put away all his clothes. He yelled that he wanted a wife that would just handle the laundry without busting his balls for where he put it." Kathy laughed. "That's when I told him that I got it, he wanted me to come into the room with my dirt-seeking locating laser, find all the dirty laundry in nooks and crannies and piled on his chair and under the bed, wash it and fold it neatly in his drawers. Then bake his cookies and lay then out with a glass of cold milk. That's when Jack called me a bitch and stormed out of the room, which was probably a good thing because it was getting ugly." The group laughed.

"Wow, you sure know how to bust a man's balls, Kathy," said Jake with a grin.

"He had it coming this time," said Susan.

"So what do you make of the exchange?" asked Evelyn.

"That's what I've been trying to figure out. I think he's acting like a child expecting me to find his dirty laundry and make sure he has a certain shirt. But at the same time maybe I was acting like a parent with what I said."

"Well yes, your comment about the laser and the milk and cookies was critical and parental. But I think you're trying to get Jack to take a look at how he plays a part in the dance between the two of you. He does seem to be looking for a parent to make sure his laundry gets handled," said Dr. Aragorn.

"That's what I thought. So why did I end up being a parent again?"

"You started out pretty good, so something must have hooked you," suggested Susan.

"What do you mean, 'hooked me'?"

"You started out taking care of whatever laundry's in the basket, and you told him you didn't know where that particular shirt was, but then you let something provoke you at some point after that. What was it? What really got you?" asked Susan.

Kathy looked down and thought for a moment. "I think it was when he called me a perfectionist. I hate it when he calls me that! I wanted to slap him across the face when he said that."

"So why is that so upsetting?" asked Dr. Aragorn.

"Maybe because I feel like he was blaming me for his shirt missing when he called me a perfectionist, as though I'm so uptight that I didn't wash a shirt that happened to be slightly out of place."

"I think he was blaming you," said Evelyn.

"Yes, and that's what hooked you?" suggested Dr. Aragorn.

"Yeah, so how do I not get hooked?"

"You may not be able to prevent it just yet. But let's take a closer look. Probably nobody likes feeling blamed, but why does it feel unbearable to you?" asked Dr. Aragorn.

"I don't know…" My God, why do these people have these questions? Does it make any difference why? She thought.

"Did anybody blame you before?" asked Karen.

"Oh my God, yes. I think I felt blamed, or something like that, whenever I did something that my family didn't like."

"Your whole family would react to what you'd done?" asked Susan.

"No, not really the whole family…I don't know if I can put my finger on it, but I just remember often feeling bad, maybe the word is blamed, when somebody in the family was upset."

"Can you think of an example?" asked Dr. Aragorn.

"Well, I remember one year I didn't do as well in school, which I think was during junior high, and my father went off on me several times for not trying hard enough in school and not having good study habits, and not taking him seriously about the importance of school. I hated it when he did that, I remember feeling like I was failing him."

"Why do you think you did poorly in school that year?" asked Evelyn.

"I'm not sure…although that might have been the year my first boyfriend broke up with me. Yes, I think it was about that time."

"Do you think that was related to your slump in school?" asked Dr. Aragorn.

"I've never thought of it that way, but maybe."

"So nobody asked you why you were struggling in school?" asked Dr. Aragorn.

"No, I don't remember that."

"You were shamed for doing poorly, when you probably needed somebody to ask a few questions and try to help you get through a rough season," suggested Dr. Aragorn. Tears began to form in Kathy's eyes. She looked at Dr. Aragorn and nodded, and then looked away and reached for a tissue. "So when Jack blames you for his shirt missing, it probably touches feelings of shame that you haven't even known about," Dr. Aragorn continued.

Kathy nodded and averted her eyes to her feet. She wrapped her arms around herself tightly. She felt the eyes of the group on her, but didn't want to return their gaze. "I wonder if you're feeling ashamed right now?" suggested Evelyn.

"Oh my God, yes. I don't even want to look at you. Actually, I can't wait for group to end so that I can run out of here."

"As bad as it feels, it's good to let yourself feel that. Last night with Jack touched way more than you'd known, and now you're getting to it, which is really important for your work on yourself," said Dr. Aragorn.

When she got to her car she opened the trunk and pulled out her trench coat and put it on. She got into her car and sat. Kathy felt an urge to look in the rearview mirror. She didn't like what she saw. Kathy combed her hair with her fingers and reapplied her lipstick, which didn't help. "Why do I look like the ugly duckling?" she wondered. As she pondered her question she found she couldn't even think about it. Her mind didn't seem to want to go there. Kathy felt mildly dizzy, and looked out the window to try to orient herself.

Jack reclined on their bed watching the news when she got home, and Kathy lay down beside him and folded her arms. When the commercial break came Jack turned towards her and kissed her cheek. "Hey Kath, what're you doing in all those clothes? Get your jammies on."

"No, I like what I'm wearing."

"Come on Kath, I'll make it worth your while to change."

Kathy waited until the news came back on until rolling out of bed. She closed the door to the bathroom and undressed and showered. It felt really good being under the hot shower. She took her time, feeling strangely reluctant to get out. She selected one of her thick flannel pajamas, and was relieved to see Jack asleep when she slowly crept into bed. Her eye caught the clock and she turned on her alarm, and was surprised. She couldn't believe she'd been in the shower forty-five minutes. It had only seemed like ten or fifteen.

Jack still slept when Kathy's alarm woke her. She quietly got ready and toasted a bagel to eat in her car on the way to the office. Jack came in as Kathy spread the creamed cheese on her bagel. "Hey Kath, leaving so early?"

"Yes, I've got a 7:30 meeting today."

"That sucks. I'm sure glad I'm not an attorney. Our meetings never start before 9:30. Anyways, what was up with you last night?"

Kathy thought for a moment before asking, "What do you mean?"

"When you were lying on the bed last night, I had to ask you three or four times before you'd answer my questions."

"Really? Oh, I'm not sure…maybe I was distracted."

"I'd say you were more than distracted. It didn't even seem like you were there. You were freaking me out."

"Hmm, well I have to go. You're taking Lily to school, right?" Jack nodded.

"Okay, see you tonight."

On the ride to the office Kathy tried to remember what Jack was talking about. She couldn't pull up any memory of Jack asking her questions. All she recalled was Jack asking her to put on her pajamas, which she recoiled at the thought of. Why couldn't she remember anything else? And what was with the forty-five minute shower? The appearance of the firm's parking garage ended her speculation for now. She stuffed the last bite of bagel into her mouth, stood, brushed the crumbs off her suit, and headed for the elevator.

After the morning meetings were over Kathy rushed through her emails. She was motivated to get to the gym on her lunch break today. She had more energy for exercise than usual. Kathy normally worked out a couple of days a week for maybe thirty minutes, but today she had fuel left in the tank after a full hour workout. Walking back out to her car she felt better, as though she'd left something behind at the gym. Maybe she had less nervous energy, she told herself.

When she got back to the office Kathy's concentration was improved. She sat down at her desk and sorted through her messages. Before lunch she'd struggled to sit down long enough to attend to her work, now she made it through an hour of returning phone calls. When she set down her phone after the last call she stared out the window. Her office window on the fifth floor overlooked a busy street, lined with office buildings and commercial stores. Kathy watched pedestrians walking in and out of buildings. She wondered what they thought about. She wondered if they thought about their lives. Was she the only one who analyzed her marriage and her life? Did anyone else feel bad about herself? Examining their faces, only a couple of pedestrians' faces evidenced emotion, or so she thought. Then a father walking with his son caught her eye. The father stopped and bent down to his young son's level and seemed to talk seriously about something. Kathy expected the boy to crumble, feeling cut down to size. However, the boy merely nodded and the father stood and they walked on.

Kathy sat in group and listened. She normally tried to contribute in some way, but tonight felt that she had nothing helpful to add. She desperately wanted to say something, and began to formulate what she might say to the others, but couldn't seem to find the words. Kathy looked up as Tom said he was finished for now.

Again she tried to find a place to begin, yet felt uncomfortable and hesitated. While she hesitated someone else jumped in. Kathy glanced at the clock and realized there wasn't much time left. She waited while Susan spoke and received feedback. Paying close attention, Kathy watched for signs that Susan was finishing her processing for the night. Then she heard Susan speak the words she'd been waiting to hear, "Well, I feel like I'm done for now."

"I want to speak," Kathy heard herself say. Her words sounded hollow, as if someone else spoke them through her like a ventriloquist. "I don't know what to say, but I need your help. I guess I'm nervous to bring anything up tonight. I don't know how to start."

"You already have started by telling us you're anxious. So what's your anxiety about?" asked Dr. Aragorn.

"I'm not sure, but I keep thinking about something that I'm embarrassed to tell you about," said Kathy. The group merely waited. "I don't want to leave without getting this off my chest so I'll just say it. I keep looking at myself in the mirror."

"You're anxious to tell us that?" asked Evelyn.

"Yes, I'm afraid you'll think I'm vain or conceited or something," said Kathy.

"So why are you looking in the mirror more often?" asked Jake.

"I'm not sure, but I keep thinking about my hair. I don't like how it looks right now… and my eyes, I think I'm getting more crow's feet around them," said Kathy.

"Kathy you're hair and eyes look the same as they've looked since you've been in the group," said Jake.

Kathy averted her eyes. She adjusted her skirt, and then shifted her coat. "You really think I look the same?"

The group members exchanged glances with one another and then Susan spoke, "Yes, I can't tell the difference." Many others echoed the same.

"Say more about what you see when you look in the mirror," suggested Dr. Aragorn.

"I look older and…well, I'm embarrassed to tell you, but I feel ugly," said Kathy.

"Well I think you're hot," said Jake with a grin. "I thought you were hot the first night you came and I still think so." The group laughed. Kathy smiled and gazed out the window.

"What have you been feeling this week?" asked Dr. Aragorn.

"I don't know, just ugly I guess. I don't get why anybody would want to have much to do with me," said Kathy.

"I don't think this has much to do with your physical appearance," said Dr. Aragorn.

"What else would it be?" asked Kathy.

"You're feeling bad about yourself, in some way," suggested Dr. Aragorn.

"Bad? Well, yes, I suppose that is what I feel…I'm not sure how come," said Kathy.

"Can you describe the bad feeling?" asked Evelyn.

"I don't know…I just don't like something about myself…maybe it isn't how I look, but…"

"I think you're feeling ashamed. I think that's what you mean when you say 'ugly'. You talked about feeling bad growing up, especially during your slump in junior high, and you often feel blamed by Jack. I think you've had a sore spot opened up," said Dr. Aragorn.

"I hate it when Jack blames me! It seems like he does that every day now. Every time something of his is missing or not where he expects to find it he questions me. I'm sick of it. Keep track of your own damned possessions. I'm not responsible for your shit anymore. And if you want a particular thing for dinner, then you go to the damn store and make sure we have it on hand. I'm sick and tired of hearing that it's my fault these things don't happen for Jack."

"Wow, I didn't realize that was such a thing for you with Jack," said Jake.

"I guess I didn't realize it until now either," said Kathy with a smile.

"Anytime Jack even comes close to suggesting something is your fault your radar alarm goes off," said Dr. Aragorn.

"Yes, I guess so," asked Kathy.

"It doesn't feel too good for anyone to be blamed, but I think Jack's touching a deep pocket of pain, or better said a deep pocket of shame within you," explained Dr. Aragorn.

"Are you saying this is my issue and Jack has nothing to do with it?"

"Oh no, it's likely Jack's playing a part in this, but I believe it stirs so much energy in you because of what it touches, which is much bigger than Jack," said Dr. Aragorn.

"But what does it touch?" asked Kathy.

"You're just beginning to explore that. All we know so far is that you left last week's group feeling ugly after you talked about your father going off on you when you slumped in school. Is there a connection there?" asked Dr. Aragorn.

Kathy examined the backs of her hands, which rested on her knees while she considered Dr. Aragorn's comment. "I do remember feeling really bad about myself as a kid."

"Does anything come to mind about that?" asked Dr. Aragorn.

"I don't know, I just remember feeling like something was wrong with me...like I was defective maybe."

"That sounds awful," said Tom. Kathy cried silently.

"I'm so sorry," said Susan.

"Our time's up for tonight, but that's something well worth thinking more about," said Dr. Aragorn.

Jack had his feet up on the table, sitting in his favorite leather chair and watching the sporting news roundup for the day. He took a swig of his beer when Kathy walked in, set his beer between his legs and smiled. "Just getting in from the groupies?"

"Yes," answered Kathy as she sat down on the coach across from Jack.

"And how was it?"

"Um... it's kind of hard to say. I guess it was okay, I mean, there weren't any lightning bolts or anything." Jack nodded. Kathy looked down at her hands and smiled.

"What's that about?" asks Jack.

"What's what about?"

"You just smiled like you've got a secret."

"Oh that. I was just thinking of something somebody said in group."

"And are you gonna tell me what it was?"

"Oh, this guy told me that I'm hot."

"That you're hot? Oh great, so you're going to group to deal with your issues and some guy's hitting on you?"

"No, it wasn't like that. He was…he was just being supportive."

"Oh I'll bet he was. And was he supportive enough to walk you out to your car? And was he supportive enough to ask for your number? And was he supportive enough to give you a goodnight kiss?

"Stop it, Jack! It wasn't like that. I was feeling like shit about myself and he was trying to help. I don't expect you to understand something like that."

"And what's that supposed to mean?"

"That means you aren't much support when I'm hurting. You just tell me to not worry about it. Or you say that it's no big deal, and that I'm making too much out of it," Kathy said.

"Yeah, I say those things to try and help you feel better. Would you rather that I not say anything?"

"Yes, I mean, no. I want you to say something, but I don't want to be told that I shouldn't feel that way. Because I do feel that way, and I need someone to help me with my feelings, not shoo them away."

"Damn Kath, you don't give me much credit do you? You never give me much credit for trying. I can't seem to do anything right for you. Have you ever considered that you might just be impossible to please? Maybe you'd be better off with this guy in group. Maybe he can give you what I can't."

"Don't tempt me, Jack."

"So you are tempted. You're admitting it. You want to have an affair with this guy. Or maybe you already are having an affair and I'm just figuring it out."

"Talk about twisting words, you take an innocent comment made in group and now you have me already hot and heavy into an affair."

"What do you want from me, Kath, because I don't seem to be getting the clue? Tell me what the hell you want from me."

"You asked how my group was. How about just trying to listen and understand what I'm saying about group tonight before you jump to any conclusions. I want to be understood. When I talk about my feelings I end up feeling fixed by you. I don't want to be fixed. I want to be listened to and feel like you get me. Is that too much to ask for?"

Jack sighed deeply, exhaling slowly as he averted his gaze. "I don't know, Kath. I do want to listen to you, and I really am trying. Maybe I can try harder, and maybe you can try to give me a little more credit when I do try. I'm probably not as touchy feely as your group, but I can listen as well as the next guy."

"Okay Jack, we'll see if we can work on it. I'll think about what you said; maybe I'm not giving you enough credit. Please think about what I said about fixing me. I don't want to be told that I shouldn't feel that way, or that I'm making too big a deal out of something. That doesn't help me." Jack nodded, and then looked at the television screen as the basketball report came on. He picked up the remote control and turned up the volume.

"Well I'm tired, so I'm going to bed," said Kathy.

"Night," said Jack without emotion. Kathy stood and started walking towards the bedroom, then stopped and turned back. She studied Jack's face, as if trying to read a densely worded book. Kathy secretly wished he'd turn and look at her, but he didn't. His eyes remained glued to the screen. The only sign of life was the beer can being lifted to his mouth and back to his lap. Kathy shrugged, and continued her journey to the shower and bed.

Dr. Aragorn held Kathy's gaze, with kind unblinking eyes. He waited while she pondered his question. "No, I suppose I never have talked about my feelings with Jack much. Probably just when we're fighting and I'm hurt or angry."

"And how does that normally go?" asked Dr. Aragorn.

"He usually explains why he did or said something."

"And does that help?" asked Dr. Aragorn.

"Occasionally it helps, but most of the time I hate it, and I just feel misunderstood. I've brought that up with Jack a few times recently. I want to feel listened to, but it's not working."

"What's not working?" asked Evelyn.

"I end up feeling like Jack's trying to convince me of something. That probably doesn't say much…it's hard to explain. Like last night, I stepped on the scale and had gained six pounds. I've already been feeling unattractive, and that made it worse. Jack was in the bathroom when I stepped off the scale, and he saw my reaction. When I tried to explain how bad I felt about my body, he said I was overreacting to retaining a few pounds of water. I wanted to slug him in the chops when he said that. I guess he saw my face get red and he backed up and said, 'Hey Kath, what'd I say? I'm just trying to be supportive.' I told him that did not feel supportive, and that I didn't feel like he was listening to me. Then it turned ugly and we had another one of our famous fights. I just don't know how to get him to understand what I want, and I wish I had more patience with him."

"It's hard to be patient when you feel dismissed," suggested Dr. Aragorn. Kathy nodded. Dr. Aragorn continued, "Jack probably thinks he's being supportive by talking you out of your feelings, not realizing it's the last thing you need. You need people to help you find your feelings, not help you put your feelings away."

"I know he's really trying, and I feel bad for him. Maybe I'm being too hard on him."

"Maybe you are, but he's not allowing much room for your pain," said Susan.

"Does Jack ever talk about his own feelings?" asked Jake.

Kathy laughed, "What feelings? He says he doesn't have any bad feelings to talk about. The only bad feelings he says he has is when I insult him during our fights. Which I know is true. Sometimes I can be critical." Dr. Aragorn smiled and nodded.

"If he doesn't have his own painful feelings, then how can he be there for you in yours?" asked Jake.

"Great point, Jake," said Dr. Aragorn. "You might be asking Jack to do something that he can't do."

"But why can't he?" asked Kathy.

"I don't see how he can allow room for you to be in pain if he hasn't experienced that himself. You can't give what you don't have. It's like trying to pour milk out of an empty carton. Oh you might get a drop or two, but you won't get much," explained Dr. Aragorn.

"Oh, so maybe I should be more understanding of Jack's feelings?" Kathy thought aloud.

"That's a good place to start, but being more inviting of his feelings is the way I would say it; although it might be tough to do if Jack doesn't allow himself to have bad feelings. But you might occasionally invite him to talk about himself," said Dr. Aragorn.

"You might watch for opportunities when he seems to be feeling something. I don't know how rarely that happens," said Evelyn.

"When Linda almost left me I couldn't tell a feeling from a hot rock," began Jake. "My first months of group, I only knew I was feeling when someone else told me, and then I could tell. Now a couple years later I can recognize my feelings a lot better, but even now I still need help getting to my feelings sometimes, especially when I'm sad. I seem to be programmed to not feel sad. Other feelings I do pretty well with. Jack might be something like me, I mean, when you talk about him most of it sounds familiar."

"At first you didn't know you were feeling at all, or do you mean you knew you were having an emotion, but just didn't know what you were feeling?" asked Kathy.

"At first I didn't even know I was feeling. I only thought," answered Jake.

"Oh my God, that does sound like Jack. I feel sad thinking about him that way. Maybe he's waiting for someone to help him feel," said Kathy.

"Maybe," said Jake.

"What do you think, Dr. Aragorn?" asked Kathy.

"I think it's possible, and worth giving a try."

The Flaming Grill accommodated about 150 patrons including both the bar and restaurant, and there were about 175 packed inside. Many were huddled around the flat screen watching March Madness, as the college basketball season culminated in a flurry of upsets and surprises. Jack sat facing the bar, and more importantly the flat screen, so that he could talk to Kathy while he casually looked over her shoulder at the game.

"So Jack, how has your week gone?" asked Kathy.

"Fine."

Kathy waited thirty seconds before following up, "Can you elaborate any?"

"There's not much to tell. It was a ho-hum week at work, grinding away on the latest game I'm working on. The old man left me alone most of the week, which was good. I had a few laughs with the guys the other night watching the games. That's about it."

"Are you feeling any better about your job, or do you still want to look for something else?"

"Oh I don't know. It's fine for now. If something else came along I'd listen, but I'm not really in any hurry to make a change. You know, it's a paycheck."

"And how are you feeling about us?" asked Kathy.

"About us? What's with the serious questions? I'm doing fine, I got no complaints. Is there something that you wanted to talk about?"

"I've just been thinking that maybe I haven't been open to your feelings, and I want to try to be more supportive," explained Kathy.

"What are you talking about? You're fine. My only complaint is when you get on me about stuff, otherwise you're plenty supportive."

"But I'm talking about feelings. Don't you ever have a bad feeling and want to talk about it?"

"What bad feelings? I don't let stuff like that get me down. I'm a positive person, and if something happens I put it in the past. I don't get down by dwelling on the past. I think that's one of your problems Kath, you can't let the past go and it weighs you down. You got to let that small stuff go."

Kathy opened her mouth to explain and felt a warning signal go off. She took a drink of her wine and decided to just nod and let it go for now. This is going to be harder than I expected, she thought.

"From down town baby, that's what I'm talking 'bout. The Cougars just took the lead with a huge three," Jack cheered with both hands raised. He saw the surprise on Kathy's face and explained, "I noticed the game on in the bar. I have twenty bucks on the Cougars to pull off an upset, and I'm just three minutes away from collecting that twenty bucks from a guy at the office."

Kathy looked over her shoulder at the flat screen, took a sip of her wine and excused herself to use the ladies room. While reapplying her make-up in the ladies room Kathy remembered Dr. Aragorn's advice that Jack may not be able to respond to a direct question about his feelings, but may be receptive to Kathy noticing when he's feeling in the moment. "I guess Dr. Aragorn's right about that," she said to the mirror. "I'll watch for such an opportunity."

Kathy couldn't wait for Tuesday, and finally it arrived. She arrived early, being the first one in the waiting room, and was the one to begin the group. "I've tried to talk with Jack about his feelings a couple of times, and it isn't working. I know what I did wrong the first time. I asked him about how he felt directly, and he acted like I was interrogating him. Then I remembered you told me to watch for opportunities when he might be having a feeling. I thought I found a chance last night when Jack came home cursing his boss. I invited him to sit down and tell me about it. Well, he sat down and continued to tell me what an asshole his boss is. I suggested that he might be angry, and he said, 'no shit, Sherlock'."

The rest of the group erupted in laughter. "Maybe you were overdoing the obvious, Kathy," said Jake.

"Yes, I realized that afterwards. Anyways, I told Jack I was trying to be a safe person for him to talk to about stuff when he needed to. I said I wanted us to be able to come to one another when something happened."

"And what'd he say?" asked Jake.

"He said that he just needed me to let him blow off some steam. I said that blowing off steam is fine, but if he wanted to get into more of what was coming up for him I'd be glad to listen. He said, 'I don't give a shit about that psychobabble. You can save that for your groupies. Like I said, I just need you to let me blow off some steam.' I was so frustrated, I mean, I'm trying so hard to be there for him and he won't have it."

"You haven't given him much time," began Dr. Aragorn, "blowing off steam's probably the only way he knows to process. You invited him to have more with you, but I doubt he knows how to make use of your offer. Remember how it took you awhile to get much out of being here."

"When Linda first talked to me about feelings, I thought she wanted me to cry with her," said Jake laughing. "Only much later did I have any idea what she meant."

"How much later?" asked Kathy.

"Oh, it might have been five or six months," said Jake.

"Six months! I can't wait that long. Oh my God, I can't keep doing this till the end of summer," said Kathy.

"You might have to if you want to have an alive marriage. Remember, you're changing the rules of engagement for the marriage. You didn't start out connecting emotionally, and it won't happen overnight. If you expect it to, you're setting you and Jack up for failure," said Dr. Aragorn.

"Oh that's just great. So it's my fault because I'm changing the rules."

"You're adding blame to my words," countered Dr. Aragorn.

"But aren't you saying it's my fault?"

"No, you and Jack together created the marriage the way it is, and it will take both of you to make it more alive. I'm suggesting that you're asking Jack to make a huge change in the way he relates to you, probably the way he relates to anybody, for that matter. This level of change will likely be disorganizing for him, and for you by the way. And you've had some time with us to begin to prepare to relate to people in a different way, and Jack hasn't. And for awhile you were planning to drop out of group. In all fairness to Jack, he'll need some time and some help to do what you're asking him. Think of the nights you've left group feeling like your head was spinning," said Dr. Aragorn with a smile.

"There've been several of those," Kathy admitted with a sheepish smile.

"And Jack doesn't have the support of a group like you," added Evelyn.

"Okay I get it, I think. So how do I go about this with Jack then?"

"Does Jack know what you want with him?" asked Susan.

Kathy thought a moment before responding, "I don't know if he does. I told him I wanted him to feel free to come to me when he wants to talk."

"But that makes it sound like it's for him," said Evelyn.

"Yes, I'm offering him to come to me if he needs to process."

"Has Jack given you reason to suspect he feels the need to process with you?" asked Evelyn.

"Well, he said he wants me to just let him blow off steam."

"That's fine but he's probably not asking to process. He's asking to merely get the bad feelings out," suggested Dr. Aragorn.

"Isn't it the same thing?"

"Oh my goodness, no. My guess is he just wants to get the bad feelings off his chest, but I don't hear him asking you to help him look at where that's taking him on the inside. You're confusing him going off on his boss with establishing an inner life. You're getting ahead of him, and he may get there and he may not," said Dr. Aragorn.

"He may never get there? What if he doesn't? Then what do I do?" asked Kathy.

"You're getting ahead of yourself. We'll cross that bridge when we come to it. For now it's enough to try to connect with your husband more intimately, and I think it might help to tell

Jack directly what you want from him. I doubt he has any clue," said Dr. Aragorn.

"Take it from me, I'm pretty damn sure he has no clue. I didn't have any clue how to process **or** notice a feeling, not to mention have that kind of conversation. Give the guy a break," said Jake.

"But he better get a clue, or he'll lose Kathy," said Susan.

"That's not fair to Jack! The poor guy hasn't had any help. Give the guy a break!" said Karen.

"Then he better get some help real soon," countered Susan.

"How do you want him to do that?" asked Karen.

"He can get himself into therapy, like Kathy has," said Susan. "Wait a minute…I guess your reaction pisses me off…I still wish that Lane had given me a chance to get help for myself. I'd love to have had the opportunity that Kathy's giving to Jack."

When Kathy got home she found Jack parked in front of the flat screen as usual. She sat down and said hello, and then waited for the next commercial. When it came she said, "Hey Jack, when your show is over I want to tell you about something, okay?"

"Sure Kath, you got it." Kathy went into the room and got ready for bed. She prayed for help finding the right words. The last thing Kathy wanted was to put Jack on the defensive like she'd done before. She finished asking God for help and turned on her light and picked up her novel.

Twenty minutes later Jack jumped on the bed and snuggled up to her. "So, what's on your mind? Maybe a little play?" Jack said as he massaged her thigh.

Kathy took a deep breath and exhaled slowly while she pushed Jack's hand away. "Not exactly, but something related. I've been trying to talk with you about feelings, but I think I've been going about it all wrong."

"Oh Kath not that again, I told you I don't have anything like that to tell you about. I don't hold on to shit like that."

"I know. I get that now. I haven't been direct with you. The truth is I want to talk about my feelings with you, and if you want to talk about your feelings too that'd be great, and if you don't have any to talk about that's fine. But either way, I need to be able to talk with you about what's going on inside me. Connecting emotionally has never been a part of our marriage, and I've been really missing it."

"What does 'connecting emotionally' mean? I gotta be honest with you Kath, I'm trying to be open, but that sounds like a load of psychobabble crap to me."

"Okay, but hear me out, Jack. What I mean is I've not been paying enough attention to my own feelings, probably my whole life, and now I have to. I get it now that I've been missing out on something really important to me. I've always wanted there to be somebody I could go to, and especially when I'm hurting. But not just that, I want to talk to someone even when I'm feeling good. I'm realizing that it's like breathing for me, I don't pay too much attention to it until my supply's turned off."

"What are you getting at, Kath? Are you saying you can't breathe in this marriage? I mean, I don't think I'm that demanding, am I?"

"No Jack, it's not that. I'm trying to tell you more about me. I want you to listen and to know what's going on for me. Can you understand that?"

"You talk to me all the time Kath, I don't get it. Seems to me you feel free to tell me stuff whenever you want. I'm not saying you can't."

"That's not what I mean. Yes, I talk to you about many things, but I don't talk about what's most important to me, at least not until recently. I'm not saying you don't listen to me, but I'm not sure that you hear what I'm most trying to say. And partly that's because I haven't been expressing myself well."

"Okay, so bring it to me."

"Really? You'd be okay with that?"

"Of course I would. I mean I blow off steam with you whenever the old man at the office gets on my back."

"Well, but that's," and then Kathy caught herself. "Okay Jack, I'll take you up on your offer. I guess I'm trying to do it right now, but maybe not so well. I've been lonely in our marriage. And I'm not saying that's your fault. I know I haven't been talking about the right things, the things I've needed to talk about. And I intend to do that now."

"How long have you been lonely?"

"I didn't know it then, but I've been lonely our whole marriage," said Kathy. For an instant Jack looked like he'd been kicked in the gut.

He sucked in a quick breath. "Oh my God, Kath, I didn't know you'd been that unhappy."

Kathy threw her arms around Jack and cried on his chest, "Oh thank God you get it. Thank you for not being defensive and hearing what I had to say. I was so afraid you'd be mad."

Several fragments of thought came to Jack's mind, yet none of them came into focus clearly enough to articulate. He merely held her while she cried. Kathy noticed the tension leaving her body, as she sank into Jack's body more deeply. Her breathing became slower and deeper, and that was the last she knew.

They awoke the next morning with Jack in the middle of the bed and Kathy with a creak in her back. She rolled over and found her book underneath her back. Kathy sat up in bed and rubbed her back. She rolled over to get out of bed and Jack grabbed her arm and pulled her back. "Turn over on your stomach and let me work on your back. Is this where you're sore?"

"Yes, oh yes, that feels great." Jack worked his hands firmly into her lower back, and then made his way down to the soft area below. A few minutes later he eased her panties off, and then removed her nightgown. He took his time and massaged every part of her body. At some point Kathy could no longer stand it and turned over, pulling him down onto her. After Jack entered her he asked, "So how are you feeling now?"

Kathy smiled and punched him in the shoulder. "You better watch it, or I'll give you a feeling you don't want in your manhood," she said. They laughed together.

The River: Day 4

Mid-morning they walked the boat into the campsite cove. Kathy was still asleep, and didn't awaken until Jack unzipped the tent and tickled her bare foot. She pulled him into the tent and embraced him gratefully. As Jack stood up his foot kicked something hard. He reached down and picked up his hunting knife. Surprised, he showed it to Kathy, "Were you sleeping with this?"

"Of course I was. I was scared being in this dark place alone. I thought I heard something out there. I'm really glad you're back," admitted Kathy.

"Oh, really…I guess I'm not used to you being like that…at least not recently," said Jack.

"Look Jack, I really enjoyed last night. It reminded me of better times."

"Yeah, and maybe we can have better times again," said Jack.

"Yes, maybe…I'd like that," said Kathy.

"Yeah I know. Nothing's changed between us. I get it…I had hoped that maybe you were…I don't know, maybe…"

"Jack I'm so sorry to confuse you…I did want to be with you last night…I guess I was scared and…well I guess I was worried about you. And when you came down that hill I was so glad to…"

"Yeah I get it. Never mind. Nothing's changed."

"Jack, I care about you, but I just don't want…"

"Look I get it! You don't have to keep saying it," said Jack. And with that Jack turned and left the tent. He paused and then came back in. "I guess you should know, we can't fix the boat.

We brought the boat back, and we're going to pack it up and try to float back to the truck."

"How did you get the boat back if you can't fix it?"

"We paddled from the sand bar, and then walked it up the shoreline. That's why we were gone so long, it took forever to walk it back."

"So we're floating all the way back? How long will that take?" asked Kathy.

"Not sure, but probably not too long. But that's probably a Mike question."

Stacy and Mike sorted through the ice chests, taking inventory. Mike's face became grim as he saw the state of their ice blocks.

"Damn. I'd hoped these blocks would last the week, but they're already more than half melted. I wonder...wait I know what happened. These have been out in the sun the past two days I've been dealing with the boat. Shit! Oh my God, the chicken is sitting right on top of the ice. Hey Stacy, do you think it's still okay?"

Stacy dug her fingers into the chicken breasts, which gave little resistance. Then she smelled the chicken and made a face. "The chicken's definitely not okay. I won't eat it for sure. We'll just have to use up the most perishable items first, like the eggs, before anything else spoils. I'll make the rest of the eggs for breakfast," suggested Stacy.

"Okay, yeah. Probably the hot dogs and hamburgers are okay for now, if we keep 'em at the bottom of the ice chest. If the milk goes sour we can still make pancakes out of it. I'm going to drain off some of the water and then get them out of the sun," said Mike.

Having eliminated their hunger for the moment, they packed up everything into the boat, making sure that the ice chests were completely shielded from the sun under the cabin. While the others packed, Kathy walked down the beach with her piece of wood. She retrieved Jack's hunting knife and continued her whittling. When she'd heard that Mike only had one paddle, she'd decided to make one. Kathy had felt helpless and useless the past two days the others had been working on the boat, and wanted to contribute to their situation. By the time the boat was completely packed, Kathy finished. She approached Jack and handed him his knife and her finished product.

"Hope this helps," offered Kathy.

"Wow, look at that! You made us a second paddle," said Jack and smiled from ear to ear. "Hey Mike, look at what Kath made."

"You made that? That's awesome! Thanks Kathy," said Mike.

"I didn't know you knew how to do stuff like that," said Jack.

"There's much you don't know of me," returned Kathy with a smile and a wink.

Mike inspected his repair job on the hull and was satisfied that it held. They all took their seats in the boat and shoved off from shore. Jack and Mike manned the paddles and pulled them into the river. Once they left the protection of the cove the boat caught the current of the river. Mike and Jack stopped paddling, and the boat barely moved. Mike scanned the river as he stood, shielding his eyes. As he looked to the middle of the river he noted the speed of the water.

"Let's get the boat out into the middle and see if we can find a stronger current," said Mike.

Seventy-five yards further out they stopped paddling again, judging that they'd made the middle of the river. Now the boat rode the current at twice the speed. Satisfied, the men stowed their paddles on board.

"Alright ladies and gentlemen, now the adventure begins," pronounced Mike with a grin.

"Too bad we don't have a sail," said Stacy.

"Hey, there's an idea. Any chance we could rig a sail?" asked Jack.

"But with what? I got plenty of rope, but I don't know what we'd use for a sail," answered Mike.

"Any kind of cloth would do," said Jack. Both men sifted through the under cabin to see what might work. The only thing close was their clothes.

"We can use my shirts," offered Jack.

"Naw, I don't think it would do much," said Mike.

"So how far back is it?" asked Kathy.

Mike shuffled through his dash storage and found the river's map he searched for. He unfolded it and pored over it. Jack leaned over Mike's shoulder.

"I think this is the cove we camped in, and there's the sand bar," said Mike pointing to spots on the map. "Let's see," said Mike as he fished through his dash again, pulling out a ruler this time. "According to my estimate, we're fifty-one miles from the marina," Mike announced.

"Fifty-one miles! Oh my God that's far," said Kathy.

"That doesn't sound too bad, we ought to make that in two days tops," Jack guessed.

"Well, maybe," Mike responded.

"Yeah, we can kick back, drink a few beers and enjoy the company of good friends," suggested Jack.

"Sounds good to me," said Stacy.

Jack dug out one of the ice chests and handed everyone a beer, and then cracked it open and put his feet up on the gunwales. "Hey man, ain't this the life?" said Jack.

"I don't know if it'll be as easy as that, we'll see," said Mike.

"Oh my God, you act like this is all part of this grand adventure we're having. Do you realize that this might not be a beer flotilla? What if we can't get back in time?" asked Kathy.

"In time for what? You're always in such a hurry, Kath. We're on vacation. Relax!" said Jack.

"Vacation? I think the vacation ended when the boat broke down. Don't you?" returned Kathy.

"Come on Kath, don't make such a federal case out of this. Relax and enjoy the ride. This ain't so bad, you know."

"I don't know what it'll take to wake you up from Neverland. Maybe if the boat sank, but…" Kathy caught herself in mid sentence, "Oh what am I doing?" she said. Then privately she thought, Why am I acting like a total bitch? Then Kathy said, "Oh my God I don't want to be like that. I'm sorry, Jack, I don't want to act like that."

"Forget it! It's no big deal. Let's just have a good time while we're out here," said Jack.

"I'd like to enjoy myself too, but I just want us to be realistic that we do have a problem with no working boat," said Kathy. Jack waved her off and took another swig of his beer.

They floated in silence, each with their own thoughts. Mike studied the map. Stacy worked the paddle to keep them on course. Jack worked the beer. Kathy tried to relax. Satisfied that the boat floated well in the river's current, Stacy turned to Kathy and asked, "So how did you and Jack meet?"

A smile emerged on Kathy's face. She took a swig from her water bottle and said, "I worked my way through law school with a part-time job hosting events. Our company mostly planned and hosted large parties, and I usually worked the information booth. I was working a trade show in Vegas, and this tall, good-looking guy approached me at the booth. Jack worked as a programmer for a small time video gaming company, and was sent to Vegas by his company to learn about the latest developments in graphic design. The trade show had been huge and Jack was soon lost trying to find the booths he'd been asked to visit. So I pulled out a map of the show and expertly directed Jack to his sites. I even drew him a map, since he didn't seem to be getting my directions," Kathy said with a laugh.

"Oh that was all part of the act, which ended up working quite well I might add," Jack said. "At first I got a 'don't even try to get me cause I'm out of your league' attitude from Kathy, which inspired me to bring out my best material. I hunted her down at the end of the day and offered to buy her a drink, which she reluctantly accepted after pretending to not be interested. I knew that was all an act."

"Are you sure about that?" said Kathy playfully.

"Most often my considerable skill and charm works right away, at least if they're not lesbian."

"That's right, Jack usually found his way into women's beds the first night or two. On rare occasions he needed three or four dates to seduce them," added Kathy.

"So my interest went off the chart when Kathy resisted my best delivery and best material," said Jack.

"He'd met a few women who turned him down. Jack just wasn't used to not getting what he wanted if he secured initial interest. Jack was on the verge of begging when I relented," concluded Kathy.

"Begging? Dream on, and don't flatter yourself. I've never had to beg."

"Oh I can remember a few times when…"

"That doesn't count! I was just playing around with you," argued Jack.

"Uh huh," said Kathy with a smile and a wave of her hand.

Throughout the day the men paddled occasionally to keep the boat in the middle, and also had to negotiate a couple of bends in the river. Kathy read her magazines and nervously twirled her hair, Stacy read a novel, Jack made beer cans into animal shapes, and Mike kept an eye on the river.

Late in the day Mike examined the sky in the west, and then looked down river where they were headed. "I think we ought to camp for the night. It'll be dark soon," said Mike.

"No let's keep going. We can get a couple more miles easy," said Jack.

"It's not worth the risk."

"What risk? We're just cruisin' down at what, probably three miles an hour," said Jack.

"But once it gets dark we won't be able to see anything submerged. It wouldn't take much to reopen the crack in the bow. The patch job's okay, but I don't want to test it more than we have to."

And with that Mike slipped an oar in the water and pulled for shore. Jack reluctantly grabbed the other oar to help. When they reached shore Jack stumbled out of the boat in good spirits. Mike poured over his map. "So let me guess, we made twenty-five miles today. Tell me I'm right," said Jack.

"Jack, you're not going to believe this, but we only made fifteen miles today," answered Mike.

"No way, you must have made a mistake! We can't be moving that slow," shouted Jack.

"Come take a look at the map and I can show you where we are," countered Mike.

"Naw, I don't need to see it. You'll see, we'll be at the truck by night fall tomorrow," said a confident Jack. Mike shook his head and put the map away.

Jack walked up the beach carrying the tents, and tripped over the anchor line doing a face plant into the sand and gravel. "Shit! Who in the hell put that rope there!" Kathy rolled her eyes.

"Ah, give it a rest, Kath. I saw you do that eye thing," Jack growled.

Kathy picked up the tent and marched up the beach with it. She began to set it up.

"Come on Kath, don't be like that. I'll set up the tent for us. Don't be a bitch," said Jack. "See what I mean, Mike, this is the shit I get, day in and day out with her?"

Kathy threw the tent down, turned on her heels and fired back, "You leave him out of this! This is between you and me."

"Ah, it ain't worth it. You won't listen anyways, so why bother?" Jack retorted.

"You see, this is one of the reasons our marriage doesn't work so well," said Kathy.

"What do you mean? Because I tripped and fell?"

"Of course not, Jack, because you won't talk things through with me when there's a problem between us."

"Oh, go put a cork in it," said Jack with a wave of his hand. He turned and went back to help Mike unpack the boat.

Jack rolled his eyes as Mike glanced up at his approach. "You see what I have to put up with?" Jack asked. "What am I supposed to do? Nothing will make that bitch happy. Am I right or what, man?"

Mike paused and thought a moment, "Look, I'm your friend and you always got my support, but I'm not going to take sides between you two. And anyways she's got a point."

"Come on man, anybody can see she's unreasonable and there's no pleasing her," argued Jack.

Pointing to himself, Mike said, "No, this anybody can't see that. I see two people struggling to work out a tough marriage. I know you'd like to see it that way, but it isn't as simple as one bitch and one nice guy. Maybe it's time you take a closer look at your part in your marriage problems. I've been trying to tell you that for months."

"Ah shit, now you sound like Kath. You're almost as bad as she is."

Mike stared into Jack's face a moment, and then went back to unpacking the boat.

Kathy walked down the beach by herself. She rubbed her hands across her face and groaned, and said aloud, "Why do I let myself get pulled into those fights with Jack. I just hate it when I do that! I know I make it worse when I react like that." Kathy sat down on a rock and looked out at the moving river.

Mike set up the stove and pulled the food off the boat. He was lighting the stove when Jack walked up. "Look man, I'm sorry. What I said was stupid," apologized Jack with his eyes on the sand.

"Apology accepted...You know what Jack, whenever I try to get you to take a closer look at your marriage, you blow me off."

"I don't blow you off! I think about what you say," said Jack.

"Well I don't hear about that part."

"What, you want me to fill you in each time I think?"

"Let's just forget about it," said Mike. "Hey, lend me a hand with barbequing these burgers."

"Oh yeah, you got it," said Jack.

Stacy finished washing the dinner dishes and sat down next to Mike. Mike reached out and held her hand and gave her a smile. "Hey, how are you holding up?" asked Mike.

"I'm worried. Did you see what's left in the ice chests? We don't have much left to eat."

"What's left?" asked Mike.

"About a dozen hot dogs, a little bit of turkey, less than a half block of cheese, and a bag of potato chips. There was half a milk left, but it soured so I dumped it."

"Even too sour for pancakes?"

"Yes. There's no way I'd use that milk for anything," said Stacy.

"That's it? Damn, I didn't know we were that low on food…how long do you figure that'll last us?

"Two days tops, but probably not even that. Oh I forgot, we've still got a few protein bars," answered Stacy.

Stacy and Mike stared off at the darkening river as they contemplated their situation. Mike rubbed his face with both hands and sighed. "Do you think we should start rationing?"

"Maybe we should…how long do you figure till we get back to the truck?"

"Two days minimum, and that's if everything goes well."

"I think we should talk it over with Jack and Kathy," suggested Stacy.

"Agreed. Hey Jack, Kathy, come over here a minute."

Kathy and Jack had been sitting in the boat, quietly arguing interspersed with long silences. They stepped out of the boat. "What's up?" asked Jack with a grin.

"Stacy and I were talking, and we thought you should know that we're almost out of food."

"What do we have left?" asked Kathy.

Stacy ran through the inventory.

"Oh that's just great! So to cap off a perfect camping trip, we're all going to go on a forced diet of hot dogs and chips," said Kathy.

"We got a lot of beer left," interjected Jack.

"Well that's just even greater. Then you can be on a beer diet so there's more hot dogs for the rest of us," said Kathy.

"Beer and chips sounds alright to me," said Jack jovially.

Kathy turned to leave in disgust. "Kathy, wait a minute please," asked Mike.

"Mike and I were wondering if we should do some sort of rationing," said Stacy.

"Put me down for the turkey and cheese. I don't care what you do with the beer," answered Kathy.

"Oh, so you get the best food, huh?" said Jack.

"Well, she asked what I thought," retorted Kathy.

"Wait a minute, I think we should plan ahead. We'll set aside so much for tomorrow and so much for the day after. And should we allocate anything for the third day?" asked Stacy.

"Naw, we'll be back before then. We don't need anything after tomorrow night if you ask me," Jack said.

"I say we save the protein bars for the third day, and eat everything else the next two days," suggested Stacy.

"That's fine by me," said Kathy.

Kathy pulled on her sweatshirt, told Jack of her plans, and headed up the beach for some privacy. She sat down on the sand and pulled her knees up to her chest. Why do I keep allowing myself to get into it with Jack? she thought. I hate being like that! I don't want to be a bitch to Jack. God knows he's taken enough from me already...I wish I would think a bit before responding when he says things that get to me...Maybe the stress of this whole trip is weighing on me more than I thought...thank God for Mike and Stacy. At least they're really nice. Maybe if I can remember to think before I speak. It's just so easy to go off on Jack.

Kathy stood and slowly walked to the end of the cove and stared at the water. I hope we're going to be okay, she thought.

34 Weeks after the River Trip

"Last month I told you all that we'd made it. I thought Jack and I were over the hump and on our way to a great marriage. I'd never been so hopeful about my marriage, at least since the first year. And then the last few weeks everything seems different."

"What happened?" asked Susan.

"Oh my, how do I explain? At first I felt like Jack was actually listening to me. He seemed to be trying. I don't remember quite how it happened, but last week I had some conflict with my boss at work. I brought it up with Jack over dinner, and I didn't have two sentences out of my mouth when he's telling me to resign. I asked Jack to hear me out, so he waved me to continue. Anyway, once I got the whole story out he told me my boss was abusing her power and that I should at least resign, and possibly file a harassment suit against her and the firm. I tried to tell Jack that I didn't want any advice, and that I just wanted him to hear me. And then he went on to elaborate the reasons why I shouldn't tolerate that kind of abuse. Finally I got so frustrated I raised my voice and asked him if he was hearing what I wanted. He said he did hear me and was trying to be supportive like I've asked. Oh my God, I must have spent the next hour trying to explain the kind of support I wanted. I told him that I wanted to feel heard and understood, not told what to do. I don't know if he was just being stubborn, but he didn't seem to get the distinction. Anyway, at some point I finally gave up and said I wanted to go read by myself. He followed me into the bedroom and said I was punishing him by running away. I told him I would think about that, but I just didn't know what else to say, and that I was too frustrated to try anymore tonight."

"What'd he do?" asked Jake.

"He marched out in a huff and slept on the couch. To be honest I was relieved he slept somewhere else. I'm so disappointed, I thought we were really getting somewhere, and now it seems like we're back to square one."

"Oh Kathy, that sucks! Although I still envy the bastard, especially after you made love to him four times that one week," said Jake with a mischievous grin. A faint smile crossed Kathy's face.

"What made you think you were really getting somewhere?" asked Dr. Aragorn.

"Like I said, Jack seemed to be listening to me."

"And what gave you that idea?" asked Dr. Aragorn.

"Because there were several times when I'd bring up something about work or a friend that I was having a reaction to, and he listened."

"But tell us what you mean that he listened," pressed Dr. Aragorn.

"What else is there to say? I mean, I'd be talking and he shut up and didn't interrupt me."

"And how did he respond after you were done telling him?" asked Dr. Aragorn.

Kathy looked down at the ground and rubbed her knees with her hands while she thought, "I guess he didn't really say anything."

"Because he listened and didn't give you any advice, you took that as him hearing you," suggested Dr. Aragorn.

"Well, yes, I guess so."

"It doesn't sound to me like he's hearing you. I get that him being quiet and avoiding the advice might be an improvement, but that isn't the same as being heard and known by him," said Evelyn.

"I agree. Jack learning to keep his mouth shut has given you the false impression that he knows what you're going through," said Susan.

"Oh my God, I don't want that to be true," sobbed Kathy, putting her hands over her ears. "Don't tell me that!" She shook her head softly. After several minutes Kathy wiped her face with a tissue and looked up, "Okay I'm done. Someone else can process."

"Wait a minute Kathy, are you shutting us out?" asked Dr. Aragorn.

"I don't know…maybe…So how will I know if he's truly hearing me? I don't want to be fooled again."

"It helped me to know my husband heard me when he could tell me in his own words what I was saying," said Evelyn.

"I can tell when my wife has her own reaction to what I'm trying to tell her, and then I know I'm getting through," said Jake.

"But how can you tell what her reaction is?" asked Kathy.

"I can usually see it on her face, but the true test is I can feel it," said Jake.

"There probably isn't one magic way to know, but I think your heart will tell you if he's truly with you or not. You might also ask some questions," suggested Dr. Aragorn.

"Like what questions?"

"Like Evelyn was saying, you might ask Jack to tell you what he's hearing you say. Or ask him what he thinks you're feeling," said Dr. Aragorn.

"I can usually feel it, no matter what he says. I can feel when there's life in his words," said Evelyn.

"I'm not sure I know the difference," said Kathy.

"Then we'll help you to know," said Dr. Aragorn.

Jake and Kathy headed out to the parking lot together. At first they walked in silence, and then Kathy spoke, "You know it's tempting to just give up on Jack."

Jake turned to look at Kathy in surprise, "What do you mean give up on him?"

"I can't believe I'm saying this, but I've been thinking about leaving Jack and moving in with my sister."

"Wow, for real?" Kathy nodded solemnly.

"How long have you been considering that?" asked Jake.

"I'm not sure that I'm seriously considering it, but I've fantasized about leaving him off and on the last year or two, but I've been thinking about it more the last month…probably since things started going bad again. I just can't go back to living like that. It's just way too lonely." Kathy stopped and stood next to her car with Jake leaning against his own car, which happened to be next to Kathy's. And then Kathy continued, "At the same time, I don't know if I can do that to Lily."

"Do what to her?"

"Leave her daddy. I picture her being so hurt if I told her. She'd be so mad at me I don't know if she'd ever forgive me."

"Would you take her with you?"

"I've wondered about that. I'm not sure that I could take her. Jack is the one who picks her up from school four to five days a week," said Kathy.

"You can't pick her up?"

"Sometimes I can, but often my work demands make it impossible."

"Oh man, so you'd likely be leaving her with Jack then," said Jake.

"Oh my God, don't say that! You make it sound like I'd be abandoning my daughter." Jake just looked at Kathy and waited.

"I would just have to figure out a way to take Lily with me, but how?"

"Damn, I don't know Kathy. You might have to leave her with Jack, unless you can do something with your work schedule."

"Oh my God, there's just no way I could tell Lily that I'm going and that she's not coming." Jake shook his head slowly and started to mouth words, but nothing came out. Kathy cried softly.

"Have I ever told you why my wife almost left me?" asked Jake.

Kathy shook her head and said, "I don't think so."

Jake continued, "Linda couldn't bear the loneliness of our marriage. She felt like we were roommates that occasionally slept together. At first I had no clue what she meant. When she explained that I didn't know her, I told her that of course I did. I said I could name dozens of things about her. Like what kinds of food she liked, her habits, the kind of movies she was into. That just frustrated her. Anyways, it took me a long time being in the group to understand that I mistook knowing about Linda, for knowing Linda."

"Oh my God, do I wish Jack would say that to me," Kathy said as tears gently formed in her eyes. Several people walked past on their way to parked cars.

"Why don't we sit in my car," suggested Jake. Kathy nodded and climbed into the passenger's seat. "I don't know if I'll ever hear something like that from Jack. Right now it's hard to imagine."

"I get that, but give him a chance. As a recovering rock-head myself, I get that Jack probably has no clue what you're talking about. Likely he thinks he's being a great husband, and that you just don't appreciate what you've got."

"Maybe I don't appreciate what I've got."

"Maybe, but you do need your marriage to grow."

"I wonder if Jack would get into therapy."

"Have you ever asked?"

"No. I've never even thought of it until now. It's not likely, since he's not a fan of our group," said Kathy.

"Why not?"

"He thinks it's feeding my not appreciating him…you know Jake, you have to stop making comments about being envious of Jack." Jake laughed. "No, really, I'm not kidding," said Kathy.

"Why is that? I thought you enjoyed my little comments."

"I do, I mean, I do and I don't. It feels good that you find me attractive, but it reminds me of what I don't have. Whenever you say something like that I wish I was married to someone like you."

"Oh Kathy, I'm so sorry. I had no idea my comments had that kind of, I mean, that I stirred up, well, you know what I mean...I guess the problem is I'm attracted to you, and maybe you're attracted to me. I've known that on my end since the first time you spoke in group. But I didn't realize..."

"Yes it's true. I didn't like you at first. In fact, I wrote you off as a clown the first month or two, but you've grown on me lately. Maybe I'm seeing your depth and it seems like you get many of the things that I say."

"Oh Kathy, I had no idea about my comments. I'm flattered that you're attracted to me, but I don't want to be...to be a distraction. I'm trying to help you make your marriage work, not be a problem...I suppose I say some of those things because you talk about feeling ugly, and I want you to know that at least this man finds you quite attractive. But now that I know, I'll drop the flattery."

"Please don't drop it completely. I mean, I really do like it when you say those things about how lucky Jack is, but maybe just say them when I feel like crap about myself. Those are the times when I really need to hear something like that."

Jake and Kathy laughed together, and then Jake said, "Okay, I'll think a bit more before I speak. Well, I ought to be heading home, so I'll see you next week."

"Okay Jake, bye."

On the drive home Kathy kept thinking about sitting in Jake's car. She brushed the thoughts away, but they stubbornly returned, again and again. Kathy relented and found herself picturing Jake leaning towards her. At first she and Jake kiss tenderly. Then they recline the seats and make out passionately. Just as zippers and buttons begin to be manipulated Kathy shook her head and thought, what am I thinking about? I don't want to have an affair...but it would be really great to be physical with a man that I have that kind of connection with. Maybe I could just have an affair and stay with Jack. Maybe that would make it bearable to stay...my God, I can't believe I'm even thinking that way! I'd feel like crap about myself if I did anything like what I'm picturing. Maybe I can go home and be with Jack...although Jack is not the person really I want to be with right now. Maybe if I go home and Jack and I talk first, then I might be in the mood to…well, we'll see what happens when I get home.

As soon as Kathy got inside she quietly opened Lily's door. She crept over to her bed and laid a hand on Lily's back, which gently rose and fell in rhythm. Tears reemerged in her eyes as she sat with Lily. She pictured Lily's little face as Kathy explained that she wouldn't be living here for awhile. Kathy violently closed her eyes, as if slamming them shut would purge the image from her mind.

As she closed Lily's door a faint sound leaked out of the bedroom. Kathy paused as she closed the garage door and looked in the living room, but she saw no Jack. Then it dawned on her that the sound she heard was Jack in the shower. She set her purse down and went into the bedroom. She opened her closet and hung up her coat and put her shoes in their place, and then lay down on the bed and waited. Presently Jack emerged from the bathroom with his hair messy and a towel around his waist and did a double take at the bed, "Oh, I didn't hear you come in."

"I just got home before you got out of the shower. So, how was your day?"

"It was fine…had lunch with Mike. He and Stacy want to double date with us some time. I tell you, Mike might have met the girl of his dreams this time. He's a great guy, and will make a great catch for some lucky girl."

"Oh yeah."

"Yeah, I'm looking forward to seeing them again."

"Would you say Mike's your best friend, or one of them?"

"I haven't really thought about it, but yeah, I'd say Mike would be right up there. Why do you ask?"

"No particular reason, just wondering. Maybe I ask because you seem to have so much respect for him."

"Definitely, I can't think of anyone I respect more than Mike. So hey, how about tomorrow night?"

"For what?"

"To meet up with Mike and Stacy for dinner."

"Sounds okay. Oh, wait a minute, I can't. I'm meeting some people from group for dinner tomorrow."

"Really? I didn't know you saw them outside of group."

"Yes, on occasion."

"What about Lily?" asked Jack.

"I thought I'd take her with me."

"Can't you cancel them?"

"I don't want to cancel them. I'm looking forward to seeing them."

"Can't you just reschedule them?"

"Jack, it's tough to get six people together at the same time. Maybe we can meet with Mike and Stacy another night."

"Damn Kath, are those people more important than me?"

"Come on Jack, that isn't fair. I already had plans with them before you and Mike talked."

"So you'd rather be with them than me."

"Damn it, Jack, knock it off, it's not about picking somebody over you. It's about having previous plans. I feel like you're trying to manipulate me out of my plans, and I don't like it."

"Take it however you want. I just want my wife to be with me and my best friend. Is that too much to ask?"

"Oh damn it Jack, I don't want to talk about it anymore. On my way home I was looking forward to being with you, but this isn't at all going how I'd pictured."

"If you weren't being so damned stubborn it might be a different conversation."

"Oh my God, I'm done. I'm getting in the shower and going to bed."

"That suits me just fine."

The hot water spraying the back of her neck felt heavenly. She stood motionless in the pulsing stream. Kathy was thankful that the shower kept Jack from seeing her tears. She wouldn't give him that satisfaction tonight. "Dear God, I wished it weren't like this with me and Jack," Kathy said aloud. Then she thought, I wonder what I could've done different…maybe I should've just cancelled on my group…or at least not been so defensive…but I really want to see them tomorrow. At least they seem to get me. It seems like Jack rarely does. I wonder if he ever will. Right now it sure doesn't seem likely.

When Kathy emerged from the bathroom Jack was gone. Just as well I suppose, I don't want to try again tonight, thought Kathy. She picked up her novel and read until she felt tired enough to sleep.

All afternoon Kathy found herself thinking about dinner with the Tuesday night people. Her work required a bit less energy than usual, and before the day seemed half over it was time to leave and meet her new friends. O'Dell's Irish Pub was lit up in green neon lights, with the bar patio extending out under the sign on the right side of the door. Kathy stepped across the threshold holding Lily's hand and waited for her eyes to adjust to the dim lighting. "Now how come we're going here, Mommy?"

"Because we're meeting some of Mommy's friends for dinner and Susan's bringing her little girl too. Her name is Jamie, and maybe you and Jamie can color together." They wondered around for a minute before Kathy spotted them in a booth in the far corner. Jake slid over to make room for her as sat down next to him. Across the table sat Tom between Susan and Karen. A chorus of 'hi's' all around as Kathy sat down.

"Susan, is there room for Lily to sit next to Jamie? I think they might have fun coloring together," said Kathy.

"Oh sure, uh…"

"Here, I'll move and you two can sit next to Susan and Jamie," offered Karen.

"Thanks Karen. That would be great."

"Anyways, it feels really strange to not be depressed. I mean, it feels really good, but I don't know what to do with myself. I'm so used to not having much energy, and I'm so used to avoiding people, that it's weird to talk to people I don't really know," said Tom.

"That's so great Tom, you're coming to life," said Susan.

"Yeah, I've never seen you look this good, and have this much energy," added Jake.

"I don't know if I've ever felt this much energy either, except maybe when a woman would agree to go out with me. But that didn't usually last long; usually by the end of the date, you know," said Tom.

"So have you been out with anybody lately?" asked Kathy.

Tom flushed and grinned, looking out at the bar for a moment, "Well, I wasn't going to say anything yet, but I've been out with somebody new, I mean it's just one date so far, but we'll see."

"Tell us about her," asked Karen.

"Well, she's one of our clients and I've actually known her a long time. I'm embarrassed to tell you this, but she gave me her cell phone number about six months ago, but I wasn't ready to call her."

"Six months ago? Tommy Tommy Tommy, you operate about as fast as frozen maple syrup," said Jake.

"Lay off him, Jake. So maybe he's not the smooth operator you are," said Karen.

"Thanks Karen. You can be a real jerk sometimes, Jake. Anyways, I made a business call to her a couple weeks back and, well, it just seemed natural to ask her out for a drink, so I did."

"Tom, you slick operator. I know, I'll call you the Tomenator from now on," said Jake. Everyone laughed. Tom laughed, but with a flushed face.

"Come on Jake, don't embarrass me. I'm new at this," pleaded Tom.

"I'm just playing with you Tommy, and I'm proud of you. Aside from all the friendly ribbing, I couldn't imagine you asking anyone out a year and a half ago when we first started group, and now you're doing it. I think that's just great," said Jake.

"I wish I could do that," said Karen.

After a pause Jake asked, "You mean ask out a woman?"

"No! Talk to guys. I get so shy around guys that I can't talk and I end up saying stupid things," said Karen.

"Like what?" asked Susan.

"I don't want to give you any examples, you'll think I'm an idiot," said Karen.

"Don't worry, we already think you're an idiot," needled Jake.

"You can't be much more awkward than I've been, I mean, the story I told you is just one date," said Tom.

"And I haven't even been dating hardly at all," added Susan.

"I date, but it's with my wife, so that doesn't count," said Jake.

"No way, I'm not giving you any examples. Let's just say I freeze up and don't know what to say to guys. The truth is I get anxious, and when I'm anxious I can't really talk. Words won't even come out of my mouth. I wish I could just relax and be myself," said Karen.

"Have you considered alcohol?" asked Jake.

"What do you get anxious about?" asked Susan.

The waitress came up and Kathy ordered a glass of red wine and a Caesar's salad for herself and something off the kid's menu for Lily. A couple others ordered a second round with their dinners. The waitress left and all eyes returned to Karen.

"I was hoping you'd forget that you'd asked me a question," said Karen with a smile.

"Yes, but wouldn't you also be disappointed if we forgot about you?" suggested Kathy.

"In this case maybe not. Well yeah, I probably would," admitted Karen. "Anyways, I don't know why I get anxious, but I do whenever a good-looking guy is around."

"I get nervous around guys too," said Susan.

"Yeah, but you can still talk," countered Karen.

"Yes, but with your hot runner's body you have something to be confident about. Look at me, carrying around extra luggage in my buns and thighs. No matter how much I diet, I can't seem to drop the last twenty pounds. How do you look like that at forty?" asked Susan.

"Just double your anxiety to my level and you'll drop it easy," said Karen. "But seriously, I run twenty miles a week to stay at this weight."

"I don't know if I could get myself to do that, I mean I hate running. It's all I can get myself to do to walk around the block three mornings a week before work," said Susan rolling her eyes.

"For me it's depression that does it," said Kathy. "When I'm depressed I eat less, not more. I completely lose my appetite and sometimes get nauseous when I'm down."

"Aren't you the lucky one. When I get depressed I eat chocolate like I won a lifetime's supply on The Price is Right. A good depression is usually good for about ten pounds for me," complained Susan with a twinkle in her eye.

"Anyway, getting back to Karen, you've talked in group about feeling like others look at you through a microscope. Do you think you feel that around guys?" suggested Susan.

"Yes, I've thought about that. I know that's a thing for me, but I can't seem to stop being anxious just the same," said Karen.

"I get anxious that guys will think I'm just a fat, middle-aged lady and look no further," said Susan.

"But the guys that take the time to get to know you will realize how much you've got under the hood," said Jake.

Susan reached across the table and put her hand on Jake's, "Thank God for you Jake, but I don't know if any other guys on the planet think like you," said Susan.

"Sure there are, take Tommy here for example, he would only be with a woman with a great soul," said Jake. "Right Tommy?"

"I don't want to pump myself up or anything, but yes it's true. Although I've been lucky to get any second dates, I wouldn't want a second date with a woman who didn't have a great heart," answered Tom.

Susan put her arm around Tom's shoulder and said, "Too bad we can't date group members." Tom blushed and looked down at his food.

"Well, just drop out of group and then you can go after Tommy," suggested Jake with a wink.

"No, because then I'd probably commit suicide if I dropped out of group right now, so I wouldn't be around to enjoy the romance," said Susan.

"I guess that would be a problem," admitted Jake.

"I wish I had a little romance myself," said Kathy.

"Still going badly with Jack?" asked Susan.

"Yes, but please don't use his name in front of you know who," Kathy whispered. Then raising her voice slightly she added, "We fought again last night and this morning. He tried to talk me out of meeting with you guys tonight so I could double date with him and his buddy. This morning I asked if he'd consider getting into therapy," said Kathy.

"And what'd he say?" asked Jake.

"He told me that I was the one with the issues and that he didn't need no head shrinking."

"Typical man," said Evelyn with some energy. "No offense to present company," she added quickly. Jake waved her off.

"I'm sorry, honey," said Susan. "He still thinks all the issues in the marriage are about you."

"I guess so...I don't know how much longer I can go on like this. I've been thinking about..." Kathy glanced at Lily, and satisfied that she wasn't paying attention took out a pen and wrote 'leaving' on her napkin, and then showed it to the others.

"Oh no, really?" asked Karen.

Kathy nodded, "Yes, I can't go on like this forever. I mean, we'll have a good week or two and I get my hopes up, and then everything just seems to go down the toilet and I get depressed again. I just can't keep getting my hopes up, it's too painful," she said as she dabbed at the corners of her eyes.

"How serious are you?" asked Susan.

"I don't know...sometimes I think I'm ready to do it and I get excited, and then I get scared and depressed. I don't know if I can bring myself to actually go through with it."

"That's a big decision," said Karen.

"Yeah no shit, that's huge," added Jake sympathetically.

"Have you thought about a trial separation?" asked Susan.

"What do you mean?" asked Kathy.

"To try out living apart for a few months and see how it goes, without making any permanent decisions," explained Susan.

"It might wake him up," added Karen.

"Yeah, it might take you leaving for him to realize what he's about to lose," said Jake.

"Yes, but I'm not considering leaving to wake him up, but because I can't keep living like this."

"Of course you are, but the benefit of a trial separation is for both of you to reevaluate the marriage, not just you. Lane and I did a trial separation," added Susan.

"Did it help?"

"We ended up getting divorced anyways, so it obviously didn't save our marriage, but it did give us an opportunity to see how it would be to live apart. I found that I was incredibly relieved, but that I also missed Lane. Lane was just relieved. He said he felt free for the first time since we'd been married. But I think the separation helped us to be sure that we wanted to divorce. I still had mixed feelings, but for Lane it just confirmed it," said Susan.

"That scares me. What if we separate and then he decides he's better off without me. I can just see him shrugging his shoulders, and then starting to date other women and never looking back," said Kathy.

"You don't imagine you mean much to him, do you? You don't think he'll miss you at all?" asked Susan.

"I don't know. I just don't know. I can see him going either way. He might try to talk me into coming back. I wonder if he might try to prevent me from leaving," said Kathy.

"And what if you stay, then what?" asked Jake.

"What do you mean?"

"I mean what do you think will happen if you just stay and gut it out?" asked Jake.

Kathy stared into her glass of wine while she swirled it around, and then said quietly, "I don't know, probably nothing changes…I wish I knew what would happen if I stayed, and what would happen if I moved out for awhile."

The others nodded knowingly. And then Jake said, "Sorry honey, I broke my crystal ball last week, or I'd let you borrow it."

After a pregnant silence Karen asked, "Kathy, has anything really changed since you joined us?"

"Oh my God, yes! I've changed a lot, well at least some. I'm not being a parent to him much anymore. I also feel lonelier in my marriage. I mean, I think I've been lonely all along, but I'm now aware of it. I'm much more aware of myself. Most of my conversations with him feel empty. Sometimes I feel like he's listening to me, but I can't really tell for sure."

"Your relationship with your husband isn't evolving, is it?" suggested Susan. Kathy looked away and wiped the corner of her eyes, and then shook her head. "That's an awful realization to come to," added Susan.

"My God, no shit," said Jake shaking his head slowly.

"Does he know you're considering leaving?" asked Susan.

"I don't think so. I mean I haven't told him?"

"Why not?" asked Susan.

"Oh my God, I think he'd hit the roof if I told him. I don't know what he'd do. He might even tell me to get the hell out."

"So you're scared to tell him," said Jake.

"Yeah, I am. I'd have to leave if I told him."

"Then what keeps you from being ready?" asked Susan.

"Are you saying you think I should leave him?"

"Oh no, I'm not making any suggestions. But you're telling us how empty your marriage continues to be, so I'm wondering what keeps you there," answered Susan.

"First of all there's her," Kathy said as she nodded to Lily. "I don't know if I can put her through that, and then I keep hoping he'll change. I keep hoping he'll finally get it and realize how lonely the marriage is for me. I keep hoping he'll see that I want a partner. I keep hoping he'll get that I want a soul mate, not just someone to eat and sleep with."

"Can't put who through that," asked Lily.

"Oh Lily, we're just having an adult conversation," said Kathy. Kathy grimaced as she looked back at the others, "I guess I've said enough for tonight."

"Well preach it, sister! I haven't met too many men that get any of that. I keep looking for just one. Well, it's time for me to go home and get to bed. I'll see you all next week," said Susan.

Kathy fidgeted in group. She felt light-headed and in her stomach it seemed like a squadron of bees were buzzing as they tried to fly in formation but were only somewhat successful. Jake talked through some conflict he'd had with Linda, and Kathy struggled to listen and participate. The best she could do was track with Jake off and on. She refocused on Jake as he said, "I just hate the idea that you all think I'm being arrogant about this, when I do think I get Linda's desire to have kids."

"But if you understand her desire to have kids then why does she feel like you don't understand?" pressed Susan.

"Maybe she's mad because I'm not telling her what she wants to hear, that I'm ready to start trying," countered Jake.

"You understand the data, that she wants to try, but I'm not sure you're hearing her heart," said Susan.

"So what am I not hearing?"

"That she's afraid. She's telling you she's afraid she won't be able to get pregnant right away and that you might wait too long," said Susan.

"But that's crazy! We have all the time in the world."

"And that's what sounds arrogant to me Jake, I think you're dismissing the fact that Linda's 36 and has some reason to be concerned about waiting too long," said Dr. Aragorn. Jake folded his arms and crossed his legs.

Kathy put her hand over her nose. She didn't want to distract Jake, but her tears flowed with more and more fluidity. Dr. Aragorn turned and glanced at Kathy, and then turned back to Jake and said, "I can tell you're trying to hear Linda in this, but I sense there's something getting triggered for you that's preventing you from completely taking in what she's saying."

"Well, I guess I'll have to think about it. I don't want to be defensive, but so far I'm not seeing it," said Jake.

Dr. Aragorn nodded to Jake, and then turned towards Kathy. Kathy noted his gaze and wiped her eyes and nose and then spoke, "Hearing Jake talk about having kids got to me. I've been thinking a whole lot about leaving Jack, but…" And here her tears returned with a vengeance. "I just don't think I can do this to Lily."

"Do what to Lily?" asked Susan.

"Put her through a divorce…even more than that I don't want to leave her."

"Leave her? What do you mean?" said Dr. Aragorn.

"I don't think Jack will leave, so I'll have to be the one who goes. And I think I'd have to leave Lily at our condo anyways," said Kathy as she began to sob. "Because of my work I can't pick her up from school most days, and I can't even take her much either. Oh my God I wish I could take her with me, or better yet I wish Jack would move out, but I don't know what I'd do about Lily's school.

"You can't work something out with your boss?" asked Evelyn.

"I talked to my boss, and even though she's willing to be somewhat flexible with me, there's just no way I could count on being available to get her on time. I'd have to rely on Jack to do it. I hate that! I just hate that! I even thought about quitting my job, but…"

"Oh God I can't even imagine," said Evelyn. The others nodded and waited.

After a time Dr. Aragorn spoke, "I'm so sorry, Kathy." Evelyn, sitting next to Kathy, put her hand on Kathy's hand. Kathy squeezed Evelyn's hand.

"So what are you imagining Lily will go through if you move out?" asked Dr. Aragorn.

"Like her mom's leaving her behind."

"As though you'd be abandoning her," said Dr. Aragorn.

"Of course! What else will she feel if I leave? I will be leaving her."

"Stay with me on this. I want to get past the concrete fact that yes, you'll be physically leaving living with her, which you do have to face. But what are you picturing that will do to her?" pressed Dr. Aragorn.

"She'll feel afraid…lonely…hurt, maybe mad at me. Maybe she'll feel like it's because of her that I'm leaving."

"You expect her to feel emotionally abandoned, not just physically abandoned," said Evelyn.

"Yes, what else could she possibly feel?" said Kathy.

"Most kids would have a whole assortment of feelings, but I don't know that they'd all feel abandoned," began Susan. "Like my daughter, she misses her daddy, and sometimes asks for him, but I don't think she feels abandoned."

"Wait a minute, I think there's more to this," began Dr. Aragorn. "How do you imagine it is for Lily right now?"

"I don't follow," said Kathy.

"Is there any cost for Lily if you stay?" asked Dr. Aragorn.

"How can there be any cost for her if I stay?"

"What kind of mom do you think Lily gets right now?"

"I hope a mom that loves her," said Kathy.

"Yes I'm sure of that, but what kind of mom does Lily get while her mom lives with Jack?" asked Dr. Aragorn.

"Well, at least she gets a mom that's there for her."

"Yes, but that's not what I'm asking. What kind of mom does she get while you're there with Jack?" asked Dr. Aragorn.

Kathy paused and pondered his question. "Well, I suppose sometimes she gets a depressed mom…sometimes she gets a lonely mom…and I think sometimes she gets a happy mom."

"How often does she get the depressed or lonely mom?" asked Dr. Aragorn.

"Damn, that would be hard to say…"

"Come on Kathy, you've been depressed most of the time since you joined this group," said Jake.

"I have?"

"You didn't know that?" asked Dr. Aragorn.

"I guess I didn't realize it was that bad. I mean, haven't I grown some since I started here?"

"Sure you have. And I don't mean to suggest you're depressed in the same way as when you started. It's actually been growth for you to come to feel how lonely and disappointed you've been. You're probably more lonely and disappointed and less depressed," said Dr. Aragorn.

"What's the difference?"

"The difference is that you're allowing yourself to feel how lonely and how disappointing your marriage has been for you. When you were depressed, your marriage felt bad to you, but it didn't seem to me that you were able to get to some of the important feelings that you're aware of now," explained Dr. Aragorn.

"I suppose Lily gets a mom that's mostly lonely and disappointed in her marriage."

"And what kind of mom do you imagine she'll get if you separate?" asked Susan.

"I hadn't even thought of that…I would hope I'd be less disappointed…maybe I'd be less frustrated too. I do get frustrated with Jack, and I'm sure she sees that. So what does that mean? Does that mean I should leave Jack?"

"That means staying or leaving your marriage is a complex issue with no simple answers. You've been worried about how it will affect Lily if you leave, and I'm sure it will affect her, but I'm not sure that you've considered how it affects her that you're staying," said Dr. Aragorn.

"Oh my God, it sucks no matter what I do! Lily will be affected no matter what. I'll be affected no matter what. Jack will be affected no matter what."

"Yes," said Dr. Aragorn.

"What you're saying just makes it even more complicated."

"Maybe you'd hoped we would tell you what the right decision is?" suggested Evelyn.

"Yes! I so wish you could…but I know you won't."

"It's not just that I won't, it's that I can't know the right decision for you, and I hope that no one else in here tries to," said Dr. Aragorn.

Kathy dropped her face into her hands as she cried, "I know none of you can, but I still wish you would. I hate it that I have to decide myself...but I guess I suppose I wouldn't like it if..." She lifted her face and stared over Dr. Aragorn's shoulder.

"It's an awful decision to have to face, whatever you decide," said Evelyn.

Mike and Jack walked out of the Staples Center, high-fiving each other. The Lakers had won a close game in the closing minutes of the fourth quarter by coming back from eleven points down. Both men were excited, talking rapidly and reliving the final minutes of the game. It's exhilarating to be part of a packed house when your team's playing well.

On the way home the excitement of the game began to wear off and Jack stared out the window. Mike noticed Jack's change in mood and said, "Hey man, what's up?"

"What do you mean?"

"You've got something on your mind," said Mike.

"Naw, not really."

"Come off it man, I know you better than that. The only time you're that quiet is when something's on your mind," pressed Mike.

"Well...Kath wants me to go to marriage counseling with her."

"Really?"

"Yeah really; what do you think?" asked Jack.

"It can't hurt, so why not?"

"Why not? Because that head-shrinker has already got Kathy brain-washed, and he isn't doing that to me," said Jack.

"Oh come off it man, brain-washed? Do you really think Kathy's the type to let someone easily influence her?"

"Well, he's done it," said Jack.

"I doubt it. Kathy's got a good head on her shoulders. She thinks things through pretty good. Isn't that right?"

"Normally I'd agree with you, but this guy's got her spouting some psychobabble that don't make any sense," said Jack.

"So even if he has, you're afraid he'll get inside your mind without your permission? Come on Jack, why would he want to do that?"

"I don't know, but he's got Kathy singing his tune," said Jack.

"And what tune is that?"

"The tune that we've got marriage problems, or some bullshit like that," said Jack.

"Maybe you do have marriage problems. I mean, Kathy's unhappy enough to go to therapy, and ask you to go to marriage counseling."

"The only problems we got are in Kathy's head. We'd be fine if she could just stop carrying a grudge. She keeps on harping on the same old crap again and again," said Jack.

"Look man, this guy isn't going to brainwash you, so what's the harm in giving it a try. At least you can show Kathy that you're giving it a go."

"I don't know man…maybe it would get her off my back," said Jack.

"It might…And do you really think the only problem is Kathy?"

"Of course I do. Why do you ask? You know that Kathy's a real handful."

"Hey man, it takes two to tango, right? How can it all be in Kathy's head? Do you play any part in the problem?" asked Mike.

"Now wait a minute, you're saying that I'm the problem here?"

"No, I'm not saying you're THE PROBLEM, I'm saying that you and Kathy might both be playing a role in this. Isn't it a bit arrogant of you to say it's all Kathy?" suggested Mike.

"Hey screw this! I don't need one of my good buddies telling me I suck as a husband. I would have thought you'd back me up on this. It's hard enough with Kathy riding my ass."

"Now wait a minute, it's because we are good buddies that I'm try to help you deal with this. Take a step back and look at this objectively. How many wives ask their husbands to go to marriage counseling when there's no problem? Come on man, you're in denial," said Mike.

"Just forget it, Mike. You don't get it. I'll have to find somebody else to give me some feedback."

"Oh, don't be that way. You know I'm trying to help you out. Don't close me out," said Mike.

"Just forget it. I don't want to talk about it anymore."

The River: Day 5

The next day broke cloudy and humid. Without the sun to wake the campers, they all slept late. All four were weary from the difficulties they'd encountered, and all but Kathy were physically fatigued as well. Kathy ran her hands through her hair and made a face. Kathy pulled Stacy aside. "Stacy, are you going to bathe?"

"Definitely before we break camp today," answered Stacy.

"I just have to wash this morning, but how can we do it privately?"

Stacy looked around their new campsite. "Tell you what, let me grab my toiletry bag and we go find somewhere right now," suggested Stacy. Stacy told Mike where they were going, and off they went. Jack noted their departure with alarm.

"Hey wait a minute Stacy, what's for breakfast?" asked Jack.

"We went over that last night. There's nothing for breakfast. We finished off the pancake batter yesterday," Stacy explained.

"How do you expect me to load up and then paddle the boat on an empty stomach?"

"Oh Jack, just go have a couple of…wait a minute, I'm sorry. I don't want to go there," said Kathy.

"No, good idea, I think I will," said Jack as he opened the ice chest. Jack cracked open his first beer, and when he turned to display it to Kathy, she was already gone.

Mike and Jack broke camp and loaded up the boat. Mike checked the patch on the hull, which continued to hold. After they finished their work, Jack opened another beer. He offered one to Mike, who declined. "No, I'll wait to have one with my lunch in a few hours."

"I can't believe we agreed to wait until noon before eating anything. That was stupid," said Jack.

"Maybe, but it would be even more stupid to eat all our food and have nothing left to look forward to eating," returned Mike.

"Oh Mike, we'll be back long before we run out of food. You worry too much, man."

Mike fetched his dirty laundry, which by now was everything he'd brought with him. He went down to the river and washed all his clothes, and then his body as well. Jack watched while he drank his third beer. Mike looked up and noted Jack's idleness. "Hey, go and tell the ladies it's time to shove off. We're burning daylight," said Mike.

Jack headed off in the direction he'd seen the ladies leave. He expected to find them in the next cove, but was surprised to see no sign of them when he rounded the point. He threw back the last swallow of beer, crushed the can, and then threw it into the river. As he neared the next point, he heard voices. He stopped in his tracks and strained to hear what the ladies were saying. Not being able to discern any content, he crouched and crept closer. He lay down on the sand dune separating his cove from Kathy and Stacy's cove. Jack pulled himself up on all fours to the crest of the dune. He waited until he heard their voices again, trying to judge the distance from him. They sounded far away, and he slowly raised his head above the edge of the dune.

First Jack saw ladies' clothes lying out on brush near the water, and he ducked back down, being surprised at the close proximity of them. He raised his head again and found Kathy and Stacy washing their hair, standing in waist deep water-nude. Jack ducked back down, fearing being discovered. He slid back down the down and hiked fifteen yards away from the water where he found low brush. He crawled through the brush until he reached the top of the dune. Jack peeked over the edge and smiled as he found the ladies still bathing nude. He took stock of his camouflage, and nodded with contentment that he was well hidden. Jack leisurely watched Kathy and Stacy repeatedly dunk themselves under water, washing out the shampoo. The cool water shone in the morning sun as it ran off their bodies.

"Wow, I didn't realize what a hot body Stacy's got," he whispered.

Just as the words left his mouth he dropped to the sand. Kathy turned around and looked his way. When Jack raised his head, Kathy had turned back. Jack watched as they dried themselves and redressed. When they were fully clothed he scampered back down the dune and retreated forty yards. Then he called to them, "Hey Kath, hey Stacy, where are you! Come on back, it's time to go!"

"Okay, we'll be right there," called back Stacy.

Jack waited until they rounded the top of the dune. "Oh, there you are. Hey Mike wants to head out."

"Yeah, we're done," answered Kathy.

They drifted down the river at a slow pace. Mike eyed the dark clouds moving in from the east. It appeared to be raining in the distance. The wind had been gentle when they awoke, but had been freshening all morning. Mike worried about what they might be in for, but kept his concerns to himself. He removed his hat and wiped his forehead with his arm. He turned to Stacy and said, "I've definitely got less energy today. I can't paddle as much without feeling wiped out."

"I'm feeling the lack of breakfast myself," said Stacy.

Around noon they beached the boat and fired up the stove to cook hot dogs. Hot dogs, chips and beer or bottled water was on the menu today. In spite of their poor fare, they all fell to their lunch with eagerness. After eating his last bite, Mike hiked up to a low hill and looked east. He hurried down the hill and began loading the boat. "Hey Jack, give me a hand. I want to get going before the storm hits."

"What storm? The weather seems pretty nice to me. The clouds are keeping it cooler," said Jack.

"Cooler's great, but we'll see what comes," said Mike as he loaded the stove under the bow. The ladies climbed into the boat and Mike and Jack shoved off.

The wind came up soon after they launched, and blew them along at a faster pace. Mike and Jack had to man the paddles constantly, since the wind blew them downriver and towards the western shore. They had to paddle constantly to keep from getting blown onto a western beach. It began to sprinkle.

"Here we go. I'm afraid we might be in for a pretty good storm," said Mike.

"It might help us. I mean it is blowing us faster to the truck," observed Jack.

"Yeah, if we can keep off the shore. I'd prefer no wind," said Mike.

"You worry too much man, the storm's gonna help us out," said Jack.

The wind strengthened and the sprinkle turned to a downpour. The boys had to pull harder on their paddles to keep the boat headed downriver, and not headed diagonally. The wind blew even harder in gusts. Mike looked up at the bimini, the boat's canopy, and saw the canvas straining to the point that he feared the aluminum bars might bend.

"Stacy, help me take down the bimini. I'm afraid we're going to lose it!" yelled Mike over the wind.

Mike and Stacy unlatched the bimini from the windshield. Just as they did a gust of wind ripped the straps out of their hands, flinging the bimini to the stern, slamming into Jack and knocking him overboard.

"Jack! My God, Jack's overboard!" screamed Kathy.

Kathy searched the water from the stern of the boat. Mike dug through his under cabin. Jack's wild eyed face surfaced, looking startled and alarmed. He sputtered and waved them to come get him, surprised at how far away from him the boat already was. Mike scrambled to grab a rope and tie it to his throw ring. He threw it as far as he could towards Jack. He tied the other end to a cleat. The river was covered with whitecaps and two-foot swells. Jack saw the ring hit the water five yards in front of him. He put his head down and dug into the water and swam for the floating ring. When he looked up again he was astonished to find the ring further away. Mike realized the wind blew the boat faster than Jack. Mike reached for the paddle. The boat became a sail for the wind, blowing them twice as fast as Jack, who provided little sail for the wind.

"Stacy, grab the other paddle! We have to slow the boat down for Jack. The wind's blowing us away from him," yelled Mike.

"Hurry up! He's getting farther away!" yelled Kathy. She cupped her hands and screamed, "Swim harder, Jack!"

Mike and Stacy strained at their paddles, trying to paddle upriver. Jack took a deep breath and put his head back down and swam with all he had. He looked up and the rope was closer, but still out of reach. Jack didn't have much strength left. Panic began to surge through his veins. He treaded water for a few minutes and tried to ignore the panic, and then swam with all his strength.

Mike tore off one of his seats and riffled through the storage area. He pulled out another rope and glanced at Jack. He tied the end of the second rope onto the rope attached to the floating ring to give Jack more rope and more of a chance, since the wind didn't push the ring as fast as the boat.

Jack was desperate for the salvation of the ring, but resisted the temptation to cease swimming and look up. He dug a little deeper and swam another ten yards before he felt something hit his shoulder, and raised his eyes to see the ring. Mike pulled him in.

Once Jack was safely aboard, he collapsed onto the boat. Mike fell back into the seat spent, and then glanced at the western shore, and saw it fast approaching. As he surveyed the shoreline, the next half mile was nothing but rocks. He grabbed his paddle and pulled at the water. "Stacy, we have to keep us off the shore until we can find sand. If we hit those rocks we're through!"

Stacy nodded and picked up her paddle and went back to work. Kathy dug out a towel and wrapped up the shivering

Jack. The storm had lowered the temperature dramatically. "I was so worried about you! You almost drowned," said Kathy and she held onto Jack.

Minutes later Stacy's arms burned and the energy quickly ebbed from her body. "Hey Jack, I can't paddle much longer. Can you take over for me," asked Stacy.

Jack stood and took the paddle from Stacy. His arms felt like spaghetti noodles. He used his body weight to lean into each stroke. When he looked to the shore he saw an outcropping of rock jutting into the river. "Mike, look at that!"

Mike nodded and both men strained at their oars. Their arm and leg muscles shook and begged for rest. Mike could see they weren't going to make it like this. "Jack, dig your paddle deep into the water and hold it against the side of the boat! Our only chance is to steer ourselves around that rock point," yelled Mike over the wind. The boat responded to the twin rudders by steering towards the edge of the rocks. Stacy saw that they weren't going to make it and jumped onto the gunwale and pushed off the rocks with her legs. However, the hull groaned as it scraped along submerged rock. "Dear God, let the hull hold out," pleaded Mike.

As they cleared the point Mike glanced over his shoulder at the shoreline while continuing to hold his paddle against the gunwale. A sand beach approached on the western shore, and they steered the boat onto it. Once on the beach, Mike scampered around and made the boat fast to the shore, tying his strongest rope to a boulder on the beach. Then he dug his two anchors into the sand. He and Jack piled up several large rocks on top of the anchors to help hold them fast. The exhausted men joined the ladies underneath the cabin where they were already huddled in towels. Moments later the rain was joined by hail.

At first the hail were only the size of buckshot, but quickly turned to large marble sized balls of ice. It made such a sound when it slammed into the boat that it sounded as though the fiberglass were cracking. Soon the bottom of the boat was all white with ice marbles completely covering the carpeting.

"Mike, all our stuff's getting drenched," said Kathy.

"I know, but what can we do about it now?" Mike responded.

"Couldn't we cover it with the canopy?" asked Stacy.

"I'm not going out there in the hail. Maybe after it stops hailing Jack and I can tie the canopy over our gear," answered Mike.

Three hours later it finally stopped raining and hailing. The sky reflected patches of grey cloud and blue sky. Mike handed Jack the other bucket and the two men began bailing buckets of hail back into the river. Kathy and Stacy scooped hail with their hands. Everything in the boat that wasn't under the cabin was wet, and even some of the stuff under the cabin was wet, thanks to the wind.

They decided it was too late in the day to try to make it any further downriver, and none of them had any energy left anyways, so they set up camp. With the sand wet, they were all covered with sand by the time camp was pitched. They rinsed off in the river and shivered under damp towels. It was still cold. When he stopped shivering, Mike pulled his map out and spread it on the boat dash. He was making his calculations. Jack joined his friend in the boat.

"Let me guess, don't tell me, we made twenty miles today," estimated Jack.

"I wish. Jack, you get the optimist of the year award. We made twelve miles today," answered Mike.

"No way! That can't be right. The wind had to have helped us more than that. Let me see that map." Mike showed Jack the landmarks he used to calculate their position.

"Jack, the wind was mostly pushing us into the shore, remember? And if we're here, that means we're still twenty-four miles from the truck," said Mike. The women overheard their conversation and joined them.

"No! My God, Mike, what are we going to eat? We're down to four hot dogs, and the turkey's gone," said Stacy.

"How we can have nothing left? Didn't you plan for a week's trip?" asked Kathy.

"I know we planned for seven days of meals, so what did we have planned for the end of the week?" asked Mike.

"Barbecued chicken for dinner and roast beef sandwiches for lunch the last two days," answered Stacy.

"So what happened to the chicken and roast beef? Didn't you get them out of my freezer?" asked Mike.

"The chicken we threw away. Remember it was spoiled," said Stacy.

"Oh yeah, but what about the roast beef?"

"Was I supposed to get that? I got the frozen hamburgers out of the freezer, but I didn't see anything else."

"I thought I told you they were in the back, behind the orange juice?"

"Oh my God I'm sorry, I didn't get them. I never saw the roast beef," Stacy apologized.

There was silence amongst the campers as they took in this new revelation. "I guess that explains what happened to the food for today and tomorrow. Maybe I didn't tell you about the roast beef in the first place," groaned Mike.

"Maybe, or maybe I just forgot," acknowledged Stacy.

"Well, I guess it doesn't matter now. But what are we going to do for food?" asked Mike.

"When will we be back to the truck?" asked Kathy.

"Probably tomorrow night," hoped Jack.

"I doubt it. I think the day after is the earliest," said Mike.

"Great! So we've got four hot dogs for two days," moaned Kathy.

"And a bag of chips and a case of beer," added Jack.

Kathy dismissed Jack with a wave of her hand and barely restrained herself from rolling her eyes, and then turned and walked off in a huff. Jack shrugged his shoulders, "Well, be that way. I choose to look on the bright side." The other two just watched Kathy hike over a low hill upriver.

After a prolonged silence, Mike stood and rummaged through his under cabin. "What are you doing?" asked Stacy.

"I'm going to try to catch some fish. I can't just sit here. I have to do something." Mike grabbed his fishing pole and tackle box and headed off upriver. Mike hiked back upriver a couple of coves, until he came to the rock outcropping they almost ran aground on. It seemed a likely place to catch some fish.

Mike sat down on a rock and waited for a bite. He hadn't heard her approach and was surprised to hear a voice. "How do you put up with his childishness? I suppose you've done better at being his friend than I have at being his wife," said Kathy.

"Sometimes he does get to me," laughed Mike.

"Do you ever get so frustrated you want to just delete him from your life?" asked Kathy. Mike turned to look Kathy square in the face. "I know you're having a rough go of your marriage," he said.

"I figured that Jack would tell you." Kathy sighed. "I know that you're Jack's friend and that we don't know each other well, but I could use a friendly ear right now."

"Sure I'm listening," said Mike, "but I want to warn you that I'm not interested in taking any sides."

"That's fair enough. I'm not looking for someone to take my side, just to hear me out. There's no way for me to reach anybody out here. I get no cell service." Mike waved Kathy to continue as he checked his line.

Kathy sighed and said, "I keep hoping that we'll be able to work it out. I get so frustrated all I want to do is strangle him. Some of the things he does with money leaves me wanting to pull out my hair…but I guess money doesn't matter so much right now. I'd gladly pay fifty dollars for a nice salad…anyways, I keep hoping he'll finally grow up and be a man, and then I realize that it's not really happening. I suppose I'm just so frustrated. I mean I wanted to pick up a handful of sand and throw it in his face when he said we'd be back to the truck tomorrow, no problem."

Mike reeled in and recast his line. "Yep, everything you're saying is true about Jack."

"You mean you see it too?" Kathy asked eagerly.

"Of course, I've saw how Jack handled money in college."

"I'm so glad you see it too. Sometimes I still wonder if I'm just crazy. Everyone else seems to love fun-loving Jack, and why am I such a bitch that I can't see what a great guy I've got."

"Yeah he can be a lot of fun to be with," said Mike.

"I almost didn't come on this trip. I feared it'd be another nightmare of a trip for us. Do you think I made a mistake by coming?"

Mike looked away and thought before responding. "I don't really know, Kathy. I don't want to betray Jack's confidence, but I don't think he'd mind me saying that he certainly is hoping this trip will help you guys with your marriage."

Kathy sighed deeply and said, "Oh maybe I shouldn't have come."

"Kathy, I can't say whether that's true or not, but maybe this trip will somehow help you two…I don't exactly know how, though."

"I hope so." Mike and Kathy sat in silence. Tears formed in the corners of Kathy's eyes, and slowly made their way down familiar tracks. Mike saw her tears and said, "I know you're both going through hell. I'm sorry for what a rough season's it been." Kathy nodded in appreciation.

"I don't want to pry Mike, but…well I sometimes wonder if Jack sees any of his own problems? I just thought, well, I thought you might know."

"Man, that's a hard one. Sometimes I get the feeling that he sees some of what he's doing, but then he'll say something and it doesn't seem like it at all. I guess that's probably not much help to you, but I don't feel free to get into the specifics for the sake of Jack's confidence in me."

"Oh I totally understand. I wouldn't want you to betray his trust in you. And actually what you said is helpful."

"I can tell you that I've confronted Jack quite a bit, and he does seem to think about what I say, well at least sometimes he does…can I give you a little feedback?" said Mike.

"Oh, please do."

"Sometimes you can be a bit judgmental," suggested Mike.

"You think so?" said Kathy. And then Mike almost dropped his fishing pole.

When Mike left to go fish, Jack and Stacy got the stove out and prepared for what little cooking they'd do when Mike and Kathy returned. After a few minutes there wasn't anything else to do, so Stacy pulled out her book to read before it was too dark. Jack paced back and forth across their narrow strip of beach. When Stacy next looked up Jack was standing next to her.

"I don't know what I'm going to do with Kathy," Jack began. Stacy waved him to sit down next to her as she closed her book.

"I thought if we got away from it all for awhile, maybe we could get back to the way it used to be for us…damn, it seems like it's gotten worse out here, not better at all. It seems like we keep fighting. I don't know how to stop it. I wish Kathy would just get off my back. Sometimes she's the biggest bitch I've ever met! Is there anybody more critical than her?"

"She can be critical. I've seen that on this trip," sympathized Stacy.

"That's putting it mild! You're seeing her in her better moments. You ought to see her when there's no one else around to keep face for. She says things to me that I wouldn't expect from my worst enemy, not that I really have any enemies. What do I do? I don't know how to get her off my back. You're a woman, any ideas?"

"You know, Jack, sometimes you provoke her pretty good."

"What do you mean?"

"When we're down to our last four hot dogs, mentioning the case of beer makes it sound like we ought to have a party tonight, you know?"

Jack laughed nervously. "Well there are nutrients in beer, you know?"

"That's exactly what I mean. If I were your wife, that would piss me off to hear that when all I've had is a hot dog and a few chips all day."

Jack laughed again. "Maybe you're right. I'm just trying to keep our spirits up. It's not like we're going to die or anything."

"Probably not, but Jack, there is a good chance we're going to run out of food before we get back. Some people starve to death in situations like this, you know?"

"Maybe, but you make it sound so dramatic when you say it like that. I mean come on, we've got all the water we need, a boat that floats and protein bars to keep us going until we get back."

"That's probably how it's going to happen, but Jack you're not acknowledging that it might not go that smoothly. Bad things happen to people. Maybe Kathy just wants you to acknowledge that. I'm not too fussy about food, but a diet of protein bars and water for a couple days doesn't sound too appealing to me either."

Jack sighed and got up. He went back to the water's edge and resumed his pacing the shoreline. Stacy watched him go, and felt more empathy for Kathy. Then she reopened her novel.

"I got one! I got one!" Stacy and Jack saw Mike coming over the low hill holding a bucket up for all to see. He grinned with satisfaction and triumphantly marched into camp, with Kathy walking slowly behind him with a smile on her face.

"Hey man, let's see what you got," said Jack. Jack and Stacy peered into the bucket to see one trout, appearing to be about a foot long.

"I know it ain't much, but at least we got something else to eat besides hot dogs again," said Mike.

"No, it's great," said Stacy.

"Absolutely! Let's fire it up. I'll light the stove," said Jack.

"Should we cook up the last four hot dogs also?" asked Stacy.

"Yeah, let's make it a feast," gushed Jack. "We'll have surf and turf tonight."

"I don't know, maybe we ought to save some meat for tomorrow," said Mike. "What do you ladies think?"

"I know I might regret this tomorrow, but I say we eat up tonight. I mean, it's not like four people will be feasting on four hot dogs and a small fish," answered Stacy.

"Sounds fine to me," replied Kathy when they looked at her.

"Alright, so we cook 'em up," said Jack.

The fish lifted the spirits of all, even though nobody had more than a bite or two. Mike and Stacy joined Jack in enjoying a beer with dinner. Jack enjoyed enough beer for him and Kathy together. Kathy picked up a folding chair and walked upriver to the low hill and sat down alone with her thoughts. "Now what's she doing? Kathy's so antisocial," complained Jack.

"Give her a break Jack. This hasn't been exactly a fun vacation for her," said Mike.

"What? So now you're on her side?"

"I'm not on anyone's side. I can see how the marriage sucks for both of you," said Mike.

"I thought you were on my side, man. I mean, what are friends for if you can't count on a buddy taking your part in something?" countered Jack.

"Look Jack, you're one of my best friends. But what kind of friend would that be? You want someone to just tell you what you want to hear, even if you got a blind spot?"

"Oh, so now you're calling me blind?"

"Just forget it. You're not getting what I'm saying," said Mike.

"That's exactly what Kathy always says to me."

"Well, maybe there's something to it," suggested Mike.

Kathy set aside her magazine. It was too dark to read. Her thoughts returned to her conversation with Mike an hour earlier. There was something about talking with him that felt good to her, but she couldn't quite put her finger on it. Kathy thought, there's a noticeable difference talking with Jack versus talking with Mike...I like the way I feel with Mike a whole lot better than the way I feel around Jack. I so often feel mean-spirited with Jack, but I don't feel that way when I talk to Mike...I wonder what the difference is...It sure is nice to feel more like a woman to Mike. It sure would be great to be with a man that I feel feminine and attractive around...maybe I'll find that someday...hopefully with Jack.

40 Weeks after the River Trip

The TV droned on in the background. Jack stared at the screen without really seeing it. He was stunned. He couldn't believe what his wife had just told him. He awoke as if from a hypnotized state. It startled him to see the late show on the TV. "How long have I been sitting here?" he said aloud. Jack picked up the phone and dialed. A groggy voice answered. "Hey Mike, something's…uh, something just…something's come up. Can you come over?"

"Jack?"

"Yeah man, it's me. Can you come on over right now?"

"What time is it?" asked Mike.

"Don't know…it's…"

"Damn, it's 1:00 in the morning!"

"It is? Hey man I'm sorry it's late, but I need to talk."

"Can't it wait for the morning?" asked Mike.

"No."

Mike paused and Jack heard shuffling sounds on the line, and then Mike's voice, "Alright man, I'll be right over. This better be important." Jack set the phone down and looked at it as if he expected something further. Then he returned his eyes to the TV screen and waited.

A knock on the door jarred him out of another altered state. At first he was startled, and then he remembered about Mike. The moment Mike saw his friend's face he knew something was seriously wrong. Mike's concern for his friend went off the chart. He'd only seen that look on his face twice before. The first time was when Jack had learned of his favorite grandmother's death. Mike had been there that night too. Jack and Mike roomed together in college and were just finishing off a pizza in their apartment when the call came in. The happy and carefree Jack who answered the phone hardly resembled the Jack who hung up. It had taken Mike hours to get Jack to come out of his stupor. At first Jack wouldn't even move, and then he moved but didn't talk, nor did he respond to anything Mike said. It wasn't until past 2:00 am that Jack finally spoke. All he said was, "She's gone."

Jack's mother had gone back to work when he was young. Fortunately Nana lived with them after her husband's death, and became a second mother to him. Truth be told, Nana became his first mother. She took him everywhere she went. There were few boys in the neighborhood close to Jack's age, so he spent most of his time with Nana. Jack was one of those rare boys who actually enjoyed going to the mall. It was like Jack and Nana had been surgically attached at the hip, at least until Jack started school. And even then it was as though the Siamese twin surgery had only been partial.

The second time was when Jack's dad died. Mike had received a call Saturday morning while he was reading the paper and sipping his coffee. Mike dropped his paper and jumped in the car right away. He arrived to find Jack in an altered state. Jack sat in a chair with his dad's red hat in his lap. Mike tried to rouse him, but it took almost an hour before Jack would talk with Mike.

Mike found the same Jack tonight. Jack looked through him with unseeing eyes. The color in his face had drained to a dull gray.

"Jack, my God what happened? You look like somebody died!"

"Yeah," said Jack in a monotone.

"What do you mean? Jack, tell me what the hell's going on."

"She's gone."

Confused Mike asked, "Who's gone?"

"Huh?" said Jack.

"Jack, look at me." Jack semi-focused his eyes on Mike's face. Mike asked, "Jack, who died?"

"Died? Nobody died."

"Jack, you're not making any sense. What the hell happened?"

"Kath's gone."

"She's what?"

"Little while ago…first she got home from work, like any other night, and then she's packing a bag and gone."

"Gone where? Come on man fill me in, you still aren't making much sense."

"It's Kath, she left me."

"You mean she moved out?"

"Yeah, that's what I been saying."

"My God, what brought that on?"

"Don't know…she just did it."

"You mean tonight was the first you heard of it?"

"Yep."

"Damn, I mean I know you and Kathy were having some problems, but I had no idea it was to this point!"

"Neither did I."

"Did she say why?"

"Something about that she can't live like this anymore."

"That's all she said? What does that mean? There's got to be more to it than that."

"I don't know what else to tell you, I mean, she didn't really say much. She just asked me if I'd ever thought about leaving her."

"And have you?"

"Of course not; you know that! I'm committed to my marriage."

"Let me get this straight, this is the first time she's mentioned leaving."

"Yes, damn it! That's what I'm trying to tell you! This was totally out of left field. I don't know what got into her. I think it must have been that psychobabble group she joined. Ever since she started with that shrink and his groupies she's been different, saying weird stuff that nobody thinks about. I think they put it in her mind that she's unhappy and had to make a change. I think we would be just fine if they hadn't brainwashed her. That damned shrink, I outta send him a Christmas card and thank him for taking my wife away from me."

"Now wait a minute Jack, weren't you and Kathy having problems before she started that group? I mean, you've been talking to me about issues with her for over a year now."

"Yeah, but nothing like this. We had some minor issues to deal with until this psychobabble group blew things out of proportion."

"Maybe they weren't as minor as you thought. I remember a few times hearing you tell me stuff about you and Kathy, and thinking it didn't sound good at all," said Mike.

"Then why the hell didn't you say something!"

Mike looked away a moment before responding, "I tried to."

"Then how come I don't remember anything about that?"

"Because you didn't want to hear about it man! The times I tried to say something about this being a bigger deal than you was saying, you'd brush me off and change the subject."

"Oh shit."

"Look man, I'm really sorry Kathy left. I'm sure it's a kick to the balls. And I'm here for you. But look, now it's time that you let some people help you with your marriage. No more blowing me off. You're going to lose your marriage if you don't. It might already be too late."

"What are you talking about? How can you help me with my marriage? Kathy's the one with the problem. She's the one that left. Why don't you go talk to her?"

"Now come on Jack, this is Mike you're talking to. Don't pull that bullshit on me. There's no such thing as a marriage problem with one person at fault. Now level with me. What the hell's been going on?"

"What do you want me to tell you? I told you when Kath started that psychobabble group. That's when..."

"Come on man, I know you were having problems before that...look, I don't want to lay it on you too heavy now, with your wife just leaving and all, but you have to start leveling with me. You're talking like everything was just fine until Kathy started the group, and I don't buy it. If everything was so great why did Kathy join it?"

"I don't know, because she's got issues!"

Mike rolled his eyes, and then sighed. He threw up his hands and leaned all the way back into the couch. Mike's voice became barely audible as he said, "Look I can't help you if you keep feeding me that steady diet of bullshit. Maybe you really believe that crap and maybe you don't, but you're shutting me out. I'd like to help you out. Damn, we've been friends for over ten years, but I can't if you won't let me in. So if you want to keep up the game that this is all about Kathy you go right ahead, but I'm going back home to bed unless you start talking straight right now."

"Shit man, you really know how to bust a guy's balls," Jack began as he brushed the hair out of his eyes and then crossed his arms. "Alright, so maybe I'm not the best communicator in the world."

"What does that mean?"

"Kathy tells me I don't listen too good. She says I try to fix her."

"And do you?"

"I don't know...I guess I've done that a few times."

"A few times? Come off it Jack, how many times have I told you that when I want your advice I'll ask for it?"

Jack laughed. "Yeah well, I guess you have said that."

"So you've been hearing that from both of us. And what have you done with the feedback?"

"What am I supposed to do with it? I stopped giving you advice didn't I? And I tried to stop giving Kath advice."

"Maybe that's a start, but I think you have to take a deeper look at this one. Whatever you're doing obviously hasn't been enough."

"So now you're taking Kath's side. Is that it?"

"Come on man, you know me better than that! Of course I'm on your side, but I'm not going to blow smoke up your ass and pretend that the only problem is that you married a bitch."

"Well maybe I did marry a bitch. Just maybe that's the worst of my crimes is picking the wrong girl."

"Look Jack, maybe I'm being too hard on you right now…it's late, and I'm tired…I know you just took a pretty good hit," said Mike.

Jack nodded, and put his hands to his head. "I don't know what else to say man."

"Get some sleep, and we'll talk more tomorrow…I'm really sorry, buddy," said Mike. Jack nodded.

"I'm leaving…we'll talk tomorrow. I'll call you and check in with you," said Mike.

"Yeah."

Kathy sat in the food court at the mall. She picked at the salad in front of her, but didn't make much of a dent in it. Her stomach had been squeamish all day. She worked at her desk through lunch without noticing until she smelled food from down the hall. Kathy normally drank iced tea, but sipped a cola today to sooth her acidic stomach. She checked her watch about every fifteen minutes. Kathy kept reliving last night, as though the movie was stuck in a groove and kept repeating the same scene again and again. After lunch she spent a couple hours trying unsuccessfully to work on a file, and then she gave up and just replied to a few emails and left the office. Images of last night crowded every other thought out of her mind. Kathy brought the case file home with her, thinking she might work on it. However, she knew she wouldn't feel like it.

Tears welled up in her eyes as Kathy sat in the waiting room. Susan, who sat next to her, wordlessly put her hand on Kathy's shoulder and smiled sympathetically. The group sat down in Dr. Aragorn's office and all eyes turned to Kathy. She noticed everybody looking at her and said, "I guess it's obvious that I'm…last night I asked Jack if he's ever thought about leaving me. He said, 'why the hell would I think about that', and then asked me why I was asking. It seems like the most obvious question to ask, and I was totally taken off guard. I started stumbling over my words, and then he knew. Oh my God, he was so mad when I admitted it. He told me that 'this damned crazy-making group is brainwashing my mind and is going to cost us our marriage.' I said 'no, it isn't them. It's MY idea to try living apart. I want a trial separation.' You would have thought I told him I'd taken out a hit on his head. He said to 'just pack my bags and get the hell out right now!' I begged him to wait, and that I wanted to talk it out more, but he wouldn't hear of it. He said 'there was nothing to talk about, that I'm throwing away our great marriage and to just get on with it! Have you even given a single thought of what this will do to Lily? You're ruining her for life!' I almost died when he said that. I slumped to my knees and started crying. I didn't want to, but I couldn't help it. Oh my God, Jack got even madder. Even though I didn't want to leave yet, I was afraid to stay, with him that angry. I thought he might do something crazy. I mean, Jack's never hurt me or anything, but I've never seen him like that before, and I didn't know what he might do…I didn't know if I should wake up Lily and tell her, or check and see if she was still asleep or what…but I just couldn't tell Lily, so I packed a suitcase and went to my sister's," said Kathy as heaving sobs overtook her.

"Oh God, Kathy, I'm so sorry," said Jake. Dr. Aragorn looked at Kathy with watery eyes, but didn't speak. Karen handed Kathy the Kleenex box. Susan put her hand on Kathy's arm. Then another thought occurred to Jake, "He didn't lay a hand on you, did he?" Kathy shook her head without looking up.

"I couldn't sleep last night. I guess I dosed off sometime after two a.m. I could barely work today. Oh my God, am I being stupid? Am I throwing away a perfectly good marriage? Am I ruining my daughter's life? Am I being unbelievably selfish?"

"Give yourself some time, Kathy," began Dr. Aragorn. "You've just left and you're reeling. You'll need time to get your feet under you. You'll need to see what you and Jack do, and how it is to be separated."

"But what if I'm making a huge mistake? Oh my God, my head's spinning."

"Then you'll find that out. Allow yourself time to absorb the changes. The benefit of a trial separation is to see if it's a mistake," said Dr. Aragorn.

"But what if I've already ruined my marriage by leaving, even leaving temporarily? I'm afraid Jack's already done with me."

"If Jack's already done with you then there wasn't much holding you together in the first place," said Susan.

"Exactly!" said Jake. "If my wife had given up on me that easily I'd be long since divorced. How can you make a good marriage if it's that quickly broken?"

Kathy looked at Dr. Aragorn, who was nodding. "Kathy, you're really anxious and scared and probably disorganized. And you need to be. You're separating for now to give your marriage a last chance, and it took great courage to do so. You'll need time to get back on your feet. You're not being patient with yourself."

Kathy sat with her head in her hands. Her sobbing had receded to gentle crying. She dabbed at her eyes and nose, and then looked around the room. "I'm really thankful for you guys. I couldn't do this on my own…I don't know if I can do this even with you."

"You'll get through this. I know it doesn't seem like it right now. Did you know that I almost killed myself when Lane left me?" asked Susan.

Kathy shook her head, and Susan continued, "Yes, that's right. I had some valium for anxiety, and not one, but many nights I sat with a bottle of wine in one hand and a bottle of valium in the other. One night I poured half the bottle of pills into my hand and took a big drink of wine. I was about to take the pills when the phone rang. I think I would have gone through with it if the phone hadn't stopped me. I can't tell you how many times I almost ended it all."

"I don't think about taking my life, but…but I feel like I'm losing it, like I'm going crazy. My head feels like it's spinning, my hands are sweaty, I can't concentrate worth a damn at work, and I'm so depressed I don't care if I shower or eat. Am I losing it?" Kathy asked looking at Dr. Aragorn.

"You're not going crazy. You are disorganized and anxious and need our help more than ever. Stay with us, stay with your process, and we'll help you get through this. Trust me on this," said Dr. Aragorn.

"But how can you promise me that it will all work out okay?" asked Kathy.

"I can't promise you that. But I, and we can help you navigate this difficult road," explained Dr. Aragorn.

"But I want to know that it will all be okay in the end!"

"I know, Kathy…I know," said Dr. Aragorn softly.

"How long until you felt normal again?" Kathy asked Susan.

"I've never felt normal again," said Susan with a gleam in her eye. "To be honest, I didn't want to return to normal. My normal wasn't anything I wanted to return to. I wanted to do better than normal. I've had to face that I needed to work hard at my own growth if I was ever going to be happy. I didn't want to admit it to myself, but I never was happy before. I thought I was, but I was fooling myself, because I couldn't accept how disappointing my life was."

"Oh my God, you're scaring me," said Kathy. "Do you mean you had to get divorced to be happy?"

"Oh no, I don't think so. I still believe that if Lane and I had both been willing to do the hard work and make significant changes, we would have been able to make a good marriage. But no amount of taking the old marriage and giving it a tune-up and a paint job was going to do it. We needed an overhaul, a rebuild, but I think we could've done it. You're leaving Jack for yourself, but it might be the best gift you've ever given him."

Kathy looked over at Susan. "You're looking at me like I've just lost my marbles, but I mean it. You're giving you and Jack a chance for something truly grand. You're giving you two the opportunity for genuine intimacy and richness. Now I don't know if Jack wants that or not, and I guess we're going to find out."

"I doubt Jack sees it that way," said Kathy.

"Probably he doesn't, but I think Susan's right, the current version of your marriage is never going to work for you, and now you and Jack have the chance to make a new version," said Dr. Aragorn.

"I hadn't thought of it that way, but I think my wife and I have been trying to make a new version of our marriage. I'd like to think we have made a new one, but I'm not so sure. I'm worried that all we're doing is making a new and improved old one," said Jake.

"What if it is a new and improved old one? Maybe that's good enough," suggested Kathy.

"I wish it was, but I don't think so. You see, Linda and I hardly ever talked before, and now we do talk pretty regularly, but I don't think that alone will do it. We need to do better than talk, because Linda needs to feel like we're emotionally connecting somewhat regularly. And I need to feel like I can be honest with her. I used to just tell her what I thought she wanted to hear, but it pisses me off when I do that now. In fact, it used to piss me off back then too, but I just didn't realize it. I have to feel free to be honest or I won't want to connect with her. I worry that what we're doing isn't different enough to work for long," said Jake.

"But that sounds really good," said Kathy.

"Yeah, I can talk a good game, that's part of my problem. The real issue is whether I'm actually living it," said Jake.

"That's what I wanted! It still angers me that Lane wouldn't make a new marriage with me. Damn it, I wanted Lane to want a different marriage, but he never did," said Susan.

"Why not?" asked Kathy.

"I still don't really know. I think the bastard just wanted a younger and thinner wife...but I'm not sure that's totally fair," said Susan.

"I wonder if Linda would be open to me marrying you as well. You know, I've been considering becoming a Mormon. They make it pretty attractive with the polygamy and all," said Jake to Susan.

Susan smiled and looked away sad, and then said, "At first that seemed funny, and even an appealing offer, but I think I'm angry with you for making light of my pain."

"Oh damn it, I'm sorry Susan. I know I can overuse my humor," admitted Jake. Susan nodded.

"Maybe you feel uncomfortable that you've been able to save your marriage and Susan hasn't," suggested Dr. Aragorn.

Jake rubbed his scruffy beard and looked down at his feet. Then he said, "That could be, I guess I do feel bad for Susan, and also for Kathy. It doesn't seem fair. I was such a shit to Linda early on, that if anyone deserves to lose his marriage, it's me."

"Do you wonder if Susan and Kathy are jealous of you?" asked Dr. Aragorn.

"I don't think so. At least I hadn't thought that…are you jealous of me?" asked Jake.

"Wait! I don't want either of you to answer that," said Dr. Aragorn to Susan and Kathy. Then he turned to Jake, "I want you to first wrestle with that yourself before we ask them. It's something important to think about."

After a moment of silence Dr. Aragorn looked to Kathy, "Have you talked with Jack since you left?"

"To be honest I'm more concerned about talking to Lily. I still haven't told her that I won't be coming home for awhile. Oh my God, I just cringe inside whenever I think about telling her. And I don't even know what to say. I keep trying out different words, but nothing seems right. I feel like I might vomit every time I think about telling her."

"You're terrified of telling her," said Evelyn.

"Do I have to? Don't even answer that. I know I have to. I just don't know how to bring myself to do it."

"So what words come to mind for Lily?" asked Dr. Aragorn.

"Umm…Mommy's decided to leave Daddy. Mommy and Daddy might get divorced, but I still love you."

"Oh Kathy, you don't have to say something like that! No wonder you're so anxious. I mean you'd probably be anxious anyway, but pressuring yourself to say something like that has got to be making it worse," said Dr. Aragorn.

"So then what do I say?"

"Well, you might say something like 'Mommy and Daddy are trying to work something out between us, and I'll be spending more time over at Aunt Jane's for awhile. But I want you to know that I'll still see you almost every day. And I want you to know that this has nothing to do with you. Mommy and Daddy both love you very much, and we love each other, but we need to try something different to make things better,'" suggested Dr. Aragorn.

"That's all? Wouldn't I be lying by telling her that? You make it sound like I'm just going on a women's retreat for the weekend."

"So it's better to tell her everything now? What's the benefit to Lily of telling her that you are considering divorcing her daddy?" asked Dr. Aragorn.

"Because it's the truth."

"So you're lying by not telling her that you're considering divorce? Yes it's the truth, but I think you risk upsetting her and scaring her unnecessarily by saying anything about divorce at this point. She'll probably be upset no matter what you say, but I think you can help her adjust to the changes a little at a time. You can be honest without having to disclose everything," said Dr. Aragorn.

Kathy rubbed the back of her head, and then put her face into her hands before saying, "Oh my God, I don't know what to think! I definitely don't want to scare her, but..."

"Kathy you're going to scare her if you don't tell her something very soon. She's going to wonder why you didn't come home tonight. Don't pressure yourself to say everything tonight, but you have to tell her something," said Susan.

"Definitely tell her something tonight. Otherwise you leave it up to Jack to explain it to her," said Evelyn.

"Oh my God, I can't leave it up to him. I mean, he's so angry he might say almost anything."

"Okay, so what can you say tonight?" asked Dr. Aragorn.

"Umm...maybe just that Mommy's going to be at Aunt Jane's for awhile and that I'll still see her almost every day."

"Okay, that's plenty for now, but I want you to be prepared. What if she asks you why?" said Dr. Aragorn.

"I'll just tell her that Mommy and Daddy are having a disagreement and that I need some time away right now."

"That sounds good. A comment like that lets her know that you'll be away, and that it has something to do with Mommy and Daddy and nothing to do with her, which you might want to add, by the way," said Dr. Aragorn.

Kathy nodded her head slowly. "Okay, I guess I can do this. You guys pray for me."

"You're welcome to call me right after you talk to Lily," offered Susan.

"Thank you. I think I will."

"Have you talked to Jack since you left?" asked Jake.

Kathy shook her head and said, "I'm afraid to call him. I wanted to come here first. I don't know if it would be good to call. I kind of think it'd be better to let him cool off for awhile. I'm afraid of what he'll say."

"And what are you afraid he'll say?" asked Susan.

"I'm afraid he never wants to talk to me again."

"He might say that, and that would mean he's not ready to talk yet," suggested Dr. Aragorn.

"But what if he never talks to me again?"

"Then you'll have found out what you needed to know," said Dr. Aragorn.

Kathy nodded sadly and said, "That's the answer I'm afraid of."

"And maybe it's enough to just talk to Lily for now and leave Jack for another day," suggested Dr. Aragon.

On her way out to the car Kathy dug her cell phone out of her purse and speed dialed the house. She glanced at her watch and saw that it was Lily's bed time. The greeting with Jack's voice came on. Kathy waited for the prompt and said, "Jack, it's me. Look I know you're mad at me, but I need to talk to Lily tonight. Please, as a favor to Lily, please keep her up until I can get there and talk to her. I'll be there in ten minutes." Kathy dialed Jack's cell number and it went straight to greeting.

Kathy parked in front of the house. She took several deep breaths and walked to the front door. She knocked, and then let herself in with her key. Jack manned his usual perch, beer in hand. He glanced up as Kathy walked in, nodded and turned back to the TV. Kathy paused, unsure what to say. She stuttered, "Is Lily still awake?" It was a statement about her intent as much as a request for information.

Jack responded by taking another sip of his beer and keeping his eyes locked onto the screen. Kathy thought about repeating her question, but she was sure he'd heard her. She turned towards Lily's room. Lily's room was dark when she opened the door. Kathy turned on the lamp and crept to the bed. Lily turned over and said, "Hi Mommy," through sleepy eyes.

"Hi honey, I guess I woke you up."

"That's okay, Mommy."

"How was your day?"

"Fine."

Kathy rubbed her hands on her pants while she gathered her thoughts, and then began, "Lily, you've probably noticed that Daddy and Mommy have been mad at each other?"

"Yeah."

"Well, I've...Mommy and Daddy are working on not being mad at each other any more, and Mommy's decided to stay over at Aunt Jane's for awhile. I'm hoping it will help Mommy and Daddy to get along better."

"You're going to live with Aunt Jane?"

"That's right, honey."

"You don't want to live with me and Daddy any more," said Lily as her eyes widened.

"Oh honey, I so want to live with you! And I want you to know that you'll still see me almost every day."

"But I want to live with you, Mommy. I don't want you to live at Aunt Jane's. Can't you find a different way to not get mad at Daddy?"

"Oh my God…" and Kathy began to tear. "I know you do, honey…I wish there was another…oh Lily, I don't know how to explain it to you."

Lily began to cry, rubbing her hands in her eyes, "You don't want to live with Daddy?"

"Well, I do want to live with Daddy, but…oh honey, this doesn't make any sense to you does it?"

Lily shook her head, and then said, "How come you and Daddy can't get along? Aren't you trying to play nice?"

Kathy laughed nervously. "Uh well, yes Daddy and Mommy are trying to play nice, but sometimes…oh Lily I don't know if I can explain this to you. It's not exactly the same as playing nice with the kids at school. You don't live with the other kids at school."

"It's harder to play nice if you live in the same house?" asked Lily.

"Well no, I mean yes it is. That probably doesn't make sense to you, but there are some Mommy and Daddy things that I can't explain until you're older."

Lily stared into Kathy's eyes, weighing the information. "Can I come and live with you at Aunt Jane's?"

"Oh my God, Lily, I so wish I could take you with me. I don't think…" And then Kathy looked up and saw the fear in her daughter's eyes and stopped. She couldn't complete her sentence. And then she added, "I don't know honey, we'll have to see. But for now I'll come as see you almost every day. And sometimes I will take you with me over to Aunt Jane's."

"But I don't want you to go," said Lily softy as she wiped at her eyes with her fist.

Kathy turned away and dabbed at her eyes with a tissue, and then turned back to Lily. "Honey, why don't you turn over and I'll rub your back while you fall back to sleep."

When Lily was a baby and even a toddler Kathy often soothed Lily to sleep by rubbing her back until she submitted to sleep. At first Kathy began doing so out of desperation, having an upset child who protested whenever she left the room. But over time it became part of a bedtime routine whether Lily was upset at bedtime or not. In time, mother became more attached to the bedtime routine than daughter. When Lily was asleep before Kathy could get home she missed her bedtime ritual with Lily. The night after her first day of kindergarten Kathy began to rub Lily's back, when Lily turned over and said, "Mommy, I think I'm too old for you to rub my back anymore. Would it be okay if we stopped doing that?" That was the last time Kathy rubbed her back at bedtime, until tonight. And tonight Lily accepted her offer.

As soon as Kathy reached the end of the street she called Susan. "Please pick up, please pick up, Susan," Kathy said aloud. She let out a groan when Susan's greeting came on. Kathy hung up and hit redial. On the third ring she heard Susan's voice, "Hello?"

"Oh thank God you answered," said Kathy.

"Did you tell her?"

"Oh my God, I just did!"

"And?"

"And…" Kathy began to cry softly, which turned into sobbing heaves.

"Oh Kathy, I'm so sorry…my God this is tearing you up," said Susan. Susan waited until Kathy's sobbing eased before asking, "So tell me what happened."

"I didn't really know what to say. When I tried to explain it…it just sounded lame. And I could tell it sounded lame to Lily. And when she asked me why I was going, oh my God, I didn't know what to say," said Kathy as she pulled the car to the curb. Her sobbing returned.

"Oh Kathy, you poor thing," said Susan as tears came to her own eyes. Images of telling her own daughter came to mind, and she relived that memory.

Kathy's sobbing lessened and she said, "How do you explain to a six year old why you're leaving her daddy? Oh my God, there's just no way…"

"Oh I know. I remember fumbling for the words to tell Jamie. I felt like I was killing her little soul."

"She wanted to know why I wouldn't take her with me…I couldn't think of anything to say to that, but I had to tell her something. When I saw the look in her eyes I almost told her she could come."

"Oh Kathy, what a nightmare…I don't know what else to say."

"I know. Maybe there isn't anything else to say…it does feel good to have you listen."

"As awful as tonight was, I do believe you and Lily will get through this," said Susan.

Kathy was silent for a moment, before she said, "You're probably right, but it doesn't seem like it right now. I'm afraid Lily will never get over this."

"You can call me whenever you want. You will need us more than ever now."

"Thank you, Susan…well, I guess I'll go now…good night."

Kathy waited for Jack to answer the door, not letting herself in this time. She feared his anger erupting tonight. For the first time since the separation she was taking Lily for the weekend. Jack opened the door, nodded and walked past her to his car, started his car and drove away without a word, leaving Kathy standing speechless in the doorway. Kathy stared after Jack until his car was out of sight, and then closed the door and felt relieved; at least he hadn't exploded. She'd take winter anger over summer rage any day. Kathy shrugged and went to Lily's room.

Lily stood in the middle of her room with an open suitcase on the bed and most of her clothes piled in or near the suitcase with several items on the ground under her feet. Her favorite bear safely tucked under one arm. Lily turned and ran to Kathy when she saw her, "Hi Mommy! We're having a sleepover tonight, right?"

"That's right, Honey."

"I don't know what to bring, so I decided to bring everything I can fit in my Little Bears suitcase."

"We're going to have to leave some of this at home," said Kathy as she laughed. "I couldn't fit all this in my car, not to mention your Little Bears suitcase."

"Okay Mommy." Mother and daughter knelt together at the bed and decided what to bring, returning most of the clothes to drawers and closet.

Aunt Jane and Brian met them at a pizza parlor. Lily and Brian immediately pleaded for money to buy tokens, and then off they went to play the video games. Since Jane's husband often worked late, the four of them had done this many times. Kathy felt grateful for the familiar outing, wanting the weekend to not feel too different to Lily. Kathy worried that the first weekend at Jane's might be upsetting for Lily. In an attempt to minimize the drama of the separation, Kathy had couched the weekend as a slumber party with Aunt Jane and Brian.

The kids had to be pulled away from the Ms. Pacman game when the pizza arrived at the table. The pizza commanded little interest for Brian and Lily until the tokens ran out. It made little difference whether the pizza was hot, cold or anywhere in between. Kathy and Jane had miscalculated and given them too many tokens this time. On occasion they'd underestimated the token disbursement and had fussy kids complaining that the pizza took too long. Better too many this time, Kathy figured.

Kathy consciously tried to act like it was any other Friday night. However, she found herself monitoring Lily, looking over at her every few minutes to see if she seemed upset. Jane noticed and placed a hand on Kathy's arm and silently mouthed, "She'll be okay." Kathy gratefully squeezed her sister's hand and wiped away tears. She turned her head away from Lily.

After the pizza was gone and only three crusts with teeth marks remained, the two kids begged for more tokens and were soon back at the Ms. Pacman joysticks. Jane turned to her sister and smiled, "So how are you holding up?"

Tears welled in the corners of her eyes. Kathy dabbed at them with her napkin and shook her head. Then she said, "I don't know if I can do this. It's like someone's reaching into my stomach and trying to tear it in half…every time I look at Lily I start to cry."

"Oh honey, Lily will be fine. Little kids are indestructible," said Jane.

"She might look like it, but I'm afraid this is killing her on the inside."

"Oh don't be dramatic, she'll be just fine. She's got a mom that loves her and that's all that matters."

Kathy stared at her sister blankly, and then looked away.

Kathy occupied the guest room at Jane's, which was furnished with a small desk, a dresser and a day bed large enough to comfortably sleep Kathy. All of the furniture was painted white. Kathy unrolled Lily's sleeping bag on the floor next to her bed. Lily hadn't seen her mother grab the bag out of

the closet in her room and was surprised by its appearance. "No Mommy, I want to sleep with you," Lily said emphatically with an energy that surprised Kathy.

"You don't want to sleep in your Sleeping Bears bag?"

Lily stared at her sleeping bag and then back at the day bed and then had an inspiration. She picked up her sleeping bag and dragged it onto the bed next to the wall. "I want to sleep in my Sleeping Bears bag AND I want to sleep with you!"

"Okay Honey, that will be fine."

Lily positioned Kathy's arm around her before nodding off to sleep. Kathy shifted uncomfortably in bed, though being careful to keep her arm on her daughter. She gladly took a little physical discomfort this time, which was easily offset by the comfort of having her daughter next to her. Just the same Kathy lay awake longer than usual adjusting to her company. Even though she'd slept with Jack for years, they normally rolled to their separate corners of the bed when they finished whatever intimate gymnastics they may have enjoyed.

The sun shining in through the window reached her face and woke her. Kathy rolled over to get her face out of the sun and heard children's playful voices. She tried to take in the familiar and yet strange sound, and wondered where she was. The one child's voice sounded quite familiar, and soon Kathy placed it as Lily's. "Am I at home?" she said aloud. Kathy wondered if she had awakened yet, or was she still dreaming. Then she pushed up on one elbow and surveyed the room, recognizing the surroundings of Jane's guest room, and then she remembered she'd brought Lily over. Excited, she climbed out of bed and pulled on a sweatshirt.

She found Lily and Brian playing video games on the living room TV, and Jane sipping coffee with her nose in the paper. Jane looked up over the top of her reading glasses and smiled. "Thought I'd let you sleep in a bit," said Jane.

"What time is it?" asked Kathy.

"Late for you." Kathy studied the kitchen clock and was surprised to find that it was already 9:43, as she rarely slept past eight on any day that she wasn't ill. Kathy went over and rubbed Lily's back and said, "Morning."

"Mommy, don't mess me up. We're about to beat the boss," Lily responded.

"Okay I'll leave you two to your important work."

Kathy sat down across from her sister and picked up the local paper. She glanced at it absentmindedly and set it down. She found Jane staring at her and said, "It sure is strange having Lily here overnight...and really nice. When I went to say good morning to her I didn't know what to expect. I was so relieved she seemed fine that I almost gave her a bear hug."

"She's fine, Kathy. You're too worried about her."

Kathy poured herself a cup of coffee and refilled Jane's cup, and then sat back down. "So what do I do with her today?" asked Kathy.

"What do you normally do on a Saturday morning?"

"Uh well, I guess I normally drink coffee and read the paper while Lily plays with her toys or watches TV, and then I usually take her to the mall or the park and lunch."

"Then that's what we'll do."

The cars moved slowly down the crowded street. Kathy stared at them without really seeing them. Something about them drew her attention. She was jarred out of her reverie when her secretary's voice came out over the speaker, "Kathy, it's your sister on line two. Shall I take a message?"

"No, thank you, I'll take it." Kathy lifted the receiver and punched the button and with little energy said, "Hi Jane."

"Hey little sister, how's it going?"

"Okay I guess," answered Kathy.

"Still haven't heard from Jack?"

"No, not yet."

"He'll call you back eventually. The bastard sure is taking his sweet time. How long has it been?" asked Jane.

"Ten days."

After a strained silence Jane added, "Want to meet me at the mall?"

"No, I've got a hundred emails to catch up on. I'll probably be here another couple hours.

"Kathy, the last ten days you've been working twelve hour days, except when you're with Lily. If you don't let up you're going to kill yourself. I'm worried about you."

"It keeps my mind off Jack…well, sort of. It's just too painful to sit at your house and think about us all night. I pick up my cell phone every half hour to see if I've missed his call, and when I have to use the bathroom I take my phone with me. I never used to take my phone to the bathroom."

"I know, honey. I wish there was something I could do for you."

"There isn't. I just keep trying to distract myself so I don't think about my marriage."

"Kathy, you have to just forget about him, at least for now."

"But I can't! I wish I could."

"It does you no good to fret about Jack. There's nothing you can do until he calls you back."

"So how do I stop fretting? You don't get it. I can't! I push the thoughts away and they just come back. That's why I like working right now. It gives me a break from feeling haunted."

"If Jack doesn't call you're eventually going to have to move on with your life."

"But how do I move on with my life, Jane? Tell me how to do that! Should I start dating? Maybe I should go find a few guys to sleep with. Would that be moving on with my life? Right about now I'd love to do that. Do you think I like torturing myself with ruminations about my marriage? It's tempting to drink myself into mindless oblivion every night. I might even do that tonight if you keep on me."

"Okay, okay, you don't have to get mad at me. At least come to the mall with me and let me help distract you," offered Jane.

A lengthy silence ensued before Kathy answered, "Okay, but I'll need at least an hour to get to the most important emails. I want to bring Lily with me."

"Alright, I'll see you at the usual spot in an hour."

Tom spoke about his new dating relationship, and his anxiety and his efforts to treat himself with respect with this new lady. He was excited and hoped things would work out, but didn't want to get his hopes up too high. Kathy tracked Tom's processing, but made no comments. She felt numb and weighed down as though she'd been walking in cement boots. Her face felt imprinted in place, while her ears rang with a low din. She sat without moving and watched the group.

The group paused. Dr. Aragorn turned to Kathy and asked, "You haven't said anything tonight, Kathy. So where are you?"

"I don't know...I guess I'm just listening."

"You don't seem present tonight," added Dr. Aragorn.

"I don't feel here either. I think I'm checked out."

"What's that about?" asked Dr. Aragorn.

Kathy sighed and said, "I've been so anxious the last three weeks, it's really a welcomed relief to be checked out. I want to be *not here*. At least I can work and sleep now."

"Any word from Jack?" asked Jake.

Kathy nodded and said, "Yes, he called last week. He wasn't as mad. He just said I'm making a mistake throwing away a perfectly good marriage, and that I'm kidding myself if I think I'll find somebody better."

"And that's it?" asked Jake.

"And he said to get my act together and let me know when I'm ready to come back home."

"Just like that?" said Susan. Kathy shrugged her shoulders.

"You can't go home like that," said Evelyn.

"When Jack first asked me to come back I almost jumped in the car and drove a hundred miles an hour to get there. The thought of being back living with Lily sounds really good. I actually started packing my bags and had them all loaded in the car, but after I thought about it I realized that nothing's changed. No, I'm not ready to go home. I told Jack that we had to talk some things out before I could come back. He said, 'then let's talk'."

"So now what?" asked Susan.

"We've talked a couple times since…I don't know, Jack says he's willing to work on our communication, but when I try to address the issues something just doesn't…I don't know."

"Doesn't feel right?" asked Dr. Aragorn.

"Like when he says he gets that I'm lonely in the marriage and that he wants to understand me, I get confused. I mean I really want that to be true, but something just doesn't feel right. I suppose Jack gets that I'm lonely, but it doesn't really help to talk about it. I don't know what else I want him to do. I mean he's saying the right things."

"Maybe you hear the words, but don't feel it," suggested Dr. Aragorn.

"Yes, that's it. I don't feel him being…moved or impacted in any way. It's like he's cold."

"Yeah, he's gets the data, but doesn't let your loneliness penetrate him," suggested Evelyn.

"Maybe Jack doesn't know how to feel," said Karen.

"He sure felt when I told him I wanted a trial separation. I was afraid of him he felt so much," said Kathy.

"Yes, but he may not allow himself to be affected by your feeling. That isn't the same as being angry at the threat of you leaving," said Dr. Aragorn.

"Give the guy a break! You're expecting too much out of him. Maybe he feels as much as he can," said Karen.

"But Kathy needs more," countered Susan.

"But what if he's doing the best he can? What if he can't do more?" said Karen.

"Then he better learn in a big hurry, or he's going to lose his wife," said Susan.

"How's he supposed to learn? Who's teaching him how?" asked Karen.

"Kathy's given him plenty of chances. She's invited him to go to therapy on his own, she's offered to go with him to therapy, and she suggested books on communication. What else do you want her to do?" said Jake.

"I don't know…it just feels like you're not being fair to the guy. I know how it is to not know how to feel. I can barely feel now and I've been in group for a long time. Poor Jack hasn't had any professional help. It pisses me off that you're all dismissing him so quickly," said Karen.

"What would you have us do for Jack?" asked Dr. Aragorn.

"I don't know for sure…maybe give him another chance," said Karen.

"But what kind of chance?" asked Evelyn.

"What if you brought him in for a session with Dr. Aragorn? Have you done that yet?" asked Karen.

"No, I haven't. I doubt he'd come, but I guess I could offer," said Kathy.

"That's not a bad suggestion. Jack might be more open to coming in now that you've left. He knows you're serious now," said Dr. Aragorn.

"I really feel for the guy. He probably doesn't know what truck hit him last month," said Karen.

"I do want to give us every opportunity to save our marriage. I really don't want to get divorced. It's hard to imagine things being different with me and Jack, but maybe if he'd come in to see you," said Kathy to Dr. Aragorn.

"I sure am thankful that Linda gave me another chance. If she hadn't given me several chances, we'd be divorced," said Jake.

"What kind of chances did she give you?" asked Karen.

"At first she tried talking to me about the issues. In fact, she brought it up a number of times. Looking back I'm surprised how patient she was when I was totally defensive. After a few months of getting nowhere she asked me to go to couples therapy. Of course she'd been in individual therapy a couple years by then. I went one time to see a marriage therapist and wouldn't go back. The therapist was on Linda's side. Well, at least at the time it seemed like she was, so I quit. At that point Linda said to either find my own therapy or to pick another marriage therapist. She added that if I chose neither, then she would choose to move out. So that's how I ended up in this group. One of my buddies had been in therapy with Dr. Aragorn and recommended him."

"At least you were willing to give therapy a try. So far Jack hasn't been willing to even consider it. Every time I've asked he says he doesn't need no headshrinker. But I suppose I'll ask one more time," said Kathy.

Kathy braced herself for Jack's response. She expected a volcanic eruption, complete with lava flow.

"Oh you're kidding, right? Why can't we just work this out on our own? I feel like I'm willing to learn to communicate better. Why do we need a shrink for that?" asked Jack.

At least it wasn't as bad as she expected. "Jack, how well have we done on our own so far?" countered Kathy.

"Maybe we just haven't worked at it enough. Isn't there a communication book we could read together or something?"

"Just come in for at least one session with me, and we'll see how that goes. Maybe Dr. Aragorn can suggest a book, but I don't think we can do it on our own."

"Oh my God, I can't believe I'm considering seeing your shrink."

"Stop calling him that! You make it sound like he's some quack."

"Well, no comment…alright, alright, I'll agree to see him once, if you agree to come home."

"No Jack, I'm not making any deals with you. I'm not coming home until we make some genuine progress."

"Then why should I bother seeing your shrink, huh?"

"This isn't Let's Make a Deal. I won't come back until things are different between us. Look, he's really helped me. Give him a try."

"What do you want to be different? I don't know what else you want me to do. I think I'm listening way better than I was, and you're not giving me any credit for that," said Jack.

Kathy exhaled deeply, and then she said, "I know you're trying to listen. You are better at letting me talk without interrupting me or trying to fix me. But it just…it just seems like something's missing…I don't feel like I impact you."

"What sort of impact do you want? Do you want me to cry about your feelings, because that's not gonna happen."

"No Jack, you don't have to cry, although that would be nice if that ever happened, but I don't get any reaction from you, except when you offer advice. You just look at me."

"Are you saying that I'm cold and don't have any feelings?"

"The thought's crossed my mind, yes."

"We aren't going to solve anything with you insulting me. Come on Kath, give me some credit for trying."

"I know you're trying. But it's not enough for me. I'm sorry Jack, I wish I could tell you that what you're doing is great and that I'm so thankful, but I'm not."

"Well maybe you just need one of those touchy feely guys, like the ones in your shrinker group. I'll never be one of those faggots, so if that's what you need then don't bother coming back. Just go ahead and file!"

Kathy started at the loud noise, and pulled the phone away from her ear. Then she put the phone to her ear again and heard silence. She closed and dropped her phone into her purse and put her face in her hands, shaking her head slowly back and forth. Kathy slowly lifted her head and gazed out the window, a dull glaze to her eyes. The traffic on the street below flowed with the slowness of maple syrup that's begun to congeal. The cars moved in chaos, some moving this way and some that, as if the drivers didn't know where they were trying to get.

Jack threw his phone on the couch. It bounced off the cushion and landed on the brick fire place hearth, cracking the case. He picked it back up and cursed under his breath. Then he checked to see if it still worked. Seeing that it did, he phoned Mike.

"This is Mike?"

"Hey man, it's Jack."

"I was wondering when I was going to hear from you again. Sure took you a long time to think it through. What has it been, a week?"

"Yeah, but don't bust my balls about it. Look I've taken about as much crap from Kathy as I can handle."

"So have you decided to let me help you?"

At first Mike only heard silence on the other end. Then Jack replied, "Yeah man, of course. Was that ever in doubt?"

"It was on my end. I didn't know if you'd drop the 'it's all Kath's fault bit' or not."

"Okay okay, but don't bust my balls about it."

"Alright man, so what can I do you for?" asked Mike.

"I need your advice. Kathy wants me to go see her shrink. What do you think?"

"Why not go?"

"Because this is the quack that's put all these ideas in Kathy's head and caused her to leave."

"You don't think she made that decision on her own."

"No, I think that shrink and his groupies have brainwashed her."

"Now come on Jack, is Kathy the kind of person who's easily influenced and allows others to do her thinking for her?"

"Well…"

"Of course that's not her. I'm sure she's been influenced, but until she starts selling purple flowers in airports we have to assume she's making her own decisions."

"So you think I should go see her shrink?"

"I can't see how it could hurt, and it might even help. Maybe he can help you and Kathy work things out. Have you considered that possibility?"

"Not really."

"Jack, you're a great guy and you've been a good friend, but you sure can be a stubborn son of a bitch. Give the guy a chance before you write him off as a quack. What benefit is there to deciding that before you've even met him?"

"Yeah, I suppose you're right. Maybe I will give him a try, but I'm only going to one session unless that shrink shows me he knows what he's doing."

"If nothing else, you'll be showing Kathy that you're willing to try."

"I have tried! What do you think I've been doing?"

"Look man, let's not go there. I'm sorry I brought it up." Jack remained silent.

"So how come it's been a week since I heard from you?" asked Mike.

"Because you pissed me off. And I didn't want you to take any more shots at me."

"Did you think anymore about what I said the other night?"

"What did you say?" asked Jack.

"Well I guess you just answered my question."

"Come off it man, I need a friend in my corner right now."

"Look Jack, you need a friend who cares enough to give it to you straight. And the way I see it you've got a serious blind spot. That is, you think the whole problem's Kathy. And until you give that up, you have no chance of saving your marriage. So you might as well head on down to the attorney's office unless you're going to rethink this."

Jack was quiet as he mulled over Mike's words. At first he wanted to fire back at Mike and tell him he was full of shit. Fortunately he thought a moment longer and a ray of light clicked on in his mind. And then Jack responded, "You sure know how to kick a guy when he's down. But maybe you have a point. I do think Kathy's the one with the problem. Maybe that's not totally fair to Kathy."

"I'm not trying to kick you. I'm trying to help you look in the mirror. And that's huge!"

"What's huge?" asked Jack.

"You seeing the marriage problems as not just about Kathy," said Mike.

"I'm still not sure that we have any serious marriage problems."

"Now you're scaring me, Jack," said Mike.

"Yeah, well I better go. I have a phone call to make," said Jack as he hung up.

The River: Day 6

The campers awoke to the bright morning sun shining directly into their tents. They had inadvertently set up their tents facing east. Both couples had left their outer flap unzipped to allow more air in, since it was warm and humid, leaving the sun with only a mosquito screen to penetrate through to shine on their faces.

"Ugh, who turned on the damn lights so early," complained Jack.

Jack zipped closed the outer door and rolled back into bed. It became so warm in the tent that he and Kathy got up fifteen minutes later. Mike and Stacy were already folding their tent and bedding.

"Good morning campers, ready for another fun adventure on the river," chirped Jack.

Mike and Stacy just grunted at him. They'd been awakened even earlier by the sun. Mike threw the tent and bedding into the boat, and then went down to the river with a bar of soap for a river bath. Stacy joined him in her bathing suit. Kathy hiked over to the next cove to take her bath in private. Jack dove into the river to cool off. Mike, Jack and Stacy finished loading up the boat, and then looked around for Kathy.

"Hey Jack, where's Kathy?" asked Mike. "I'd like to get going."

Jack shrugged his shoulders.

"I saw her walk off with her bathing stuff that way," said Stacy pointing upriver.

Jack didn't respond.

"Jack, you want to go find Kathy?" suggested Mike.

"If you want her, go get her yourself," barked Jack.

"Okay. Can you pull the anchors while I'm gone?"

Jack nodded.

Mike climbed the low hill and stopped in his tracks when he caught sight of Kathy. Her hair was wet and her dirty clothes were folded on a rock next to her shampoo and soap. She sat on a nearby rock with her head in her hands. Her shoulders heaved silently.

"Oh Kathy," said Mike under his breath.

Kathy looked up through red eyes when Mike put a hand on her shoulder. I'm alright," cried Kathy.

"I'm sorry, Kathy." Kathy scooted over for Mike to sit down. Mike left his hand on her back.

"Hey, you want to talk about it?" offered Mike.

"I don't know what to say...I'm just really sad," sobbed Kathy. Mike nodded.

"Ever since we talked yesterday I've felt on the verge of crying. I still can't believe how things are between me and Jack." Mike just listened.

"I don't know, I feel like a loser, since me and Jack..."

"Come on, aren't you being a bit rough on yourself?"

"God, it's nice to hear that," said Kathy as she turned and laid her head on Mike's shoulder.

Mike was momentarily taken by surprise, but recovered and put his arm around her shoulders. Mike didn't know what else to say, and sat in silence. Kathy continued to cry softly.

The quiet moment was suddenly interrupted by a shout. "What the hell are you two doing? I should have known all along something was going on! I would expect this of Kathy, but I thought you were my friend! To hell with you both, I'm out of here!"

"Wait! Jack!" called out Mike, but Jack had already turned and left.

"Jack, you're way out of line this time!" shouted Mike. But Jack was already out of sight over the small sand dune. By the time Kathy and Mike crested the dune there was no sign of Jack.

Mike and Kathy rounded the next hill to see Stacy reading her novel in a chair by the boat, but no Jack. Mike hiked over to the next cove downriver, but didn't catch sight of Jack there either. Coming back he said, "Stacy, where's Jack?"

"Jack? How would I know? Didn't he come to find you guys?"

"Yeah, he found us. He accused us of doing something behind his back," explained Mike.

"Doing what behind your back?"

"When I found Kathy she was crying. I sat down and put my arm around her. And that's how Jack found us. I guess he figured the worse."

"That's just great! So where in God's creation is he now?" asked Stacy.

"I don't know, but let's find him. We have to get going," said Mike. All three spread out and searched for Jack.

Kathy searched downriver, and walked along the river's edge. After walking a half mile she encountered a wall of rock. She hiked inland in search of a way around the rock cliff, but after a quarter mile gave up and turned around. Low lying brush scratched up both her legs, and eventually the brush became too thick to penetrate. Kathy considered swimming around the rocky point, but decided against it. She figured Jack would not have gone to that much trouble. Kathy washed her legs in the river, and turned around and hiked back to camp. When she arrived at camp she found it abandoned, guarded only by the boat. She paced around for a few minutes, and then decided to make herself useful and finished loading the boat, except for the stove which was heavy.

Stacy had taken the upriver route, while Mike followed a trail inland from their campsite. Mike swept his eyes from one side of the trail to the other, and every so often stopped to listen for sounds. Forty-five minutes later he crested a hill. The hill afforded him a view of the river, several miles in both directions. Movement caught his eye downriver, but when he turned his head he couldn't detect any sign of Jack. Eventually

Mike gave up and hiked back to camp. He found both women sitting in the boat when he returned. Both women stood as they saw him approach. Mike shook his head.

"My God, you didn't find him either?" said Kathy.

"Kathy, I'm worried. I can't find Jack anywhere. And I looked from the top of that hill several miles in each direction," said Mike.

"Oh my God," said Kathy.

"I don't know what to do," began Mike. "I mean, you both looked upriver and downriver three or four coves, right?" Both women nodded. "I don't know where else he could be."

"Is he hiding from us?" said Kathy.

"Even if he is, so what do we do?" asked Mike.

A long silence ensued. Each of the three looked from one face to another. They looked at the hills, upriver and downriver, expecting to see Jack grinning at them. But he didn't appear.

"This is going to sound cold, but we have to leave. If we wait much longer, we all risk starving to death. It's already well past midday and we haven't even left camp. When we get back to the truck we can send out a search party for him," said a sober Mike.

"Oh God, I don't know if I can leave him here," said Kathy.

"Mike's right. We have to go. And you aren't leaving him. He left us, right?" reminded Stacy.

"Oh my God, I know you both are right, but…Jack? Jack! Come out! This isn't funny anymore! You've gotten our attention! Come back, you son of a bitch!" shouted Kathy.

Tears welled up in Kathy's eyes. She wiped them on her sleeve. Stacy put her arm around her neck and pulled her close. "I know, Kathy. I know this is hard on you. Maybe Jack will show up," consoled Stacy. Kathy nodded and wiped her eyes.

Mike hiked up to the low hill behind their campsite and called out, "Jack, we're leaving now! If you want to come with us, get your but down here now! We're leaving in five minutes!"

Stacy helped Kathy climb into the boat, and then she stepped into the boat herself while Mike slowly pulled and loaded the anchors. Mike surveyed the surroundings one last time, and then looked at the women. They both nodded. Mike pushed the boat into the river.

All three constantly scanned the western shoreline, searching for any signs of Jack. The winds were light and Mike was able to keep the boat in the middle of the river with ease. Conversation was almost non-existent. Stacy picked up the other paddle to help Mike. Kathy kept her eyes fixed to the Western shoreline. They remained floating downriver the rest of the day. There was no reason to stop for lunch, since they had nothing to cook.

At mid afternoon they all inhaled a protein bar. None were close to being sated, yet they would survive for now. Mike opened a beer, bringing water to his eyes. "Damn Jack, where the hell are you? Are you playing a trick on us, or what?"

Stacy put her hand on Mike's shoulder. "Hey Babe, I know you're worried about Jack, but it might be good for us to start fishing again," suggested Stacy.

Mike wiped his eyes with his hand. "You're right. I'll get the pole going."

Mike sat in the back of the boat, fishing pole in hand. His eyes followed the train of the shoreline, barely noticing the presence of the pole. Stacy rubbed sun screen on his neck, face and arms. Conversation in the boat remained sparse. Stacy and Kathy took turns minding the oars while Mike fished. He slipped down in the seat so he could rest his head against the back of the seat, holding the pole with one hand. Twenty minutes later Mike slept. The women decided to leave him be, knowing he was exhausted. They were all tired, but Mike had been bearing the heaviest physical labor since they arrived at the river.

By late afternoon all three of the boaters were asleep. The gentle current lulled them peacefully. They were jolted awake by a thud. They startled to consciousness and looked around. The bow of the boat rested against a high cliff wall, with the boat turning to the side. Mike grabbed his paddle and pushed off the cliff, and then pulled with all he had towards the nearby eastern shore just beyond the cliff. Stacy picked up the other paddle and helped Mike make a safe landing. Mike jumped off the boat and immediately inspected his hull. The fiberglass was spider-cracked and scrapped up, but remained sound for now. The sun hung just over the western hills, and the campers decided to make camp for the night.

"Damn, we might have sunk the boat, falling asleep like that. I can't believe I let myself fall asleep," said Mike.

"We all fell asleep Mike, not just you," consoled Stacy.

"I'm responsible for the boat. I have to stay awake. What happens if we lose the boat?"

"All right, so we designate one person to be on watch next time," suggested Stacy.

"Everybody get back in the boat, I want to paddle over to the western shore and camp there," said Mike.

"Why? Because of Jack?" asked Stacy.

"Yeah."

They made camp on a thin strip of sand and pebbled beach. They each had their ration of one protein bar. Nobody talked much. Kathy regularly scanned the hills behind them.

"I'm heading down to find a good fishing spot. I'm can't go much longer on protein bars," said Mike. He gathered his pole and tackle box and found a rock outcropping downriver to fish from.

"Okay, we'll set up the tents," suggested Stacy. Kathy slowly stood and helped Stacy unload the tents from the boat.

"You thinking about Jack?" asked Stacy.

"Of course."

"Where do you think he is?"

"Oh my God, I wish I knew. As much as I'm going to be mad, I hope he's just punishing us or something. Maybe he's shadowing us down river along the shore, or maybe along the ridge of the hills," said Kathy.

"But what if he's hurt?"

"I doubt it. It's just like Jack to do this. He thinks he's teaching me a lesson."

"Do you think he really believes there was something going on between you and Mike?" asked Stacy.

"No. Jack's just punishing me for everything he hates about me. He knows Mike was just trying to comfort me…I think. He may be immature, but he's not stupid."

"Even if he's punishing you, what's he eating all day?"

"What's he eating? What are any of us eating?" countered Kathy.

"Has he ever done something like this before?"

"Yes. We were car camping in Yosemite last year. We got in a fight and I told him I was going home. So I got in the car and drove off. An hour down the road I cooled off and realized I couldn't just leave him out there, and I turned around and went back for him. I got back to the campsite and he was gone. He was gone and all our gear too. I could swear that he was watching me. I could almost feel his eyes on me. So like an idiot, I waited at the campgrounds until dark, and when he didn't show I drove home."

"And what happened to Jack?"

"I got home, and there was no Jack. But there was a voice mail from a ranger station saying they'd found his body. At first I was freaked out, and started crying and wailing. And then I listened to the message again, and realized it was Jack disguising his voice. He arrived home a week later with a big grin on his face."

"Oh my God, that's a dirty trick! And he made you wait a week before knowing if he was still alive?"

"That's my husband, and my guess is he's doing the same immature game right now. That's why I'm not giving him the pleasure of looking for him anymore. He's not doing that to me again. If he comes back, he comes back; and if not, there's nothing I can do about it anyway."

Mike returned from his attempt at fishing. "Catch anything?" asked Stacy. Mike turned his bucket upside down in answer.

"Don't know if I can catch anything with these lures. I don't have any bait," said Mike.

"What did you catch yesterday's fish with?"

"The piece of hot dog that fell in the sand. How many protein bars do we have left?"

"Seven," answered Stacy.

"How much further do we have to go?" asked Kathy.

"About thirteen miles, but I can't be sure," Mike replied.

"Thirteen miles, so we should be back by tomorrow night then?" asked Kathy.

"That would be my guess, but again, I'm not sure about the distance. It's hard to tell without mile-markers. I'm going on terrain alone. Sometimes it all looks about the same out here."

"We better be back by tomorrow night, because we'll be eating Jack's beer by then," said Kathy.

52 Weeks after the River Trip

Kathy sat still and gazed out the window at the traffic. When the phone rang she started and answered, "Hello?"

"Let me know when the appointment with your shrink is," said Jack without emotion.

"Okay...so you agreed."

"Look Kathy, I'll go one time and see what happens. I make no promises after that, got it?"

"Okay, but..." Kathy was interrupted by a click in her ear. And the line went dead. Kathy thought about calling Jack back, but thought better of it and emailed him Dr. Aragorn's address and the appointment time.

Kathy fidgeted while she sat in Dr. Aragorn's waiting room. She kept checking the door, waiting for it to open, wondering when it would. Kathy looked up as the door opened. Jack's face had the appearance of smooth blacktop, almost featureless. Kathy smiled hesitantly and said, "Thanks for coming."

Jack nodded without looking at her and picked up a sports magazine from the table. Kathy glanced at her watch and realized they still had eight or ten minutes yet to wait. She grabbed her own magazine. Kathy flipped through the pages without really seeing what was on them. It was as if her hands knew what to do and didn't need her eyes to participate in the project.

Jack followed Kathy into Dr. Aragorn's consulting room. Kathy turned her head to look at him over her shoulder. Jack walked with his head down and arms folded across his chest. A flash of pleasure emerged on Kathy's face. She felt guilty for enjoying Jack's discomfort, and made sure to put her smile away before she faced Jack. Kathy sat in her usual spot on the couch. Jack sat at the opposite end of the same couch. "So Jack, what brings you in today?" began Dr. Aragorn.

"Ain't it obvious, man?"

Dr. Aragorn smiled briefly before saying, "I know Kathy invited you to come, but that doesn't tell me much about why you're here."

Jack eyed Dr. Aragorn as if he were a dull child. "Because Kathy made an appointment," said Jack with a half grin.

"Yes, I know why Kathy's here, but why did you agree to come in?" asked Dr. Aragorn.

"Look man, do I have to spell it out for you? Silly me for expecting that Kathy had filled you in. I'm here because she won't come home unless I come see you once."

"You don't want to be here, do you Jack?" asked Dr. Aragorn.

Jack shifted in his seat, looked at Kathy as though she might answer for him, and then said, "No, not really. I think we can work it out on our own. I don't get why Kathy won't just work it out with me."

"What do you think she'd say if you asked her that?" said Dr. Aragorn.

"She'd say we can't work it out on our own."

"That's right, Jack. We've tried, God knows I've tried to work it out with you, and I can't," said an exasperated Kathy.

"It shouldn't be this hard. Why can't you work it out with me? I mean I listen without cutting you off, I don't give much advice anymore. What else do you want from me?"

"I want you to listen with more than your ears."

Jack rolled his eyes and sighed, and then turned to Kathy and said, "Come on Kath, I patiently listen to your feelings, what else is there to get? You just don't give me any credit. I am listening to your feelings. You just won't give me a break. I think you want me to be crying and wringing my hands and afraid and bummed out. You want a woman with a dick."

Kathy threw her hands in the air and said to Dr. Aragorn, "What do I do with that? No matter what I say..."

"Hang on Kathy, let me talk with Jack," said Dr. Aragorn interrupting her. "Jack, you're trying to give Kathy what she wants and don't know what else to do."

"Yes! That's what I've been trying to tell her."

Dr. Aragorn turned to Kathy, "Okay, I think we can agree that Jack's made progress and is certainly trying to give you what you want." Kathy hesitated and then nodded. "And I think we can agree that he's hearing your words." Kathy nodded reluctantly. "Maybe what's missing for you is you want to know that your feelings affect Jack?"

"That's it. I can tell you hear my words," said Kathy turning to Jack. "I don't think it makes a difference to you whether I'm hurting or feeling great or whatever. Your expression doesn't change."

"That's not true. I don't want you to be hurting. Maybe I don't act like one of your groupies, but I don't want you to be down. That's why I try to help."

"But that doesn't help me. You try to help by making it all go away. I want you to know me."

"Come on Kath, you want me to be like your sister and get all hysterical about it. I can't do that. It's not my style." Kathy looked at Dr. Aragorn and shrugged, pleading him for help with her eyes.

"Okay Kathy, try to tell Jack about yourself now," said Dr. Aragorn.

"What's the point? I'll just be disappointed," said Kathy.

"Try it with me here so I can see what happens," directed Dr. Aragorn.

Kathy took a deep breath and exhaled slowly. "Okay, here goes. Jack, I'm lonely in our marriage. Looking back I think the marriage has been lonely for me since day one, but I didn't realize it until recently. I uh, I just can't bear to continue the way it is. Something has to give."

Jack glanced up at Dr. Aragorn, who nodded for Jack to respond. "What do you want me to do man, I've heard that crap a hundred times."

"I'm sure you're not hearing any new data, but humor me by telling Kathy what you're getting," said Dr. Aragorn.

"I know I know, our marriage has been a total waste and we never should have gotten married."

"You hear Kathy trashing your marriage, is that it?" asked Dr. Aragorn.

"Yep, what would you hear in that?" Jack fired back.

"I hear a woman who's awakened to how lonely she's been for a long time," answered Dr. Aragorn.

"Well ain't that a nice pack of psychobabble, putting a nice bow around a box of shit," said Jack.

"Do you hear Kathy saying you've been a failure as a husband?" asked Dr. Aragorn.

"Of course I do. What else could I get from that?"

Dr. Aragorn addressed Kathy, "Is that right? Do you think of Jack as a failing husband?"

Kathy looked down at the floor as she gathered her thoughts. "Yes, I do think Jack has failed me as a husband. I've needed a partner and I've never gotten that."

"You're devaluing Jack, Kathy," said Dr. Aragorn.

"Am I? Or am I just saying what I'm feeling?"

"I think you're deeply disappointed in how your marriage is, but right now you're laying it all at Jack's feet and dismissing him."

"That's it! I've been trying to tell you that for months now," said Jack. Kathy sighed deeply and looked out the window. She glanced at Jack with shinning eyes, and then turned back to Dr. Aragorn.

"Oh my God, I don't what to do that to Jack. I'm sorry, Jack." Jack's jaw fell open, and then he recovered and folded his arms and smiled.

"Well I don't hear 'sorry' too often," said Jack.

"So Kathy, let's see if we can get to what's behind your devaluing. How do you feel about your marriage right now?" asked Dr. Aragorn.

"I'm disappointed in how it is between us. I often feel like I have a roommate, but no husband…and I hate to admit it, but I know I haven't been an ideal wife either. I know I've helped make the problem."

"See what I mean," said Jack to Dr. Aragorn.

"See what?"

"She gives me no credit. She calls me a disappointment as a husband."

"Is that all you heard? I also heard Kathy say something about herself as a wife," pressed Dr. Aragorn.

"What, that she hasn't been ideal? That ain't much of an admission."

"Kathy may not be giving you your due credit, but this time you aren't giving her hers. Kathy knows she's created the marriage with you. And this time I don't hear her devaluing you. She's telling us how the marriage is for her," said Dr. Aragorn.

"I don't know doc, all I ever hear about is what I'm doing wrong, and what I'm not doing right. I don't ever get anything about her part in the problems."

"You feel blamed for everything," said Dr. Aragorn.

"Of course I do."

"So when Kathy talks about being lonely in the marriage, you hear what a good-for–nothing-husband you've been," suggested Dr. Aragorn.

"What else could I hear? Isn't that what she's saying?"

"That's not what I hear," said Dr. Aragorn. Then turning to Kathy he asked, "You've been lonely since before you met Jack, haven't you?"

Kathy nodded as she looked down, and then spoke softly, "Yes, it's true. I hate to let this be true, but I've felt lonely my whole life. It's only since I've started the group and begun to make friends with them that I've felt like somebody knew me. I mean, I've had some friends in college and maybe law school that got me some, but I haven't felt anything to this degree before."

Dr. Aragorn turned to Jack, "What do you feel as Kathy talks right now?"

"I hear that her life sucks and always has."

"Okay, but what do you feel as you listen to her?"

"I feel like that sucks."

"That's not a feeling. You're telling me what you think. Dig deeper. What do you feel as you listen to Kathy?" said Dr. Aragorn.

"Look man, I don't know what you want from me, I feel bad for her that her life has sucked, and I keep thinking that I know it's coming. I know she thinks it's my fault that our marriage sucks, and she thinks it's my fault that her life sucks. She's just not saying it yet."

"You have some sympathy for Kathy, but what competes with your sympathy is feeling blamed. Whenever Kathy talks about feeling bad, you hear that it's your fault," said Dr. Aragorn.

"That's right. Everything bad in her life is always my fault. I'm always disappointing her. No matter how hard I try, it's never good enough. I'm tired of taking the rap for it. If you're unhappy then deal with it yourself. Don't lay that on me!" said Jack.

"Is there something familiar about taking the rap for someone else's unhappiness?" asked Dr. Aragorn.

"Yeah, I just got done telling you. It's familiar our whole marriage."

"But before you met Kathy, have you been blamed for somebody else's life that sucks?" asked Dr. Aragorn.

"Look man, I know I'm supposed to start crying and tell you that my mother or father beat me since the day I was born, right? But I don't want to get into that psychobabble bullshit with you. I don't have any bad memories like that. Not everything was perfect, but on the whole I had a helluva good home life."

"Jack, I'm sure that Kathy has done some blaming of you, and I'm pretty sure that she's hitting a sore spot in you. No one likes to be blamed, but you've got your radar tuned in for it. You expect Kathy to blame you, even when she doesn't. Let me help you understand what's getting triggered in you," invited Dr. Aragorn.

Jack eyed Dr. Aragorn, then looked away and rubbed his stubble. He looked back at Dr. Aragorn and said, "Look man, there probably is something to me expecting to be blamed, and it probably has happened before. But I'm not interested in getting into my childhood and all that psychobabble. Save that for the people that want to be here. But I do want to stay married to Kathy, and if you can help us to communicate better and to get past this blame thing, then I'm all for that."

"Fair enough, if you can accept that what you're feeling is partly about Kathy sometimes blaming you, and partly about you being sensitive to being blamed, then that might be enough for us to work with," said Dr. Aragorn.

"Alright, so we understand each other. Is that good enough for you, Kath?" asked Jack.

Kathy glanced over at Dr. Aragorn and then looked at Jack and said, "Yeah, I guess that's a good start."

"A good start? Look Kath, this is the whole problem with us. You don't give me much credit no matter what I do."

"No Jack, I'm saying what you're offering is okay. I'm not discrediting you this time. I know I've done that to you before, and I'm sorry about it, but I accept what you're offering."

"Then why doesn't it seem like it?"

"Kathy, what was your reaction when you heard Jack's offer?" asked Dr. Aragorn.

"Wary, I suppose. I'm reluctant to get my hopes up. I've gotten my hopes up many times only to have them dashed against the rocks. I want to give us a chance, but I feel cautious about going through that again."

"Fair enough," said Dr. Aragorn.

"Fair enough? She isn't giving me a chance," complained Jack.

"Jack, you have to let Kathy have her feelings. You're taking any unpleasant feeling as discrediting you, which doesn't give Kathy much room to have any bad feelings."

"If you say so doc, but I don't see it," said Jack.

"Okay, let's set that aside for now. So Jack, getting back to

Kathy feeling lonely, let's pretend that Kathy sees you as having no part in her loneliness, then what is your reaction to hearing about her being lonely her whole life?" asked Dr. Aragorn.

"I guess my reaction is that sucks for Kathy."

"And what feeling goes with the thought that it sucks for Kathy?"

"Look doc, I don't know what you want from me. I feel bad for Kath, I don't want her to be lonely."

"Explain to me what feeling 'bad' for Kathy is like," said Aragorn.

"You don't know what bad feels like?"

"I know what it feels like to me, but then again I might use bad when I feel guilty or sad or ashamed, so I'm not sure what you mean by bad."

Jack looked at Kathy and then back at Aragorn. He wiped his sweaty palms on his jeans and then said, "Look man you got me. I don't know what else to tell you. I just feel bad for Kath when she's down."

Dr. Aragorn pondered Jack's response for a moment and then turned to Kathy and said, "And how does that land on you?"

"Well, I can tell that Jack feels something for me. I believe he doesn't want me to hurt. I have to admit it's not as much of a reaction as I'd like, but it's better than what I've received before."

"See doc, that's what I mean, I give it my best shot and I still walk away with a 'D' on my report card," complained Jack.

"I don't hear her giving you a 'D' there. I think she's taking in and appreciating that you're offering her something," suggested Dr. Aragorn.

"I don't know doc, maybe you give her too much credit there. I just don't get that."

"You know I wonder, have you ever felt appreciated by Kathy?"

"Oh yeah I did at first, when we were dating and first married…back then it seemed like Kathy thought I was a pretty cool guy. I don't know what happened, but I haven't seen that in quite a while."

"And what did she seem to appreciate about you?" asked Dr. Aragorn.

"I don't know man, ask her."

"No, I'd like to hear from you on that, Jack."

"Well I don't know, she laughed at my jokes, she told me I was good looking...a couple times she said I was fun and easy going."

"A number of things. I'll bet you miss feeling appreciated," said Aragorn.

Jack smiled sheepishly and averted his eyes while nodding slightly.

Mike opened the door to find Jack standing there. He knew Jack had an appointment with Kathy's therapist today, and stepped back and waved Jack into his condominium. Mike went to the fridge and pulled out two beers, handed one to Jack and sat down. He opened his beer and took a swig, wiped his mouth and commented, "So by the looks of you, it didn't go that great."

"I don't know man, he's a shrink, what'd I expect?"

"You expected it would help you get Kathy back."

"Yeah I suppose. And that's just the thing, I don't know if it helped or not. I mean...I guess the shrink was alright. He tried to get into the psychobabble thing with me, but of course I didn't go there, but he let it go more than I would've thought. I was hoping he'd give us some sort of communication technique to take home and try, but he didn't. I just don't know if we got anywhere."

"What did happen?"

Jack wiped the neck of his beer on his sleeve and took a swallow of his beer. He stared at the wall as though he were trying to focus on something difficult to read. Then he said, "Beats me man...we talked about Kath being lonely, you know, the usual topic." Jack chuckled to himself and then said, "At one point I lost my cool and accused Kathy of being lesbian. I tell you man, I do know Kath enjoys sex with a guy, which I can personally vouch for, but in some ways I think she is a lesbian. I mean she wants me to be like a woman, all touchy feely and emotional. I think she wants the sex with a guy but everything else with a woman."

"Get out of here man! You don't really think…"

"Yeah I do! Her biggest beef has something to do with me not knowing her, or being impacted or something. It beats the hell outta me what that means. I do listen to her, and more than the average Joe. Only thing I can figure is that she wants me to be all upset and dramatic like on those soap operas."

"Come off it, Jack! That can't be what she wants," said a grinning Mike. "Now tell me what her exact words were."

"I'm serious! She said she wants me to FEEL her feelings, or some such bullshit."

Mike threw his head back and laughed. "I think there's more to it," began Mike.

"Come on man, I get that she's upset. I'm not that much of a caveman."

"No, I don't think you are getting it. I think she wants you to listen with your heart and not just your head," suggested Mike.

"Oh now isn't that a nice package of shrink-speak! I've never heard any of that crap from you before. I'd thought I could at least count on you to talk like a real man."

"Now you do sound like a caveman. Don't you read anything besides the sports page? I've been doing some reading, and many modern women want a modern man who does more than sports, beer and fix the toilet," said Mike.

"Besides that and sex what else is there?"

"Jack, you're scaring me. You've got no chance to save your marriage thinking like that. Now that is caveman thinking. Look man, I've had to learn the same lesson. I've been a rock head in more relationships than I can count, and lost most of them because I thought like that. The only reason I'm able to be with a quality woman like Stacy is because I've learned there's a whole other world out there, and it's called having an inner life."

"A what? Mike, now you're really scaring me. Are you preparing for a sex change or something?"

Mike waved him off and said, "You can still be a guy and know that a feeling exists. It doesn't make you a woman or a faggot or anything else like that because you look in the mirror. It's like what Socrates said, 'The unexamined life is not worth living'."

"Now you're quoting fucking Socrates to me? When did…"

"Come on Jack, I realized I had to change if I wanted more out of life. Don't get me wrong, I still enjoy a nice beer and the ball game. But I want more with my lady than that. At first I did all that reading and such because I wanted to catch a quality woman. Actually, the last lady that I dated gave me a book on what women want from a man. Funny thing is she gave it to me the night she broke it off with me, and said something about maybe I'd have a better chance with the next one if I read this. I was so pissed off that I just tossed it in the corner of my room. Months later I was cleaning out my room since I couldn't see the color of the carpet in my room anymore, and I can across this book. I thought it'd help me pick up women, so I read it. After awhile I realized that the book was talking about something pretty cool. I wanted that kind of relationship for myself. The kind of woman that settles for sex, beer and baseball is not the kind I want to be with."

"Now you're not making any sense! What else is there to life, and don't quote fucking Socrates to me."

"I said an inner life. That means you notice something inside your skin. That means you have reactions to life. That means you think about things. That means you have conversations about real life. That means you self-reflect some. That's what else there is. And I tell you man, when I have that kind of thing with a woman, the sex is unbelievable."

"You mean you found an aphrodisiac?"

"No! Well yes and no. It works like an aphrodisiac, but you can't use it that way. But if you work on making a deep life with your lady the great sex comes with it."

"Now you've got my attention. So how do you do this deep aphrodisiac thing?"

"That's just the thing, it's not really a do thing. I don't know how to tell you to go about it, but I think it's what Kathy means. It's like when I keep telling you to stop giving me advice. I don't want you to fix my situation, but just support me while I go through it. Sometimes I just need a buddy to hang in there with me, and maybe not even say too much, but just to know what I'm going through, maybe say a word or two of encouragement. When I lost my job last year there was nothing you could do about it. You kept trying to tell me how to make my resume better and where to look for job postings and how to network. All of that is fine, but I really just wanted you to tell me that you knew it sucked and that I'd get through it. That's it!"

"That is the same kind of shit Kath keeps telling me."

"Yes! But it isn't shit. That's the point you're missing. You can still be a man's man and add another dimension. We're not in the Stone Age any longer, and a man can have sensitivities."

"I got sensitivities right in my manhood."

Mike rolled his eyes and said, "Thinking like that is the fast track to divorce. Look man, you have to learn to do this or you've lost Kathy. Isn't it worth your marriage to dig a little deeper?"

"Yeah of course I want to save my marriage, but that's just not me man. I don't get the inner tube life, or whatever you call it. That's what you and Kath don't get. That's just not me!" Jack looked over at Mike, and saw a look on his face he didn't recognize. Mike didn't seem angry, but he certainly wasn't happy about what Jack had said either. Jack couldn't quite place it.

Jack and Kathy followed Dr. Aragorn into his office and sat down in their assigned seats. Dr. Aragorn looked from one to the other, and waited. Jack looked over at Kathy and shrugged.

"I don't know if we're getting anywhere," began Kathy. "I mean we've been coming together for a few months now, and I feel like we keep having the same conversations. I feel lonely,

Jack feels unappreciated, and there we sit at an impasse...I don't know how to get past that, and I guess I'm looking to you Dr. Aragorn to help us out of this, if you can."

"I think we're making progress," said Jack. "Come on Kath, you have to admit I've been working my ass off to listen better, right?"

"I know you've been trying, but I don't feel like anything's really different. Maybe we just want different things out of a relationship?"

"You know Kath, that's the same old shit you always give me. I work like hell to try to please you, and all I get is 'nice try but no cigar'!"

"No, hear me out Jack! I'm not saying that! I'm wondering if we really are just different kinds of people. You don't feel the need to talk about how you're doing. You are happy to tell me about your day and you're good. I'm not like that. I need someone I can talk through my day with, at least on some days."

"Come on Kath, you're just repackaging the same old shit. I'm a loser as a husband, and you're the long-suffering wife that just can't get her husband to get with the program."

"No Jack. I don't think you're a loser! I truly believe you try hard to do what I'm asking for. But if you're a lion and I'm a tiger, no amount of counseling will change our spots. I don't think it is an effort thing. I used to think you didn't care about me enough to change, but I don't believe that anymore. Maybe we're just different types of animals."

"Oh I get it, kind of like in Kindergarten. You're in the tigers group, and I'm with the rodents. Come off it! Who are you trying to fool? Everybody in Kindergarten knew the tigers were the high achievers and the rodents were the retarded losers!" Kathy threw her hands in the air and gave Dr. Aragorn a pleading gesture.

"Kathy you're wondering if you and Jack are just not a good fit. In the past I've confronted you on devaluing Jack as less than you, but today I'm not hearing that. Today I think you're wondering if you and Jack are just too different to make it work," said Dr. Aragorn. Kathy nodded, and looked down. She feared looking Jack in the eye.

"You know doc, when we first started coming here I expected you to be on Kathy's side, and after a few meetings I had to admit that you weren't. But now I think you really are on Kathy's side, and it pisses me off. You're just gonna sit there and let her throw our marriage in the garbage," said Jack.

"For my money the more interesting question is- are **you** going to throw your marriage in the garbage and give up without much of a fight?" countered Dr. Aragorn.

"What else can I do, doc? I mean I'm working my ass off here trying to do what she's asking. Tell me what to do and I'll do it."

"Jack, maybe there's nothing else to do. Maybe at some point we have to face the music and admit that we're not well suited to be together," said Kathy.

"You're devaluing me again," said Jack.

"I know I've devalued you in the past, which I'm sorry about, but I don't think I am this time. I'm not angry, Jack. I'm sad. I'm sad that we're both trying hard and it's not working."

"No Kath, you just don't appreciate all that I do for you. You know, you're not a picnic to live with either. I just think you can't be pleased no matter what I do."

Kathy opened her mouth to respond, and then changed her mind. I can't make him understand…why keep beating my head against the wall…it probably just frustrates him anyway, she thought. Kathy looked down at her hands and breathed out audibly.

Kathy sat in her car at Dr. Aragorn's office. She whispered inaudible thanks for her group. Kathy pondered what to say tonight. Maybe somebody can give me some new perspective. I sure don't know what else to do, she thought. She got out of her car and walked into Dr. Aragorn's office.

"We've been going to couples therapy for six months now, but I don't really see much change. I mean the issues seem clearer, but… I don't know, I keep thinking about divorce. Oh my God, it's sad to say that out loud. It's the last thing I wanted. I really thought Jack and I would find a way to…I don't know, I just can't believe it's maybe come to this," said Kathy as her eyes shone.

"God knows you've tried hard, Kathy," said Evelyn.

"No shit, I think you've worked harder on your marriage than I have," said Jake.

"But maybe I haven't tried hard enough, or long enough. What if the change between us is right around the corner and I give up too soon?" said Kathy.

"Now wait a minute Kathy, what gives you any inkling that a significant change is imminent?" asked Susan.

"Nothing," said Kathy almost inaudibly.

"You can go on hoping that way for the rest of your life. Do you want to wake up at 60 or 65 and still be hoping like that?" asked Susan.

Kathy looked down and paused before saying, "Yes, I've thought about that, which is a horrible thought…but there's another side to this. At times I think about Jack's strengths…I really like a number of things about Jack…I'm not sure I want to let go of that guy."

"Like what?" asked Karen.

"I like the really generous man that volunteers his time at Jimmy's school. Jack teaches the developmentally delayed kids at his brother's school how to play baseball. I really respect that about Jack. You should see how patient he is with those kids… that's the guy that I don't want to give up."

"That's quite admirable," said Jake.

"Yes, and he's a great dad to Lily…I really like how gentle he is with her," said Kathy.

"That's all worth considering," said Dr. Aragorn.

Kathy shook her head slowly. "And on the other hand, I don't know if I can break up our family. I just don't know if I can do that to Jack, and Lily," said Kathy softly.

"But can you do that to Kathy?" challenged Susan.

"Can you ask yourself to stay in a lonely, disappointing marriage for the rest of your life?" added Evelyn.

Kathy shrugged and said, "I guess not."

"You guess not? Now Kathy, think about what that would be like for you. Think about how it was for you when you were living with Jack. Remember, you're separated and don't have much contact with him now," said Susan.

"And don't forget that Jack said he doesn't want to go to any more couples sessions unless you come home, and that he thinks he doesn't need them," reminded Jake.

"I wonder what other people are going to think," said Kathy.

"What do you expect?" asked Dr. Aragorn.

"That I'm a quitter, and that I wasn't committed, and that I didn't keep my marriage vows, that I'm a nut-job who can't make a marriage work to a great guy."

"And you'd believe that kind of crap," laughed Jake.

"Kathy, people are going to have all kinds of reactions to your divorce, and you'll need to be able to tolerate it. I've had to bear feeling like crap in many people's eyes, and it hasn't been easy. Some people at my church were especially rough on me," said Susan.

"I just dread telling Jack. Oh my God he's going to kill me."

"And what if he wants to kill you?" asked Evelyn.

"I don't know if I can tolerate him feeling like that about me for the rest of my life."

"You'll have to, and you'll be able to," said Susan.

"I hate being the bad guy in all this," said Kathy.

"And who says you are?" asked Jake.

"I suppose I do."

"Other people may very well make you the bad guy, but that will be okay if you're not the bad guy inside yourself," said Dr. Aragorn.

"I know I can be rough on myself," Kathy whispered.

"There you go. It's good to be mindful of that. Don't allow your guilt enough rope to put around your neck. YOU are making yourself the bad guy," said Dr. Aragorn.

"I suppose I've hung myself with that rope many a time…I don't want to do that, but I do feel guilty for wanting to divorce Jack."

"And we'll help you deal with that," said Susan.

Mike pulled into the parking lot and turned off his car. He kept thinking about something he heard in Jack's voice, and Mike had a sinking feeling in his gut. Jack wouldn't say what happened, but Mike knew if couldn't be good. He got out of his car and stepped into the bar. He found Jack staring into his beer at the end of the bar. Mike sat down and said, "Hey buddy, what's up?"

"Well man, it's over," said Jack without emotion.

"What's over?" asked Mike.

"Kath's going to file."

"Oh man, I'm so sorry."

Jack waved his hand as if batting away a fly. Then he looked back at Mike with vacant eyes. Jack's skin looked ghost white and his face expressionless. If he didn't know Jack well, he wouldn't have known if he was awake or even alive.

"You look awful," said Mike.

"Thanks man, that makes me feel really good."

"You know what I mean. I can tell you're hurting."

"Oh yeah, that. Well it don't do no good to dwell on it. It is what it is. She's made her decision."

"You want to talk about it?" invited Mike.

"There's not much to talk about. She told me about her decision, and then I let her have it. I told her she's throwing away a perfectly good marriage because she's looking for a guy that acts like a woman, and that until she gets over that the only guys she'll find are guys that can't get a hard on with her since they have no balls. At first she was all pissed off, and then she tried to make nice and comfort me for hurting me. Of course I wouldn't have none of that. She didn't get to play nice after being a bitch and all. And that's about it."

"I'm so sorry, buddy," offered Mike. Jack nodded.

Mike waited before asking, "And now what?"

"What do you mean 'now what'? Now I get divorced and move on with my life," said Jack.

"Just like that? You mean you're not going to fight for your marriage?"

"Wait a damned minute! I just spent the last six months going to her shrink for marriage counseling. Does that sound like I'm not fighting for my marriage?"

"Look man, I know you've tried hard to work it out with her. But are you really ready to give up now?"

"What the hell else is there to do?"

"What have you done with my feedback over the last six months?" asked Mike.

"What feedback? The feedback that I have to be a SENSITIVE MAN?" said Jack enunciating each syllable.

"That's right."

"Come on man, you know that isn't me. That's fine if it gets you off, but that's not me. I like who I am, and I want to stay this way."

"Is it really how you want to be, or are you afraid?" asked Mike.

"Afraid? Come off it man, afraid of what? Fear's got nothing to do with it."

"Some men fear appearing anything like a woman."

"What kind of bull is that? I'm secure about my manhood. What the hell do you mean?"

"I mean that I read somewhere that a real man has got a good bit of feminine characteristics too."

"Where did you read that? In some women's magazine?"

"You know Jack, if you'd stop shooting down my ideas for a minute and actually thought about what I'm saying, you might get something out of it."

"Look man, all I'm saying is that's all great for you, but I don't buy it."

"Well I guess that's it then," agreed Mike.

"That's what I've been saying. That's it!"

The group sat down and all eyes were on Kathy. It was like time stood still until she spoke. Kathy was in jeans and a sweat shirt with her hair pulled back in a pony tail. She wore not a stitch of make-up. "I told him," Kathy said quietly as tears streamed down her face.

"How did it go?" asked Susan.

Kathy's mouth formed soundless words as the fountain of her eyes poured forth. She gave up trying to speak and submitted to sobs. Jake and Susan put their hands on her shoulders in support. No one spoke. They all merely sat with her. In time her sobs eased, and then she was able to speak.

"Jack was so angry at first, but this time I wasn't scared he'd hurt me. He yelled at me. Then he broke and I could see the hurt on his face. Oh my God, I almost took it all back when I saw the look on his face. It was like I'd told a little boy his mother was going away and would never come back...I got up to comfort him, but he wouldn't let me. I had to make myself stay on the couch. I so wanted to go to him. He was hurting so bad, and I knew he didn't understand why I decided to...he kept asking me why, and I didn't know what to tell him. All the reasons I had in my head seemed to have seeped out of my mind. I tried to explain at first, and then I gave up when I saw him getting more upset, and I was so confused I don't know if what I was saying made sense...oh my God, I can't believe I told him."

"It took courage for you to go through with it," said Dr. Aragorn.

"No shit. I so respect you for doing what you knew you had to do," said Jake.

"You had to do it, Kathy," said Susan. Evelyn nodded.

"Oh my God, my head is spinning. I still can't believe I'm really getting divorced. I've been so upset the last two days that I haven't been in the office. Thank God I have plenty of personal days saved up. I don't know when I'll be able to work again."

"You'll know when you need to know. For now you're off," said Dr. Aragorn.

"Kathy, give yourself the time you need. My God, you've just made a huge life change," said Susan.

"Oh yeah, I don't know if I'd be able to work for a month," said Karen.

"You'll need a lot of time and space to let this enormous change sink in. You're disorganized and just beginning to get your mind around it," said Dr. Aragorn.

"I keep thinking about something Jack said. He told me that what I'm really looking for is a woman, and that normal guys aren't into what I want. I keep wondering if he's right."

"In a sense he is. I believe a mature man has a sensitive woman in him, and a mature woman has an assertive man in him. I doubt that's what Jack means, but I think you do want a man who can be sensitive like a woman," explained Dr. Aragorn.

"I'm sure that's not what Jack means," said Kathy with a laugh.

"There's nothing wrong with wanting a sensitive man, so don't feel bad about asking for that," said Evelyn.

"Jack also said something else…it seemed like the strangest thing to say, I mean at a time like this, and I didn't know what he meant. He asked if I want him to have an 'inner tube life'. What is that?" asked Kathy.

"An inner tube life? Are you sure those are the words," laughed Dr. Aragorn. "It sounds to me as if it might be life in the country with a good inner tube out by the watering hole."

"Does he mean internal life, or inner life?" suggested Susan.

"That's probably what he meant," agreed Evelyn.

Kathy shrugged her shoulders and asked, "So what does that mean?"

"That's what you've been developing since you joined us," began Susan. "An internal life involves getting to know yourself from the inside out. It means living inside your soul and not just your body. It's what every soulful person has done, spent time self-reflecting.

"Kathy you've become a soulful person, and you've been asking Jack to grow with you and develop himself too. You've needed your marriage to grow with you. Jack has consistently told you he's not too interested in being soulful. You've found out what you need to know," said Dr. Aragorn.

Kathy nodded and wiped at her eyes with a tissue before saying, "I just know that I can't keep living like I used to live...but I sure wish Jack and I could have worked it out somehow." Many heads in the room nodded.

Mike tried Jack again on his cell. No answer. Mike checked and there was still no response to his text messages. His first text had been sent over two hours ago. He looked up at Stacy and said, "He's still not answering. I'm going over there. It's not like Jack to not respond to a text message. I'm worried about him."

"Do you want me to come with you?" asked Stacy.

"No, I don't know if Jack would open up with you there."

"Why isn't he texting you back?"

"I'm going to find out. I'll call you."

"Do you think he's still sleeping? I mean it is Saturday."

"It's almost noon. He never sleeps past ten."

Mike knocked again on the front door, this time with more energy. He raised his fist to knock a third time when he heard footsteps. The door opened to reveal a man whose hair looked like he'd slept on a bus for three days, his eyes were ringed in dark circles, and the Dodgers sweatshirt he wore may not have been washed this year.

"Shit Jack, when did you last shower," said Mike as he pushed past his friend and sat down on the couch? Jack followed slowly and plopped himself in his leather chair.

When Jack didn't answer he tried again, "What the hell happened?"

Jack rubbed his eyes and stared out the window a moment as if he were bored with the subject. Then he said, "I called her, and she still wants to end it."

"Oh man, I'm so sorry."

Jack shrugged as his eyes wandered back to the window.

"How are you doing with all this?" asked Mike.

Jack shrugged and looked vacantly at Mike.

"What did you say to her?" asked Mike.

"I just told her we have a nice family and that she was making a huge mistake that she'd regret for the rest of her life."

Mike asked, "What did she say to that?"

"Nothing really," said Jack.

"Look man, I don't think that's the best approach."

"What do you mean? I'm just telling her what I feel."

"You're telling her what you think, and you're putting her on the defensive by telling her she's an idiot."

"I didn't say that."

"Not directly, but you might as well have," countered Mike.

"It doesn't matter anymore. She's done."

Mike exhaled deeply as he ran his hands through his hair. He searched his mind for something to say to his friend, but was drawing a blank. There's got to be something I can say, I can't just let him give up, he thought. Mike looked over at Jack, who continued to stare out the window, not moving a muscle. Then it came to him, "I got it!"

Jack didn't seem to hear, and didn't move. "Jack, I got it! Invite her to get away with you!"

Jack turned his head towards Mike and regarded him with a semi sideways stare, the way a dog looks at you when it seems to be trying to understand. "What the hell good would that do?"

"It would give you one last chance with her," explained Mike.

"I don't know man, I don't know if I give a damn any longer."

"You can't really mean that," countered Mike. Jack merely shrugged and stared at his hands, as if seeing them for the first time.

"If you can truly say you're ready to give up that's fine, but if there's any fight left in you then think about it," said Mike.

"Do I look like a guy who has any fight left in him?" Mike bit his lip to suppress a laugh. It didn't seem like the time to laugh, but when Jack saw the contained smile he burst into laughing himself. It was as though somebody just plugged Jack back into the socket. Jack stood and paced the room. "So where should I take her?"

"I don't know."

"But you said you had an idea."

'Yeah, but I haven't gotten that far yet," admitted Mike.

"It probably doesn't matter, I don't think Kath would agree to go anywhere with me."

Mike shrugged his shoulders, and then Jack continued, "But I can hear you saying it. I have to try. I can't give up on my marriage until I've given it my all, and I think you've given me one last card up my sleeve...but where to take her, that's the...I've got it! I'll take her to the Saint Casius Hotel for a spa weekend! What do you think?"

Mike's less than enthusiastic expression negated the need for a verbal response. "No good?" asked Jack. Mike shook his head.

"Wait a minute. What if I took her somewhere with you and Stacy? You guys have a great relationship, right? Maybe if she sees how good it can be with you and Stacy, and sees that I'm just like you, and that if you can do it so can I. What do you think?"

"I don't know Jack...I mean, Kathy doesn't really know me, and she only knows Stacy a little bit."

"Man, you sure know how to throw a bucket of water on a guy," said Jack.

"Look man, I don't mean to be a downer, but I think you have a better chance going somewhere with Kathy alone...Is there anywhere you've been with Kathy that you've had a great time?" asked Mike.

"Well, our best vacations were when we went snow skiing."

"There you go! Take her away to the romantic mountains for a ski trip," enthused Mike.

"Yes, I'll get her away from Lily and her sister and all the places with the bad memories, and we'll have a chance at a fresh start!"

"Go for it, man!" said Mike.

Kathy went back to work the next Monday. She tossed and turned much of the night before, as she had been most nights. She dosed for an hour or two and then woke. Then dosed for another couple hours and woke. Kathy finally turned off the alarm and got up at six. She made a tall coffee and got to the office early. Kathy didn't even want to know how many emails she had. She was relieved to see that her secretary had weeded through most of them. Two hours later she was almost done

with the urgent emails when her cell phone rang. Without looking at the caller ID she picked up, "This is Kathy."

"Hi Kath, its Jack."

Kathy's blood froze and her muscles tightened. After taking a moment to find her voice she said, "Yes?"

"I want you to consider something. No, I mean I want you to do me a favor..." Kathy concentrated on breathing, as she realized she'd been holding her breath.

"Jack, I already told you I'm not..."

And then Jack cut her off. "Just hear me out before you say anything. I want us to take a vacation together, and then reevaluate our situation. And it would be just the two of us. My parents said they'd watch Lily."

"Oh my God Jack, I can't go through that again. You don't know how many hours I've spent thinking about this and..."

Jack jumped in, "Kath listen, forget the reevaluate part. I just want you to go away with me for a week and see what happens. No pressure." There was a long pause while Kathy tried to think. Her head was spinning so fast she struggled to put two thoughts together. Finally she was able to ask, "Where do you want me to go with you?"

"I want you to go to Vail with me. It would be good to get away from everything, you know, all the bad memories and reminders, and get out in nature and just see."

"Oh Jack..."

"Kath just think about it."

After a lengthy pause Kathy said, "Okay, I'll think about it, but I can't promise I'll go."

"Great, but don't think too long."

"But Jack I don't want you to..." But Kathy was interrupted by the line going dead.

Kathy stared at the phone. She closed the phone and set it down. She dropped her head into her hands. I can't believe I told him I'd...oh my God, what was I thinking. I just can't... Kathy picked her phone and dialed Susan, who fortunately picked up. She relayed Jack's request and then asked, "So what do you think? Should I go?"

"Well...I'm not sure what to say. I guess I surprised that you're considering something like this, after how much you've thought about your..."

"I know, I can't believe I'm considering it either," said Kathy.

"It might be confusing for both of you, to agree to a trip at this point," said Susan.

"Yeah, I suppose that is a risk..."

Susan asked, "So what would be the benefit of going?"

"I don't know, maybe if I go I could feel like I gave us every opportunity to...I don't know."

"Maybe going would help you with your guilt? Is that what you're saying?"

"Yeah, maybe that's it...I still feel bad about going through with this. At times I feel like it's all my fault that we're getting a..."

Susan cut her off, "Don't do that to yourself! It's not all your fault, and in your better moments you know that, right?"

Kathy paused before responding, "Well, yes I suppose I do know that in my heart of hearts."

"So my question for you is this. Are you just considering going to appease your guilt, or is there more to it?"

"I'm not sure, but probably it's partly about my guilt, and maybe partly I'm curious how it would be to go away at this point...maybe it would help Jack to see that we don't have anything to save anymore."

"It might be a good idea for you to sleep on this, before you decide anything for sure," suggested Susan.

Two days later Kathy picked up the phone and called Jack. He picked up right away. Kathy said, "Jack, I'll agree to go, but only on two conditions. Number one, this doesn't mean I'm reconsidering the divorce. I've already made up my mind on that."

"I know Kath, I understand..."

"Now hear me out Jack. Condition number two is that we don't discuss our divorce on the trip, agreed?"

"Well, what if we..."

"No Jack, I won't go if you don't accept my conditions."

Jack paused before saying, "Okay great. This is going to be so great for us. You'll see how great we are together. I think you've forgotten..."

"Now Jack, I don't want any pressure. This isn't going to be a marriage retreat. I'm thinking of it as a way to go into the divorce as friends."

The River: Day 7

Mike woke with a start. He thought he heard something in camp. Crawling out of his tent and standing up, he turned on his flashlight and scanned their campsite. Nothing. He walked over to the boat and shined the light into the boat, and then walked to the far end of the beach. Something didn't feel right. Mike sat down on a rock and watched. He waited for a half hour, and nothing stirred. Satisfied that nothing was amiss, he went back to bed.

The next morning Mike and Stacy were putting away their tent, and in spite of their empty stomachs, were having some fun with each other. When they got the tent in the bag, Mike tackled Stacy to the sand. She rolled over on top of him and pinned him down. Stacy raked sand into his hair. Mike rolled her over and rubbed sand on her belly. Then they got up and went down to the river to bath.

"Hey, what's all the racket over there. Can't a guy get a decent night's sleep around here?"

"Jack! You're back!" said Mike.

"'Course I'm back. You didn't think I'd leave you alone with these two beauties for long, did you?"

"Where the hell have you been?" demanded Mike, turning more serious.

"I was shadowing you all along," Jack replied.

"You mean you were watching us the whole time?" asked Stacy.

"Of course he was. What did I tell you?" said Kathy.

"It was all in fun. I hope I didn't give you all too much of a scare," said Jack.

"Who are you kidding? You definitely were trying to give us a scare, and probably especially me. You were punishing me again, like on the Yosemite trip," said Kathy.

"Oh Kath, don't be like that. I was just having some fun," insisted Jack.

"Jack, it wasn't fun for us. I was worried about you," said Mike.

"So was I," added Stacy.

"I go away for a day, and now everybody's on Kathy's side. Is that it?"

"Like I told you the other day, it's not about taking sides, man. It's about calling it like it is. The way I see it, you and Kathy both got your parts in this mess," said Mike.

"Hey, what's with all those protein bar wrappers? How many did you eat?" accused Kathy.

"I just ate my ration from yesterday and this morning."

Growing concern grew on the other three's faces as the implications of Jack's early morning meal set in.

"Wait a minute, exactly how many did you eat?" demanded Kathy.

"Four. I had three when I got in last night, and one this morning when I woke up."

"Four! My God Jack, we only had two each yesterday!" exclaimed Kathy.

"You selfish son of a bitch, you ate double your share!" accused Mike.

"How many are left?" asked Stacy.

Jack bent down and picked up the box and fingered through its contents. "It looks like there's three left."

"Three! That means you don't get another single bite! This has to be the height of your selfishness. You said we got plenty of beer, and now that's exactly what you get to live off today," said Kathy.

"Come on Kath, I can't live off just beer. I got to have something else coming today. Tell her, Mike."

After a pause Mike responded with a dour face. "I'm afraid Kathy's right, Jack. You just ate your ration for today."

"You can't be serious," said Jack. Jack looked to Stacy for help, but she averted her eyes.

"Stacy and Kathy, you each get one more protein bar, eat it whenever you want," said Mike as he handed them their bars. He put the other bar in his pocket.

"Well I'm full. I don't want another one of those boring cardboard bars," said Jack with a shrug of his shoulders. "I'll catch some real food," said Jack as he picked up the fishing pole.

"That'd be great," said Mike.

Jack walked to the point at the downriver end of their beach, and commenced fishing. Mike and Stacy helped Kathy fold up her tent and finish packing up the boat. Thirty minutes later the boat was ready to go. Mike went over to where Jack fished. "Any luck?"

"Nothing yet," answered Jack.

"We're all packed up and ready to go."

"Uh huh."

Mike waited a minute, but Jack merely continued fishing. "Hey Jack, I want to get going. If we leave now we stand a good chance of getting back by nightfall," pressed Mike.

"Hey man, I ain't ready."

Mike paused to contain his rising temper. "So, when do you think you'll be ready?"

"I don't know, man. I guess whenever I catch my breakfast."

"So, you want the rest of us to just wait until you're ready to go?"

"That's right. If I have to wait to eat, then you all might just have to wait to go. Fair is fair, right?"

Mike breathed out slowly, buying time. "Look Jack, the sooner we leave the sooner we get back, and the sooner we all get to eat."

"Hey don't hassle me, man. You're getting on my nerves, just like Kathy. You're starting to sound like her."

Mike looked away and scratched his head, and then turned and went back to the others, who had overheard most of the conversation. Kathy started towards Jack, with a look of fury on her face. Mike stopped her.

"Kathy, please don't. Let's just let him be for a bit," pleaded Mike.

"I'm not about to let that selfish child make the rest of us wait until…" And then she caught herself, and said, "Oh here I go again. I don't want to go there…okay Mike, I'll leave him be for now."

"Kathy, God knows we're all frustrated with the situation we're in, and we don't need any more conflict. We can give him an hour," said Mike. Kathy nodded.

Kathy took a few deep breaths, grabbed her magazine and dragged a chair over to the shade. She set the chair down and she tried to distract herself with the magazine. Mike ran his hands threw his hair and shook his head slowly. He looked up at Stacy. Tears formed in Stacy's eyes, and she threw her arms around Mike and quietly wept.

"I know Babe, I know," Mike offered.

"What are we going to do, Mike? I just want to get off this cursed river. And I'm getting really hungry."

"I know. I'm hungry too. We'll be back soon."

"What are we to do with Jack and Kathy? They're getting worse."

"I don't know…I haven't seen Jack like this before."

"My God, I feel like we're two parents on vacation with their two teenagers, and don't know what to do with them," said Stacy.

Mike laughed nervously. "That's a scary thought."

Mike and Stacy had intended to give Jack an hour to fish, but fell asleep lying on their towels. Mike awoke groggy to the wind freshening in his face. He gazed at the sky to the east and furrowed his brow as he saw the dark clouds. By now it was almost noon and Jack continued to fish unsuccessfully, while Kathy remained at her post with her magazine. Kathy could see Jack at the end of their cove, and had eyed him every few minutes. She often reminded herself to take deep breaths, breathing out slowly. "I'm really doing pretty well with Jack today," she thought.

"Hey guys, we best get going while the going's good. Hey Jack, Kathy, let's go! Take a look at those clouds blowing in," said Mike.

Jack gazed up at the sky, and then reeled in his line with leisure. Kathy didn't bother looking at the incoming clouds, but folded her chair up and climbed into the boat.

Everybody else climbed aboard and Mike pushed his boat out into the river. Jack helped Mike paddle out into the swiftest moving water. Mike kept eyeing the storm over his left shoulder. The wind remained mild, yet pushed them back towards the western shore and slowed their progress.

Kathy sat in the front seat, reading her magazine and rationing her spoken words as if they were edible. She didn't trust herself to say much right now. She knew she was still upset with Jack for ditching them yesterday, as well as his tantrum this morning.

A moment later a gust of wind slammed into the boat, ripping Kathy's magazine out of her hands and into the water. Mike had been standing up, and narrowing avoided falling into the river by grabbing onto the gunwale of the boat.

"Wow, now that's some wind," said Jack with a smile.

"Yeah, and it's blowing us directly into the western shore. We best pick out a beach we can crash land on, because we're going to hit the shore one way or another, and there's nothing we can do about it," said Mike.

"But can't we ride the wind for awhile and make better time?" suggested Jack.

"Don't want to risk it. The winds might be 50 miles per hour any minute."

"How about that one?" suggested Stacy as she pointed to a beach a half mile downriver.

"Looks good. Okay Jack, let's aim for that beach," said Mike.

After a laborious thirty minutes of paddling, both men stopped for a breather. "I can't do this much longer man, I don't have any energy left," said Jack.

"Me neither. We have to dig deep. We're almost there," encouraged Mike.

Both men redoubled their efforts, until Mike collapsed onto his knees. "Mike!" cried Stacy. "Are you okay?"

"I've got nothing left," Mike gasped between breaths.

Stacy took the paddle from his hand and took his place at the side of the boat. Ten minutes later Stacy and Jack had the boat pointed at their target beach. The waves had grown to three feet, with white caps topping each one. The waves splashed over the side of the boat. The wind had strengthened to gusts of forty miles per hours. Each time a wave hit the boat water rushed over the sides, and soon the entire floor of the boat was drenched.

"Everybody hold on, we're going to hit the beach hard," warned Mike.

The boat slammed into the beach. Mike and Jack jumped out with an anchor each. A wave of water came over the stern, drenching Stacy and Kathy. Mike and Jack worked feverishly to get the boat secured. They set the upriver anchor first. Just as they stood to run to the other side, a wave pushed the stern of the boat towards the shore. The boat now lie parallel to the shore, with the stern moving further and further up the beach with each crashing wave.

"Help me hold it off, Jack!" yelled Mike above the wind.

Mike and Jack plunged into the shallows and leaned their shoulders into the side of the boat. They were able to hold the boat from getting any closer to the shore, but failed to push the stern an inch back out. The next wave pushed the boat against their tiring shoulders, moving the boat another yard closer to the beach. Stacy leaped out of the boat and ran to help the men. Kathy stared with wide eyes from her perch onboard, and then went back to bailing water out of the boat.

The threesome began to inch the boat back out, but their progress only lasted a moment. Another gust of wind caught the boat and threw another series of waves at the boat, throwing the weakening campers back.

"We can't hold it off! On the count of three, we let go and make for the beach! One, two, three," yelled Mike.

All three rushed up onto the shore, with the boat following a moment later. The outdrive of the boat dug into the gravel and sand, and the next wave swamped the boat.

"Get everything out of the boat," ordered Mike.

All four campers scrambled to unload everything. The other three handed gear to Mike, who threw it up onto the beach as far as he could throw. Mike wasn't worried about damaging anything at this point. All their gear was soaked already. They finally collapsed onto the sand, exhausted from their efforts. They lay on the ground and rested, also seeking refuge from the strong winds. The wind pelted them with gravel and sand. Mike dug four towels out of their pile of gear, and each wrapped themselves up in a towel and lay down again.

A couple hours later the winds decreased, and the campers got up. Mike and Jack approached the beached boat. The wind whipped waves had pushed the boat several yards above the water line, now lying at an angle beyond parallel to the shoreline. The men stood with hands on hips, amazed at the storm's work. Mike went down on his knees to examine the hull. At first glance it looked okay. He crawled around to the other side and gasped at what he found. A softball sized hole lay gaping in the right side of the bow. "Oh my God, look at that!" said Mike.

"That's a tough break, man," agreed Jack.

"A tough break? The boat's done," countered Mike.

"Can't we patch it?"

"No, it's too big."

"We patched the other one."

"This one's way bigger. I don't have the right stuff to patch a hole that sized," explained Mike. "I would need plenty of fiberglass and resin…maybe even a piece of plywood."

Stacy and Kathy walked up to see what the problem was. "Oh my, that's huge," said Kathy. Mike nodded.

"So, can you fix it?" asked Stacy.

"Not out here I can't," answered Mike.

"Then what are we going to do?" asked Kathy.

Jack looked at Mike, and Stacy and Kathy's eyes followed. "I don't know. We better put our heads together and figure out a plan. The one thing I can say is that the boat's done. We'll have to leave it here," said Mike.

"Then how do we get back," asked Kathy with wide eyes.

"If we can't use the boat, then we have to hike out of here," said Stacy.

A pregnant pause ensued while all four considered the implications of Stacy's obvious conclusion.

"Stacy's right, there's nothing else we can do," said Mike.

"Can't we build a signal fire and wait to be rescued?" suggested Jack.

"Unlikely. They probably won't be patrolling this part of the river for another week yet," answered Mike. "Who's going to see it?"

"Maybe a plane or helicopter passing by might."

"How many planes and helicopters have you seen pass by?" offered Kathy.

"I don't know, I haven't been monitoring the air traffic too closely, and I suppose you have?" countered Jack.

"Oh God, I don't want to do this again," said Kathy as she turned and walked away.

"Yeah, just walk away. It's what you're good at," quipped Jack. Kathy ignored Jack's comment, and sat down in a chair.

"Alright, so how about if I build a fire and just see," suggested Jack.

"Fine, but we have to make more of a plan. I'm not counting on the fire," said Mike.

"I agree. We can't just wait around when we have no food. We might starve to death if we don't get back soon," said Stacy.

"Okay we hike out, but I'm not leaving before we give the signal fire a go," said Jack. And with that he went in search of wood and tender.

Mike and Stacy went over to where Kathy sat with arms folded. "Jack's building a fire," said Mike.

"That's so Jack. He's playing Cowboys and Indians while we're sitting here miles from food," said Kathy.

"I say we decide what to bring with us when we go," suggested Mike. The two women nodded and the three sorted through their gear, making a pile of things to bring. The first few things were obvious. They all wanted to bring sleeping bags in case they spent another night out here. No one wanted to bother carrying the tents. Extra clothes were quickly discarded. The tough decision was the stove and propane.

"What about the stove?" asked Stacy.

"We might want it if we catch anything," said Mike.

"Really Mike, what could we catch out here?" asked Kathy.

"Maybe fish."

"You only caught a fish when you had bait," reminded Stacy.

"Yeah, but what if I find something I can use as bait?"

"What can you find out here? I haven't seen many bait shops," said Kathy.

"Don't talk to me like a child! I know what's out here. I come out here every year. Now it's not likely, but I might catch a lizard, and the fish might bite on that," said Mike.

"You're right, I'm sorry Mike," apologized Kathy.

"I accept, Kathy. Now, I'll carry the stove. I've got some rope in the boat that I can use to make straps out of. We've got two backpacks, and we can use a couple of these bags as packs as well," said Mike.

Mike, Kathy and Stacy finished packing the four bags with the items they decided to bring. By the time they finished Jack had a good fire going, which he'd ringed with rocks. The fire produced a dark smoke, and they all moved upwind to get out of the way. Jack smiled with pride, "Hey, not bad, huh?" Then Jack went off in search of additional fuel. He brought back an armful of wood and dropped it next to the fire. Mike glanced at Stacy and Kathy. Stacy held his gaze, while Kathy averted her eyes.

"Hey Jack the fire's great, but we need to get going," said Mike.

"I'm not leaving yet. I just got it started. It'll take a couple hours for anyone to see it and come get us," returned Jack.

"So you want to just sit here on our hands and wait a couple hours?" asked Kathy.

"You damned right I do, and…"

"Wait a minute, both of you," interceded Mike. Turning to Kathy, "Please, let me do this," requested Mike. Kathy put her hands up in surrender and nodded. Mike turned back to Jack.

"Jack, the fire just might bring somebody, but I don't want to wait around much and see. I'm so damned hungry I can't think about much other than food. My stomach feels like it's sinking into my knees. We gotta go soon, man," Mike pleaded.

"I know, man, I'm hungry too. And this is our best chance to get food. I say we give it two or three hours," said Jack.

Mike shook his head, "I can't wait that long."

"You just might have to," said Jack.

Mike shook his head slowly, and ran his hands through his dried out hair. "I don't know, man, we might have to split up then."

"You mean you'd leave me here?" asked Jack.

"That's right. If you won't come, then I suppose…"

"I can't believe you'd…"

"Look man, you have to make your own decision, and so do I. I'm leaving real soon, and if you want to stay, then…"

"I've got an idea! What if we leave a note in case somebody comes?" suggested Stacy.

Mike nodded his head, and Kathy said, "That's a great idea!"

Jack crossed his arms and looked away at the river. "How come nobody likes my plan? Nobody ever likes my ideas," pleaded Jack.

"Look man," began Mike when he was interrupted by Stacy, who put her hand on his shoulder. She could feel Mike's frustration building.

"Walk with me, Jack," said Stacy as she took Jack's arm and walked him away from the others. Jack reluctantly allowed her to lead him, while slowing Stacy's hurried pace to a leisurely stroll. Stacy waited until they were well out of hearing.

"Jack, the fire's a great idea, brilliant even. You came up with something that none of the rest of us thought of, even Mike, and it might just save us. You've alerted others that we need help, and now your work is done. We simply leave some kind of instructions on how to find us, and we can get a head start on the hike back. Worse case, we hike a couple miles unnecessarily, and best case we get ourselves closer to the truck in case we get there before help gets here," reasoned Stacy.

Jack searched Stacy's eyes while he weighed her advice. "You're the only one that understands me. Mike and Kathy just think I'm an idiot with dumb ideas. Nobody else gets what I'm trying to do with the fire…Maybe you're right; I suppose we can start hiking back if they know where to find us."

"Yes! Maybe you can write the note explaining which way we headed."

Jack left his gaze to linger on Stacy's face, and then nodded his assent. He surprised Stacy with a hug, and then turned back to the others with Stacy in tow.

"Alright, who's got paper and pen? I'll write a note to the park rangers that find my fire later today. Then we can go," announced Jack.

"Sounds good," said Mike. Kathy stared in disbelief.

"Where should I leave the note?" asked Jack.

"I think," began Mike, but he was cut off by Stacy.

"Leave it wherever you think best," suggested Stacy.

Jack smiled ear to ear. He walked around the campsite evaluating several possible sites for his note. Jack circled the fire a couple times, then considered a rock monument in the middle of the beach, and then examined several locations on the boat. He finally settled on the dash board of the boat, weighing it down with a rock. Then Jack pulled up one of the seat cushions, and retrieved his dad's red hat, putting it on his head tightly, pointing backwards.

"Okay, I've got my lucky hat, I'm ready to go," said Jack.

Each of the campers picked up a bag and put it on their backs. Mike picked up the stove, while Stacy grabbed the fishing pole and Jack the small ice chest. They started to walk downriver, and Mike turned and looked back at his boat. An empty pit weighed heavy in his stomach, and a mist formed in his eyes. He turned and caught up with the others who hadn't stopped.

Mike led the way and they followed the shoreline. At times they waded through waist deep water to get around rocky outcroppings, or brush and low trees that crowded the water's edge. Sometimes they hiked away from the water to get around brush too thick to walk through and water too deep to wade.

No one spoke much. None of them had much energy for conversation. After an hour they stopped and drank water. The clouds had blow over leaving a scorching late afternoon.

"I don't think I can walk any farther without eating something," said Kathy.

"We still have the last three protein bars," reminded Stacy.

"This might be as good a time as any to eat them. But it means we won't have anything to eat tomorrow," said Mike.

"You mean we won't get to the truck tonight?" asked Kathy.

"There's no way. We've got to be a good six, seven miles out yet," answered Mike.

"What if we just hike all night? We'd be there by morning, right?" suggested Jack.

"Maybe, but I don't want to hike after dark. It'd be too dangerous," said Mike.

"I'm not hiking after dark either, but I will take my last protein bar," said Kathy. Jack folded his arms and looked away.

Stacy fished through her bag and produced the precious protein bars. Kathy promptly opened hers and savored each bite. Mike took his and put it in his bag. Stacy opened hers and broke off a piece for Jack. He looked at her in surprise, and then accepted her offering and ate. Stacy broke off a piece and put the rest in her mouth. She offered the last piece to Mike, "Take this and we'll save yours for later."

Mike took the broken off piece and ate without comment. They finished their bottles of water and took a dip before shouldering their packs again. Dusk was still an hour or two away and they resumed their march.

Jack had his pack on first, and turned to look up towards the hills a couple hundred yards off the river. As he surveyed their outline he noticed a faint path running along them. He realized he hadn't seen it before as it was at best barely discernible, and in spots undetectable.

"Hey man, let's take that trail along the hills. It looks way easier than scratching through these bushes down here," suggested Jack. Mike followed his finger and pondered the possibility.

"It does look easier to walk, but I wonder if it'll take us far from the river. I don't want to lose sight of the river," said Mike.

"No way man, we can see the river from there no problem. Let's go," said Jack eagerly. No one else had much energy about any particular path, and they all filed off behind Jack, who had already begun the walk up to the base of the hills.

The walking was easier at first, with little or no brush to negotiate. Once they began climbing the hill they began to slow down and perspire more. It felt twenty degrees warmer away from the cool water, but was probably only five or six degrees hotter. And as rugged as the river's edge may be, it was relatively flat. Walking along the hill top the path rose and fell with the uneven terrain, and the hikers expended much of their precious energy. Mike brought up the rear and paused halfway up the hill and looked down at the river. He was tempted to turn around, feeling out of breath, but decided against debating the issue with Jack for now.

They hikers stopped to rest at the crest of the hill, sitting down on small boulders. Mike and Stacy wiped their perspiring faces with their shirt tails. Kathy didn't have the energy to bother with the sweat dripping into her eyes, and Jack opened a beer and remained standing.

"Come on you guys, let's keep going. The more we stop the later we'll get in tonight," encouraged Jack.

"I can't take another step right now. I'm so hot I feel like I'm melting," said Kathy.

"You need a beer. Let me get you one," offered Jack.

"No. I don't want a beer," said Kathy evenly. She opened her bag and pulled out a water bottle, and took a long draught. "Just give me a couple minutes and then I'll be ready. You're probably in better shape than me, Jack."

Ten minutes later they resumed the trail. Jack took the lead, Mike brought up the rear and the two ladies walked shoulder to shoulder in between. They struck out at an easier pace.

"You seemed different with Jack just now," said Stacy.

"Yes. I've been thinking about it all day."

"What do you mean?" asked Stacy.

"I hate being a bitch to Jack. I don't want to be like that anymore…I keep trying to stop myself. Sometimes it seems like I can't keep myself from saying those things…as though another person is speaking out of my mouth. It's so strange. It's like two or three different people live inside my head, and I'm the host trying to get them all to get along with each other. I'm working on it. I'm probably freaking you out by talking like that."

"Hardly, I think that's so great," said Stacy. Kathy smiled weakly.

Both women walked in silence, each with their own thoughts. Kathy felt an emptiness permeating her stomach. She felt heavier, and hiking became more effortful. Kathy looked around her, and everything appeared to be shades of grey. She looked ahead and saw Jack, and almost ran up to him on impulse to hug him. Yet she restrained herself. It didn't seem right.

Stacy thought about her relationship with Mike. She turned around and looked at Mike, who smiled at her. Stacy smiled back. A sense a dread came over her.

"Since you've been honest with me, I'll put myself out there too. Watching you and Jack scares me. Maybe it's best to never get married, if that's what I have to look forward to."

"It's good to give marriage a second thought, but I don't want to scare you off too much. Some people are happily married, I think there's at least one or two couples out there," laughed Kathy.

Stacy glanced over at Kathy, and seeing her face, laughed as well.

"I sure wish I'd given more thought to our relationship, before we got married that is. A good friend, Sophia's her name, tried to get me to take a closer look at things between me and Jack, but I wouldn't listen. I brushed her off as being too serious."

"What did she say?" asked Stacy.

"Sophia said I didn't know myself well enough to choose a marriage partner yet. Oh my God I was naïve. I couldn't hear the wisdom in her words. I thought she was being high and mighty, but the truth is she was worried about me."

"What a great friend! She reminds me of some new friends that I have," said Stacy.

"How so?"

"Well, they kind of seem like what Sophia was to you. There are six of us from work that go out for a drink after work every Thursday night. I don't even remember how we started doing it, but we've been at it awhile now. Anyways, we started talking about work issues, and then it moved into more personal stuff. I look forward to it every week. It's helped me a lot to have someone to talk to, besides Mike that is," said Stacy.

"Really? That sounds great. I wish I had something like that."

"So are you still in contact with Sophia?" asked Stacy.

"Oh yes, I've recently reestablished contact with her. I suppose I'm just learning to listen to wise people like her. It's too bad she lives out of state or I'd see her regularly."

"What does Sophia say about you and Jack now?"

"She's been saying for a long time now, 'you already know there's a problem'."

"What does that mean?"

"That means Sophia knows that I have to find a way to somehow make a change in our marriage."

"Ohhh, got it."

Kathy felt dizzy. Her legs felt weak. She put her hand on her forehead, and then stopped moving. "I don't think I can go any further."

"Hey Jack, we have to stop. Kathy can't go on, and I can't go much further either," Stacy called out.

Jack turned around and stopped. He and Mike joined the women. Jack could see Kathy's ashen face and supported her arm.

"We better find a place we can camp for the night," said Mike.

"I guess so. I was hoping we'd just keep going until we got back," said Jack.

"There's no way we can do that," said Stacy.

"Let's hike down to the water and find a beach to sleep on," said Mike.

Kathy fell asleep as soon as she slipped down onto her sleeping bag. Stacy lay down next to her. Jack and Mike stood and stared helplessly at the women. "Hey man, I'm so hungry I could almost eat sand. Let's go catch some fish for dinner," said Jack.

"With what? We have no bait," said Mike.

"Come on man, have a little faith. We'll catch something."

"I'll come and keep you company."

Mike followed Jack down the beach and sat down on a large rock. Jack set down the tackle box and cast his line. The men sat in silence at first. The demands of the day had depleted their energy, and they melted into the sand and rock.

Later Mike stood and waded into the water, and slowly washed his face and hands. He dried himself off with his shirt. "How are you holding up?" asked Mike.

"I'm okay. I don't know if I can be any more hungry, but I'm alright."

Mike nodded. "I'm so hungry I feel like my stomach is eating itself. I have to eat soon. Right now I can't take another step. Dear God, how did we get ourselves into this mess?"

"It'll be alright, man, you'll see," said Jack.

"Maybe if we'd packed more food we'd be okay…maybe if I'd made sure the boat was secured before I went to bed the first night…maybe…"

"Don't go there, Mike. Don't do that to yourself. It is what it is, and we'll just have to make the best of it."

"I don't know if I can hike tomorrow, unless I get something to eat," said Mike.

"You'll be able to after you sleep."

"How do you know?"

"Because I know that we'll be able to do whatever we have to," said Jack.

"But what if we run out of gas and just can't walk a step further?"

"Then we rest some until we can hike again. We'll be back tomorrow for sure," said Jack.

"I hope so."

"I know so."

Mike hung his head down and nodded slightly. He rubbed his face with his hands and breathed deeply. He walked over to Jack and put a hand on his shoulder and said, "Thanks man, I needed to hear something like that. I have to go lay down." And Mike retreated to unroll his sleeping bag. Jack nodded, and returned his focus to fishing.

78 Weeks after the River Trip

There was little traffic along the Interstate 5 after midnight. Jack piloted the car while Kathy slept next to him. Jack drove with his right arm resting on his skis, which lay across the center armrest. He tried to remember the last time he'd skied out of state. His mind worked slowly as he was tired. After searching the radio dial again, Jack pulled out his CD case and selected Jethro Tull. He figured he'd need music with some energy to keep him awake another hour until they got into Las Vegas.

Kathy stirred and repositioned herself when the first loud strains of Aqualung filled the car. Jack put his arm back on his skis and thumped the steering wheel in tune with the music with his other hand. Jack had been looking forward to this ski vacation for weeks now. He hoped that the romantic mountains of Colorado would help revive the romantic flames between him and Kathy. Jack was thankful, and a bit surprised that Kathy agreed to go. He also wanted time off from work. For the last year and a half, Jack worked full time for the first time in his life, learning to write software for a video game company. He'd spent much of his adolescence in front of a screen playing video games, so the job seemed the natural thing to do after graduating from college. Jack found the work laborious, not because it was difficult for Jack, but because he was required to work almost a serious forty-hour work week. Throughout college he'd taken light course loads and graduated in six years. During college he'd never worked more than ten hours a week at various on-campus jobs. Most Christmas breaks between semesters he and his buddies had gone skiing or played in some other playground. Jack didn't need much money for his lifestyle, and so he wasn't motivated to work many hours.

Jack's college buddies couldn't believe his good fortune at getting paid to play with video games. They chided him with questions about when he was going to get a real job. Jack would simple grin and tell them they were green with envy. Although Jack enjoyed his job, except for the demands, it didn't pay well. Fortunately Kathy's job as a junior partner in a law firm paid well, and had provided most of the funds the family needed. She was well-respected by the senior partners and had earned several raises.

Although he couldn't actually see the city yet, the powerful Las Vegas lights lit up the sky ahead. It looked like a gigantic flashlight shining straight up at the night. Jack drove over the last hill before the sprawling city of Las Vegas came into view. He took the first exit and pulled into the parking lot of the first large hotel-casino he came to. He parked far away in the corner and turned off the car. He thought about waking Kathy up, but decided against it as she seemed to be sleeping peacefully. Jack climbed into the back of the SUV and fell asleep within five minutes.

A sudden sound pulled Jack out of his dream in which he was winning a bundle at a casino table with a beautiful blond on his arm. The voice repeated the sound several more times until he realized they were words, and words directed at him from Kathy, "Hey Jack, where the hell are we?"

"We're in Vegas, baby. Ain't that great?"

"But why are we sleeping in a parking lot?" asked Kathy.

"Oh I didn't want to wake you. We didn't get in until about two."

"Oh my God, I'm all stiff from sleeping against the window. I have to get out and walk around and use the ladies' room."

"Okay Kath, I'll come in with you."

Jack rubbed his face, trying to get the blood flowing in his brain. He felt like he'd slept about fifteen minutes. His eyes burned. He slowly extracted himself from the car, which seemed to take about thirty minutes. Kathy handed him his tooth brush and they headed towards the hotel. It felt good to walk. The stiffness slowly melted from both their bodies.

Kathy came out of the ladies' room and looked around for Jack. She figured she must have beat him out, and leaned against the wall to wait. Kathy closed her burning eyes to rest them, when a moment later she heard a familiar voice. "That sounded like Jack," she said aloud. She turned towards the men's room, but saw no Jack. Then she heard his voice again and turned around to find him at a blackjack table. As she approached she noticed his toothbrush and toothpaste sticking out of his hip pocked, his hands rubbing against each other and an eager grin on his face. His grin fell when he saw Kathy. "What are you doing here? I thought we were washing up and then finding a place for breakfast."

"Oh sorry Kath, I guess the tables distracted me for a moment."

"Then undistract yourself and let's go."

"Come on Kath, I'm on a roll! Just give me another half hour."

"I'll be in the car. I'm not standing around while you gamble away the vacation money."

"Okay Kath, I'll just play this last hand," said Jack with a sheepish grin. Several other faces at the table were now looking his way. Jack was dealt a 9 and a 7. He asked for another card and busted with a 6. "Oh man, so close," Jack said. He cashed out and followed Kathy over to the restrooms, stuffing his wallet back into his pants. Kathy waited outside the restrooms while Jack attended to his dental hygiene.

By late afternoon they were close to Vail, driving alongside majestic, snow-covered mountains. The snow cover came all the way down to the roadside, having been blanketed with snow all week. The sun glimmered off the bright snow, dancing in an inviting way. "Man, I just can't wait to get out on the slopes. It's going to be great conditions. Look at all that snow, will ya," enthused Jack.

"Yes, it sure looks nice," agreed Kathy.

"What do you say we hit the town as soon as we get in?" suggested Jack.

"Okay, but I do want to get settled into the room first."

They drove into a quaint, yet new looking village. Above them loomed Vail Mountain, huge and imposing. The crowds wandered the streets, carrying shopping bags and most wore mittens or gloves. Some adorned themselves with expensive fur coats and boots, while many wore ski apparel. As Jack and Kathy got out of the car it began to snow lightly. It was cold and the snow was so light and dry that it seemed to have no weight. Kathy was amazed at how she could brush the flakes off her jacket without leaving a trace.

Kathy and Jack wandered through the village, stopping at some stores and merely pausing to glance into the window of others. Jack followed Kathy around the stores they entered, waiting for her to be ready to go. By early evening they came upon an inviting steak house and sat down for dinner by the window. The snow continued to fall upon the village, thicker than when they first arrived. They sat mesmerized by the winter wonderland before them, watching as the footprints slowly filled in.

"It's so beautiful here," Kathy said.

"Yeah, it's really cool here," agreed Jack. "I want to be the first ones on the slopes tomorrow. You game?"

"Sure, as long as you don't wake me up too early."

Although Kathy still nursed her first glass of wine, Jack topped her off and emptied the bottle into his own glass. The food was excellent. Jack ate a steak filet topped with a blue cheese sauce, while Kathy had the grilled salmon. As the meal went on Jack talked with more and more animation. "I can't believe old man Flanders makes me come in every day by 9:00 sharp. I mean come on, are we in junior high or what. He told me just this week that if I'm late again he'll write me up and put it in my file," said Jack.

"How late have you been?" asked Kathy.

"Not that late, I'm always there by 9:30 for sure."

"Nine-thirty? That's pretty late, Jack."

"Come on Kath, Joe comes in after 9:00 every day."

"But didn't you tell me he has special permission because he takes a bus to work?"

"Yeah but still, if he can come in late then I should be able to."

"But it's not the same, you have your own car, and Flanders lets you leave early to pick up Lily from school," Kathy pointed out.

"Wait a minute, whose side are you on? Are you taking Flanders side against me?"

"No Jack, I'm not taking sides, I just think you and Joe have different situations, that's all."

"Maybe so, but Flanders should still be fair about it. If Joe can come in late, then I should be able to come in late too. He's got to understand that I'm not used to getting up early in the morning. Nine a.m. is almost the middle of the night. Anyways, unless he lightens up I'll start looking for a new job right after we get back in town."

"Really, you're going to quit your job? You just started there a year ago!"

"Come on Kath, I can't be tied down to a bummer job like that. Try to understand," Jack pleaded.

"I just don't think you've given the bummer job much time to see. I mean, it worries me that you might jump from job to job. And how many jobs will let you leave early to get our daughter from school? We need for you to have a flexible situation since I normally can't get to Lily's school by three."

"You make it sound like I have trouble holding down a job."

"Well Jack, you've never had a job you kept for more than a year. We've been married seven years and you've had five jobs. What conclusion am I supposed to come to?"

"Come on Kath, that isn't fair. I'd just graduated from college a couple years back when we first married, and I wasn't on my feet yet and I only had a part-time job at Vlad's Video Games. Then I tried working at the bank when Father got me a job there, but you know that just wasn't my thing. And then my next job was temporary all along, working at Gamer's Games Unlimited, so it isn't fair to count that one. And then I worked for that asshole at the wireless phone store. I mean nobody could deal with that freak. And then I ended up where I am with Flanders. So you can really only count this as my first real job."

"That's exactly what I mean Jack, you just got your first real job in the time I've know you, and you're already thinking of quitting. What am I supposed to think? I don't want to stay in a marriage where I'm supporting my husband forever. This is part of our problem."

"Wait a minute Kath, it's not my fault you've got a great job and make more money than me. I'm glad for you and everything, but you have to give me time to find my own great job."

"And what about Lily? How will we get her from school?"

"I don't know, but I'm sure we'll work something out."

Kathy looked away out the window and pursed her lips tight. She knew this conversation backwards and forewords. She didn't know how many times they'd discussed Jack's career, or lack of one, but it was more than the number of her fingers. Kathy felt a bit mean getting on Jack's case like that, but at this point she planned to divorce Jack, so she wasn't as concerned. Kathy's thoughts were interrupted by Jack, "Kath, all I ask is that you give me more time to find my way, okay?"

Kathy nodded and smiled weakly. She didn't know what else to say. Sometimes she felt like a pushover allowing Jack to continue to not make a significant contribution to the family finances. Then Kathy reminded herself that it may not matter to her much longer what Jack did with his job. Once the divorce was done, she wouldn't care what he made.

The next morning Jack stood with hands on hips, impatiently waiting to leave. He'd been ready for twenty minutes, while Kathy was just pulling on her after-ski boots. "Okay I'm ready to go. I've got my ski boots, do you have my skis and poles?" asked Kathy.

"Yeah, I've got 'em. Let's go," answered Jack. Jack held the door open while Kathy squeezed through with her boot bag in hand, goggles around her neck. Jack picked up the ski bag and his ski boots and they were off for the lifts.

They bought their lift tickets and found a locker downstairs. Kathy unzipped the ski bag and pulled her own skis out. She fished around inside the bag and only found Jack's skis and poles. "Hey Jack, where's my poles?"

"They should be in the bag."

"Well they're not. Look and see for yourself." Jack stood with his ski boots on and looked into the bag. "Your right, they aren't here. I wonder where…oh wait a minute. I know what happened. I left them in the back of the SUV."

"Why are they in the back of the SUV?" asked Kathy.

"I couldn't fit them into the ski bag with both sets of skis in there."

"Oh that's just great. So now one of us has to walk back to the car and get them."

"I get them Kath. I'm sorry," offered Jack.

"No, I'll get them myself."

"Come on Kath, that isn't fair. Let me go get them. It was an honest mistake. I just forgot to get them out of the SUV last night when we unpacked. I'll just take off my ski boots and go get them."

"No no, I'll get them. Give me the keys to the car," insisted Kathy. Jack reluctantly took the keys from his pocket and handed them to Kathy, who turned quickly and left. "Kath, I really don't mind…" But she was already gone and not listening.

Kathy returned with the missing poles and set the car keys down on the bench without comment. She sat down with a huff and quickly put on her own boots, grabbed her poles and skis and headed off towards the stairs with Jack in tow. "Hey Kath, I'm really sorry about the poles, but can we just let it go and have a good time?" asked Jack.

"Yes we can, but I guess this just reminds me of so much of what is wrong between us."

"Come on Kath, don't be like that."

"How do you want me to be after having to walk a mile in the snow to fetch poles that we should have had with us?"

"I would have gone to get them myself if you would have let me," Jack offered lamely.

"No, I wanted to get them myself," Kathy said with a sigh and with less anger.

The first hour of skiing was strained and with little conversation between the two. Eventually the ice melted amongst them and they settled into a fun day of skiing in excellent conditions. Both Jack and Kathy were accomplished skiers and carved up the fresh snow until their legs gave out in the afternoon. It was a Monday, and the slopes were not crowded.

Kathy and Jack walked back to their hotel holding hands after a nice time at dinner. Kathy wondered why she let him hold her hand, but her mind was a bit fuzzy after two or three glasses of wine. Kathy normally only drank one or one and a half glasses. Although Kathy kept saying 'no,' Jack insisted on refilling her wine glass several times. Kathy knew it wasn't a good idea, but drank the wine anyways.

Before she could think about it much more, Jack massaged Kathy's back side as they ascended in the elevator alone. Kathy pushed Jack's hand away firmly. But Jack persisted and playfully rubbed her backside again. She pushed his hand away again, but this time without conviction.

Jack fumbled with the room key, flustered in anticipation while Kathy continued to tease him with making faces. Jack finally got the door opened and pulled Kathy onto the floor of the room. Kathy kicked the door shut and they pulled at each other's clothes. When Kathy got Jack's pants off she grinned as she said, "Jack's been a bad boy and now he's going to get punished." Kathy roughly massaged Jack in a way that excited him even further. Their physical pleasure climaxed in a thoroughly enjoyable make-up session.

They lay back on the pillows exhausted and satisfied, laying arm in arm. Kathy sighed and said, "You know Jack, the best part about fighting with you is what happens after."

"You ain't kidding," agreed Jack.

"But I wonder if this was a mistake. I'm not sure why I let us end up in bed. Maybe I'm drunk," said Kathy.

"No Kathy, don't ruin tonight. It was great, and could be a sign of good things to come for us."

"I don't know…I mean this doesn't mean that anything's changed between us."

"Just give this trip a chance. Let's see what happens. I might have to just pick a fight with you tomorrow as well," said Jack.

"You'd better not," Kathy said playfully.

"Maybe tomorrow I'll just forget your skis this time."

"And if you do then you'll owe me big time."

"Oh, we'll see about that," said Jack.

"No way, buster. If you forget my skis you won't deserve anything. Maybe I'd give you a spanking though."

"Then I'd turn you over my knee and give you a bare-assed spanking," countered Jack.

"You just try it buster."

"I just might," said Jack.

Kathy got into the shower and put her hands over her eyes. My God, what am I doing? I'm such a whore! I can't believe I just did that! I'm planning on divorcing Jack, and I let him seduce me? My goodness, what was I thinking? Maybe I did have too much to drink? Maybe I should say something to him…but what?

Jack and Kathy walked to the ski lodge the next morning. Jack tried to hold Kathy's hand, but she gently pushed his hand away. They chatted pleasantly while swinging the skis over their arms. They followed the arrow pointing downstairs to the ski lockers. Kathy sat down in front of their locker and began to unlace her after-ski boots. Kathy glanced up as she noticed him fishing through his pockets. "Don't tell me you forgot the locker key," said Kathy.

"No I got it. I just don't remember where I put it."

"You forgot the key," said Kathy as she rolled her eyes and sighed.

"Hang on Kath, just give me a minute and I'll find it. Don't be like that."

"Look Jack, I'm trying to be patient. But it's pretty tough after you forgot the poles yesterday."

"I didn't forget it! I just don't know where I put it, that's all." Kathy looked away and breathed out loudly. She restrained herself from saying anything further for a couple minutes, which required considerable effort.

"Alright, do you want me to go back to the room and find the key?" asked Kathy.

"Here it is," said a grinning Jack as he pulled the key from inside his ski gloves. "See, if you'd just back off and give me a chance I'd find the key. I knew I had it. You just don't have any faith in me."

"Maybe I'm not…well, I suppose there's something to that," said Kathy as she caught herself before getting reactive.

"You're too hard on me, Kath. You expect me to be perfect…just like we talked about in your shrink's office."

"Yes, but I don't expect perfection anymore, just responsibility."

"What's the difference?" asked Jack.

"I don't want to go there, Jack. This isn't helpful to either one of us."

"You see, this is exactly your problem, you treat me like I'm stupid."

"Well, let's just drop it."

"So you never forget anything? You never make any mistakes then?"

"You know…about last night," began Kathy.

"No, don't say anything…" said Jack.

"No, I just don't know if it was a good idea, given…"

"But Kath…"

"Just forget it. Let's just go skiing before we fight again."

Jack put his after-ski boots in the locker, grabbed his skis and poles and walked off towards the lifts. Kathy slowly raised her head, rubbed her face, and slowly closed the locker. She took care to put the locker key in a zipped pocket, double checking to make sure it was safe. She picked up her gear and shuffled after Jack.

By the time Kathy caught up to Jack outside, he had just finished putting on his skis and moved off towards the lift line. Kathy got into line behind an older couple, and excused herself as she slid in place next to Jack. He looked up at her, but she did not return his gaze. Jack thought, Oh no, I hope Kath's not going to punish me all day again. This might be one of those long days that I hate.

Jack searched his mind for just the right thing to say. He dreaded a day without talking. He waited until they were on the chair lift. "Look Kath, maybe I shouldn't have tried to get you into bed. I'm just trying to give us the best chance to save us. Kathy nodded and squeezed his arm with her gloved hand. Jack exhaled in relief and thought, thank God! He knew the day would be okay, maybe not great, but at least okay. Jack pat Kathy's thigh, leaving his hand there. She turned to him and smiled weakly, tears glistening in her eyes, and then pulled her hand away. Jack smiled and then scanned his environment. He looked up and saw the deep blue sky, decorated with a few wispy clouds.

"Looks like a beautiful day. The news said it's going to get up into the thirties today, which sounds perfect for skiing," said Jack, wanting desperately to change the subject. He hoped Kathy would go along with him and let the issue go.

"Yes, it's lovely. I'm glad I wore my warm jacket, or I'd be freezing."

"Yeah, you still like that jacket I got you?"

"Oh yes, I love it," said Kathy as she straightened her jacket and scarf.

"So where do you want to ski?" asked Jack.

"Let's go over to chair five."

"Okay."

Clouds blew in after lunch, turning the day from bright to gray. The lift lines were short, and Jack and Kathy had taken many runs, and both were feeling tired. But the conditions were so nearly perfect, that neither wanted to stop. "My legs are starting to shake when I ski. I think I better stop for the day," said Kathy.

"Okay, let's make this our last run. I'll race you to the lodge," suggested Jack.

"No, I don't have it in me to race. You go ahead and I'll meet you at the locker."

Jack skied off the lift and put his pole straps on without stopping. He waved at Kathy without bothering to turn and took off at high speed. Jack had been skiing most of his life and was an accomplished skier. Kathy got off the lift and stopped. She adjusted her hat and goggles before pushing off towards the lodge. She skied slowly and stayed away from the moguls. Kathy was almost to the bottom when she saw a skier on his back off to the side of the run. She stopped to see if he was okay. As she got near the skier seemed familiar, and suddenly Kathy realized it was Jack.

"Oh my God, Jack, are you okay?"

"I don't know. I think I tweaked my ankle pretty good. Can you take off my left binding? I don't think I can stand up with my ski on."

"Oh sure." Kathy bent down and released Jack's binding. "Here, lean on me and I'll help you stand up." Jack pushed off the snow with his right arm and held onto Kathy's arm with his left. He winced as he stood. Kathy saw the look on his face. "Oh Jack, you're hurt bad. I'll flag down a ski patrol."

"No, I don't need the ski patrol. I want to see if I can make it down to the lodge on my own."

"Jack, you're hurt. You might have broken your ankle. You need medical attention."

"No I don't. The lodge isn't far, and I want to get myself down."

"Jack, don't be stubborn. How are you going to get yourself down with that ankle?"

"I'll ski. I'll ski real slow and easy."

"You're hurt, and you might make it worse if you try to ski on that ankle. Don't do this to yourself. Let the ski patrol take you down."

"Come on Kath, let me decide for myself."

"Okay…you're right, I guess it's up to you," Kathy said.

Jack bent down and put his ski in position next to his right ski. He slowly put the toe of his boot in the binding, and then pushed down on the back of the boot with the heel of his hand to lock the boot into the binding. He put on a brave face, although Kathy could tell it hurt. Jack glanced at Kathy, and then looked over his shoulder and pushed off with his poles. He skied like a beginner, traversing back and forth across the slope until he reached the lodge entrance. He carefully took off his skis and limped to the locker. Kathy carried her own skis and poles.

It took Jack twice as long as normal to take off his left boot. He massaged his left ankle. After he put on his walking boots, he tried walking back and forth to test the ankle. "You know, it isn't too bad walking in these boots. I think I can walk back to the hotel."

"Why do that to yourself, Jack? I can easily walk back and get the car and come get you. Let me do that for you."

"No, there's no need. I can walk fine."

"I swear, I don't know if I've ever met someone as stubborn as you. You could easily have made your injury way worse by skiing the rest of the way down, and now you want to walk a half mile back to the hotel."

"Come on Kath, I'm the one who's hurt. You can't feel the injury, I can. Let me decide what to do."

Kathy sighed and nodded, "Okay, I don't want to mother you anymore. And you're right, it's your decision."

Jack propped himself up on the bed with a bag of ice on his ankle, having successfully limped the half mile. He picked up the remote control and found the football game. He looked over at Kathy, who stood next to the bed with her arms folded over her chest. "If you want to do something for me, you can go get me a six pack and some dinner," Jack said. Kathy picked up her purse and walked to the door without saying anything. As she was closing the door Jack called after her, "Make it a case of beer; that way you can have a couple." Kathy nodded and shut the door.

An hour later Kathy walked through the door with a pizza and salad in her hands. She set them down on the bed next to Jack. "Don't eat the salad, it's for me," Kathy said.

"Hey, where's the beer?"

"Give me a minute. I couldn't carry the pizza and the beer at the same time. If you're in such a hurry, you can run down to the car and get it yourself."

"Okay, okay. I can wait," said Jack.

"I'll be right back," said Kathy. Kathy returned with a case of beer. She took the ice bucket down the hall and filled it up. She handed a beer to Jack, took one for herself, and put four more on ice. Kathy sat down next to Jack and began to pick at her salad. Jack was already on his second slice. "How's the ankle?"

"Not too bad right now. Although with the ice it's pretty numbed out." Kathy nodded.

"The pizza's good. Where'd you get it?"

"Just some place in the village that was across the street from the grocery store where I got the beer." Jack nodded. He reached over and patted Kathy's leg. She turned towards Jack and smiled weakly, and gently pushed his hand off her leg. She didn't want to fight anymore, but Kathy also didn't want to be physically intimate tonight. She might not want to be intimate with Jack ever again.

"I might even be able to ski tomorrow," said Jack. Kathy shook her head.

"Come on Kath, don't give me that look. You know I hate it. I really might be able to ski tomorrow. I'd probably have to take it easy, maybe just ski intermediate runs, but I think I might be okay by the morning."

Kathy shook her head with her eyes shut. "I don't even want to talk about it. I'm just trying to let you decide for yourself.

We'll see what you want to do in the morning."

Jack shrugged his shoulders and grabbed another slice of pizza. "You'll see, Kath. Hey, hand me another one of those beers." Kathy picked up a beer and shook it over his head, dripping water and bits of ice on his head. Jack laughed and slapped Kathy on the thigh as he took the beer from her.

"Watch it Kath, or I might have to punish you later for that." Kathy rolled her eyes and headed off for the bathroom.

"Oh you just wait and see," Jack called after her.

Jack woke in the morning. He stretched and got up. He'd forgotten about his ankle until he put his full weight on it, and limped. It was mostly stiff, but he felt a stab of pain when he planted his left ankle to change directions on his way to start the coffee machine. Jack climbed into the shower, directing the stream of hot water to the outer side of his ankle. The hot water felt good. Maybe after I get the blood circulating in my foot I'll be okay, he thought.

He'd put half his ski clothes on when Kathy woke. She rubbed her eyes and looked at him. "So it looks like you've decided to give it a go?" asked Kathy.

"I'm going skiing. Come on and get in the shower," answered Jack.

"Wait a minute, so you're actually going to ski on that ankle?"

"Sure I am. It's a little sore, but I'll be alright if I take it easy."

"And what does 'take it easy' mean?"

"I'll just stick to the blue squares and stay off the black diamonds."

"Oh my God Jack, you're...well, okay, do whatever you want."

"Come on Kath, don't talk to me like that. I know what I'm doing. My ankle isn't that bad, it's just a little sore."

"Alright let's see. Stand up and put your full weight on it." Jack stood. "Now go up on your toes." As Jack went up on his toes he grimaced in pain. "You see Jack, you're in a lot of pain. Don't you think you might make it worse?"

"It didn't hurt that bad, you're exaggerating my injury."

"Don't treat me like I'm an idiot. I saw the look on your face, and you were in serious pain," said Kathy.

"It only hurt a little."

"A little? Come off it Jack, people don't make faces…never mind," Kathy said.

"It's my ankle and it's up to me if I ski, and I'm skiing today."

"Okay Jack, you go ahead and ski, but I think I'll stay back."

"And what does that mean?"

"That means I'm not skiing today. You do what you want."

"Come on Kath, don't act like that. You're making too big a deal out of nothing."

"I'm trying to hold myself back and not go there. And I'm trying to take care of myself here. And I think taking care of myself right now means that I'm not skiing today. I don't think I would enjoy skiing today," said Kathy.

"If you weren't so damn critical then things would work out for us."

"Oh I see, so once again, all the problems in our marriage are my issues," said Kathy.

"Exactly!"

"Jack, this is part of the reason I want a divorce. You don't take any responsibility for our marriage struggles."

"No I don't. I'm perfectly happy with how our marriage is. You're the one with the issues. If you didn't act like such a bitch, we'd get along okay," said Jack.

"A bitch? Yes, you've make it clear that's what you think of me. If you think I'm such a bitch then why did you marry me in the first place?"

"I guess that was a mistake. If I'd known you'd turn into such a control freak I wouldn't have married you."

"And this is another of the reasons why I want to divorce. This isn't working between us," said Kathy.

"Well good, we agree on one thing. I've had enough of this. I'm going skiing. You do whatever the hell you want," said Jack. He picked up his gear bag, grabbed a beer from the ice bucket and slammed the door behind him.

Jack carried his skis out of the lodge and stood facing the three lifts in front of the lodge. I guess I'll start out with the beginner chair to loosen my ankle up, he thought. He slowly made his way towards the triple chair and winced with each step. He struggled to carry the weight of the ski boot with his bad ankle. He dropped his skis on the snow. It was still early and the sun shone through the tops of the pine trees. He breathed in the crisp, cool air deep into his lungs. "I love that pine tree smell," he said aloud. Jack slid his left ski up and back on the snow. The ankle felt a bit sore, but seemed strong enough to ski.

The chair lift dropped him off at the top of the gentle slope. Jack tightened his boot buckles and made his left extra tight, and then pushed off with his poles. His ankle felt good until he made his first turn, shooting pain through his foot. As he continued down he scaled back to more gentle turns, and as his first run ended his ankle loosened a bit. It seemed to hold up better under the gentle turning. At the bottom Jack decided he was ready for the intermediate runs.

If it had been icy conditions it would have been a short day of skiing. The cold conditions and fresh snow created soft, yielding snow, not requiring much effort to turn his skis. Jack skied the sides of the runs, avoiding the moguls in the middle. He slowly stretched at the bottom of each run while waiting in line. "So far so good. I'm gonna make Kathy eat her words," Jack said aloud.

Around midday Jack stopped for lunch. He ordered a cheeseburger, fries and two beers and sat down in the lodge. His ankle hurt, so he took off his left ski boot. His whole foot throbbed as though his heart were located in his foot. Jack massaged his foot and ankle while he ate. He hoped the beer might provide some deadening of the pain. The longer his lunch break went on, the more his ankle became sore. Damn, maybe it's hurting more as it thaws out, Jack thought. Maybe I'll head back to the hotel...Although I don't want to go back right now, because Kathy will just say "I told you so." I won't give her the satisfaction. Maybe I'll just have another beer or two before I head back, so it'll look like I skied most of the day. Jack glanced at his watch and noted that it was only 1:15.

At 3:00 Jack stepped through the door of their hotel room. The room was empty. Jack picked up a note on the bed that read,

Jack,

I went shopping.
I'll be back in time for dinner with you.

Kathy

Jack tossed the note on the night stand and walked down the hall for fresh ice. He took off his boots and socks and turned on the T.V. He stocked the ice bucket with six beers, opened one, and put his foot up on ice. Jack picked up the remote control and found an old Clint Eastwood movie.

When Kathy got back to the room she found Jack asleep with the remote on his chest and a full complement of four empty beer cans serving as paper weights for her note on the night stand. She looked at his ankle and rolled her eyes, breathing out loudly. She walked over to the case of beer and noticed that many of them were gone. "My God, did I marry an alcoholic," she said to no one in particular. Jack stirred, knocking the remote to the floor. Kathy stood and pondered her thoughts. I suppose I was a little tough on Jack over the whole ankle thing. I really do want to let that be his thing and stay out of it. After a few minutes she shook her head and shrugged her shoulders, and started the bath water.

Jack opened his eyes and turned his head towards Kathy as she emerged from the bathroom with a towel around her. He rubbed his eyes with his fingers and smiled as though awakening from a pleasant dream. "Hey Kath, come over here and give me a kiss," invited Jack. Kathy pursed her lips and paused to think, and then walked over to the bed and kissed Jack with a smack. Jack pulled her back for a longer embrace and a wetter kiss, which she allowed. As Kathy pulled away Jack groped at her behind, and Kathy slapped his hand away as if he were picking at a dessert intended for later. "No Jack, get in the shower. I'm starving."

Jack stretched and extracted himself from the clutches of the bed. Although his foot hurt, he deliberately walked without a limp in spite of the pain, turning his face away from her. He examined his foot in the shower, and was surprised to see that it had swollen to twice its normal size, and had turned the color of a ripe plum.

At dinner Jack and Kathy sat sipping red wine. Kathy worked at her salad while Jack gulped down his soup. They sat in a restaurant with dim lighting and rich burgundy velvet booths. Jack enjoyed how the candle light danced in Kathy's blue eyes. She looked beautiful in her black sweater and tight jeans.

"So, how was skiing today?" asked Kathy.

Jack grinned and said, "It was alright."

Kathy sized him up, glancing at him sideways before asking, "And how did your ankle hold up?"

"It was fine. I was able to ski okay. I just stayed off the steeps and took it easy, you know."

Kathy nodded knowingly. "It was pretty swollen when I got back to the room from shopping."

"Yeah, it swelled up a little," agreed Jack.

"A little? It was twice the normal size!"

"Oh you're exaggerating. It isn't that bad. I can't even feel much pain."

"Is that why you didn't lace up your left boot, because it feels fantastic?"

"Okay, so it's a little sore," Jack admitted.

"Are you glad that you skied today?"

"Come on Kath, don't be like that. Why do you like to rub it in like that? Yeah my ankle's sore and I could barely ski. Okay I admit it. Are you happy now, or do you want me to go on and on about what a stupid idiot I am for skiing today? Would that make you happier?" Kathy pursed her lips, but didn't say anything.

The waitress brought their entrees. They ate in silence, looking out the window at the village. Couples walked past the window hand in hand or arm in arm. Kathy turned away from the window and eyed her salad, slowly lifting her fork to her mouth. After swallowing she said, "God Jack, you make me sound like some sadistic bitch that's out for blood."

"Sometimes you are a sadistic bitch out for blood or something. I don't even know what you want from me. I don't think I can please you no matter what I do. Even my breathing seems to offend you."

Kathy averted her eyes as tears welled up in them. She wiped her eyes with her napkin. Jack reached out and put his hand on hers. Kathy pulled her hand away. Jack sighed, and then reengaged with his steak. When the waitress came by he took the last swallow of wine and ordered another glass. The remainder of the dinner was draped in silence.

They walked back towards the hotel. Jack reached out and took Kathy's hand. She allowed him to hold her hand, yet her hand remained limp in his. After walking this way for several minutes Jack broke the silence, "Come on Kath, talk to me. I hate it when you shut me out."

"I don't know what to say. I'm not sure it would be helpful to talk more about it…we've been over all this, and we don't seem to get anywhere. I don't want to fight anymore. Let's just leave it be…I'm sad at what's become of us.

"I'm sorry I was mean back in the restaurant. I didn't mean what I said," offered Jack.

"Yes you did. Don't pretend that you didn't feel every word you said."

"Come on Kath, I was angry. I said things I shouldn't have said."

"Yes you were angry, but you meant it. At this point I'm no longer looking for an apology. It's too late for an apology." Both walked in silence as they pondered their evening.

"I don't know what else to say, Kath. I'm sorry about in the restaurant. Can we just get past it?"

Kathy thought for a moment before saying, "I think I can set it aside for now. I would like to enjoy the rest of this trip, as much as we can."

"Can't we just forget about tonight and start fresh?"

"What do you mean?" asked Kathy.

"Just pretend like tonight didn't happen. Maybe we can go back to the room and have a great make up session in bed. That might do it."

Kathy frowned in response, and then added, "No, I don't want to confuse either one of us. And I don't feel like making love tonight."

"Why not?"

"It just doesn't feel right tonight. And I still think that last night was a mistake…especially given where we're at…maybe coming on this trip was a mistake…maybe I felt like I had to give you this one last trip."

Jack let Kathy's hand go, and then folded his arms across his chest. Kathy pulled her collar up against the wind and cold and walked with her eyes on the snow in front of her. Kathy turned towards Jack and said, "I want to walk around a bit. I'll be back in the room in an hour or so." Jack didn't hear her and kept walking towards the room.

Jack reached the hotel door and turned around to see where Kathy was while he held the door for her. She wasn't in sight. Jack let go of the door and retraced his steps, looking for her. Thirty minutes later he found her walking slowly in the village. "Hey Kath, what're you doing?"

"I just want to be alone for awhile and think. I'll meet you back at the room later. Didn't you hear me tell you that?" Jack looked into her face as if trying to read a difficult puzzle. Then he threw his hands up in the air and turned to go back to the hotel.

Kathy walked around the village without noticing her surroundings. Her mind seemed clouded. Why did I come on this trip...I already knew the marriage was over...I suppose Susan was right, that I feel guilty and pressured myself to go on this trip for Jack...I don't know, did I have some magical hope that things would be different...possibly...I wonder if that's why I had sex with Jack last night...I still can't believe I did that...maybe this trip has just confirmed it for me...nothing is changed. We're done...at least I'm done."

The River: Day 8

The morning sun shone its golden rays upon the camper's faces. Mike sat up in his sleeping bag, while the women turned over and buried their faces in their bags. Jack continued sleeping with the sun shining directly on him. Hunger pangs beat within Mike's stomach, with each heartbeat echoing through an empty drum. He lay back down, but couldn't return to the welcomed distraction of sleep. The pain in his stomach kept him awake. He put his hat over his face to protect him from the sun and waited for the others. The thought of his last protein bar burned its image in his mind's eye. He could think of nothing else.

Should I eat it before the others wake up, he wondered. No. I can't do that to them…well, maybe I'll just take one bite, and save the rest for the others. No, if I take one bite I might not be able to keep myself from finishing it off…what if I take one bit, and then wrap up the rest and put it away in my pack? No, whom am I kidding? If I take one bite, I'll eat the whole thing, I just know it.

Mike was interrupted in his internal debate when Stacy whispered, "Hey Mike, are you awake?"

"Yeah, I've been up awhile. My stomach won't let me sleep anymore."

"I don't think I can hike a single step if I don't get a bite of that last protein bar," Stacy responded.

"I haven't thought of anything except that bar. I hope it isn't all melted. Let me check."

Mike pulled the last bar out of his pack, his mouth watering in anticipation. It felt soft in his hands. "It's melted. I'm going to put it in the water to firm it up a bit. I don't want to lose a single gram of it on the wrapper."

Stacy watched with eyes riveted to the silver wrapper as Mike placed the bar in a bucket of cool water, and then set the bucket in the shade. Jack and Kathy stirred and sat up. They rubbed the sleep from their eyes. Mike noted their awakening and said, "I've got breakfast cooling in the fridge."

"What breakfast, man?" asked Jack.

"The only breakfast we got left, the golden protein bar."

"Oh yeah, let me at it," said Jack as he pull himself out of his sleeping bag.

"Let's give it a minute to firm up while we pack up. It was a bit melted from yesterday," said Mike.

"Firm it up my ass. It's not gonna taste any better firm or melted. I can't even think until I get some of that in me."

"Come on Jack, let's just pack up and wait a minute. It won't kill us to give it a minute to cool," interjected Kathy.

"Lay off Kath, you wait all you want, I'm going to eat my fourth now!" Jack angrily rolled up his sleeping bag, tied it up and threw his few possessions into his bag. "Okay man, I'm packed. Break out the grub, man."

"Wait a damn minute, Jack! I don't want us to miss a single molecule of the only damn food we have left!" countered Mike. Mike stood as he said this and Jack approached him nose to nose, fists clinched.

Stacy tried to intercede and said, "Come on you guys, don't…"

"Shit Mike, every time I open my mouth you're backing me off. It's like I can't do anything right in your eyes!" said Jack.

Kathy felt the impulse to jump on Jack verbally, but checked herself just as she opened her mouth.

"It's not about you, Jack! I'm just trying to make the most of the bite we have left. And it's probably the only bite we'll get all day," said Mike.

Jack shrugged his shoulders and said, "Whatever man," as he turned and walked away.

Mike turned away and folded his arms across his chest, scared he'd almost come to blows with his best friend. My God, I've never come that close to…oh shit. Now is not the time for me to get into it with him, even if he is acting like an asshole, thought Mike.

He eyed Jack briefly while he made a decision, and then slowly retrieved the precious bar from the bucket. It had firmed up slightly, but he would have liked to give it more time. Jack snatched the bar from Mike's hands and tore open the wrapper, with Mike now fearing to protest, after what had almost transpired. The bar was indeed soft, but mostly in one piece. Jack broke it in half, handed one half to Mike, and then ate half of what was in his hand. He gave the rest to Kathy. The other three ate eagerly, with Mike licking the microscopic remains off the wrapper.

Jack went down and submerged himself in the river, washed his face with his hands and returned to their gear. He lifted his pack, put on the straps and was heading for the trail when he felt Mike's hand on his shoulder. Jack brushed Mike's hand away, and Mike said, "Hey buddy, I don't want it to be like this between us…I'm sorry for jumping on you, I'm just nervous about not having any more food."

Jack hesitated, eyed Mike for a moment, and then said, "Don't worry about it man. It was nothing."

"No, it wasn't nothing. That's what worries me," said Mike.

"Look man, don't make more of it than it was. We're both a little jumpy and that's it. Let's forget it and get this damn nature hike over with, okay," said Jack. Mike nodded.

They hefted their packs to their backs and walked slowly downriver along the water. The morsel each had eaten failed to alleviate their hunger, in fact they felt hungrier. Mike thought it a cruel trick to give his stomach one bite of food, as if teasing his stomach. He wasn't sure if it was his imagination, but Mike did find more energy in his weary body. He walked with less pain, whereas the last hour of the day's hike last night required an immense effort. Although his body might have more energy, his mind didn't seem to benefit any. Few thoughts arose, and he seemed to be in a daydream state with soft focus. Mike walked on without conscious planning, merely responding to the river's terrain involuntarily. Jack led the way and Mike brought up the rear.

By midday the sun had heated the oven they walked in to one hundred degrees. Mike didn't take any notice of the temperature, and was surprised when Kathy suddenly slumped to her hands and knees in front of him. Stacy gave a cry, and lowered Kathy's head into her lap. Her eyes were unfocused and her face beet red. Mike focused his thoughts through sheer effort, making himself concentrate on Kathy's face.

"What's wrong with her?" asked Jack.

"She's going into heat stroke. We have to hydrate her and get her into the shade," said Mike tonelessly.

Mike surveyed their environ and located a low, wispy tree. "Jack, help me lower Kathy into the water, and then we have to find her some shade. Stacy, get her some drinkable water. We have to cool her down immediately." Stacy rolled out a towel under the tree, and Jack and Mike lowered her in the river. Kathy started at the cold water, but didn't resist. Jack kept his arm around her shoulders to keep her face out of the water. After about ten minutes Mike helped half carry and half support Kathy walking up to the towel, where she lay next to Stacy. Kathy's flushing had lessened slightly.

"I have to get back into that water myself," said Mike in a low voice. Jack followed Mike into the water, while Stacy remained with Kathy. The men sat in the water, grateful for the rest. Neither of them had much energy left after hiking the past three hours on essentially no food. They slowly rose from the water and joined the women under the tree.

"How long till Kathy can get back on the trail?" asked Jack.

"I don't know, but definitely not yet. We should wait until her color returns," said Mike.

"Hey man, I want to get back tonight. I'm not spending another night out here. Let's get back on the trail as soon as Kathy possibly can," said Jack.

"I don't know if Kathy can hike again today at all," said a concerned Stacy.

"She'll be a whole lot better off once she gets some real food in her, and something besides water to drink," countered Jack.

"Now hold on Jack, Kathy just fainted from being overheated. We can't just throw her back on the trail. It's dangerous! People die from being overheated," Mike warned.

"Look man, don't lecture me. I get that Kath needs to rest, but we have to get back tonight. She'll be fine in a couple hours."

Mike looked over at Stacy, who returned his glance with worried eyes. "Why don't we all get some much needed rest, and reevaluate in a couple hours," suggested Stacy.

"Sounds good to me," said Jack lightly. He reached over to the small ice chest and pulled out a beer. "Anybody else want one?" Mike and Stacy eyed the warm beer and shook their heads. The ice had long melted and all that remained was warm beer, slightly cooled by the river water Jack continually freshened. "Suit yourselves," said Jack with a shrug.

Mike awoke to the sound of a bird's cry. He rolled over and checked his watch. They'd been asleep two and a half hours. Mike rubbed his head, as he'd awakened to a headache. He felt hot and light-headed. He reached over and placed his palm on Stacy's forehead. She felt warm too. "Come on, we have to get in the water and cool off," said Mike. Stacy didn't stir.

"Stacy! Can you hear me? Wake up!" Stacy looked at Mike with dreamy eyes. She rubbed her eyes and turned over on her towel. "No Stacy, don't go back to sleep. We have to start moving soon," urged Mike. He helped her sit up.

"I don't feel too great," she said.

"I know, Babe. Let me help you into the water. That might help." When Stacy was settled sitting in the river Mike returned to where the others lay. Jack was already awake and sitting against the tree, "Hey Jack, help me get Kathy into the water. We have to keep cool, especially Kathy."

Jack helped Mike lift Kathy and carry her into the water. She woke with a start when she hit the cool water. "Oh my God, that's cold!" Mike examined Kathy's face carefully. "You still look red to me. What do you think, Stacy?"

"She looks flushed to me too, but better than before," confirmed Stacy.

"So now you're going to tell me that we can't take her anywhere today," voiced an angry Jack.

"Don't you care about Kathy's condition?" asked Mike.

"'Course I care about my own wife! Don't give me that shit. But I also care about getting us all back to civilization! Now isn't the time to coddle somebody's sunburned face."

"That's not a sunburn, Jack. She's overheated! We have to wait till she's ready or she might die before we get back," shot back Mike.

"She might also die if we don't get her some food soon!"

"We can go for awhile without food. That's not as pressing as us keeping cool and hydrated," said Stacy.

"I'm surrounded by idiots! Look, I'm hot too. It's hot out here. We're going to be hot until we get out of the sun, and the sooner we do that the better. We're all going to be a whole lot better once we get back to the truck and get a real meal, right?"

When neither Mike nor Stacy responded, Jack huffed off back to the tree and opened another beer. Kathy was holding her head in both hands. "Oh my God, I've never had a headache like this," moaned Kathy.

"Kathy, you've got heat-stroke. We have to keep plenty of water in you and keep you cool," began Mike. "Hey Stacy, go back and get Kathy's hat." Then he turned back to Kathy, "You have a headache because of the heat-stroke. Your head will get better after you cool off and rehydrate." Kathy nodded that she understood.

"This water's too cold, help me get out," complained Kathy.

"No Kathy, it's important for you to cool down," replied Stacy.

"I'm so cold! I'm too cold already," said Kathy.

"Kathy, your flushed face and headache tells us you're not as cool as you need to be. Just be patient for a bit longer. You feel cold but you're still overheated," soothed Mike.

Kathy nodded. "I don't think I can hike anymore today," said Kathy.

"Okay, then we'll just sit tight," answered Stacy as she looked to Mike.

"We can spend the night here. That tree will provide good shade from the morning sun."

Kathy shivered as she lay dripping wet on her towel. Stacy sat next to her, while Mike walked over to where Jack sipped on his warm beer.

"Hey man, how you holding up?" asked Mike.

"It isn't that I don't care for Kath, I love her, but I'm antsy to get back already. I just can't take the delays. If it isn't the boat getting a hole in it, then it's running out of food. If it isn't that then it's running out of ice for the beer, and if it isn't that then somebody's overheating and we have to sit on our hands twiddling our thumbs while we starve to death. I just can't take it much longer, you know what I mean?"

"I know Jack. I never knew hunger could feel like this. I mean, I thought I was hungry yesterday, but yesterday's nothing like today. I keep seeing pictures of cheeseburgers and chocolate milk shakes."

"For me it's a steak with a mushroom, blue-cheese sauce, fries and a cold beer…I don't want to be insensitive, but when will Kath be ready to walk?" asked Jack.

"Jack, you're not going to want to hear this, but probably not till the morning."

"No way, man! Tell me you're pulling my leg."

Mike closed his eyes and breathed out slowly. "I wouldn't joke about something like that in a situation like this. Kathy's still recovering from heat-stroke, and I think it would be dangerous to ask her to move."

"What if I carry her?"

"Carry her? You can't be serious. How can you have the energy to carry her? I can barely carry myself."

"Look man, I'll do whatever I have to so me and Kath get back. And if I have to carry her the rest of the way, then I will."

"I still think we ought to wait till morning. She can probably walk on her own by then."

"This is truly unbelievable! Whatever man," said Jack as he got up and walked away.

Mike went back to the women. He sat on the towel next to Stacy. Mike glanced over at Kathy, who still didn't look good. "Hey Stacy, how are we doing on waters?" asked Mike.

"I think we only have a couple left."

"Damn. I guess I better boil some more water then."

"What for? Isn't your water warm enough for you?" asked Stacy.

"Very funny." Mike went down to the water and returned with his metal bucket full. He gathered fuel and lit a fire. He hung the half-circular handle over a tepee of sticks he'd made.

"Really Mike, why are you boiling water?" asked Stacy.

"The water looks crystal clear, but it actually contains microscopic bacteria that'll make you sick if you drink it. Boiling the water kills the germs so that it's safe."

"Good thing we brought you along on this trip then."

Mike looked at Stacy affectionately and hugged her. "I so appreciate you keeping your sense of humor, even in a situation like this."

"It's the only way I can keep from either going crazy or killing someone. And if I had to pick someone right now, it would be Jack," said Stacy. Mike laughed.

Mike had saved twelve empty water bottles in his pack, and refilled them with boiled water once it had cooled enough. When they abandoned the boat, Mike had known they'd run out of water sooner or later, and knew they'd need to drink often to keep hiking. Jack approached as Mike replaced the bottles in his pack.

"I'm going to make a go of it," said Jack.

"Make a go of what?"

"It's cooling off now, so I figure it's a good time to make for the truck. I can…"

"Now wait a minute…"

"Hear me out, Mike," said Jack. "I can travel faster on my own. I'll go for help and bring the rangers back to you guys here."

"But it'll be dark in less than two hours. How will you hike in the dark?"

"I'll figure it out. Look man, I can't just sit on my hands while we starve to death. I have to do something."

"Jack, don't do it! It's a suicide mission. What if you don't find the truck or the marina?"

"Look man, you don't have to agree with me, but I have to do this. I'm going crazy sitting on my ass while we're dying of heat and hunger."

"Does Kathy know you're going?"

"No, not yet."

Both men were silent, each contemplating their plight. Jack pictured jumping in the truck and driving to the restaurant they passed just before turning off for the marina. Mike kept wondering if Jack would make it. "Look man, I'm worried about you. You don't know the river, it's got to be a good five miles yet, and you'll only have a half moon's light."

"I still got my flashlight," said Jack.

Mike nodded and turned his head away. "My God, how did we get into this?"

"I'm heading over to tell Kath, and then I'll get going. I want to use whatever light's left."

Jack found Kathy still lying on her towel under the tree. At first Kathy didn't stir when Jack spoke. Jack knelt down and shook her shoulder. Kathy groaned and turned her head. She shielded her eyes from the low sun when she looked up. "Hey Kath, I'm going to make a run for it."

"You mean you're going on alone?"

"Yep. I figure you need to rest up, and I can make better time on my own."

"Oh Jack, please don't go. I'm afraid I'll never see you again."

"Don't be silly Kath, I'll be fine. And I can bring back help. You might not be able to get much farther."

"Something about this just doesn't feel right to me, but...I wish you'd think this over some more. What if you get lost?"

"I'm taking the extra map with me. How hard can it be to find the marina? I mean I know it's on the west side of the river and can't be more than four or five miles away."

"That's a long ways when you haven't eaten more than a bite all day."

"Look Kath, I'll be fine, and I want to get going while I still have daylight. You sit tight and I'll bring back the cavalry, okay?"

"I still don't like it, but I guess it's up to you."

"That's right, now you're getting it. This is a good idea, you'll see."

Jack bent down and kissed Kathy on the forehead, and with an ear to ear grin turned to go. He picked up his ice chest of warm beer and put on his red hat. Jack pulled off his hat and ran his fingers over his dad's signature across the front of the hat. "Help me out here, dad. I figure I can get half way back before I lose the light," said Jack. He waded into the river, dumped out the lukewarm water and dipped the ice chest into the river.

"Here, take these," offered Mike as he handed him two of the bottled waters.

"Thanks," said Jack as he stowed them in his ice chest.

"We'll follow the river, so look for us along the shore when you come back."

"Will do, man," said Jack.

Jack slapped Mike on the back, and then headed for the path in the hills. The other three watched him stop at the top of the first hill and wave. Then he disappeared over the hill.

"You think he's going to make it?" asked Stacy.

"Dear God, I hope so. I'm mostly worried about him getting lost after dark," said Mike.

"Well, he seemed determined to go no matter what anybody said."

Mike nodded sadly, and put his arm around Stacy. "We need more fuel for the fire. I plan to keep it going all night, in case anybody sees it."

Mike and Stacy wondered around the surrounding area, gathering all the dried wood they came across. By the time they were done they had a large pile on the beach. They collapsed on the beach, exhausted. Mike rubbed his temples with both hands. Stacy put her forehead on her knees. "I can't believe how much it took out of me just to gather a few sticks," said Stacy.

"I know. I've never felt this tired before."

"Mike, will we be able to walk tomorrow?"

"Right now I couldn't walk a mile if my life depended on it. And it might," said Mike as he laughed nervously.

"We're in trouble, aren't we?"

"Yeah…I don't know how we'll get back the last five miles, with no food."

"Is there anything out here we can eat? There's got to be something edible in this God forsaken desert," said Stacy.

"Lizards, birds, maybe a cactus I suppose. I don't have the energy to catch anything, and I don't know where the nearest edible cactus is. I guess we could keep an eye out when we're hiking tomorrow."

"That doesn't sound too promising."

"No, it isn't," said Mike. Mike went to the edge of their cove and shaded his eyes. He scanned the horizon, looking for anything moving. No movement caught his eye.

Kathy woke first the next morning, having been asleep for over twelve hours. She sat up and looked around. The sun didn't seem to be in the right place. She reached over and shook the others. "Hey Stacy, Mike, wake up. It's morning." Mike and Stacy rubbed their eyes. Mike sat up. "Oh my God, the sun's been up for hours. It's got to be mid morning."

"I thought the sun seemed awful high in the sky," said Kathy.

"We overslept. I meant to get us on the trail early before it gets too hot. We have to conserve our energy. Let's get going!"

"Do we have to leave already," asked Stacy who was still prone.

"Absolutely! We have to go before it gets any hotter," said Mike.

Mike threw a bucket of water on the smoking embers and rolled up his and Stacy's sleeping bags, almost with her still in it. He threw his things into his bag, and helped Stacy and Kathy pack as well. They reluctantly headed out after Mike.

At first they made good time, as they were eager to get back and felt refreshed from a good night's sleep. Over the next couple hours they felt their energy drain out of their feet, like syrup out of an almost empty bottle. The rising sun and their declining energy took its toll. They dropped their packs and retreated to the refuge of the river and sat down.

"How are you holding up, Kathy?" asked Mike.

"Oh, okay I guess. I do feel strange though. The last half hour I felt like I was walking through quicksand."

Mike nodded grimly. "How about you, Stacy?" asked Mike.

"I'm alright. I might need to walk a bit more slowly the rest of the day."

"I think we better wait for it to cool off some before we try to hike anymore." Both women nodded without saying anything. All three remained sitting in the water.

After four o'clock they resumed their trek. At first they made fair progress, but they began walking more slowly before long. Kathy noticed her muscles not only grew tired, but began to hurt. In less than an hour she fell behind Stacy and Mike, who walked in front. They talked quietly until they were interrupted by a soft voice.

"Hey guys, wait up. I have to stop," Kathy yelled in a whisper.

"What's up, Kathy? You getting tired?" asked Mike.

"Yeah, but there's something wrong with my legs."

"What do you mean?" asked Stacy.

"They really hurt," she said as she rubbed her thighs.

"We have to get you into the water. I'm so sorry, I should have had you back in the river before now," said Mike.

They dropped their bags and collapsed into the river. Mike looked across the river and felt dizzy. He washed his face and rubbed his eyes, and then looked again. He still felt shaky. He glanced over at Kathy and Stacy. "Do I look as red as the two of you look?"

"You are red, but not as red as Kathy," answered Stacy.

"Kathy, you do look flushed again. Are you having headaches?" asked Mike.

"Yeah, but not as bad as yesterday. At least I don't think so. I'm having trouble remembering how yesterday was. I'm not thinking about much besides food."

"We better cool you way down before we move again," said Mike.

"I have to lie down," said Kathy as she swooned. Stacy steadied her with her arm.

"Mike, help me get her into the shade."

Mike stood, and immediately fell back to his knees, holding his head. He felt woozy and the river seemed to be spinning.

"What's wrong, Mike?" asked Stacy.

"I don't feel so good. I'm dizzy and feel like I might throw up."

"Oh my God, are you sick? Do you want me to do something?" asked Stacy.

"No, just give me a minute." Mike sat in the water with his head in his hands and his elbows on his knees.

Mike slowly stood, and walked onto the beach and made a place for them to lay in the shade. He moved at half speed. Then he and Stacy supported Kathy as she slowly walked up the beach. All three lay down in the shade. Kathy fell asleep immediately. A few minutes later Mike sat up and looked around. "Hey, where's my boat?"

"Your boat? Mike, we left that two days ago," reminded Stacy.

"We did? Oh yeah, I remember now. How did I forget?"

"Mike, are you sick?" asked Stacy.

"I don't know…I sure don't feel too good."

"Mike, I'm really scared. What's happening to us?"

Mike appeared to be concentrating, as he rubbed the sides of his head. "I don't know. I have to lie down and rest for awhile."

Mike turned over and vomited onto the beach. He turned back over and fell asleep. Stacy felt alone. Mike and Kathy slept. Stacy was too troubled to sleep. She worried about what would happen to them. Are we going to get back? Are we going to get out of this alive? Dear God, please help us, if you're there at all! And Jack, is he okay? Did he make it back alright? Stacy felt light-headed and lay back down.

Mike woke to a tingling feeling. At first he couldn't place the sensation, and then realized it was his legs. He saw ants crawling on his legs, and swatted them away. He was relieved to feel better. The women still slept. He slowly stood and made his way into the river to cool off. The water felt too cold at first, but nice once he adjusted to it. Mike went over to his pack to fetch some soap. As he dug through his pack his eye caught the glint of something silver. He reached for it and pulled out a forgotten protein bar. "What are you doing here, my little friend?" he said aloud.

Mike glanced over at the women, who still slept. He began to tear the wrapper open, and then stopped. I can't do this. I'd be so angry if one of them did this to me. I can't even let myself think about it. The bar felt soft, so Mike put it in a bucket of cold water.

After washing up, Mike hiked up to the top of the hill behind the beach. He shielded his eyes from the westering sun and peered downriver. He thought he recognized the bend in the river and the rock sticking out of the water. It can't be much further. Mike returned to the beach and made a fire and boiled more water to replenish the water bottles. He'd made a decision.

He figured there was about three hours of daylight left. Mike gently woke the women. He winced as he saw how hot and sweaty they appeared. "Ladies, you have to drink water." He handed each a full water bottle.

"I'm not thirsty," said Kathy as she pushed the water away.

"Kathy, you have to drink."

"But I'm not thirsty. I don't want it."

"You can't go on thirst. Part of having heat stroke is losing your thirst. It means it's even more urgent for you to drink," insisted Mike.

Kathy and Stacy both drank part of their bottles. "Drink the whole bottle, and then we have to talk," said Mike.

"Talk about what," asked Stacy as she finished off her bottle.

"I found something," said Mike cryptically.

"Found what?" asked Stacy.

"I found another protein bar. I'd forgotten that I still had one in my pack."

"Let's eat it. Where is it?" said Kathy.

"Wait a minute, we have to decide something. I'm worried that we're not going to make it back in our weakened state. It's starting to cool off, but we've still got maybe three hours of sun left. I think one of us should eat most of the bar and make for the truck."

"And leave the other two here," asked Kathy incredulously.

"Yes."

"I can hike. I think we should all go," suggested Kathy.

"Kathy, we still have at least three miles to go in ninety-something degree weather, and one protein bar amongst us. Stacy's in the best shape of all of us, I say she eats the bar and makes for the truck," countered Mike.

"Me? But I don't even know where to go. It's only my second time being out to the river, I don't know if I can find the truck." Mike ran a hand through his greasy hair and looked downriver, and then said, "I hate to say this, but it might be even more than three miles back."

Kathy slowly shook her head as tears ran down her face, "My God, how did we get ourselves into this situation." Stacy took one look at Kathy and began crying herself.

All three sat in silence. In their state of heat exhaustion their thinking was confused. "Mike, I think you should be the one to go. You know the river and are the strongest of us. I don't have any confidence that Kathy or I would make it," said Stacy.

"Normally yes, but Stacy, I just got done vomiting a couple hours ago. That's not a good sign."

"I think Stacy's right. Mike, you eat the bar and take a bunch of waters and go get help. We'll stay here in the shade and pray to God that you make it," said Kathy. Mike grimaced and scratched his head.

"Mike, you're the only one who can find the truck. You go!" said Stacy.

"Okay, I guess what you're saying makes sense. But I'll share the bar with you both," said Mike.

"No. You need the strength, you eat the whole thing and get back here quick," said Stacy.

"But that would be selfish of me to eat the whole thing. We're all starving out here, how can I eat the whole thing?"

"I'd love a bit of that bar, but I'd rather have you get the energy so you can get back to us quicker," said Kathy.

"But what if you starve to death before I can get back?"

"That's why you need to eat the whole thing so you can hurry," said Stacy.

"Oh my God, I can't believe we're talking about not making it. I can't get my mind around this," said Mike.

"I'm thinking clearly for the both of us, and we're wasting daylight. Eat the bar, take water and go. Now!" pushed Stacy.

"Okay, okay. I'll do it, but only if you both have one bite of the bar," said Mike.

"No, just eat the whole thing and go before I shove it down your throat," said Kathy.

Mike got up and put his hat on. He picked up two water bottles and retrieved the protein bar. "Alright, I'm going." Mike opened the bar and ate two-thirds of it, and handed the rest to the women. "I'll only go if you two finish it off while I'm watching."
Kathy took the bar and winked at Stacy. She bit off a third of what was left, and then handed the bar to Stacy. Stacy ate half of what was left and handed the rest to Mike.

"Okay, we each had a bite. Now eat the last part or we're going to pin you down and shove it through your teeth," said Kathy with a smile on her face.

Mike smiled weakly and popped the last bite in his mouth. He embraced Kathy, and then Stacy. "I love you, Stacy." Then with a hand on each of them he gave final instructions. "Keep out of the sun, stay wet as much as you can stand, and keep drinking water. You should both drink about four bottles a day, okay? Whether you feel thirty or not you have to keep drinking." Both women smiled and nodded their heads.

"You just hurry back for us," said Kathy. And with that Mike bent down for his waters and left. He took ten steps and came back to his pack. "You're not taking that with you?" asked Stacy.

"No, I forgot the keys to the truck, and a life jacket."

"A life jacket, won't that make you hot?"

"Yeah, but I have to risk it. I might need it."

Mike walked along the river, keeping himself wet. He hadn't gone a half mile when he almost turned back. He felt strangely empty. The thought of leaving Stacy and Kathy out there without food was almost unbearable. Pictures of them slowly starving to death crowded his mind. He tried not to think about that, but the thoughts came just the same. He felt like an insensitive jerk who'd just abandoned his family in need.

He kept glancing up at the hills above him to the right, hoping to see Jack. Mike knew there was little chance of seeing Jack, since he'd left well before him. He hoped Jack was already in the truck and on his way to getting help. However, Mike kept looking to the hills anyways.

An hour later Mike sat down in the water. At first his thoughts were unfocused, and then he had a sudden urge to hurry back to the women. He stood and started walking back upriver, and then sat down again. He looked upriver and then downriver. What good would it do for me to go back? But how in the hell can I just leave them there to die? Maybe I should just lay down for a little bit and get some more strength…no I can't. If I do that I might not get up again…I have to keep going. Out of mere will he required himself to stand and begin walking, although every cell of his body screamed for rest.

By now he paid little attention to the terrain, and stumbled and fell many times. Each time required a herculean effort to rise. Mike rounded a point on the river and came across a tall cliff, sheer to the water's edge. He hiked away from the river to find a passage around, but soon gave up. Mike saw that he might have to hike a half mile to get around it. Climbing the cliff was out of the question, and he didn't think he would make it the half mile around. Mike put on his life jacket and waded into the water and began to float. It was the only option he had the energy for. He hoped the river's current would carry him awhile, and not require him to swim much. The only energy required was to keep his mouth above the water so the waves didn't fill it.

Kathy and Stacy remained in the shade while the sun drew near the western hills above them. They conserved energy by not moving around much, with the exception of getting wet whenever they fully dried. Kathy licked her dry lips, which only served to make them hurt. She looked at Stacy, and wondered if her own lips also looked like they belonged on a corpse. Her muscles were stiff from lying, and she sat up. Kathy's head swam with dizziness. For a moment she thought she would

vomit, but it passed. Sitting up sapped her energy faster and yet her back hurt to lie down.

"I keep wondering how the boys are faring. I don't like some of the images that I see," said Stacy.

"I picture Jack lying at the bottom of some cliff, broken and bleeding. I had a bad feeling when I saw him take to the hills. He was in such a damn fool hurry to get back, I'm afraid he might do something stupid. He's always been in a hurry to do things without really thinking them through. Of course I know I can overanalyze and wait too long sometimes, which drives him crazy."

"What are you afraid he might do?"

"Push himself too hard, or maybe climb a cliff that's too steep to climb without ropes, or maybe lose his way in the dark. It's not like Jack knows the area well like Mike does. Most likely thing is for him to get lost and miss the truck completely."

"Maybe he'll find a road and run into somebody," suggested Stacy.

"Maybe, but I don't know if there are any roads out here."

"I'm worried about Mike. I mean I don't think he'll get lost, he knows the river almost as well as the rangers. I'm more afraid he'll get sick again and not be able to keep going," said Stacy.

"A protein bar in two days isn't much to go on," agreed Kathy.

"Oh don't bring up food, I'm trying not to think about it," laughed Stacy. "I should probably be worried about myself, but I'm more afraid of losing Mike. I haven't met anyone one else like him."

"There's got to be other guys like him out there."

"I don't know if there are. I've met plenty of guys, but none that I've loved nearly as well as Mike. I tell you Kathy, in my twenties I always picked the pushovers. I was always in control and the guys did whatever I wanted. It sounds great, but after a while I always got tired of them. I got bored and I hated being the one always in charge. I decided I'd never be in a relationship like that again. Then when I was in my early thirties I kept finding guys who were in charge. Even though I felt controlled, I sort of liked it. I respected them more than the wimpy ones. But I could only let them call all the shots for so long and then I would stand up for myself. That point was always the end of the relationship. They say I'd changed and leave me. I didn't know what to do. It was depressing. It didn't work for me with any type of guy. I figured I was fated to go from one relationship to the next the rest of my life or be alone. I was alone for a long time. It was about then that I met a new friend at the office. She introduced me to some of her friends, and they had an amazing impact on me."

"How do you mean?" asked Kathy.

"It's hard to describe how Angela does it. At first I thought they were a bunch of women bitching about their men. But later I got it. Those women were trying to figure out why they were unhappy in their relationships, with guys and their families. They all met for happy hour after work on Fridays, and after a few weeks I was hooked. These women became my best friends. They helped me see that I didn't know how to be in a relationship where me and the guy could both have some power…a relationship where both of us had a say in things, with nobody in charge of everything. It was about then that I met Mike."

"How did you meet him?"

"He was roommates with one of the happy hour gals. Mike came to our Christmas party, actually as somebody else's date, and that's how I met him. We ended up talking for two hours after the party. In fact, his date got mad and asked another guy to give her a ride home," said Stacy with a laugh.

"That's so funny. So what's different with you and Mike?"

"Mike's the first guy with whom I've been able to hold onto my own opinions without running him over. If I get controlling with Mike, he tells me to back off. Now Mike can be controlling too, you've seen that, but when I stand up for myself he respects that."

"Wow, that's a really great arrangement," said Kathy.

"I just can't lose him after how hard I've worked to be in a relationship like this," said Stacy.

"I'm jealous of you. I wish I had a relationship like that. God knows I tried hard to make something like that with Jack. We just can't seem to pull it off."

"I'm sorry, Kathy."

"Yeah," said Kathy as tears ran down her face. She brushed them aside with her wrist.

"Maybe you'll be able to work it out with Jack. Or meet another great guy if not."

"I don't know if I will. Right now I don't even want to think about other guys. I'm trying to figure out if I can be with the guy I'm still with," said Kathy.

"You'll figure it out."

"I don't know. Right now it's hard for me to even imagine it working out with Jack and me," said Kathy.

The shoreline drifted by like the view from a panoramic wide-angled lens. Mike felt cooler in the water, and his head seemed clearer. He felt a little more energy, since he didn't have to move much to keep floating downriver. The down side was that he made slow progress. Just ahead loomed another sheer cliff of more than two hundred feet, and the current pushed him straight for it. The river bent around to the left, which would leave him fighting the current. He loosened the straps of his life jacket and stuffed the water bottles inside. He took a few strokes, checking to see if the bottles were secure. Satisfied that they were, he tucked his head and swam to the left. After a few strokes he gave up. He simply didn't have the energy to swim.

With little strength to do anything about it, Mike ran into the cliff wall. He pushed himself along the rock wall until he rounded the point. He landed on the shore just downriver from the cliff. Mike sat down in the shallow water and drank half a bottle of water. Then he picked himself up slowly, to avoid dizziness. Mike's head did swim, and he braced his elbows on his knees until his head cleared. Cleared actually overstates the change. His head merely settled enough for him to walk. He resumed walking along the shore. By now the sun had drifted behind the western skyline and it was dusk. The dim light provided enough illumination for him to continue at a steady yet plodding pace, which was all that his body could muster anyway.

After scraping his shins on a couple rocks he couldn't see, Mike slowed his pace. Darkness now enveloped him. He didn't have a flashlight. His batteries had run out several days ago. Mike didn't look at his surroundings, keeping his eyes intently on the ground just before his feet.

His eye suddenly caught a dim light up ahead. "Who could have a light on out here," he wondered aloud. Excited, Mike moved with more energy, hoping to see somebody around the next hill.

Mike crested the low him and looked down on two streetlights. Befuddled, he took in his surroundings as much as the lights allowed. He saw a rock jetty, a dock and a faint outline of a building in the distance. "Where the hell am I?" Mike descended the hill, losing his footing halfway down, and rolled the last twenty yards to the bottom. He lay still and tried to focus his eyes. He rolled onto his knees and stood. The nausea overwhelmed him and he vomited. He felt better. Mike steadied himself and slowly crossed the asphalted ground. What the hell is this place? Mike stopped and turned around 360 degrees. There's something familiar about this place, but I just can't think why. I know I've been here before.

A low sign stood in the darkness, just out of the light. Mike approached the sign and read, Marble Canyon Marina. "Marble Canyon Marina? It can't be. If I'm at the marina, then I just walked right past my truck. Although my truck might not be there anymore if Jack... how did I walk past the truck, or at least the spot where I left it? My God, I'm not thinking clearly."

Mike's head hurt, and he felt faint. He looked around and headed towards the closer of the two buildings. The sign on the door read, Marble Canyon Ranger Station. He knocked on the ranger station door. No answer. He leaned against the door to brace himself for a more forceful knock. There was still no answer. Mike cupped his hands and peered through the draperied window, but only saw a dark office. "Damn!" Then Mike felt his head spinning and he slumped to his knees. Everything turned black and he knew no more.

80 Weeks after the River Trip

Kathy filed for divorce upon returning from Vail. It seemed anticlimactic, and yet monumental at the same time. She knew in her heart that she'd decided months ago. And yet it still startled her how strongly she felt when she actually walked out of the court house, having filed the paperwork. Kathy had fantasized about this day for months and months, like a thirsty wonderer longs after a mirage at which he never arrives. At first Jack responded with anger and accusations. By the next day he shrugged his shoulders, though Kathy knew he was hurting. She felt bad for him. In her worst moments she felt mean and sinful, and struggled with her guilt. In her best moments she felt free and alive. It felt strange to be depressed, guilty, excited, hopeful and scared, all at the same time.

She continued with her Tuesday group. Kathy always looked forward to it. At times she thought about quitting, but it didn't seem to be the right time. Kathy wanted their support through the divorce process. And she still felt helped by them, making it tough to quit. She wanted to get back on her feet more solidly before she stopped. At times Kathy couldn't imagine being without their help, and wondered if she might continue indefinitely.

"I've mostly been depressed, even more so since I filed...I don't have much energy for anything right now. About the only thing I get excited about is seeing Lily...and coming here," began Kathy.

"You're grieving," suggested Dr. Aragorn.

"I grieved for a long time," said Susan.

"I suppose I am grieving, but I mostly feel depressed...I sleep most of the weekends, at least the weekends that I don't have Lily. I don't bother to wear much make-up...I haven't been returning many calls...just the ones that I have to for work...I've stopped working out," said Kathy.

"This is not the ending that you wanted," said Evelyn.

"Yeah, you had so hoped that you and Jack could work something out," said Jake.

"You've got to be deeply disappointed," said Susan.

"I'm disappointed in Jack...and myself...when I started therapy I was expecting that I'd learn some new skill or technique, and we'd work it out," said Kathy.

"You really tried hard," offered Tom.

"No shit Kathy, you put so much energy into giving your marriage a go," said Jake.

"I still don't totally get why it wasn't enough...I suppose I might never have it all figured out," said Kathy.

"That's likely," suggested Dr. Aragorn.

"It's still frustrating," said Kathy.

"Kathy, you need to grieve for awhile. And yet, I wonder how much of this dark place you're in is you punishing yourself," said Dr. Aragorn.

"I don't know...I guess I'll have to give that some thought...It does feel good to be with all of you tonight. I'm still depressed, but maybe not as bad as when I got here tonight," said Kathy.

The next Tuesday night Kathy felt a lighter. Her depression didn't seem as bad, and she had more energy. Thought of the future kept coming to her mind, which she hadn't been thinking about till this week.

"You are beginning to feel some hope," suggested Dr. Aragorn.

"Yes, I suppose I am...I think I'm also starting to feel a little less guilty about Jack. I've thought a lot about how you all keep telling me that I'm punishing myself for the divorce...I know you're right, that Jack made his own choices, as did I…I suppose I'm ready to start making a new life for myself…I don't want to be depressed anymore…I want to start living again."

"Good for you, Kathy, it's time," said Evelyn.

Kathy smiled. "You know, I'm embarrassed to say this, but I've been thinking more and more about other guys. I notice myself looking at guys, wondering if they're single…I guess I'd like to start dating."

"It's about time you let yourself out of solitary confinement for good behavior," quipped Jake.

Kathy laughed, and it felt really good. Then she said, "And if any of you know somebody that might want to date me, then let me know."

"Good for you Kathy, it's about time," said Susan. "I'd like to see you take off your black dress and go on with living."

"So how do I meet guys? I haven't even thought about dating for a long time. I don't remember how I used to do it," said Kathy.

"You can start by taking that ring off," suggested Jake.

"Oh yeah, I didn't even notice…do you really think it matters?"

"Are you kidding? The kind of guys who will approach you while you're wearing that ring are not the guys you'll want to be with. So you start by letting guys know hunting season has begun," said Jake.

Kathy slid the ring off her left hand and dropped it in her purse. She rubbed the purple ring line on her finger. "It feels so strange to not have anything there."

"You'll get used to it," said Susan with a smile. "I felt naked without mine for a few months. I would unconsciously reach for my ring to play with it and be surprised when it wasn't there."

"Okay my ring's off, so how do I meet guys to date?"

"I'll take you clubbing. Sometimes that works for me," said Susan.

"You mean going to a bar?" asked Kathy.

"Not just any old sawdust-filled bar. I'll take you to some nice places where you can meet nice guys. I'm sure you don't want to meet drunken braggarts," said Susan.

"I think I'll pass. I want to meet a guy that I can really talk with," said Kathy.

"Those guys are hard to find," said Susan.

"There's a few of them out there. Sometimes I'm not so sure, but I hope I'm becoming one of those," said Jake.

"I'd love to meet a guy like you, Jake," said Kathy sheepishly.

"Damn, don't tempt me, Kathy. I'm trying to make my marriage work," said Jake. Then he added with a wry smile, "Perhaps we could just have a weekend fling and not tell my wife."

Kathy laughed, "Now you're tempting me." Both Kathy and Jake looked to Dr. Aragorn, who shook his head and smiled. "It's a good thing Dr. Aragorn has a rule about dating group members," said Kathy.

"You'll be safer going out clubbing with me," said Susan.

"Yeah, no doubt," agreed Kathy.

"I don't do much dating, so I couldn't really tell you. But if you find the formula, then let me know," said Karen.

"Are there any single guys at the office that you might be in to?" asked Jake.

"Oh my God, I don't know if I'd want to date anybody there…that might be more complicated than I want."

"How about in your condo complex?" asked Jake.

"I don't know, I haven't even thought about it…I guess I haven't really looked around anywhere. I haven't even thought about other men until recently. But I want to go there now. I thought about what you were saying last time Dr. Aragorn, and I want to move on with my life. I definitely want to start dating. I haven't been out on a single date, and Jack and I have been separated almost six months."

"So it's time to open your eyes and start looking around," suggested Dr. Aragorn.

Kathy smiled and nodded and said, "It feels good to finally be ready. I don't know why I've waited this long."

"You were struggling with your guilt," suggested Evelyn.

"And the shock of the divorce," added Susan.

"And you've been depressed ever since you filed," said Tom.

"I guess I've had trouble imagining myself being with another guy. I was at the gas station last week. There was a nice-looking guy filling up at the pump behind me, and he made some comment to me about the weather. I responded briefly, but I didn't say much. The guy smiled at me, and I smiled back but then turned my head back to the pump. A moment later I realized that he might be flirting with me. I looked up and he was already gone. I'm so used to being off the market that it didn't even register that I had an opportunity with this guy until it was too late. I suppose I'm keeping myself married to Jack in my mind. I'm done with that. I so want to be done with that."

"You have new eyes now, Kathy. It will be interesting to see what you notice, now that you'll be looking at men in a different way. And men will feel the difference in how you look at them," said Dr. Aragorn.

"Well, I certainly won't be leering at them," said Kathy.

"You don't have to leer at men for us to know that you're interested," suggested Jake.

"Then what's the difference. I don't imagine I'll be checking out men's body parts much," said Kathy.

"You will be letting men know that you're open," said Dr. Aragorn. "A sensitive man will know when you're inviting something romantic."

"But I'm an old-fashioned girl. I won't be asking any men out on a date."

"Okay, so you'll wait for the man to do the actual asking. However, except for the men who are the most clueless about social cues, I believe that dates are invited by both parties. Some cavemen barge on in, even when they're being told to go away. But most men are watching for cues. The man may do the asking, but the woman invites the asking," said Dr. Aragorn.

The River: Day 9

Mike awoke to the sound of low voices. He stared at an unfinished wood-planked ceiling. To the right he looked out a window onto dirt and low brush. Further to the right was a simple desk with a telephone and some papers. Mike sat up and immediately lay back down, feeling faint. His head spun. Then he raised himself with more caution, and paused to allow his head to settle down. He successfully swung his feet onto the floor. Mike waited while his head slowed its spinning again. He'd been sleeping on a cot. A familiar dull headache greeted him, and he rubbed his temples with both hands. Behind where his head had lain the door was ajar. Mike called out, "Hello, is anybody there?"

A kindly man dressed in a green uniform appeared in the doorway. He wore a smile and was soon joined by a woman with a long pony-tail under a green cap. "Well, look who's awake," said the female ranger. Seeing Mike's confusion, the male ranger added, "We found you lying across our doormat when we opened-up at seven this morning. You were in such bad shape we put you straight on the cot."

Mike nodded. Understanding began to dawn. "Oh yeah, I made it to the marina last night. I must have fainted after I got here," said Mike.

"What in God's name happened to you? We searched and didn't find any kind of car or boat," asked the man.

"Uh, I walked. We had some…uh, do you have anything to eat? I haven't eaten much in a few days."

"You betcha," said the woman who soon returned with a bag of trail mix and a water. She handed Mike the goods and said, "This is Ranger Pete Johnston, and I'm Ranger Barbara Anders, but you can call me Barb."

Mike gave them his full name. Then he stuffed a handful into his mouth, barely chewing before shoving another mouthful in. He couldn't remember food tasting this good. The rangers exchanged glances. "Hey, so what the heck happened to you? How come you haven't eaten in days?" asked Barb.

"We had trouble with our boat…in the storm…awhile back…my girlfriend and my friends were, hey wait a minute, we have to go rescue them. They're still out there! Let's go!" Mike rose and took two steps for the door, but collapsed as his legs didn't support his weight.

"Now hold on there, partner. Just settle back down and tell us what happened. You're in no condition to be rescuing anybody. We'll get to your friends soon enough," said Pete.

"But they're in trouble! We have to go now! Don't you get that"…

"Now just sit back down and relax. We'll get to your friends as soon as we know the story," said Barb.

Mike reluctantly sat back down. "Like I started to say, my girlfriend and friends and I were boat camping upriver a ways, and we got caught in a storm, a pretty bad one. Anyways, the boat got marooned and we tried to hike back. The thing is, we were pretty far upriver…"

"Did you say upriver, because that part of the river ain't open yet," said Pete.

"Yeah I know," said Mike sheepishly. "Anyways, we ran out of food a few days ago and…we couldn't hike much, especially in the heat of the day. So yesterday I left the women on a beach and hiked the rest of the way last night. I stumbled onto your front door sometime well after dark."

"So your friends are still on the river?" asked Barb.

"That's right. And they have no food."

"Where exactly are they?" asked Barb.

"I don't know exactly. They're about five miles upriver on the western shore."

"Alright, let's go," said Pete.

"Wait a minute, my buddy's out there too. I don't know where he is, because he set out a day before me trying to get back, but I don't know if he made it. Jack didn't find you, did he?"

"No. You're the only person to stumble in here," said Pete.

"So what about my buddy then?"

"We'll look for him too then. Let's go," said Pete.

The rangers led Mike to their waiting boat. They had the engine going and the ropes untied before Mike climbed in. A moment later they were heading upriver. Mike brought the trail mix and waters along for the others. All three fixed their eyes to the western shore. Mike surveyed the landmarks along the way, trying to figure out exactly where he'd left the Kathy and Stacy. Mike craned his neck to see the speedometer, and noted they were traveling at better than 40 miles per hour. Twenty minutes later they'd gone more than ten miles upriver with no signs of them.

Barb slowed the boat to idle speed and turned to Mike. "You sure you left 'em no more than five miles from the marina?" she asked.

Mike thought for a moment, his mind still foggy. "I can't be sure, but I don't think it's this far."

"We better keep heading upriver then to make sure," said Pete.

The ranger brought them back up to cruising speed and they continued on upriver. They didn't see anything unusual for awhile, and Mike began to feel sure they'd passed them. Then something caught the ranger's eye and she piloted the boat towards shore. When they were got closer Mike recognized the object. He called aloud over the engine noise, "That's my boat!" The ranger drove into the cove for a closer look. No one was in sight.

"We must have passed them! This is where we left my boat a few days ago," said Mike.

Without a word the ranger had the boat turned around and roared back to cruising speed. Pete said something to his partner, and then she slowed the boat and pulled in closer to the western shore. Mike grabbed another handful of trail mix and leaned over the gunwale to search the shoreline more intently. Fear mingled with anticipation as Mike wondered what they'd find. "Dear God, let us be in time," Mike whispered under his breath. Mike's fear increased with every passing minute he didn't see Stacy and Kathy.

Stacy woke when the sun came over the eastern mountains and crept over her face. Her stomach ached. Although she'd been lying down for twelve hours she didn't feel rested. In fact, she felt almost exactly the same as before she nodded off. She felt weak. She'd tossed and turned all night. Stacy rolled over and saw that Kathy still slept. Stacy turned back over and tried to go back to sleep, but couldn't. The pain in her stomach quickly removed all hope of returning to the bliss of unconsciousness. Her muscles felt sore all over, so she decided to walk. When she stood she became faint, almost falling, but steadied herself on one knee.

After walking down to the water and cooling off, Stacy had expended the energy she had and went back to where Kathy lay. When she knelt next to her Kathy stirred. Kathy's eyes fluttered open and she smiled weakly. Her face was pale and drawn. "My God, do I look that bad?" Stacy whispered.

"What?" asked Kathy.

"I'm hoping I don't look as bad as you."

"I was wondering the same thing yesterday. My God, I feel like I didn't even sleep. I'm so tired, I could go back to sleep right now," said Kathy.

"I know, me too. We have to drink some water," said Stacy. She stood more carefully this time and retrieved two water bottles.

Kathy sat up and took the water bottle from Stacy. She drank slowly with her other hand on her forehead. Stacy sat down next to her and raised her water to her lips. They stared out at the river and sat in silence. "I sure hope the guys got through. I don't know how much longer I can go without food," said Kathy.

"I've been trying to picture where Mike might be. I try to think of him in his truck, but bad images keep coming to mind," said Stacy.

"What if neither one of them got through?" Kathy wondered aloud.

"I just can't go there. It's too awful to even think about."

"I know," began Kathy, "but what do we do if they didn't?"

Stacy thought for a minute before responding, "I don't know. I don't think I can hike today. Dear God, the guys have to bring back help soon!"

"But what if help doesn't come soon? How long do we wait?" pressed Kathy.

"Oh my God, I don't know. It's hard for me to even think about that. I can't imagine we could make it back to the truck, and even if we did, I don't know if I could find it. Could you?"

"Maybe we could find somebody at the marina," suggested Kathy.

"Maybe, but if we leave here how will they find us?"

"I don't know. But if we just stay here, we know what happens if no help comes, right?"

"Okay okay, so how long do you propose we wait then?" asked Stacy.

"I say we wait till midday, and then start walking if nobody shows."

"Kathy, it's probably five miles more and we have nothing to eat! I don't know about you, but it's a major effort for me to just walk down to the water."

"What's the alternative? Do we just wait here to die?" asked Kathy.

Stacy burst into tears and threw her hands in the air. A wild expression came over her face. "I don't know, Kathy. My God, I don't have any answers. I just can't bear to think that neither one of the guys got through. Do you know what that means?"

"Yes, I do. It means they're both dead…and we are too."

"How can you say that so matter-of-factly? These are our guys! This is your husband we're talking about! Maybe you don't care about him anymore. Is that it?"

"Now wait a minute, that's not fair! Even though things are tough right now, I still love my husband. I'm so damned tired I can't conjure up much emotion. I'm spent! Do you think I'm so cold hearted that I want him to die? Is that what you think of me?"

"I don't know what to think! I can barely get my brain to think, I'm so damn hungry! Look, don't take this personal, but I just can't take this anymore. If they don't come back today, I don't know what to do. Maybe we're done for then," said Stacy.

"Stacy, listen to me! We have to keep our heads. If we stop thinking and making good decisions, then we are done for. I'm not ready to give up. I hope to high heaven that somebody comes for us today, but if they don't, we have to have a plan. Don't give up on me. I need you to stay with me, okay?"

Stacy nodded her head affirmatively through her sobs. She held clumps of hair in both hands, as if holding her head together. "Maybe I should be more worried about my own life, but I can't stop thinking about Mike. I just can't lose him. He's the first guy that… I just can't start all over again. I don't have it in me."

"Look Stacy, I know that you love Mike, but for right now, we have to figure out how to save ourselves. You're no good to Mike if we don't make it back okay," said Kathy.

Stacy nodded with a smile and said through her sobs, "Yes, I know you're right…I'm sorry I lost my head. I don't want to die… and you're right, we have to figure out what to do if nobody comes."

"The only question is how long do we stay here and wait," said Kathy. Both of them looked to the river for inspiration as they considered their options.

"Wait a minute, do we still have our life jackets?" asked Stacy.

"Yeah we used them as pillows, remember?"

"Of course we did. Okay, we don't have the energy to hike, right?"

"Uh huh."

"Okay, so we put on our life jackets and float downriver; which will keep us cool. How much energy could that take?"

"Great idea! That's what we'll do," agreed Kathy. "So, the only other question is when do we go?"

"I think help's most likely to come this morning, if it's coming."

"Okay, so we leave before midday."

"Before midday it is. So that mean's 11:00," said Stacy. "You don't have a watch, do you?" Kathy shook her head no. "Maybe Mike left his in his back pack," Stacy said as she searched through the pack. "Here it is. It's 8:30 right now…on second thought, I don't think we can afford to wait until 11:00. It'll be hot by 11:00. I think we should leave by 10:00."

"So 10:00 it is," agreed Kathy.

Stacy and Kathy sat in the shade on their sleeping bags. They had spent the morning scanning the river for signs of help, and listening for the sounds of an engine, while trying to ignore the sounds of their stomachs. The morning's peace had been uninterrupted. Stacy glanced at Mike's watch and said with a dull voice, "Well, it's ten."

"Okay, then let's go."

"Wait, let's give them twenty more minutes," Stacy pleaded.

"No! We've been over this, and I'm not waiting on this beach all day while we starve to death. We agreed on ten, so we go."

Stacy hung her head and wiped away a lone tear. She brushed her long brown hair out of her eyes and faced Kathy.

"You're right, let's go. I guess I didn't expect us to come to this. I really believed the guys would be back with help by now." Kathy put her arm around Stacy's shoulders and pulled her close.

"I know girlfriend, I know," consoled Kathy. Kathy held Stacy without hurry.

"Do we really have to go?"

"Yes. We really can't wait any longer. I can barely muster the strength to do this now, and if we wait any longer I don't know if I'll be able to make my body move," said Kathy.

Stacy nodded while looking away. "I can't believe Mike didn't get through. I was sure he would."

"We don't know for sure that he didn't."

"Dear God, what if Mike's dead?"

"Stacy, let's worry about saving ourselves for now, and then we'll see about the guys. And we better leave while we still have any energy to swim with."

"Swim? Who said we're doing any swimming? The best I can do is keep my head out of the water while we float," said Stacy. Kathy laughed half-heartedly.

"Okay, let's do this. And put on a shirt that will cover as much of you as possible. Remember, the sun saps our energy and we have to protect ourselves," said Stacy.

Stacy and Kathy put on their life jackets. Kathy stuffed two water bottles into Stacy's life jacket, and then two into her own. Kathy looked around at their belongings. She put her hat on her head, and then tossed Stacy hers. The two women turned around and surveyed their campsite. "I suppose we'll leave the rest here," said Kathy. They walked down into the water and began to float downriver.

They floated effortlessly the first hour, and seemed to be making good progress. Stacy and Kathy held onto each other and talked. The current carried them gently onto a sandbar.

They slowly walked across it and reentered the water. An hour later they ran into a rock cliff. They slowly swam along the cliff face until they came to a grouping of rocks jutting out from the cliff. They were fatigued from the swimming and climbed onto the rocks to sit down and rest. As they sat with their backs against the cliff, they heard a low roar.

"Do you hear that?" asked Stacy.

"Are you kidding? Of course I hear that. It sounds like a boat coming this way."

They tried to stand, but couldn't muster the energy. They listened intently, wondering from which direction the sound came. All of a sudden the engine roar grew loud and a ranger boat rounded the cliff heading upriver. Stacy and Kathy tried to yell for help, but couldn't find the energy. Not that they could have been heard over the engine. The boat continued upriver. "Oh my God, they didn't see us," said Stacy as she cried. "Come back! Please come back!" Stacy collapsed in tears.

"One hell of a rescue, when they aren't even looking!" said Kathy. Kathy put her arms around Stacy, who continued to sob.

"Maybe they'll be back this way...but we have to keep going in case they don't," said Kathy.

"Why didn't they look this way? They're coming back, aren't they?" pleaded Stacy.

"I don't know, honey. Let's get back in the water while we still can."

Kathy and Stacy slipped back into the water and paddled towards the cliff's point. At one point they had to stop paddling and allow themselves to drift into the cliff wall, too tired to move. Finally they made it around the cliff, back into open water and resumed drifting downriver. They panted, both being out of breath. Kathy felt faint, and clung onto Stacy. They were relieved to see that the river held a straight course for a ways and they could rest.

Mike kept a close eye on the western shoreline. A couple of times he thought he recognized the cove he'd last slept in with Kathy and Stacy, but each time there was nothing there. Then he caught sight of something. "Hey, I see something on that beach," Mike yelled over the engine. Barb nodded and steered towards the cove. As they approached the shore Mike could make out what was on the beach. "There's one of our sleeping bags! Wait, I see three of them. This is where we slept the other night! Maybe they're still in them."

Barb beached the boat and all three scrambled onto shore. "Stacy! Kathy! Where the hell are you?" said Mike as he ran up to the sleeping bags. Yet he found them empty. "Damn, they're not here! Where in the hell did they go? I told them to wait here for me!" Mike and the rangers spread out and searched the surrounding area, but found nothing to suggest where the women might be. The rangers approached Mike, who sat on the sleeping bags.

"Mike, I want you to look carefully around and see if anything's missing. We might find something that will help us. We did find footprints leading downriver, but there's only one pair and we figure those would be yours," said Pete. Mike nodded and looked carefully through the gear on the beach.

"The only thing missing are the water bottles," concluded Mike.

"Then they must have set out for the marina," suggested Barb.

"But there should be footprints leading out of here if they did," countered Pete.

"Unless they went into the water," said Barb.

"Oh my God, they'll drown. They didn't have any energy left even yesterday," said Mike.

"Now are you sure there's nothing else missing. Think carefully now," said the Barb.

"There's nothing else missing, I've looked. The only thing missing is...Wait a minute! The life jackets are gone. We used them as pillows, and they're gone!"

"Then they're floating downriver," concluded Barb.
"Let's go," said Pete.

82 Weeks after the River Trip

Kathy pulled into the parking lot and turned off her engine. She closed her eyes and took several deep breaths and said aloud, "I can't believe I'm doing this." She glanced over at the entrance and saw a couple of women talking to a guy. "I don't know if I can go through with this. Okay, before I talk myself out of it I'm just going to grab my purse and go in."

A couple of guys looked up at her as she walked through the parking lot. Kathy turned away in embarrassment. The entrance to the restaurant featured double French doors, and Kathy grabbed the handle and pulled. Inside it was dimly lit. Right in front sat the hostess desk and behind that was a huge wooden bar with tall chairs with low backs. The bar curved across the floor like a crescent moon. Behind the bar was a huge painting of men on horses with their dogs chasing a fox. Kathy smiled. The bartenders, men and women, wore black slacks and shirts with their sleeves rolled up. The place was packed, with standing room only. Men and women brushed past Kathy, who still stood just inside the doors. The hostess asked if she could take Kathy's name.

"Oh no, I'm meeting someone at the bar," said Kathy. She then scanned the bar and spotted Susan on the right end.

"Oh there you are. Did you get lost?" asked Susan.

"No not really… just my mind maybe," answered Kathy as she sat down next to her friend.

"Now don't give up on me just yet. Let's order you a drink before you run out of here," said Susan with a smile. Kathy smiled weakly, and nodded.

"So what do you think? Nice place, huh?" said Susan.

"It's so crowded."

"Actually not really, this is an average night. It might even pick up later."

The bartender interrupted, "What'll you have?"

"Oh, uh, I don't know. I'll have whatever she's having," said Kathy pointing to Susan.

Susan wore black slacks and a nice pink blouse. She was meticulously made-up, and Kathy realized why she didn't see her at first when arrived. "My God Susan, you look great! I've never seen you like this."

"Oh I know. I never come to group like this. It's way too much work to do every time I leave the house."

When her glass of white wine arrived Kathy took a couple quick gulps, eager for help relaxing. Turning to Susan she said, "I feel like a fish out of water here. I don't think I've ever been to a place like this."

"You're kidding? Even before you married Jack?"

"I suppose I might have sat in the restaurant part of a place like this, but… maybe what's different is that I've never come to one of these to meet guys."

"You'll be fine once you get your bearings and a couple of drinks in you," said Susan.

Kathy took another sip and surveyed the room. Everyone was dressed nice and appeared to be sophisticated. Nobody seemed sloppy drunk, which surprised her. Kathy judged the crowd to be roughly late twenties to mid fifties. Several of the guys were quite handsome. Most of them seemed to already be talking to somebody, either to a woman or in some cases to a buddy. One woman sat at the bar by herself, not talking with anyone. "So Susan, now what?"

"Now we wait for an opportunity."

"What kind of opportunity?"

"Wait and see. We'll know when it arrives."

"Okay… So what do you have going this weekend?" asked Kathy.

"Tomorrow my daughter has a track meet. She's runs the mile. I sure wish I was in the shape she's in."

"She's in high school?"

"Yes, a sophomore. And then on Sunday I've got my book club."

"Book club? What's that about?"

"We read a book and then meet once a month to discuss it," said Susan.

"Oh really, I didn't know you were a reader."

"Oh yeah, I'm always reading something, usually a novel. Do you like to read?"

"I used to read more, but not as much lately. I like to read magazines and an occasional novel when a good one's recommended to me," answered Kathy.

They were interrupted by a man reaching between them and talking to the bartender, "I'll take whatever you've got on tap." And looking at Susan and Kathy he said, "So what're you ladies drinking?"

"White wine," said Susan.

"Oh, you're the classy kind," he said.

"White wine makes us classy?" said Susan.

"Yeah, I never talk to women who drink beer, always talk to women who drink wine, and evaluate further women drinking hard stuff."

"Where did you get your system?" asked Susan.

"I have years of experience at this game. I walked into the bar tonight, looked for women with white grape juice, spotted you two lovelies and here I am."

"Lucky us," said Susan.

"Seriously, you don't even realize yet," he said as he took a deep draught of his beer.

"So you avoid women who drink beer, but you drink beer yourself," observed Susan.

"Apples and oranges- you can't categorize men who drink beer. Every guy drinks beer, unless he's gay."

"Gay men don't drink beer?" asked Susan.

"Only if they're trying to look straight."

"You seem to know a lot about people," said Kathy.

"It's my job to. Everybody in marketing has to know people to be successful. If I didn't understand people I'd have to go get a different job."

"If you know people so well, tell me about me," said Susan.

"You're easy. Been divorced for awhile, somewhat picky with guys but can't afford to be too picky, stay at home mom who never had a career, can never motivate yourself to consistently exercise, but still pretty enough to attract enough guys anyway. How'd I do?"

"There's one thing you left out. I'm a hard-core beer drinker and am only drinking white wine to attract arrogant guys like you who are easily fooled," said Susan with a fire in her eyes.

The guy took a double take, and then decided Susan was serious. He looked at Kathy and then said to Susan, "I guess that's your way of telling me to take a hike."

"You got it," confirmed Susan. He picked up his beer, nodded to Kathy, glared at Susan and left.

"My God Susan, you sure got rid of him in a hurry," said Kathy.

"I hate being insulting like that, but if I didn't he'd talk to us all night and then try to pry our phone numbers out of us if he couldn't give us a ride home. And we wouldn't have a chance to meet somebody else."

"Wow, I guess you've been around this block a few times. I didn't know what to say to him."

"You would have been too nice, and I purposely didn't give you much of a chance to talk. And it's kinder to him so he can move on and not waste his whole night on us, and can maybe meet somebody else."

"I can see that I have much to learn. Although I don't know that I could be as blunt as you are. And I'm not sure that I want to be," said Kathy.

Susan laughed and said, "You don't have to be like me honey, but I can save you some time by showing you the lay of the land."

Susan looked over Kathy's shoulder, smiled and then said, "That sounds pretty good. Maybe I'll try one of those next time."

"Oh they're great, there's nothing like a margarita made from fresh squeezed juice."

"What kind of juice is in it?" asked Susan.

"Um, I think it's orange and grapefruit."

Kathy turned to see who Susan was talking to, and two nice-looking guys were just picking up their newly served drinks from the bartender. The close one said, "Hello there I'm Steve, and this is my buddy Kevin."

"My name's Susan and this is Kathy."

"You ladies come here much?" asked Steve. The two guys moved to stand directly behind Kathy and Susan's chairs, as no other chairs were available.

"I'm here on occasion," said Susan.

"This is my first time," said Kathy. Kathy winced as her voice felt rushed.

"And why is that?" asked Kevin. While Kevin was talking Steve walked behind him to stand next to Susan and began talking to her.

"Well, um, I guess because I'm just getting out of a marriage," said Kathy.

"Is that right? Me too," said Kevin.

"I'm sorry," said Kathy.

"Don't be. It's for the best. I never should have married so young. I didn't know what I wanted."

"How old were you when you married?"

"Twenty-five, but a young twenty-four at that," said Kevin.

"I know what you mean. I married at twenty-six and still was too young. I had so little idea what I wanted in a marriage."

"Does that mean you're old enough to marry now?"

"I don't know about that," laughed Kathy, "but I have more of an idea anyhow."

"I'm hoping to be ready to remarry before I'm in a walker myself," said Kevin.

"You're that far off then?"

"Sometimes it seems like it. For now I'm just trying to meet different women and see what happens. I don't want anything serious yet."

"And what are you finding so far?"

"So far?"

"So far in meeting different women."

"Oh that- I'm finding that I like the pretty ones," Kevin said with a grin.

"Anything else?"

Kevin looked away as he reflected, and then said, "I like being with women who seem to know themselves. You know, women who know what they like and what they don't like. I don't enjoy the ones who just want to do whatever I want or just talk about me. I find those women boring. Does that sound crazy? I mean what guy doesn't want to talk about himself?"

"Not at all. You want a woman who shows up."

"Right, I want to feel like there's another person in the room. You know, I don't want to just talk about me, but I don't want to just talk about her either. It probably sounds weird, but I want more than just a pretty body. I went out with a couple of beauties when I was first separated, and I was surprised to find myself looking out the window, looking at other women, and even checking my watch to see if was time to take her home yet. I thought if I just found a pretty enough woman I'd be set... I can't believe I'm telling you all this, just meeting you and all. I don't normally say this much on a first meeting."

"I don't know if you're surprising yourself more or me more. I didn't expect to meet any guys who could talk about themselves like you. My husband didn't seem to know himself too well, and didn't like to talk about himself much."

"I suppose I'm a bit of a strange guy. I don't live for sports or beer. I actually don't even like beer that much. I mean it's fine if nothing else is available."

"What do you prefer to drink?" asked Kathy.

"A nice glass of red wine, or a Margarita if it's hot outside. I love the scratch rita's they make here."

"I love Margarita's myself, but I don't think I've ever had one made from scratch."

"Here, try a sip of mine," offered Kevin.

"Okay," said Kathy as she reached for a straw from the bar. Then took a long sip and said, "Oh yeah, those are nice. Maybe I'll get one of those after I finish my wine."

Kevin glanced at his watch and then said, "Oh boy, I have to get going. My baby-sitter wanted me to relieve her by a certain time. But I've enjoyed talking with you, actually really enjoyed it. Can I call you sometime?"

"I'd like that," said Kathy as she pulled out one of her business cards and handed it to him. "You can contact me at the office." Kevin smiled and pocketed the card. Kathy watched him walk out the door.

Kathy turned her head to find Susan still talking with Steve. She caught Kathy's eye and gave her a quick smile. Kathy got up and went to the ladies' room. It felt good to walk after sitting for the past two hours plus. When Kathy returned to her seat Susan was still engaged with Steve. Kathy was glad to see that it seemed to be going well between them, just based on body language. Steve leaned on Susan's bar stool and Susan allowed his arm to rest against hers. Susan held Steve's gaze consistently and her smile invited more. Kathy finished her glass of wine and whispered in Susan's ear, "Good luck and good night. Call me after you're done with Steve." Susan nodded and waved. Steve didn't seem to notice Kathy's departure.

In the car Kathy wondered if Kevin would call. In moments she felt sure he wouldn't and reminded herself not to get her hopes up. Then a minute later she imagined him calling and them going out for a nice time together. As her home came into view Kathy felt a shot of guilt sling through her. She thought, how can I be thinking about other guys right now? It's too soon. The cell phone rang as Kathy pulled into Jane's driveway. Kathy checked the caller ID and then answered, "Hi Susan. How did it go with Steve?"

"I think pretty good. I like him and hope he calls. He asked for my number not long after you left."

"What do you like about him?"

"Mostly that he's not arrogant and took a lot of responsibility for his divorce."

"Wow, you got into the personal stuff quickly," commented Kathy.

"Yeah, I found myself saying more than I expected myself. I didn't go into details, but I did tell him the big picture of my divorce."

"What did you say?"

"Just that I'd allowed Lane and I to drift and become distant. That I didn't realize until it was too late that I wasn't taking good care of my marriage, and that I expected Lane to do it for me."

"You told Steve a lot," said Kathy.

"I guess I did. Anyways, he took it well and told me some about his own divorce. I won't go into the details for the sake of his privacy. I hope he calls me, but I do have one concern."

"What's that?"

"I noticed him looking at several of the other women while he was talking with me. I didn't like that."

"You mean noticing other women, or do you meaning checking them out?" asked Kathy.

"In one or two cases I mean checking them out. Although I wonder if I'm overstating what he did. I mean I do want to be fair, and I know it's a thing for me feeling like I'm fatter than every other woman alive."

"Well, that is a thing for you. And you'll need to see how that goes. He might have been nervous too."

"Maybe. We'll see, that is if he calls again."

"I'll bet he calls you. I saw the way he was looking at you and leaning into you," said Kathy.

"Yeah, I noticed that too. So anyways, how did it go with the other guy? What was his name?"

"Kevin. It went way better than I expected; that is until I got home and started feeling guilty for talking to another man."

"Oh Kathy, don't let your guilt get the best of you. My God, you certainly give yourself a hard time. If you don't let go of that pretty quick I'll drag you out to the clubs every night until you do," Susan said with a laugh.

"Maybe some more conversations like I had with Kevin will cure me."

"Sure it will. It's long overdue for you to get out and enjoy some other men. What good is it to you, or Jack for that matter, to continue punishing yourself. So, did he ask for your number?"

"Yes. He said he really enjoyed talking to me and wanted to get together again."

"He'll definitely call then," said Susan.

"You think so?"

"Absolutely! The few times a guy has said that to me he's always called. I've had guys call me that said less than that. Oh don't worry, he'll call. So anyway, what did you like about him?"

"Oh, that he seemed like he was really there, and he seemed to know himself pretty well, and I don't think he just wants to get laid. I don't know why, but I expected the guys at a bar to just be looking for someone to have sex with."

Susan laughed and said, "Oh honey, there are plenty of those there. That's one of the reasons I sent away the first guy. He smelled like he was in heat."

"Oh my God, really? I just thought he was arrogant."

"Well that too."

Three days later Kathy sat at the conference table in the firm's library. A handful of books lay open before her, surrounded by numerous scattered papers. In two weeks a huge lawsuit was going to trial and Kathy, as the junior partner on the case, was in the trenches doing the heavy research. She always worked hard at research, hating to be embarrassed, or even worse to have one of the senior partners embarrassed due to her lack of thorough research. It was mid-afternoon and Kathy had worked right through lunch, her stomach failing to remind her to eat, or perhaps her stomach reminding her and her mind failing to respond to the internal memo to eat.

Her secretary's voice coming over the phone's intercom broke her concentration, "A call on line three for you, Kathy. Do you want me to take a message?"

"Who is it?"

"He didn't want to say."

"Alright, I'll take it I guess. It's probably somebody from the other side on this case." Kathy picked up the phone, "Hello, this is Kathy?"

"Yeah this is Rita's friend calling."

"Rita's friend? Is this a prank call?"

"I wouldn't call it a prank call, but I would call it a practical call," said an indistinguishable voice.

Kathy could only tell the caller was male. "Look I'm really busy, if this is a sales call I'm not interested, and if it's something else please get right to the point."

"That's fair enough. I'm wondering if you'd like to go visit Rita with me?"

"I don't have time to… Who is this?"

"Let me be more specific. I'm not a friend of any old Rita, but a good friend of fresh-squeezed Rita."

"Okay mister, I'm going to hang up. I've had enough of your mysterious shenanigans."

"Kathy don't hang up," said a more familiar laughing voice. "It's Kevin. Kevin from The Hunting Room bar."

"Kevin who? Oh my God Kevin, oh I get it, Kevin from a couple nights ago, and you mean Margarita. You funny guy you."

"Yeah well, maybe I don't know you well enough yet to be calling like that, but I enjoyed it, especially the part where you almost hung up on me."

"Thank God I didn't make an ass of myself by cussing you out."

"That might have been fun. And speaking of fun, how about dinner and a movie Friday night?"

"That sounds great."

"Okay, so where do I pick you up then?" Kathy gave Kevin her work address.

Kathy washed her face in the ladies room of her office, and then reapplied her make-up. She brushed her hair and changed into more casual clothes. She always wore a suit to the office. Kevin would be picking her up here at the office. Kathy felt safer with that arrangement until she got to know him better. She'd made arrangements for Jane to pick up Lily from school.

Oh my God, I can't believe I'm this nervous…Although it's not like I've been on a date this century. I knew I was excited, but I didn't expect to be this nervous. I guess I ought to give myself some grace this time. Maybe I'll relax after I've been on a few dates…I'm probably also nervous because I think I really like this guy, I mean as much as I can know so far.

Kathy used both hands to put her lipstick on, not trusting her right hand to be steady on its own. Maybe Kevin's nervous too. I don't think he's done much dating yet either… I wonder if I should wait for him to open the car door for me, or just get in myself. Do guys still do stuff like that? Oh well, I guess I'll just play it by ear.

Kathy glanced down at her watch and said aloud, "Oh my God it's time. I better get downstairs in case he's on time."

Kathy threw her make-up bag back in her purse and marched out the door to the elevator. She checked her hair one last time in the elevator while it descended. Satisfied, she put away her compact and straightened her blouse as the elevator doors opened. A midnight blue coupe glided into the parking lot just as Kathy emerged from the building. She waved and met the coupe at the curb.

She hopped in the car without giving Kevin a chance to open the door for her, and off they went. They filled the time it took to drive to the mall with small talk. "Can you wait to eat if we see a movie first?" asked Kevin.

Kathy's stomach fluttered with nerves as she said, "No problem. I can wait." Kevin bought the tickets and motioned for her to go first into the theatre. They sat down near the aisle. Saving them from more anxious chit chat, the curtain went up and the previews started.

Kevin glanced over at Kathy, and then quickly looked away. He wanted to put his hand on her knee, but didn't know if his hand would be welcomed. He shot another quick look at Kathy, hoping for some sort of sign, but received none as Kathy stared straight ahead at the screen. Kevin leaned closer to Kathy, yet without actually touching her. The previews came and went without as much as a glancing touch.

As the movie started Kevin leaned over and whispered into Kathy's ear, putting his hand on her arm as he did. She didn't push his hand away, thank God. A few minutes later Kevin found another pretext for leaning over and saying something in her ear, this time placing his hand on hers. She responded by turning her hand over and holding his. Kevin sighed in relief, settling back into the chair in contentment. Now I can just enjoy the movie, he thought.

Kathy felt electricity go through her body, starting at her hand where Kevin touched her. She guided his hand to her knee, placing her hand on top of his. Warmth spread throughout her body. Oh my God it feels good to have a man touch me again. How long has it been? Kathy wondered privately. She settled in to enjoying the movie, but she would have been almost as happy to sit with Kevin and stare at a blank screen. The touch felt that good.

Kevin began to move his hand, and gently massaged her knee and lower thigh. Kathy was surprised at feeling aroused. It usually took a whole lot more for her to feel excited. Kathy ran her hand up and down Kevin's bare arm, as he wore his long sleeved shirt rolled up. Kevin took turns running his fingers along her leg and softly squeezing her leg. Kathy's leg began to fall asleep, so she shifted position and crossed her legs the other way. In response Kevin went to work on the other leg.

After the movie Kevin stood in the aisle and waited for Kathy to move down the stairs ahead of him. She put her hand on his shoulder and he put his arm around her waist in response. They walked arm in arm out to the restaurant across the street. Kathy enjoyed each and every step. Kathy felt no need to talk, but they compared notes on the movie just the same.

Kevin pulled into the parking lot of Kathy's office two hours later. He parked and met Kathy at the passenger's side just as she stepped out of the car. They talked between their cars a few minutes until Kathy said she was tired. Kevin embraced her and said, "I had a nice time. I'll call you." And with that he turned and waved as he got into his car.

As Kathy drove home she noted a sense of disappointment. At first she didn't know why she felt that way. After all, she'd enjoyed the time with Kevin and hoped he'd keep his promise and call again. Her thoughts kept coming back to their goodbye in the parking lot. And then it came to her as she suddenly said aloud, "I wish he'd kissed me. Even a brief peck on the lips would have been nice." The hug just didn't fit the evening, or her desire.

That night in group Evelyn talked about her spirituality. She was excited about new energy in her relationship with God, an energy she hadn't felt in awhile. On the way out to the parking lot after group, Kathy walked alongside Evelyn. "So what inspired you to get back into religion?" asked Kathy.

Evelyn laughed and said, "I wouldn't call it religion. That makes it sound like I'm working prayer beads and handing out tracks to strangers on street corners."

"Then what's the difference between religion and spirituality? Is that the word you used?"

"Yeah, that's it. You could probably get a hundred different definitions from a hundred different people. For me religion places more emphasis on proper behavior and proper belief, while spirituality is more about faith and a journey of the soul, and of course relating to God."

"Those sound about the same to me," said Kathy.

"I guess it's hard for me to put into words, but I find religion focuses more on the external, and I'm interested more in a spirituality from the inside out. Anything spiritual that doesn't begin on the inside doesn't do much for me. Don't get me wrong, loving behavior is great, but unless it comes from a loving heart I don't see much value in it."

"That's interesting. I guess I've never really thought about that kind of difference," said Kathy.

"It's fairly new for me in the last five years or so," said Evelyn.

"Five years doesn't sound new to me."

Evelyn laughed, "It seems new for me. Maybe that's because I've been on a spiritual journey for the past thirty plus years."

Kathy asked, "Maybe I'm getting too external, but what are you actually doing that's helping you in your journey?"

"That's a fair question. I've been doing a lot of spiritual reading, and I've been meditating," said Evelyn.

"Meditating? Isn't that for monks and nuns or something?"

Evelyn laughed again. "Well, I suppose that the stereotypical view, but someone told me that they believe no one grows spiritually much without meditating."

"Really! I've never heard that. Did you hear that from a priest?"

Evelyn laughed, "Oh Kathy, you really haven't thought much about your faith, have you? No, I heard this from a dear friend who has this really great, alive faith."

"Can you recommend a book to me on meditation," Kathy asked.

Kathy set down the book and stared out the window. She'd never meditated. She wondered what it would be like. Images of bald monks in orange robes sitting cross-legged and humming came to mind. Kathy sat on the floor with her back to the couch and crossed her legs. Placing her hands on her knees, she shut her eyes and waited. Now what do I do? she wondered. She waited longer. Then she started as her head rolled over onto her shoulder. I doubt that's supposed to happen. Maybe I'm too comfortable. Kathy edged away from the couch and tried again. She sat in silence for a few minutes and then her head bobbed again. I must not be doing this right, she thought.

Kathy picked the book back up and turned to the chapter on how to meditate. Then she remembered that the book recommended focusing on her breathing. Kathy closed her eyes and focused on her breathing. Initially this seemed to work. And then thoughts of Lily came to mind, and then Kathy thought about her current case at the office, and then she made a mental list of the chores she wanted to do around the house, and then she noticed her back hurting. "Oh forget it! This isn't working. I can think all those thoughts without sitting uncomfortably and closing my eyes," she said aloud.

"I'm curious about meditating. I went out and got a book after talking to Evelyn. I read something about it and thought I might give it a try, but I don't know how to do it. I don't get how it works," said Kathy.

"So you followed through on getting the book I suggested?" asked Evelyn.

"Yes, and I read the whole chapter on how to do it. I also read that the author said it helps with anxiety and peace, both of which sound really good to me. I feel…unsettled. I mean, I've decided to go on with my life after Jack, but I don't feel as much peace as I'd like, and I don't know why. I just thought if something could help me feel more settled and at rest, I'd like to try it."

"Meditation might help you with that. I've been meditating the past few years, and it helps me to slow down and be more grounded, and more present. I guess I don't get caught up in the rush as much as I used to. Sometimes I find myself racing, but usually a good meditation sitting will slow me right down."

"So how do you do it?" asked Kathy.

"Well, I suggest you read more on it, but I can give you the basics. First you sit comfortably, close your eyes, and follow your breathing in and out. And when you notice yourself thinking about something, merely bring yourself gently back to your breathing. I suppose that's pretty much the basics. The book can give you the more advanced stuff," explained Evelyn.

"You mean the whole point is to breathe? The book I read said the same thing, but I figured I wasn't doing it right. I tried to focus on my breathing, and I could only do it for maybe a minute or two. I guess I didn't bring my wandering thoughts back to my breath," said Kathy.

"That's pretty much the point, breath and pay attention. Sounds weird huh?" laughed Evelyn.

"What's the point of focusing on your breathing?" asked Jake.

"The idea is to get out of your constant stream of thinking and just be. Getting out of the thinking might feel strange at first, but really I find it quite therapeutic," said Evelyn.

"Do you ever fall asleep doing it?" asked Kathy.

"Oh sure, on occasion, but not very often anymore unless I'm really tired. Anyways, I wrote down my two other favorite books on meditation. This first author comes from a Buddhist background, but he integrates his ideas with all the major religions. Actually, pockets of contemplatives meditate in all major religions, not just Buddhists and Hindus. The second one is from a Christian background."

"Thanks."

"Kathy, do you feel done? I'd like to talk about something," said Susan.

"Oh sure, go ahead."

"I've started dating somebody. I'm really excited, and nervous. I haven't really been involved with anybody since my divorce. I mean I've dated casually, but nothing serious. And it's been over twenty years since I dated my husband, so I feel really out of practice. I don't even know how to do this," said Susan.

"That's great, Susan," said Karen.

"So who's the guy?" asked Jake.

"His name is Steve, and I met him at a night club. Come to think of it, I met him the night Kathy and I went clubbing. He teaches English literature classes at a local high school. I know it's early, but I really like him. It scares me how much I like him."

"What do you like about him?" asked Jake.

Susan paused to think before answering, "First of all, he accepts my significantly less than perfect body. And he asks about me, and he seems to really listen to what I'm saying. I expect guys to just want to talk about themselves and only offer courtesy attention to me. At first I thought he was just putting his best foot forward by asking me questions, but he's kept it up for over a month now."

"Why can't I meet a guy like that?" bemoaned Karen.

"Sounds good," said Dr. Aragorn.

"Yes, but how do I do this?" asked Susan.

"How do you do what?" asked Dr. Aragorn.

"Do I just keep waiting for him to call me? Should I call him, and if so how often? Should I ask him out, or let him be the typical man and initiate all the dates? And how physical should

I be? Should we be having full sex by now? And how vulnerable should I be with my needs and with what I want out of a relationship?"

"Wow, that just about covers all the major areas," said Dr. Aragorn with a laugh.

"Don't leave me hanging. Can't you give me some feedback?"

"First of all you're anxious. You can probably feel that, right?" asked Dr. Aragorn.

"Right," acknowledged Susan.

"So what's your anxiety about? Is it just that you haven't dated in awhile?" asked Dr. Aragorn.

"I don't know…maybe I'm afraid to blow it and lose a great guy. I don't come across one every day you know."

"Okay, so how are you going to blow it?" asked Jake.

"By…by doing…I don't know how, I'm just afraid I'll do something to miss out on a great opportunity."

"So you don't know what you're afraid of," said Evelyn. Susan looked down at her lap and thought.

"Maybe you're just anxious to be in this kind of relationship, with it having been a long time and all," suggested Jake.

"Maybe."

"Is there a problem with how it's going with Steve so far?" asked Dr. Aragorn.

"Uh, not really. I mean we're still getting to know each other, but I think it's going well."

"Alright then, so far so good," said Dr. Aragorn.

"But isn't there something we can do to help me with being anxious?"

"It might help to work with your anxiety more, as there might be more to it. It might just be that it's new and you haven't been involved with someone in awhile," said Dr. Aragorn.

"Okay, I'll give it some more thought," said Susan.

"And you might just need to allow yourself be anxious for now. Steve's already important enough for you to be anxious," said Dr. Aragorn.

"Maybe I'm nervous that I've allowed him to become important to me already," said Susan.

Dr. Aragorn nodded and smiled. "That's vulnerable." Susan nodded with a frown.

The River: Day 12

Dr. Painter cleared Stacy to be released from the hospital. He wanted to keep Kathy another night for observation. Dr. Painter was going over final instructions with Stacy, and Mike decided to walk down the hall and check in on Kathy. After Kathy finished telling Mike about feeling a little more energy, there was a lull in the conversation. Mike sat in the chair in Kathy's hospital room and waited. Kathy appeared to be mulling something over in her mind. Mike grew impatient and stood and said, "I suppose Stacy's ready by now."

"Wait a minute, Mike. I want to talk to you about something. And don't answer right away. I want you to go look for Jack, and I want to go with you," began Kathy.

"Now hold on young lady. You're not going anywhere for a couple more days," said Dr. Painter as he stood in the doorway.

"I can't stay here any longer. I have to go find Jack. I can't just leave him out there to die."

"There's no way you're leaving this hospital until you're stable. And that won't be today, and may not be tomorrow," said Dr. Painter.

"Then you must go find him, Mike. If I can't go then you have to...I mean, please go look for him!" pleaded Kathy.

"But where would I..."

"I don't know, but I can't go home until I know we've done all we can to look for...well, to find him," said Kathy.

"Well, let me..."

"Mike, please do this for me...and for Jack."

Mike rubbed his beard stubble, and sighed deeply. He walked over to the window and stared outside. "I've actually thought about doing my own search…"

"Oh thank God," said Kathy.

"I suppose I could inspect the area where the ice chest was found…I don't know what I could see after several days have passed, but I guess I could take a look…The truth is, I'm not sure that I could live with myself if I didn't try to find him. I keep thinking about it. I just can't make you any promises, Kathy. I mean, if the rangers can't find him, well, I don't know what I can do."

Kathy smiled and squeezed his hand. "Oh thank you, Mike! You don't know what this means to me."

"I think I'm doing it for both of us," said Mike.

Mike walked into Stacy's hospital room just as she emerged from the bathroom, having changed back into her street clothes. She was washed and cleaned and smelled like the Stacy he knew. Stacy's face lit up as she saw Mike and they embraced.

"It's so good to see you looking like your old self. I hated seeing you in a hospital bed with tubes sticking out of you," said Mike.

Stacy hugged him and grabbed her purse. "The nurse just finished checking me out. I'm free to go!"

"Great, let's get out of here. I feel like I've been living here the past month," said Mike.

"You feel like you've lived here? I have been living here. I can't wait to get a real hamburger in me. I heard they've got a great burger place down the street, just past your motel."

"Okay, let's go."

Stacy took a huge bite of her burger, juice dripped down her chin and she didn't bother to wipe it. She chewed languidly. "Oh boy does that taste good. Mike nodded. He took a bite of his burger and stared out the window.

"What are you looking at?" asked Stacy.

"Huh?"

"What's on your mind, Mike?"

"Oh, yeah I guess I am distracted. Did I tell you what Kathy asked?"

"No. What?"

"She asked, well actually begged me to go look for Jack," answered Mike.

"Of course."

"It's not that I'm surprised by her request, I just…"

"Just what?" asked Stacy. "Are you afraid you won't find him?"

"No, I'm afraid that I will."

Stacy winced. "Oh my God, that would be horrible if he was…"

"Yeah…but if I don't go look, then I'll always wonder."

"Wonder what?" asked Stacy.

"I don't want to sound arrogant or anything, but I think I know this area as well as many of the rangers, well maybe not the most experienced ones, but…what I mean is that I'm the one who best knows where he was last seen, so…"

"You have to go look."

"I know," agreed Mike. "I could never forgive myself if he turned up…dead, but it looked like he might have been alive for… well, you know what I mean." Stacy nodded. They sat in silence. Mike took Stacy's hand. "I sure wish you could go with me." Stacy nodded.

"Well, maybe I could go with you," said Stacy.

"Gosh Babe, I don't think it's a good idea. I mean, you just got out of the hospital, and were badly dehydrated."

"Well, maybe you're right…I wouldn't want to slow you down, especially since time might be of the essence," said Stacy.

"Yes, I'll leave tomorrow at first light."

The next morning Mike woke at the crack of dawn. He got up slowly, not wanting to wake Stacy. He slipped into the shower and stood under the soothing hot water. When he got out of the bathroom Stacy was awake. She walked over to Mike. Stacy kissed Mike on the lips and held him. After several minutes Mike whispered in her ear, "You okay?"

Stacy wiped her eyes on her sleeve and nodded and said, "I'm just worried about you going back out there...I know it doesn't make any sense, but I'm afraid something will..."

"I'll be careful. I don't want to tell you not to worry, because I know you can't help worrying, but I won't take any chances with myself. And I will take plenty of water and food."

Stacy nodded and pushed him out the motel door. "Hurry and go before I change my mind." With a mischievous grin she added, "I'm seriously considering handcuffing you to the table." Mike kissed her and shouldered his backpack, and then walked to his truck. Mike hesitated before starting the engine. Something held him back. Mike shrugged his shoulders and drove to the Marina.

Pete waited for him in the ranger station. He looked up from his desk as Mike walked in. Pete rubbed his three-day beard and pushed his hat back. "You sure I can't talk you out of this."

"No, I have to do this," countered Mike.

"If I can't talk you out of it, then I will insist that you take these with you," said Pete. He handed Mike a bag of trail mix and two liters of water.

"I've already got plenty of water, and a box of protein bars," said Mike.

"No, this is non-negotiable, partner. You take these with you or I don't allow you into the park."

Mike looked at Pete closely. "You're serious!"

"You damn right I'm serious," said Pete. "You're at risk. It's only been a few days since you stumbled into my office half dead. You take the supplies, or you can just head back into town." Mike shrugged and put the supplies into his backpack.

"Now that's a good soldier," said Pete.

Mike opened his map on the desk and said, "Now show me exactly where my ice chest was found."

Pete studied the map and skimmed his fore-finger across the page. "Right here. We found it on top of this smooth rock saddle."

"How sure are you about that?" asked Mike.

"Look kid, I've been working out here 27 years. I know this area as well as anybody. If I say that's the spot, then that's the spot."

"Hey, I don't mean any disrespect. I just want to find my friend. I have to know his exact, last known position to have any chance," said Mike.

"Then we're wasting daylight. Let's do this," said Pete as he pushed his chair back. He grabbed a set of keys off the desk and headed for the dock.

Twenty minutes later Pete beached the boat on the shore. He glanced at Mike and asked, "You sure this is the right place." Mike looked up at the empty sleeping bags and nodded. "And you've got the marine radio I gave you."

"Yeah I got it. Look, I'll be okay. I promise I'll radio if I get into the slightest trouble."

"No, you'll do better than that. I expect you to check in with me every two hours."

"Now is that really…"

"Now you listen here, partner, this too is non-negotiable. You will check in with me every two hours. And if you miss a check in, I'll assume you're in trouble, and I'll send in the cavalry," said Pete.

"Okay, I get it." Mike hopped out onto the sand and pushed the bow back into the river.

"I'll be monitoring channel 16," Pete yelled. Mike waved and nodded. The engine roared to life and Pete was gone.

Mike turned around and surveyed the cove. He walked up the beach and found the spot where the three of them had camped not long ago. Mike didn't like seeing the empty sleeping bags. Thoughts of the argument he'd had with Jack came back, and with it the regret of allowing Jack to go off alone. Although Mike knew he probably couldn't have stopped Jack from making a trek for the truck. Mike slung his pack on his back and quickly found the trail head Jack had used. The path wound up the low hills leading out of the cove. Mike followed the path with his eyes until it disappeared over the rise. He eyed the sun, guessing he had at least eight hours of light to work with, maybe more. It was still early. Taking a deep breath, Mike began his trek up the faint path.

Barely discernible sandal tracks provided Mike with a trail to follow, but he already knew the path Jack had initially taken. Tracks would be more valuable later. The trail led three-fourths the way up the hill to a game trail that roughly paralleled the peak of the hills. When Mike reached the point where the trail turned left to run along the hills he paused and looked down. The river ran about two hundred feet below him. Mike wiped his forehead with his sleeve. He perspired profusely. Mike found one of the bottles and rehydrated.

Along the ridge path Mike found evidence of Jack's tracks often enough to reassure him he was on the right path. The soft dirt gave way in spots and Mike had to move slower than he wanted to avoid slipping and sliding down the two hundred foot hill. Mike was frustrated at his pace, but knew he wouldn't do Jack any good if he ended up battered and bruised at the bottom of a slide.

Two hours later he climbed the short rise that took him to the top of a rocky bald. The range graduated down in a series of humps to form a saddle between peaks. The ground was smooth solid rock. Mike removed his pack and studied his map. He checked the landmarks several times before he was sure. This was the spot. No evidence remained that his ice chest had been found here, but with the hard terrain he didn't expect any.

Mike pulled out his water and took a few sips. He quickly inhaled some trail mix, and picked up his pack and hiked to the top of the saddle. I won't find any tracks on this hard ground. I guess I'll have to see if I can pick up his trail in the surrounding dirt, Mike thought. He surveyed the terrain in both directions. The back side sloped down to a rocky ground with no discernible trail. Mike looked back down towards the river and also saw rough ground. "Well, if I were Jack I'd keep the river in sight. But maybe I can pick up the trail from the top of this mountain," Mike said aloud. Mike pulled the radio out of his pack and said into it, "Pete, this is Mike, come in."

"Got you loud and clear, partner. Everything okay?"

"Yeah, I'm at the spot the ice chest was found. I'm looking for tracks leading out of the hard ground," said Mike.

"Well, good luck with that. The S and R boys didn't find anything. I'll expect your next call in two hours. Pete out."

"Alrightly, Mike out."

The ground turned to hard-packed dirt once Mike left the saddle. No tracks were visible. Once on the peak Mike shielded his eyes and searched for a trail heading downriver. The suggestion of a trail started fifty feet below Mike and a hundred yards downriver. Mike surveyed the area in the general direction of the marina, and found nothing else that even remotely resembled a trail. He descended as quickly as the terrain allowed.

Mike slid the last twelve feet to the trail head, but fortunately didn't lose his footing. His heart beat rapidly as he looked down to where he might have fallen. Tumbling down a hundred yards of rough terrain would not be pleasant. Having regained his nerve, Mike studied the ground for any remnant of tracks. Not far down the trail were two prints. They were faint, and Mike squatted down to get a closer look at them. Yep, those look like they might be Jack's sandals, Mike thought. The trail ran along the shoulder of the range and Mike picked up his pace, eyeing the sun's position.

At the bottom of the shoulder the trail turned down to the right towards a deep ravine. The ground was littered with small rocks and loose dirt. Man, this is sure steep! I better watch my step on this, Mike thought. He evaluated his options for descending, and didn't like any of them. From hill top to ravine bottom was a good seventy-five yards. Mike checked his watch and pulled his pack off. He called into Pete again, letting him know his location. Mike put the radio away, and bent down and tightened the laces of his boots, repositioned his pack and began his descent.

At first he did well, with only a couple of minor slides of a few feet. The trail ran along the shoulder of the hill, and angled down towards the ravine bottom. Mike continued on this path for a few miles with good progress. This gave Mike more confidence and he picked up his speed slightly. About half way down Mike put his foot on a good-sized rock, expecting it to hold him well. The rock gave way. Mike scrambled to reposition his foot on the dirt, but it was soft and Mike slipped onto his backside and slid downhill quickly. He grabbed at some brush, but Mike pulled it out of the ground immediately. Mike flipped over onto his stomach and desperately tried to get a hold of anything to slow him down, but by now he'd picked up speed and nothing but the ravine bottom was going to stop him.

Mike slid off the hill side and crashed through the branches of low lying trees and landed with a thud. At first he just laid still on his side, not wanting to even open his eyes, afraid of the condition he'd find himself in. His body hurt everywhere. He felt wet. Mike didn't understand feeling wet. He certainly was nowhere near the river. Mike braved opening his eyes. His lower body lay in a small creek.

He tried to push up with his left arm, which he was lying on, but couldn't. His arm didn't seem to have any strength, but Mike didn't know why. He gingerly rolled over onto his right side. His left arm throbbed and was covered in blood. He couldn't move his left forearm at all. With his other hand he held his injured arm against his chest. Mike examined his surroundings for the first time. He was in a narrow ravine, maybe fifteen feet wide, with dense brush and small trees. A narrow creek, only a few feet wide meandered down a gentle incline. Heavy foliage followed the creek on both sides.

Mike didn't see anything of interest to the right. He panned back to the left. Something red caught the corner of his eye across the creek. He turned his head and saw a red hat. Beyond the hat amongst dense foliage was something else, but with the dim lighting of the trees he couldn't make it out. The trees blocked out most of the sunlight.

Mike half crawled and half dragged himself across the creek to investigate. "Thank God my legs and my other arm seem okay," Mike whispered. He picked up the hat and turned it around. Upon the front of the red hat was a large, white "C".

"Oh my God, its Jack's hat...then Jack must be..." Mike dragged himself further into the brush and found a crumpled body. "It's Jack! My God, don't be dead. Jack you better not be dead." Mike reached Jack and pulled on his shoulder to roll him onto his back. It was Jack alright, but he was unconscious. Mike checked for a pulse, and found a weak heart beat. "Thank God you're still alive, you son of a bitch. Jack, Jack can you hear me!" No response. Mike gently slapped his face. No response. "Jack, wake up! Can you hear me?" Nothing. Damn, I better get on the radio, he quickly decided.

Mike noticed his pack wasn't on his back. "Damn! Where in is my pack?" Mike scanned the creek bed and couldn't find it. He dragged himself back to where he'd crash landed. It wasn't there. When he turned to move again he almost screamed in pain. I have to make a sling for my arm...but how? He carefully pulled off his tee shirt and gently tied it into a sling, and then positioned it over his neck and settled his injured arm in its nest. He pulled himself into a standing position and searched for his pack.

The pack has settled into the tree branches nearby. Mike freed it and pulled out his marine radio. It was already on channel 16 and he hit the call button, "Pete come in, Pete do you read?" His only response was static. "Damn! Pete, do you read?" Again, he was greeted with nothing but static. Damn, these hills are blocking the signal! I have to climb out of here, and with one arm. And I have to hurry while Jack's still breathing!

Mike stuffed the radio in his front pocket and climbed on all threes. He used his good arm on the ground to keep his balance. When he reached the point where he started his slide he pulled the radio out and tried again. The response was still only static. He knew he'd have to have an almost unimpeded radio line back to the marina to get a good signal. Thirty minutes later he stood on the top of the ridge. Without waiting to regain his breath, Mike called into the radio again, "Pete, do you read? Pete, this is Mike, do you read?"

"Pete here, I read you loud and clear. What's you got, partner?"

"I found him! I found Jack! He's alive, but unconscious. We have to get him out of here ASAP!"

"Roger that Mike, what's your 1020?"

"I'm on top of a ridge about five or six miles south of the position where you found my ice chest."

"Can you give me a more exact location?" asked Pete.

"No man, just get the hell out here! My map's down in a ravine with Jack! Just hurry!"

"Okay, now settle down, partner. I have the helo on standby. We'll be there in a jiffy. Stay where you are to give us a visual to land by. And monitor your radio. Pete out."

"Got it! Mike out," yelled Mike.

Mike continuously scanned downriver, looking for any signs of the helicopter. He wondered if Pete went to the wrong place. It seemed like four hours later, but it was actually only forty minutes later the helicopter approached. The radio cracked to life. "Mike, do you read?"

"Yep, gotcha loud and clear," returned Mike.

"We don't have visual. Go to higher ground and wave your arms over your head," ordered Pete.

"Will do." Mike ran up the hillside waving his good arm. The helicopter was only a few hundred yards away.

"Okay Mike, we got visual. Point to where your buddy is," said Pete. Mike pointed down the ravine.

"Got it. We'll find a spot to put her down. Pete out." Mike turned and headed back down the hill towards Jack. Fearing another fall, Mike took his time. He knew the cavalry was already on the scene and there wasn't much he could do anyways. When he got to the loose rocks where he'd fallen he saw the rangers hiking down into the ravine. Mike sat down and slid on his backside. It was painful, but better than the alternative.

By the time Mike got back to Jack the rangers knelt over him. The rangers had pulled him out of the thicket, and an oxygen mask covered Jack's face and a tube stuck into his left arm. Jack wore a neck support, and was still unconscious. "How's he look?" asked a nervous Mike.

"Don't know yet, partner. Give us a minute here," said Pete without taking his eyes off his patient.

"Anything I can do?" asked Mike.

"Yeah, keep quiet and let us do our jobs," returned an impatient Pete.

Mike knelt as near as he dared, not wanting to interfere with the rangers' work. He almost had to bite his tongue to prevent himself from telling them to hurry. The other ranger disconnected the empty fluid bag and attached another one to the tube running into Jack's arm. "Damn, I've never seen anybody go through a bag of fluid that quick."

Finally Mike heard the words he wanted to hear. "Alright Pete, he's ready to move." Pete nodded and placed a stretcher parallel to Jack's body. On the count of three the rangers slid Jack onto the stretcher. They hoisted him and carried him to the helicopter. Once Jack was safely aboard Pete reached a hand out to Mike. "Okay partner, up you go." Mike strapped himself in and away they flew.

The pilot settled the helicopter onto the roof of the Marble Hospital. Just as they touched down two medics raced out of the building and ducked under the blades of the helicopter. One of the medics grabbed the IV and then they carried Jack into the ER. Mike followed them with his eyes until the double doors closed behind his friend.

"Alright partner, let's get that arm looked at," said Pete. Mike followed Pete inside without a word. As soon as Mike was inside he searched for Jack, but couldn't catch sight of him.

"What have you got there, Pete?" asked one of the ER nurses.

"Hi Amy, it looks like he broke his arm. He's also scrapped himself up pretty good."

"I can see that. Alright, this way," said Amy as she took Mike by the good arm.

Amy led him into an empty room and pointed to the bed. "Have a seat there. I'll help you take off those pants. I have to see what all you've done to yourself," she said with a smile and without a hint of criticism. Mike relaxed a little as Amy was gentle and took her time so as to not jar Mike's arm. "Well, I can see that Pete's right. You scrapped yourself in almost every conceivable place."

Mike smiled briefly and asked, "Is there any news of my buddy yet?"

"Oh no. We won't know anything until the doctors finish their exam. They're just getting started." Amy had begun cleaning out Mike's wounds and looked up at his face and added with a smile, "But don't worry, Dr. Watson and Dr. Michaels know what they're doing."

"How long till they're done?" asked Mike.

"I know you're worried about your friend, but right now let's see what we can do about you. We won't know anything about your friend for hours," answered Amy.

Mike sighed, and then winced. "That one hurts pretty good, I'll bet," said Amy. Mike nodded.

When Amy finished cleaning Mike up she helped him into a hospital gown. "Okay Mike, let's take you down to X-ray and see about that arm. Wait right there, I'll be back in a moment." A minute later Amy returned pushing a wheel chair.

"I don't need that. It's my arm, not my legs," said Mike.

"Just assume the position. I'll decide what's necessary while you're my patient," returned Amy without a smile. Mike realized she meant business and submitted.

Mike lay on a fresh hospital bed, different from the one he'd first sat on when he arrived. He held his arm against his chest, as Amy had taken off his make-shift sling. Thoughts of Jack rushed into his mind. He pictured Jack lying on the surgery table with doctors and nurses frantically working to revive him, while the heart-rate alarm beeped urgently. Mike shook his head, trying to shoo such thoughts from his mind. However, they returned again and again.

Finally a doctor walked into his room. She was young and wore dark brown hair tied up in a bun. She smiled at Mike behind dark-rimmed glasses. "I'm Doctor Sanchez and I'll be treating your arm. I've just looked at the X-rays and you've got a clean break. The good news is you've only got one break, and the bad news is you broke it all the way through. I'll give you something to take orally for the pain until we can put you in a cast."

"You can't put me in a cast now?" asked Mike.

"No, we have to wait for the swelling to go down first. I am going to set the bone. But don't worry, I'll deaden the arm first."

"How's Jack doing? Is there any word yet?" asked Mike.

"Jack? You must mean the unconscious patient brought in on the helo." Mike nodded.

"Haven't heard a thing. Now, this will sting a bit, but just for a moment. I'm injecting your arm with something to knock out all feeling." Mike turned away and shut his eyes. He tensed as the needle went in. "Okay, we'll give it a few minutes to make sure it takes effect." Dr. Sanchez picked up a clipboard and flipped through a few pages. Then she looked back at Mike's arm. She set down the clipboard and poked him gently, "Do you feel anything?" Mike shook his head. "Good. You might feel a tugging sensation, but you shouldn't feel any pain."

Dr. Sanchez grabbed onto his hand and pulled his arm towards her, as if trying to lengthen the arm. Mike's eyes widened as he saw his arm seem to grow a foot longer. Dr. Sanchez rotated his arm and then allowed it to slowly retract. "I think I got it the first try. But I want to take an X-ray to make sure."

Mike lay on his hospital bed with his arm in a sling. Amy came into Mike's room and smiled. "Good news, Mike, your arm…"

"You heard something about Jack?"

"No Mike, the good news is that your arm's set properly. That means you can go home."

"Go home? I'm not leaving here until I find out about Jack."

"Suit yourself. Is there someone I can call who can come for you?" asked Amy.

"My girlfriend's at the Marble Motel, room 203."

"I'll give her a call. You've been discharged. Dr. Sanchez wants to see you in two days to get that cast on. And here's a two-day supply of pain meds. Don't take more than one every four- six hours." Mike took the pills from her and allowed her to wheel him to the waiting room.

Mike awoke to a gentle nudging of his shoulder. He opened his eyes to see Stacy, and embraced her with his good arm. "Thank God you're okay, though banged up I see," said Stacy. Mike relayed the day's events to her. "I had a feeling you'd find him," said Stacy.

"How'd you know?"

"I don't know, I just had a gut feeling," said Stacy. "So there's still no word?"

"No, they said it might be hours."

The door to the ER opened and a man in green scrubs approached. He walked slowly and rubbed his eyes with his forearm. He paused at the nurse's station, followed Amy's finger to Mike, and made his way over. "I'm Dr. Watson, and I assume you're Mike?"

"Yes, how is he?"

"The good news is Jack's in and out of consciousness. He awoke shortly after surgery. He came in badly dehydrated and malnourished."

"What surgery?"

"He also has two broken arms and three broken ribs. We had to place a pin in one of his arms in order to set the break. He'll be in pain, and won't be able to do much for himself with two arms in casts, but my primary concern is rehydrating and re-nourishing him."

"So what does that mean?" asked Mike.

"It means your friend is lucky to be alive. And it means he'll be on IVs for awhile," said Dr. Watson.

"Oh thank God," said Stacy. Mike sighed.

"He'll be taken care of while he's here, but he'll need someone to help him with eating, dressing and hygiene until his hands strengthen," explained Dr. Watson.

"When can we see him?" asked Mike.

"Not until at least tomorrow. I don't want him disturbed today." And with a grim smile Dr. Watson turned and left.

84 Weeks after the River Trip

"So I guess I was unconscious when Mike and the rangers pulled me out of the water. All I know is that we were floating down the river, and then I became tired…the next thing I knew was I woke up in the hospital…And after hearing my story, a really kind nurse suggested that I get into therapy. I guess she realized that I was in trouble. I suppose that's how I ended up joining you all…I think that's all there is to tell."

Kathy looked up at Dr. Aragorn and the rest of the group. Kathy had just finished telling the group about her and Stacy being rescued at the end of the fateful river ordeal. Kathy scanned the group's faces.

"My God, Kathy, you almost died!" said Evelyn.

"That son of a bitch almost killed you, pulling that stupid stunt by going off on his own," said Jake.

"It might not have come to that, if Jack had stayed with you guys," said Tom.

"It wasn't Jack's fault Kathy almost died!" countered Karen.

"Maybe not, but Jack sure didn't help by leaving the rest of you," said Susan.

"That's bullshit! It was just mother nature having a fit," said Karen.

"Maybe so, but Jack sure didn't help the situation by going off on his own. You all had the best chance of survival by staying together," said Jake.

"I hate it when everybody makes it all Jack's fault. It's never just one person," said Karen.

"That's quite a story, Kathy. Perhaps Jack didn't literally almost kill you, but I wonder if the whole nightmare is in any way metaphorical of your marriage," said Dr. Aragorn.

"Metaphorical in what way?" asked Kathy.

"Are there any parallels? Does anyone have any other thoughts about Kathy's river trip?" asked Dr. Aragorn.

"Your marriage didn't seem to produce much food, just like the river trip," suggested Susan.

"Yeah, in both cases you've been starving," said Jake.

"You all are full of it. The river nightmare is just bad luck. It has nothing to do with Kathy's marriage," suggested Karen.

"I don't know, Karen. There do seem to be parallels," said Evelyn.

"You all are reading too much into the river thing. I mean, bad things happen to good people," said Karen.

"But Jack left them not once, but twice. And the second time almost cost Jack, Kathy and Stacy their lives," said Jake.

"This is total bullshit! I hate it when you all blame Jack for Kathy's unhappiness in her marriage. I mean, it takes two to tango," said Karen.

"You're having a strong reaction to us tonight, Karen," said Dr. Aragorn.

"Everyone's going way overboard on Jack's part in this, and it makes me mad," said Karen.

"Yes, and what's all the energy about for you?" persisted Dr. Aragorn.

"Well…I hate it when anybody get's made out to be the devil."

"Being blamed is something you're sensitive to, Karen. And yes, nobody dances alone. While I don't have it all figured out, I do think there's much to consider about how this trip went down. I think Kathy needs our help making sense of the nightmare she endured. I mean let's face it, this was a near death experience," said Dr. Aragorn.

"If nothing else, the river trip shows us how painful Kathy's marriage had become," said Susan.

"Yeah, no kidding," said Tom.

"I do feel like I've been dying in the marriage," said Kathy.

"I can't believe that jerk just left you when you were fighting for your lives," said Jake.

"But he was trying to get back for help," said Karen.

"But he was trying to get help in a stupid way," said Jake.

"Maybe so, but at least he was trying. He wasn't just sitting on his backside hoping everything would turn out okay," said Karen.

"We can never know, but I wonder what would have happened if you'd all stayed together. Would the outcome have been different?" Evelyn wondered aloud.

"I wouldn't have been worrying about Jack if he'd stayed with us," said Kathy.

"But you still would have been in the same situation, not having any food and having to get back," said Karen.

"And if you'd had less anxiety about Jack's safety, you might have had more energy to make a plan together," suggested Evelyn.

"But what better plan could you have made, other than what you ended up doing?" asked Tom.

Kathy shrugged her shoulders. "I don't know about a plan at the river, but we sure could have used a better marriage plan."

"What would you have done differently?" asked Dr. Aragorn.

Kathy pondered the question before saying, "I wish Jack and I would have talked more early in our marriage. I wish we'd addressed issues before they became so big…I don't know if it would have made any difference, but it seems like we approached our marriage with naiveté. We might have done better if we'd been more adult early on. I think I kept hoping that the problems would just go away, and well, they didn't."

The River: Day 13

Dr. Painter wanted to keep Kathy one more night for observation. Mike and Stacy walked into the room to find Kathy talking with energy on the phone. She hung up and gave them a warm welcome, "Hey guys! It's good to see you."

"Wow, your spirits sure have improved since I last saw you," said Mike.

"Mike, thank you so much for finding Jack. I'm so grateful for what you did!"

"I'm grateful that I was lucky enough to find him."

"Tell me how you found him," asked Kathy. Mike recounted the events leading up to his slide down into the ravine.

"Wow, thank God you fell into just the right place, or you might never have found him."

"Yeah, he was completely hidden from view, unless you were right on top of him," said Mike.

"So who were you talking to?" asked Stacy.

"Oh, an old friend. It helped me immensely to talk with her."

"What friend is that," asked Stacy.

"Oh, Sophie, she's a dear friend from college."

"Oh yeah, I think you mentioned her while we were hiking," said Stacy.

"So there's still no news from the ER docs?" Kathy asked.

Mike shook his head. "Just the initial feedback that he's in and out of consciousness, but stable. I called ICU this morning, but they said there was no change."

"So the nurse told me you're being discharged," said Stacy.

"Yeah, I can't wait to get out of here. I want to go over to ICU and see Jack."

"I'm not sure they'll let you in," said Jack.

"We'll see about that. I can be very persuasive when I want to be," said Kathy with a grim smile.

Jack stared blankly out the window when Mike and Stacy followed Kathy into the room. Jack had been moved from ICU into a regular room. Kathy took his hand and gently squeezed. Jack turned to Kathy and gave her a mischievous grin and said slowly, "So I'll bet I gave you a bit of a scare, huh?"

"Jack, you really did. It isn't funny," said Kathy.

"You probably did it on purpose, you asshole," added Mike.

"Of course I did it on purpose. You don't think I'd allow this to be a boring vacation, do you?"

"That's such a Jack thing to say," said Kathy as she rolled her eyes.

"So I guess you'll make it," said Mike.

"Oh yeah, I could probably check out right now."

"Oh, no you don't," said Kathy.

"I already promised the docs I'd give 'em till tomorrow," said Jack.

"So what the hell happened to you? How'd you end up in that ravine?" asked Mike.

Jack frowned as he thought, and said, "Last thing I remember I was hiking along back to the truck, and it was starting to get dark. I was making pretty good time. Then I guess I slipped."

"How long after dark did you hike?" asked Mike.

"I don't know…maybe a couple hours," said Jack.

"Were you planning to bed down for the night?" asked Kathy.

"Hell no! I was gonna keep going until I found the truck or the marina, or died trying."

"You almost did die trying," said Kathy.

"Did you realize you were hiking southwest, and angling away from the river and the marina?" said Mike.

"Get out of here! Don't mess with me."

"I'm serious, you were heading the wrong way," said Mike.

"Mike, this isn't the time for jokes," said Jack.

Mike thought about clarifying, but the look on Jack's face warned him off. Mike said, "So how did you actually fall?"

"I guess I was on a steep trail, and it was getting tough to see the terrain, and then I guess I lost my footing. And I woke up here...So you found me, Mike?"

"Yeah, a couple days after you'd gone missing. I guess I got lucky, if you can call it that. I slipped into the same ravine as you," said Mike.

"You always did kind of follow me around," said Jack.

"That's very funny. You almost killed yourself, Jack. But I promised myself I wouldn't get into it with you," said Kathy. Jack grinned.

"I never asked you, how'd you know where to look for Jack?" asked Kathy.

"The rangers showed me on a map where my ice chest was found," said Mike. "I tracked him from there, and got lucky at the end."

Pointing to Mike's arm, "Don't look so lucky to me, man," said Jack.

Mike shrugged and said, "Small price to pay to save your ass."

Mike parked his truck and trailer next to the launch ramp. He turned off the key and scanned the marina, looking for Pete. Not seeing him on the dock, he and Stacy decided to head for the station. They stepped down from the truck and walked into the ranger station.

Pete was expecting them and was ready to go. They went down to the dock and climbed into the ranger boat. Pete untied the boat and shoved off. Gray clouds covered most of the sky, with a few spots of blue sky slipping past the almost seamless cloud cover. They drove the ten miles upriver in silence. Pete beached the boat next to Mike's boat.

Mike and Stacy jumped out of the boat. Mike inspected the patch on the hull. He was satisfied it would hold for now. Mike had been out the day before placing a temporary patch on his boat. He'd found the materials he needed for the patch at the marine store in town. He wanted to get back to the hospital as soon as possible, so he hadn't taken the time to do a proper job. As he reached into the boat Mike had to move Jack's bag to get at the rope underneath the seat. Jack's second favorite hat fell out of the bag. He picked up Jack's hat and held it up.

"I expect Jack to run up and grab his hat out of my hands. He wouldn't let anyone touch this hat. His dad won it for him at a carnival throwing baseballs at milk cans. Jack beamed from ear to ear when his dad knocked over all the cans in one throw. Even the booth operator was impressed. Jack was so proud of his dad's four years in the minor leagues. He must have told me a hundred times of the day his dad played one major league season. I was there the night he won the hat…we were twelve years old." Stacy put her arm around Mike's waist.

"I can't believe we almost died out here…The whole week seems like a dream…This sure isn't what I'd expected this week…I thought we'd have the time of our lives," said Mike.

"I'm sure none of us expected this," said Stacy.

"Thank God we all survived it," said Mike.

"Yes, thank God," agreed Stacy.

Mike put the hat back in the bag and zipped it up. He tied the rope to the u-bolt in the bow of the boat and gave the other end to Pete. They towed Mike's boat back to the marina and tied it off on the courtesy dock. Stacy helped Mike trailer the boat, and then they drove back to their motel with little conversation. "This sure isn't the way I thought this trip would end. I can't stop thinking about it," said Mike. Stacy put her hand on Mike's hand and squeezed.

85 Weeks after the River Trip

Kathy looked forward to seeing Stacy. She was grateful Stacy had initiated staying in contact since the fateful river trip. They'd been getting together almost weekly since they got back.

"Can you believe it, Stacy? It's been over a year and a half since the river trip," said Kathy.

"I know! That seems so long ago," said Stacy.

"It almost seems like a lifetime ago to me," said Kathy.

"So how have you been?" asked Stacy.

Kathy paused to ponder before answering, "I still feel bad about divorcing Jack. I mean, I know it was the right thing for me to do, but I'm still working on letting myself off the hook for it. I guess it's one thing to know what's right in my head, and another thing to feel it deep in my heart," said Kathy.

"How long have you been working on that?" asked Stacy.

"About twenty years."

"What? Really?

"No, I'm kidding," laughed Kathy. "I guess I've been trying to let myself off the hook ever since I made the decision to leave Jack. I've been in that therapy group since we got back from the trip, and they're helping me forgive myself, and Jack. Joining them has been the best decision I've ever made."

"Wow, that's so interesting. Has Jack done anything like that, besides the marriage counseling?" asked Stacy.

"No, he's only done the marriage counseling. I filed for divorce soon after Jack and I stopped going to marriage counseling. As you know, at first I thought it was helping, but as time went on it didn't seem like we were getting anywhere. I wanted to keep trying though, but Jack decided he was ready to quit."

"So you've been going for 18 months now. That seems like a long time to be in therapy. I mean, what do you talk about every week?" asked Stacy.

"Oh believe me, that's no problem. I've never had trouble finding something to talk about. And to be honest, it doesn't seem like I've been going that long. I know it sounds like a long time, but it took me almost the whole first six months just to learn how to make use of therapy."

"I don't want to pry, but how do you make use of it?"

"Oh I don't mind telling you…I'm just trying to think of how to put it into words. At first I didn't know how they could help me either. I expected therapy to be about getting the right advice. I suppose I thought I'd get suggestions on what to do differently. Only after several months did I realize that the main thing I get from the group is help in getting to know myself…and learning some inner skills. And that really has nothing to do with advice. It helps me to come to understand myself. At first they mostly helped me understand my marriage better, and especially my part in it. As time went on I started seeing more of the reasons why I picked Jack as a husband. I hated admitting it to myself, not to mention to Jack, that I married him partly because I wanted someone that I could control. I wanted someone that would give me a lot of power over him," Kathy said as she laughed. "I was too afraid to be vulnerable with Jack. The truth is I've never really been very open with anyone, until the group. I'm still not too good at being open, but I have found some friends that I do pretty well with…like with you. I also realized that I needed to grow, and develop some key relationship skills that I was missing. I mean, my God Stacy, the therapy's helped me change my life!"

"I've always thought therapy was for really screwed-up losers," said Stacy.

Kathy laughed aloud, "I used to think the same thing until my marriage starting falling apart. It's not like that though."

"The way you describe it, I might even try it myself."

"Is there something you're not happy about?"

"Uh, well, I guess so. I've always been a little down. I try not to think about it, but it's always there, at least in the background."

"Oh, I'm sorry," said Kathy.

"Yeah, thanks."

"Do you have any idea why you get down?" probed Kathy.

"I'm not really sure. Maybe I get it the most around guys."

"What happens around guys?" asked Kathy.

"I'm not totally sure…maybe it has something to do with feeling rejected, or something like that…especially by a guy."

"Do you feel rejected by Mike at all?

"Yeah, Mike would probably be mad if he knew I said this, but sometimes he gets quiet and…I guess I take it kind of personal and feel rejected."

"Then maybe therapy could help you with the blues. It's helped me become a different person…well at least in some ways," said Kathy.

"I wouldn't say that I'm depressed, just a bit down…at least, I don't think so…" Kathy nodded.

"So how's life after marriage going?" asked Stacy.

"It's still painful…I don't like thinking about it, and I'm still sad."

"Oh yeah," said Stacy.

"I'm often sad about it. It isn't what I wanted. When we got married I thought it would be forever. Maybe I was being idealistic, but I thought we were a perfect match."

"When did you first think it might not be forever?" asked Stacy.

"I don't think I thought of divorce at all until we'd been married for several years. Oh, don't get me wrong, it was great at first. We really had some great times the first couple years. I was deeply in love with Jack, and so jealous whenever he even looked at another woman. I guess it was sometime during the second year that the problems started. At first I just brushed it off as Jack having a bad day or something, or that I was just taking what he said too personal. But when we started fighting more often it became harder to dismiss. And then there was the bad one." Kathy paused and winced as she remembered.

"The bad one?" invited Stacy.

"I'm almost too embarrassed to tell you, but what the heck. It happened on the way home from a party. I was mad about something Jack said at the party, something about how bossy I could be. We were all sitting around a table after dinner, and someone mentioned their tough boss. And then Jack said something about me being his boss, and then laughed it off like it was a joke. I was so embarrassed that he said it publicly, but I was mostly hurt that he felt that way. So I brought it up in the car on the way home that night, and we really got into it. I won't repeat all the names we called each other, but it was ugly…Jack slept on the couch for days and I cried myself to sleep every night. Each morning I hoped our clearer minds would enable us to talk things through. I naively thought that the alcohol was talking the night of that party. The truth is that neither one of us drank that much, I was just trying to find some excuse. I couldn't face how bad it had become between us. Anyways, the next morning we tried again, and dear God, we fought the same ugly battle again. It was almost word for word. I kicked myself for what I said, but I couldn't stop myself…After that Jack started accusing me all the time of bossing him around, and I would come back with how much of a loser he was…I think it was the time we almost got into it physically that got me thinking about leaving Jack for the first time. My God, that scared the heck out of me."

"Wow, so it's been rough going for many years then," said Stacy.

Kathy nodded and paused as she thought, and then said, "Jack's decided to move back in with his mother."

"Really? Why is that?" asked Stacy.

"He said he can't afford to buy me out of the condo, and the financial deal is better for him if I keep the condo anyways. So I'm back in my condo, and Jack is settled in with his mother. He's actually living in his old room that he grew up in."

"That is so weird," said Stacy.

"At times I feel so bad for Jack, and other times I have no respect for him whatsoever. His mother washes all his clothes, cooks for him, and doesn't charge him any rent. How can he let her treat him like that?" said Kathy.

"Well, isn't that between them," said Stacy.

"I guess so...I just hate it."

"Why does it affect you so much?" asked Stacy.

"That's a really good question, and I don't know...maybe I feel like I'm supposed to be the one taking care of Jack."

"Really? Why should you be doing that?"

"I shouldn't, but I...I don't know, maybe it's the way Jack and Gran-gran look at me whenever I go over there to pick Lily up. I feel like some criminal, who's thrown an orphan out on the street," said Kathy.

"An orphan? Wait a second, who decided he wanted to live with his parents?"

"I know, maybe I'm letting them get to me," said Kathy.

"So what's with these looks?"

"It's hard to explain, it's just a feeling I get whenever I go over there...like I'm doing something wrong. I guess I feel like I married Jack for better or for worse, and now that it's worse, I've abandoned him," said Kathy.

"Aren't you taking an awful lot of responsibility for him? I mean, I feel bad for his injuries at the river too, but isn't that a bit over the top? And aren't his injuries healed by now?"

"Yeah, he's physically healed, and has been for awhile now, but what am I supposed to do when they look at me like I broke Jack's arms, along with his heart?" asked Kathy.

"I don't know what to tell you, but I don't see that it's your problem."

"I know you're right. It's the same thing my group tells me. I take on too much responsibility for Jack. It's something I've been working on for some time now. I remember when Dr. Aragorn first told me I was mothering Jack. I knew our marriage wasn't working, but I couldn't put my finger on it. Whenever I tried to explain why, I just ended up blaming Jack for being a jerk. And he can be a total jerk, but that's not the whole story. I've had to deal with some of my own issues as well. At first it made me mad whenever they talked about my part in the marriage problems, but before long I had to admit I was as much a part of the problem as Jack...They also helped me see how lonely I've been. This may surprise you, but that has been more valuable than gold, as strange as that probably sounds. So I guess it helped me to see my part in my own problems."

"That's really interesting."

"Initially I resisted the idea, but now I know Dr. Aragorn and the others are right. As strange as it sounds, it feels better to me to take responsibility for how I was being, and how my life is. But like I was saying, I think my biggest growing edge is forgiving myself," said Kathy.

"What do you still have to forgive?"

"I mean I'm still working on forgiving myself for our marriage failing, as though I did something wrong. I know I did what I had to do, but I guess I'm still working on trusting my own journey," said Kathy.

"What's your own journey?"

"I mean that in my heart of hearts, I truly believe that I followed my heart, and that I did my best to make the marriage work...and that there's nothing to feel bad about," explained Kathy.

"Wow, I'm not sure that I completely understand what you mean."

"Yeah, I'm sure some of this sounds pretty strange," agreed Kathy.

"So are you still considering marrying Mike?" asked Kathy.

Stacy blushed and looked away, before nodding. "Now wait, you haven't been married yet, right?" Kathy asked.

"No, not yet. I came close a couple times with two other guys, but I haven't walked the aisle yet," said Stacy.

"Take it from me, there's no hurry. If I had to do it over again I'd take a lot more think deciding."

"Well, you've given me something to think about," said Stacy.

"Well good. And what's that?"

"I don't know if I can put it into words, but after our many conversations, I want Mike and I to get to know one another better. I guess I want to take our time and make sure it's a good fit, before we walk the aisle."

"That sounds great," said Kathy.

"So, does Jack accept that you're definitely done?" asked Stacy.

"Yes and no. Long ago I filed and he was served, but I don't think he believes I'm serious. I think he expects me to change my mind, and come crawling back or something. He just said that it isn't over yet. I think he's dragging out signing the final papers, hoping that I'll reconsider. Actually, I really don't know for sure, but sometimes it seems like that."

"So he's in denial," said Stacy.

"I don't know that he's in denial, but I'm worried about how he'll take it when it finally sinks in."

"What are you afraid he'll do?"

Kathy glanced out at the window and pondered Stacy's question before responding. "It's hard to say what worries me...maybe that he won't move on with his life, maybe that he'll self-destruct...you know, it's a terrible thought, and I don't even want to say it, but I'm afraid it will somehow kill him," Kathy laughed nervously. "I know that sounds crazy."

"You mean you think he might take his own life?"

"No, I don't think he'd intentionally kill himself. I don't know, I just keep getting images in my mind of him never getting over it. Maybe I'm afraid he'll never deal with me leaving. Maybe that he'll curl up on his mother's couch and never get off it…maybe it's just my own fear."

"Jack gets so mad at you, maybe he'll be relieved to have it over," suggested Stacy.

"Maybe on one level he will, but I fear it'll cut him deeper, and in a way he'll never recover from. Do you know what I mean?"

"I'm not sure that I do," answered Stacy.

"Funny thing is I'm not sure that I do either."

Stacy glanced over at the shops across the street, and then said, "Hey, you want to go get an ice cream?"

"Yeah, sounds good. Maybe that'll make me feel better," said Kathy with a smirk.

Kathy got chocolate and graham cracker with peanut butter cups mixed in, while Stacy got the same thing with chocolate chips as an add-in. "So how's it going with you and Mike?" asked Kathy.

"Oh we're still doing really good ever since the river nightmare." Kathy and Stacy exchanged a glance and a smile.

Stacy added, "We seem to be more patient with each other. I think the river trip made us stronger as a couple. I mean we still have our moments, but we seem to deal with them pretty easily. Like the other day Mike was late for dinner at my place. The food was getting cold and I was getting hot by the time he finally arrived. When he got there I played like I was asleep on the couch, and he got out my smelling salts, and we both had a great laugh. And he apologized for not calling ahead, and it was over. And then we had a nice evening. It was just no big deal."

"That's great, Stacy. Wow, I'd sure like to have a relationship like that," said Kathy.

"You will."

"Well, I should probably get going. I'm supposed to be picking up Lily from Jack's in fifteen minutes."

"And don't let them get to you," said Stacy. Kathy smiled and gave Stacy a hug.

Kathy knocked on the door. Lily answered the door almost immediately. She always knew when her mom was expected. Kathy swept her up in her arms. Jack was planted on the couch watching sports, while Gran-gran leaned against the door jam with her arms folded and eyed Kathy silently. Okay, this is one of those moments, thought Kathy. Kathy waved at Gran-gran as she took Lily's hand to leave and said, "See you on Thursday." And Kathy and Lily left.

Well, that wasn't so bad...I was making too big of a deal about their looks. I guess I was letting them get to me...Maybe I was giving them too much power...I guess Stacy and Dr. Aragorn are right about that. I can just let it be their deal. However they want to look at me can be up to them...I don't have to let it be about me, thought Kathy.

The River: Day 14

The next day Mike and Stacy walked across the street to the hospital from their motel room. Mike carried Jack's bag in one hand and Kathy's in the other. They found Kathy and Jack at the nurses' station. Kathy talked to the nurse while Jack sat in a wheelchair. After finishing checking Jack out, they wheeled him out to Mike's truck. No one wanted to stay in Marble any longer. So they loaded up the truck and headed for home. It took some doing getting Jack into the truck, with two broken arms in casts and matching broken ribs. In spite of Mike's left arm being in a cast, he insisted on driving. There was little conversation in the truck. Jack fell asleep before they hit the main highway. He was doped up on pain meds.

Before Mike and Stacy arrived at the hospital that morning, Jack and Kathy discussed what they'd do when they got home. As Kathy walked into Jack's hospital room, he was just hanging up the phone. "That was Gran-gran. She said she'd be glad to have me stay with her for awhile," said Jack.

"Jack, you can stay…"

"No, it's decided. I'll stay with my mom. I'll need someone to look after me until I get these damn casts off. I can't even take a piss on my own with these," said Jack.

"Well, if that's what you want to…"

"Yes, that's settled then. And Lily will live will you at the condo," said Jack.

"Okay, that sounds…but who will pick up Lily on the days that I can't?"

"I've got that all worked out. Gran-gran will pick her up every day from school," announced Jack.

"I don't need her to pick Lily up every day. I'll let her know which days…"

"Good, so it's all worked out. So help me change back into my clothes. I can't wait to get this embarrassing gown off me," said Jack. At first Kathy didn't like Jack's plans. She didn't like the idea of Jack living with his mother. Kathy pictured Jack doing nothing, while Gran-gran did everything for him. She wasn't sure how Jack would do at his mother's, and what impact it would have on him, but she figured that was his affair. However, the more she thought about it, the better the living arrangements sounded to her. Kathy didn't relish the idea of caring for Jack on her own. That was the best part of the plan.

As they rolled back into town, all three of the conscious travelers felt more energy. It was so nice to see home again. Having survived an ordeal, the safety of home was comforting. Stacy pulled the truck into the driveway of Jack's parents. Mike had given the keys to Stacy after lunch, as it was painful for him to use his left hand. Mike and Kathy helped Jack out of the back seat. Jack grimaced, but dismissed any more help than was absolutely necessary, and walked unassisted up to the front door. Mike stood with Jack at the front door, while Kathy and Stacy remained back by the driveway. Gran-gran opened the door and gave her son an enthusiastic embrace. She looked over Jack's shoulder and glared at Kathy, and then led her son into the house. Mike brought in Jack's bags.

Stacy and Kathy got into the front seat of the truck. Kathy was pensive. Stacy studied her friend and then said, "I saw the look Jack's mom gave you."

"Oh, really? Yeah, I don't think I'm Gran-gran's favorite person right now," said Kathy.

"Why is that?" asked Stacy.

"I don't know, but she seemed awfully angry on the phone when I told her what had happened to Jack. It was almost like it was my fault he's injured."

"But that's totally unfair," said Stacy.

"I know…If Jack's living here, then Gran-gran will be seeing a lot of Lily. I'm concerned about what Gran-gran might say to Lily," said Kathy.

"What do you think she'll say?" asked Stacy.

Kathy pondered that question and then said, "I'm not really sure, but I'm afraid she'll trash me to Lily in some way."

"But that would hurt Lily," said Stacy.

"I know…I don't think she'll hurt Lily on purpose, but when someone gets on Gran-gran's bad side, watch out! There was one time that Leslie's husband, Leslie is Jack's sister, made some bad investments. They almost lost their entire retirement, and even struggled to pay the bills. Leslie had to go back to work to help keep them afloat. My God, Gran-gran treated him like he was the anti-Christ. I don't think Gran-gran spoke to him for months. After awhile he stopped coming to family events, at least until she started talking to him again.

"Wow, that's evil," said Stacy.

"Well, that's Gran-gran. I wonder if I'll get the same treatment Leslie's husband got."

The door knob turned in her hand without resistance. Jack had left the door unlocked all vacation. They had picked Kathy up at the office, on the way out of town. Kathy smiled at the memory of Jack often forgetting things like door locks, wallets, cell phones and keys. She stepped inside and took in the musty smell. Dishes filled the sink and covered the area next to the sink. The smell of a few wet, stale cheerios floating in the remnant of milk gagged Kathy. She plugged her nose and left the kitchen and went into the master bedroom. The bed was half made with clothes on Kathy's side of the bed. Jack's favorite shirt caught her eye. It felt soft and inviting in her hands. She put it to her face and gently caressed herself. She put in on.

Tears filled her eyes and the familiar texture and smell of his shirt filled her senses. She sat on the floor and leaned against the bed. Kathy began to rock gently and she buried her nose in his shirt sleeve.

"Oh my God Jack, I can't believe what we've just been through."

Kathy slowed her rocking and scanned the bedroom. A framed picture caught her attention. She went to it and stared at their wedding picture. The one Kathy had kept on her night stand. The youthful appearance of the bride and groom surprised her. She lay down on the bed, her eyes locked onto the wedding picture.

Kathy awoke with a start. She noticed the picture frame lying in her hand. She had the sense that there was some place she was supposed to be, but at first couldn't name it. "Oh my God, I told Jane I'd get Lily before 6:00." The clock read 6:17. Kathy jumped out of bed, grabbed her keys and dashed to her sister's.

Kathy thought of Lily. She'd already spent many moments thinking over what she might tell her about Jack, and had thought she'd settled on what to say. Kathy didn't want to upset Lily, but she wanted to tell her the truth.

Jane opened the door. As Kathy stepped into the house Lily saw her mom and raced over and leapt into her arms. "Mommy, Mommy you're finally back! I missed you! You said you'd only be gone for eight days and it's been way more days. Where have you been?"

"Oh honey, it's hard to explain. Daddy and I ran into some problems out at the river."

"What kind of problems?" asked Lily.

"We ran into a storm, and the boat broke, and it took us longer to get back."

"Where's Daddy? Is he out in the car?"

Kathy began to tear and hugged Lily closer to hide her tears. Jane put her hand on her sister's arm. Kathy whipped her tears away and said, "Lily, Daddy's staying at Gran-gran's for awhile. He won't be home tonight."

Lily looked her mother in the eye and asked, "When is Daddy coming home?"

"I don't know for sure. But for now it will just be you and Mommy at home, okay?"

"Why is Daddy not coming home with us?

"Because he got hurt at the river," answered Kathy.

Lily's eyes widened. "What kind of hurt?"

"He broke his arms. But Daddy's going to be okay. He just needs Gran-gran to take care of him for a little while. And you'll get to see Daddy almost all the time," said Kathy.

Lily thought for a moment and then said, "Okay Mommy."

Kathy laughed nervously and said, "Okay honey, let's get you all packed up."

Lily pushed down and ran to get her bags, calling over her shoulder, "I got my stuff all ready. I want to go home."

Kathy breathed a sigh of relief, and turned to her sister and said, "Oh thank God that's over. I was worried that she might be more upset by Jack not coming home with us."

"She'll be fine," said Jane with a soothing smile.

Lily snored in her car seat as Kathy pulled into the driveway. Kathy took her time lifting Lily out of her car seat, hoping Lily would remain asleep. Kathy didn't think she could hold herself back from crying if Lily asked about the river again. Kathy laid her daughter down on her bed and slowly pulled off her coat and shoes. She tip-toed out of the room, and closed the door behind her.

She allowed the hot water to massage her neck and shoulders in the shower. Some of the tension in her body lessened, but Kathy still felt sore as she dried off. As she pulled on her pajamas she kept eyeing the bed.

Her side of the bed was still piled up with Jack's clothes. Kathy finished her pre-bed routine and stood before her bed. She lifted a handful of clothes and smelled them. They smelled of laundry detergent. Kathy pulled back the covers and climbed into Jack's side of the bed. She tossed and turned for an hour. Finally she gave up and pushed all the clothes onto Jack's side of the bed. Kathy settled into the bedding on her side, turned off the light and closed her eyes. Although she was on her side now, she just didn't feel comfortable. Five minutes later the light was on and Kathy was picking clothes off the bed. The next thing she knew all of the clothes were folded and put away.

Kathy thought about getting back into bed, but felt compelled to attend to the kitchen. She tied a scarf around her mouth and nose, and braved the hazardous materials left over in the sink. After dealing with the kitchen, Kathy took off her scarf and walked around the condo. She felt strangely at home, and yet in a strange place. It was almost like being in a long forgotten place that she had known in a previous lifetime.

87 Weeks after the River Trip

A knock came from the front door. Lily jumped up from her drawing to answer it. She was excited to play with her friend again, and opened the door to find Jamie and Susan. Lily pulled Jamie by her coat sleeve and he was soon sitting down at the table with Lily and drawing his own picture. Kathy poured Susan a glass of nice Pinot Noir. They talked while Kathy continued to make dinner for the four of them. "Oh yummy! I might have to drink more than one tonight," said Susan as she set down her wine glass and sat at the table in the kitchen nook.

"I know, isn't it," agreed Kathy. "So how's it going with Steve?"

"I keep pinching myself to see if I'm awake. I can't believe we're still together, and with no signs of it ending anytime soon."

"That's great, Susan…I sure wish I could meet somebody great."

"Whatever happened to Steve's buddy? What was his name?"

"Kevin," answered Kathy. "I never heard from him again. That was disappointing. I liked him. At least what I knew of him after one date."

"So are you meeting anyone else?"

"No, that's just it. I don't know how to meet guys." Kathy glanced over at Lily. "I'm just not coming across anyone. Well, none that I'm interested in. Two married guys at work commented on my wedding ring being gone and asked me out, but that's not what I'm into."

"Of course not."

"How do I meet guys? Do you have any ideas? I mean, besides going clubbing with you. I don't think that's my thing."

"Have you tried internet dating?" asked Susan.

"Online dating? No, isn't that for women looking for sex?"

Susan laughed, almost spitting her wine onto her lap. "Yes, but not just that. I know several girlfriends that have met great guys online. You should try it."

"How does it work?"

"You really don't know? Come on Kathy, let's get you into the twenty-first century." Kathy rolled her eyes playfully and stirred the spaghetti sauce simmering on the stove. "Come on, leave the spaghetti sauce for five minutes and I'll show you," said Susan. When Kathy didn't move from the stove Susan took her hand and led her into the spare bedroom and sat down at the desk as she turned on the monitor. She did a Google search on internet dating sites.

"Oh my God, there's like a hundred of them," said Kathy looking over Susan's shoulder.

"I know. Welcome to dating in the current century."

"But you met Steve at a bar," countered Kathy.

"I know, but I've done internet dating off and on since my divorce. I've even met a couple of guys online that I dated for awhile."

"Okay, so show me how this works before my spaghetti starts sticking to the sides."

"Look at this one, all you do is post a profile and then you either search for guys or wait for them to contact you. Some sites even do the matching for you. See how easy it is," said Susan.

"I guess so. It just seems so impersonal to meet guys through a computer. And how does a computer match you?"

"You fill out a questionnaire and they match you based on similarities or something."

"And anyway, is it even safe?" asked Kathy.

"Oh yeah, you don't give out any identifying information until you're comfortable with somebody. And you always want to meet somewhere in public at first. And don't give out your last name or any other identifying information through which they can find you."

"If I have to be that careful, then maybe it isn't safe," said Kathy.

"No it's safe, just use common sense and you'll be fine."

After Susan and Jamie left, Kathy put Lily to bed. Kathy turned off Lily's light and quietly closed her door. She walked into the den and stared at the computer. She stood there for several minutes before finally saying, "Oh what the heck, let's give it a try." When she turned the monitor back on, the same dating site appeared on her screen. Kathy clicked on "create a profile". After filling in her basic demographic information she clicked the "finished" key, and up popped the short answer questions. "Oh my God, how do I describe the kind of person I am in 500 words or less?"

The second question wasn't any easier: "Describe the kind of person you want to be in relationship with". This could take me all night if I really think about my answers, Kathy thought. She looked at the clock and realized she'd taken thirty minutes to complete the first question. I'll just write the first thing that comes to my mind, and then I can make it better later. Otherwise I'll be eating breakfast at the computer.

Two hours later she finished writing her profile. At least she finished the first draft of her profile. She clicked "finished" and up came one last prompt- "upload picture." I hadn't even thought about a picture. I don't even know if I have one that I'd post, she thought. Kathy brought up her pictures file and began to look through them. "No pictures with Lily…no pictures with Jack…too silly…oh my God, way too embarrassing…too fat in that one…there's no way I'm posting a picture of me in a bathing suit…this one maybe, but…forget that one, I look like an idiot," said Kathy aloud.

Twenty minutes later she'd seen the last of her pictures and realized she was left with two maybes. Kathy looked at the two pictures she'd copied to her desktop. One was her picture for the law firm's company directory. It looked professional, but a bit stuffy with almost no smile. The other picture was her and Jane at a church tea. Kathy liked how she looked, but she was wearing sunglasses. So her choices were stuffy picture in which she looked boring, or good picture in which she looked fun but had no eyes. She went with no eyes.

When she uploaded the picture she realized that she could post multiple pictures, and ended up posting the work picture as well. She clicked "finished posting pictures" and the screen told her that her profile would be reviewed for appropriate content and would be available for viewing within 48 hours. Kathy turned off the computer, stretched, and went to bed.

Kathy ate her sandwich and iced tea at her desk while she went through her emails. She came across one from the dating site, wondering what it could be. It informed her that her profile had been approved and was now posted. Curious, she signed onto the dating site and was surprised to see that she already had seven emails. The first one was from a fifty year old man who looked twenty-eight in his picture. It read, "Hi Kathy, let's get together and see if we can make magic, Likable Larry." Oh my God, no on that one. Kathy hit the delete key.

The next email was from forty-one year old Dave, and it read, "Kathy, I love your picture and what you said in your profile...let's talk, Dave." Kathy felt excited and hit the "reply" key. She wrote Dave that she'd be glad to talk and gave him her cell number. Just before she hit "send" she noticed where he lived. Oh my God, he lives two hours away. No way! Again she hit the delete key.

The third email was from 39 year old Matt. Kathy checked his city immediately, and it was close. She liked his email and also was drawn to his profile. Matt also suggested talking over the phone. "I can't believe how fast these guys operate," she whispered. I'll be careful like Susan suggested, she thought. Kathy wrote that she'd be glad to talk over the phone, and that she'd like Matt to give her a number to call him at.

The next email shocked Kathy. It read, "You've got a hot bod, Kathy. Let's hook up soon, here to please Harry." I can't believe some guy would write that! Does he think I'm a prostitute? Kathy hit the delete key as soon as she finished reading his solicitation.

The fifth email was from Mick, he wrote, "Looking for a mature woman to make my fantasies come true…Give me a call." Mick left his phone number. Kathy didn't get what he meant. She began to look through his profile, and his message still didn't make sense until she came across his age, 21. No thanks, delete. I don't want to be somebody's mother fantasy, she thought.

The last two emails from guys were merely offering to connect through email, but Kathy wasn't attracted to either guy. One of them she wasn't physically attracted to, and she didn't like what the other one had to say in his profile. She deleted them both.

Kathy was about to sign off the site when her curiosity got the better of her. I wonder what some of the other guys are like, she thought. She hit the "create search" button and figured out how to initiate a search for guys in her geographical area. Kathy selected within twenty-five miles and hit "search". But nothing happened. What the heck! Why won't the damn thing search? As Kathy looked more closely she noticed a red X next to the age range box. Oh my God, I haven't even thought about that…well, I know I don't want somebody 50 like that one guy…and I don't want some kid that's 21 and probably still in college like that other one…oh what the heck, I'll put up to five years younger or older…I guess I can always change it.

The search yielded 425 profiles. Oh my…how can I look through that many…I could be here all night reading that many profiles! Wait a minute, I'll redo the search for within twenty miles and see how many I get. Kathy typed in the new proximity number and this time got 295 hits. That's better, but still…

Kathy picked up her phone and dialed. Luckily Susan answered. "Hey Susan, I'm searching on that dating site, and I got 295 hits. There's no way I'll take the time to read that many…" Susan's laughter interrupted Kathy. It took Susan some time to stop laughing enough to speak, "Oh Kathy, you are precious. Of course you aren't reading a thousand profiles."

"Three hundred."

"Three hundred, a thousand, what's the difference? You have to learn to search more specifically. Now, which site are you on?" Kathy told her. "Okay then, on that site you can search through profile summaries that show their picture, a few demographics, and a brief summary of what they say about themselves. You can scan through those pretty quick until you find one that you want to take a closer look at. Otherwise your daughter will have to move in with me for a month while mommy finds one or two guys to date."

"Ha ha, Susan. Maybe I should just hire you as my personal dating consultant to screen through the geeks and losers for me. I want you to arrange one date for me each weekend, with pre-screened guys that have a real life."

"Oh I would have paid my weight in gold for a service like that before I met Steve," said Susan.

"I might be willing to pay my weight in gold right now for that. So, you interested in the job?"

"Good luck with the search. Call me and tell me what you find," said Susan and then hung up.

Kathy spent the next ten minutes figuring out how to display the summary profiles on her search. Her frustration mounted to the point that she was about to give up, when she finally figured it out. She was reading the first page of summaries when a call came in from her secretary. Oh I guess I'll have to wait until later to do this. I probably won't be able to do it at work, she thought.

That night Kathy finished up the dinner dishes and then sat down at her computer to give the search another go. She signed on and discovered that she had another ten emails. The first one was from Matt leaving her a phone number at which to call him. The second one read, "Hey Kathy, I'm an attorney too, and am looking for someone to discuss law cases with me over a bottle of red wine. I've had a hard time finding someone like you that could share that kind of intellectual stimulation with me. Hoping to hear from you soon, Theodore." Kathy rolled her eyes and deleted the email without reading the attached profile. "My God, the very last thing I want to do on a date is talk about law," said Kathy aloud. Kathy read through the rest of the emails, but ended up deleting all of them.

Kathy dialed up another search and brought up the profile summaries like Susan had suggested. She began scanning the summaries. Many of them sounded totally uninteresting. Most were possible attractive, and a few looked really good. After reading several pages of summaries, Kathy looked out the window and wondered aloud, "What am I supposed to be looking for? I know I don't want the guys with tattoo sleeves, or the guys two hours away, or the guys young enough to be my son or old enough to be my father, but the rest…how do I decide?"

When Kathy turned back to the screen she noticed two new emails. She opened the first one. Coolguy101 wrote, "Hey I saw that you stopped by, but didn't bother saying hi. Drop me a line, Coolguy." Kathy reread the email. "What does he mean, I stopped by?" Kathy took a closer look at Coolguy101's profile and began reading. After a few lines she realized it sounded familiar. Oh I know what he means. He means I looked at his profile. But how could he know I've seen his profile?

Kathy poked around the site a bit more until she came across a page that had a button that read "see who's viewed you". Oh my God, every guy whose profile I've looked at knows...I don't want them to know I've seen their profile...Is there any way to turn off that feature? She couldn't find a way to disengage the "see who's viewed me" feature. I guess I'll just have to be more selective about who I take a look at. I don't want every Tom, Dick and Harry to write me back...Coolguy doesn't look that great, delete.

Turning back to her messages Kathy opened the second new email which was from PeterW007. It read, "Hi Kathy, you look like the type of sophisticated woman that I'm attracted to. Want to meet?" "Do I want to meet?" said Kathy. "That's a little quick for me." And then Kathy read Peter's profile, which sounded good, although a bit mysterious. He described himself as a global traveler, sometimes for business and sometimes for pleasure. As for athletics he plays golf and tennis, but said he's not into watching sports on television. Kathy loved his picture. He looked average height, athletic build and with dark features. She'd always been more attracted to guys with dark features.

After thinking about it, Kathy decided to ask a few questions. She wrote back, "What do you mean that I'm the type of woman you're attracted to? Please elaborate on that. Also, your profile says you live in Chicago. How are we to meet with me being in California? Also, what kind of work do you do? It seems a bit fast for me to meet, but I'm glad to email, Kathy."

After sending her reply she went back to reading profile summaries from her search. Fifteen minutes later she noticed she had another new email. It was also from PeterW007. Wow, that was fast, thought Kathy. The reply stated, "I'm based in Chicago, but I travel to Southern California regularly on business, so getting together won't be a problem. As for this being fast, I don't find it helpful to email back and forth. I prefer to meet right away, and then I know if a woman is what I'm looking for. I'll be in town this weekend on business. Let's meet at Chico's for a drink Friday around six. See you soon, Peter."

Kathy felt a rush of excitement surge through her. How great would it be to have a date for this weekend? I haven't been on a date in months. Maybe this internet dating thing is just what I needed to get back out there…although I don't know hardly anything about this guy…but he sounds pretty good on his profile, a professional guy who has a job that can afford to fly him across the country regularly…I suppose it wouldn't hurt to just meet for a drink. It's not like he'll know where I live or anything. Kathy wrote back that she'd meet him at Chico's at the appointed time.

When Kathy pulled into Chico's parking lot at 5:45 it was already crowded. She drove around for ten minutes before finding a space. She checked herself in the visor mirror, grabbed her purse and coat, and stepped out of the car. Kathy looked down at her black, wool slacks, and brushed away lent. She tucked in her white, silk blouse, and made sure her collar was pulled up above her navy blazer. Content with her primping, she headed for the entrance. A string of thoughts came to mind, I hope we find each other…I suppose we will since we've seen pictures…my God am I nervous…well, nothing to do but just show up and be myself, and let the chips fall as they may.

This would be her first time in Chico's, an upscale bar and restaurant that specialized in expensive, gourmet Mexican food. The place was dimly lit with candles on each table, and low lit overhead lights. The bar was behind the hostess desk, and made of dark wood with brass down-hanging lights. The host wore a white tuxedo shirt, burgundy bow tie and black slacks. He smiled and asked for the name of her party. Kathy glanced at her watch and said, "I guess Peter would be the name. I'm meeting someone here."

"Ah yes, your party has already been seated and is expecting you. Right this way please," said the host. Kathy adjusted her blouse and coat a final time as she followed him to the table in the corner, complete with a second story view of the plaza and beautiful fountain below.

As Kathy approached the table she saw Peter first. He wore a dark suite with a bright blue tie, and had his hair slicked back. His hair had been greased just enough to keep it in place, but not so much that it appeared wet. Peter focused on his smart phone and didn't see Kathy yet. When they arrived at the table the host said, "And here we are, your server will be Tony, and he'll be with you in a moment."

Peter looked up and smiled. It was more of a half smile, with only one corner of his mouth participating in the gesture. Without appearing to be in any hurry he said, "So, the beautiful Kathy at last."

"Hello," was all Kathy managed. But a moment later added, "I hope I didn't keep you waiting for long."

"Oh no, I got here early on purpose to catch up on some emails and make sure their wine selection was adequate," Peter said with the same crooked smile.

Kathy was immediately smitten by Peter's extraordinarily handsome face, but she recovered sufficiently to respond with, "And have you found the wine list adequate?"

"Oh it'll do. I suppose it'll have to do since I don't know of anything else better that's close by. I've gone to the trouble to sample today's Cabernet special. I can't say it's outstanding, but it's fair."

"You must be a regular at fine dining," said Kathy.

"If I'm inconvenienced to be away from home on business, I expect to be compensated in some way."

"I see. It's supplementary pay."

"That's one way to look at it…so you don't get out much? I would have thought a woman of your particular…talents would have numerous opportunities to dine at such establishments."

Kathy laughed briefly, although more than did Peter. "Not all my dates prefer such fine, and yet apparently sub-par establishments," said Kathy. Peter nodded with his signature smile, and then glanced down at his menu while resting on his forearms.

"Perhaps we can remedy your cultural neglect," Peter said without looking up from the menu.

Kathy smiled at Peter's comment, yet without being sure whether he was serious. "So what sort of consulting do you do?"

"It's nothing worth spending much time on. I'm a financial planning consultant, and I assist companies in achieving their financial goals, and sometimes in saving themselves from ruin."

"Do you work for yourself, or do you represent some company," asked Kathy.

"The details really are a bore, and not worthy of more of our breath. But tell me about your work; an attorney isn't it?" Kathy filled her date in on the high points of her work, yet curtailed her explanation when she noticed Peter's eyes drift away from hers. The arrival of their server prevented what may have been an awkward moment.

They ordered their dinner and Peter selected an expensive bottle of Cabernet. Their conversation throughout their meal remained unusually sparse for a first date. Peter did not seem uncomfortable with dead air spaces.

Kathy kept finding herself tempted to fill the silences with conversation, and the first hour did so, yet as the evening wore on and the wine had its desired effect, Kathy allowed the silences to linger. She also found herself thinking about her group. Kathy's therapy experience had taught her to not only allow, but make use of silences to reflect and think. Kathy glanced at Peter during the next dead space, curious to see what he did with the silences. At first Peter simply attended to his food and leisurely placed a bite in his mouth. Then he dabbed at the corners of his mouth, and languidly looked up at Kathy. His eyes moved gently over her face, without evidence of self consciousness or hurry. After a few moments of him examining her, Kathy squirmed in her seat and glanced out the window. How does he do that? I guess I'm more nervous than he is, Kathy thought. When she looked back at him, Peter still eyed her complacently.

"You don't date much, do you?"

"It's that obvious, huh?" said Kathy.

Peter laughed and said, "Yes, I suppose so."

Kathy was relieved when the waiter interrupted them to ask if they wanted coffee or dessert.

While they nibbled at a Black Forest cake, Peter mentioned he was staying at the Four Riches Hotel, and that he was surprised at the lack of attentive response from the staff.

And Kathy said, "Isn't that a swanky hotel?"

"You mean you've never been there either?"

"No."

"Then I must show you how exquisite it is. While the staff requires motivating, the décor is quite on par." And on that note Peter plunked down his card and set the bill at the edge of the table. He didn't seem to need an affirmative response from Kathy.

Peter took Kathy's arm and escorted her out of the restaurant and to her car. "Would you like to ride with me, or follow me over to the hotel?"

Kathy thought for a moment before responding, "I'll follow you over. What are you driving?"

"I'm the black BMW just three spaces over."

As Kathy followed the black BMW she wondered what Peter had in mind for the hotel. Did he just want to show her a nice hotel, or was he hoping to get physical with her? I'll bet he's hoping I'm drunk enough that I'll let him take my clothes off…well, that's not going to happen…but what if he tries to force me, I mean I don't even know this guy…it's probably stupid for me to go up to his room…I have to do something to protect myself. Should I just tell him that I've changed my mind? Oh I know, I'll call Susan.

Kathy dialed Susan's number and explained her situation. Susan said, "Kathy, I'll be honest with you, this hotel adventure sounds really fun, but I think it's a bad idea. I'm worried for your safety."

"I'm worried for my safety too, and that's why I've called you. You'll be my bodyguard," said Kathy.

"Your bodyguard? You think I can rescue you from this guy if he gets physical? I'm not exactly the security guard type."

"No, of course not. You'll be my electronic bodyguard. I want you to call the police if I don't text you by a certain time. Here's what we'll do. I'll text you his room number when I get there. And if I don't text you every 30 minutes, then I want you to call the police and give them the room number, okay?" said Kathy.

"Kathy, but a lot can happen in 30 minutes."

"You're right. Let's make it 15 minutes. If I don't text you every 15 minutes, then call the police."

"Alright, you've got it. But I still don't like it," agreed Susan. Kathy smiled and hung up.

Peter stopped in front of the valet, and signaled for Kathy to do the same. They received their claim tickets and then Peter took her arm and led her into the lobby. He swept his arm around the room and said, "Do you see the enormity of space. A fine establishment should always create an atmosphere of endless space. Nothing should have any illusion of confinement. All the artwork is originals, no prints or substitutes of any kind. And you must see the rooms."

Without waiting for a response he led Kathy to the elevators. Kathy wondered if she ought to object, but her mind seemed to be operating in slow motion, and before she reached a decision the elevator doors opened and they were heading up.

Kathy noted the room number as Peter inserted his key card. The double doors opened to a large sitting room, complete with throw rug, velvet couch, coffee table and wet bar. The slider was open enough to allow a gentle breeze to billow the see-through curtains, behind which a spacious balcony awaited. To the right a door opened to the bedroom, with a turned-down king's bed visible through the open door. Peter tossed his coat on the table near the door and loosed his tie and he walked directly to the wet bar. "What can I get to refresh you?"

"I'd say I've already had enough wine," said Kathy as she began to text the room number to Susan. Kathy texted, "room #738," and put her phone back in her purse.

"Something else then? I've got Tanqueray tonic with a twist."

"I don't think I want any more…"

"Oh but you must at least take a sip of the Tanqueray. It's absolutely exquisite after a long day."

"This room is unbelievable," said Kathy as she made her way out to the balcony. Directly below lay the over-sized pool, with all the lounge chairs spread out in perfect symmetry. Raising her eyes Kathy caught a glimpse of the lights along the shoreline several miles away.

Peter joined her on the balcony and handed her the gin and tonic. Once she took it he laid his hand lightly on her back. After a moment's hesitation he began gently massaging her back and neck. Kathy considered objecting, but it felt so good she allowed it. It had been a long time since a man had touched her, and it felt electrifying and soothing at the same time. Kathy turned her head and glanced at Peter, who wore his signature grin. He appeared completely at ease, which seemed a bit odd to Kathy, but she didn't ponder it for long.

Kathy turned back to the magnificent view, and took a sip of her drink. He did it so smoothly that Kathy didn't notice at first that Peter's hand had drifted down below her back. She turned to him and said, "Hey isn't this a little quick? I just met you three hours ago."

"I'm sorry. With a woman of your extraordinary beauty I sometimes forget myself."

Kathy regarded Peter for a moment, and then said, "Excuse me. I need to visit the ladies room." Peter smiled by way of response.

Kathy closed the bathroom door and locked it. She examined her teeth and wiped off the lipstick from her front teeth. Kathy leaned on the sink as she observed herself in the mirror and said aloud, "Kathy, what will you do with yourself tonight? Any number of things might happen tonight." She didn't ponder long before the group that now lived in her head came to her rescue. Kathy could almost hear them saying, "So what do you want to happen tonight? What do you want to happen with Peter?" And her response came just as quickly. Kathy thought, I'm enjoying myself, and I might enjoy another evening with Peter. However, I don't want him touching my behind, and I'm definitely not going to sleep with him. I don't sleep with strangers…or even acquaintances.

Having settled that decision, Kathy next pictured Dr. Aragorn asking her, "So Kathy, what kind of physical touch do you want with Peter?" This time she had to give it some thought. After a minute or two the answer came to Kathy. I want him to kiss me, and maybe hold me, but nothing more, she thought.

Kathy stared into the mirror again, examining herself as she looked into her own eyes. And the last thought came with clarity. I can do this…even though I haven't really dated in almost ten years, I have something more important…my new friends and Dr. Aragorn helped me to process the river trip and my marriage, and they'll help me navigate dating, and anything else I decide to do…they live inside me…I have what I need on the inside to pull this off. I have a resource that will always be with me.

Kathy looked at her watch and texted Susan that she was still okay. Kathy smiled at her image in the mirror, picked up her purse and walked out of the bathroom. She walked up to Peter and took his hand and said, "I'm having a nice time with you tonight. I'd love for you to kiss me and hold me. And that's all that's going to happen for tonight. Do we understand one another?"